The Yellow God by H. Rider Haggard

Sir Henry Rider Haggard, KBE was born on June 22nd, 1856 at Bradenham in Norfolk, England.

After his education he was pushed towards an Army career but failed the entrance exam. Next Haggard was positioned to work for the British Foreign Office but he seems not to have sat that exam. Using family connections, he was sent to Southern Africa by his father in search of a further opportunity of a career.

Haggard spent six years there before a return to England and marriage. He had begun to write and publish some non-fiction in Africa but it was only after studying Law in the hope it might prove to be the proper career his father wanted for him that Haggard began to write fiction, using his African experiences as the basis.

His first fiction was published in 1885 and the following year King Solomon's Mines was published. It was a phenomenal success. His career was set.

Haggard wrote well and wrote often. He managed to sympathise with the local populations even though they were exploited and manipulated by Europeans intent on amassing fortunes in money, people and resources. His writing career covered the great sprint to Empire of several European powers and both reflects and criticizes these events through his well-loved characters including Allan Quatermain and Ayesha.

In his later years Haggard pursued much in the way social reform as well as standing for Parliament and writing a great many letters to The Times.

Henry Rider Haggard died on May 14th, 1925 at the age of 68. His ashes were buried at Ditchingham Church.

Index of Contents

CHAPTER I

SAHARA LIMITED

Sir Robert Aylward, Bart., M.P., sat in his office in the City of London. It was a very magnificent office, quite one of the finest that could be found within half a mile of the Mansion House. Its exterior was built of Aberdeen granite, a material calculated to impress the prospective investor with a comfortable sense of security. Other stucco, or even brick-built, offices might crumble and fall in an actual or a financial sense, but this rock-like edifice of granite, surmounted by a life-sized statue of Justice with her scales, admired from either corner by pleasing effigies of Commerce and of Industry, would surely endure any shock. Earthquake could scarcely shake its strong foundations; panic and disaster would as soon affect the Bank of England. That at least was the impression which it had been designed to convey, and not without success.

"There is so much in externals," Mr. Champers-Haswell, Sir Robert's partner, would say in his cheerful voice. "We are all of us influenced by them, however unconsciously. Impress the public, my dear Aylward. Let solemnity without suggest opulence within, and the bread, or rather the granite, which you throw upon the waters will come back to you after many days."

Mr. Aylward, for this conversation occurred before his merits or the depth of his purse had been rewarded by a baronetcy, looked at his partner in the impassive fashion for which he was famous, and answered:

"You mix your metaphors, Haswell, but if you mean that the public are fools who must be caught by advertisement, I agree with you. Only this particular advertisement is expensive and I do not want to wait many days for my reward. However, £20,000 one way or the other is a small matter, so tell that architect to do the thing in granite."

Sir Robert Aylward sat in his own quiet room at the back of this enduring building, a very splendid room that any Secretary of State might have envied, but arranged in excellent taste. Its walls were panelled with figured teak, a rich carpet made the footfall noiseless, an antique Venus stood upon a marble pedestal in the corner, and over the mantelpiece hung a fine portrait by Gainsborough, that of a certain Miss Aylward, a famous beauty in her day, with whom, be it added, its present owner could boast no connection whatsoever.

Sir Robert was seated at his ebony desk playing with a pencil, and the light from a cheerful fire fell upon his face.

In its own way it was a remarkable face, as he appeared then in his fourth and fortieth year; very pale but with a natural pallor, very well cut and on the whole impressive. His eyes were dark, matching his black hair and pointed beard, and his nose was straight and rather prominent. Perhaps the mouth was his weakest feature, for there was a certain shiftiness about it, also the lips were thick and slightly sensuous. Sir Robert knew this, and therefore he grew a moustache to veil them somewhat. To a careful observer the general impression given by this face was such as is left by the sudden sight of a waxen mask. "How strong! How lifelike!" he would have said, "but of course it isn't real. There may be a man behind, or there may be wood, but that's only a mask." Many people of perception had felt like this about Sir Robert Aylward, namely, that under the mask of his pale countenance dwelt a different being whom they did not know or appreciate.

If these had seen him at this moment of the opening of our story, they might have held that Wisdom was justified of her children. For now, in the solitude of his splendid office, of a sudden Sir Robert's mask seemed to fall from him. His face broke up like ice beneath a thaw. He rose from his table and began to walk up and down the room. He talked to himself aloud.

"Great Heavens!" he muttered, "what a game to have played, and it will go through. I believe that it will go through."

He stopped at the table, switched on an electric light and made a rapid calculation on the back of a letter with a blue pencil.

"Yes," he said, "that's my share, a million and seventeen thousand pounds in cash, and two million in ordinary shares which can be worked off at a discount—let us say another seven hundred and fifty thousand, plus what I have got already—put that at only two hundred and fifty thousand net. Two millions in all, which of course may or may not be added to, probably not, unless the ordinaries boom, for I don't mean to speculate any more. That's the end of twenty years' work, Robert Aylward. And to think of it, eighteen months ago, although I seemed so rich, I was on the verge of bankruptcy—the very verge, not worth five thousand pounds. Now what did the trick? I wonder what did the trick?"

He walked down the room and stopped opposite the ancient marble, staring at it—

"Not Venus, I think," he said, with a laugh, "Venus never made any man rich." He turned and retraced his steps to the other end of the room, which was veiled in shadow. Here upon a second marble pedestal stood an object that gleamed dimly through the gloom. It was about ten inches or a foot high, but in that place nothing more could be seen of it, except that it was yellow and had the general appearance of a toad. For some reason it seemed to attract Sir Robert Aylward, for he halted to stare at it, then stretched out his hand and switched on another lamp, in the hard brilliance of which the thing upon the pedestal suddenly declared itself, leaping out of the darkness into light. It was a terrible object, a monstrosity of indeterminate sex and nature, but surmounted by a woman's head and face of extraordinary, if devilish loveliness, sunk back between high but grotesquely small shoulders, like to those of a lizard, so that it glared upwards. The workmanship of the thing was rude yet strangely powerful. Whatever there is cruel, whatever there is devilish, whatever there is inhuman in the dark places of the world, shone out of the jewelled eyes which were set in that yellow female face, yellow because its substance was of gold, a face which seemed not to belong to the embryonic legs beneath, for body there was none, but to float above them. A hollow, life-sized mask with two tiny frog-like legs, that was the fashion of it.

"You are an ugly brute," muttered Sir Robert, contemplating this effigy, "but although I believe in nothing in heaven above or earth below, except the abysmal folly of the British public, I am bothered if I don't believe in you. At any rate from the day when Vernon brought you into my office, my luck turned, and to judge from the smile on your sweet countenance, I don't think it is done with yet. I wonder what those stones are in your eyes. Opals, I suppose, from the way they change colour. They shine uncommonly to-day, I never remember them so bright. I—"

At this moment a knock came on the door. Sir Robert turned off the lamp and walked back to the fireplace.

"Come in," he said, and as he spoke once more his pale face grew impassive and expressionless.

The door opened and a clerk entered, an imposing-looking clerk with iron-grey hair, who wore an irreproachable frock coat and patent leather boots. Advancing to his master, he stood respectfully silent, waiting to be addressed. For quite a long while Sir Robert looked over his head as though he did not see him; it was a way of his. Then his eyes rested on the man dreamily and he remarked in his cold, clear voice:

"I don't think I rang, Jeffreys."

"No, Sir Robert," answered the clerk, bowing as though he spoke to Royalty, "but there is a little matter about that article in The Cynic."

"Press business," said Sir Robert, lifting his eyebrows; "you should know by this time that I do not attend to such details. See Mr. Champers-Haswell, or Major Vernon."

"They are both out at the moment, Sir Robert."

"Go on, then, Jeffreys," replied the head of the firm with a resigned sigh, "only be brief. I am thinking."

The clerk bowed again.

"The Cynic people have just telephoned through about that article we sent them. I think you saw it, sir, and you may remember it begins—" and he read from a typewritten copy in his hand which was headed "Sahara Limited":

"'We are now privileged to announce that this mighty scheme which will turn a desert into a rolling sea bearing the commerce of nations and cause the waste places of the earth to teem with population and to blossom like the rose, has been completed in its necessary if dull financial details and will within a few days be submitted to investors among whom it has already caused so much excitement. These details we will deal with fully in succeeding articles, and therefore now need only pause to say that the basis of capitalization strikes us as wonderfully advantageous to the fortunate public who are asked to participate in its vast prospective prosperity. Our present object is to speak of its national and imperial aspects—'"

Sir Robert lifted his eyes in remonstrance:

"How much more of that exceedingly dull and commonplace puff do you propose to read, Jeffreys?" he asked.

"No more, Sir Robert. We are paying The Cynic thirty guineas to insert this article, and the point is that they say that if they have to put in the 'national and imperial' business they must have twenty more."

"Indeed, Jeffreys? Why?"

"Because, Sir Robert—I will tell you, as you always like to hear the truth—their advertisement-editor is of opinion that Sahara Limited is a national and imperial swindle. He says that he won't drag the nation and the empire into it in an editorial under fifty guineas."

A faint smile flickered on Sir Robert's face.

"Does he, indeed?" he asked. "I wonder at his moderation. Had I been in his place I should have asked more, for really the style is a little flamboyant. Well, we don't want to quarrel with them just now—feed the sharks. But surely, Jeffreys, you didn't come to disturb me about such a trifle?"

"Not altogether, Sir Robert. There is something more important. The Daily Judge not only declines to put any article whatsoever, but refuses our advertisement, and states that it means to criticize the prospectus trenchantly."

"Ah!" said his master after a moment's thought, "that is rather serious, since people believe in the Judge even when it is wrong. Offer them the advertisement at treble rates."

"It has been done, sir, and they still refuse."

Sir Robert walked to the corner of the room where the yellow object squatted on its pedestal, and contemplated it a while, as a man often studies one thing when he is thinking of another. It seemed to give him an idea, for he looked over his shoulder and said:

"That will do, Jeffreys. When Major Vernon comes in, give him my compliments and say that I should be obliged by a word or two with him."

The clerk bowed and went as noiselessly as he had entered.

"Let's see," added Sir Robert to himself. "Old Jackson, the editor of The Judge, was a great friend of Vernon's father, the late Sir William Vernon, G.C.B. I believe that he was engaged to be married to his sister years ago, only she died or something. So the Major ought to be able to get round him if anybody can. Only the worst of it is I don't altogether trust that young gentleman. It suited us to give him a share in the business because he is an engineer who knows the country, and this Sahara scheme was his notion, a very good one in a way, and for other reasons. Now he shows signs of kicking over the traces, wants to know too much, is developing a conscience, and so forth. As though the promoters of speculative companies had any business with consciences. Ah! here he comes."

Sir Robert seated himself at his desk and resumed his calculations upon a half-sheet of note-paper, and that moment a clear, hearty voice was heard speaking to the clerks in the outer office. Then came the sound of a strong, firm footstep, the door opened and Major Alan Vernon appeared.

He was still quite a young man, not more than thirty-two or three years of age, though he lacked the ultra robust and rubicund appearance which is typical of so many Englishmen of his class at this period of life. A heavy bout of blackwater fever acquired on service in West Africa, which would have killed anyone of weaker constitution, had robbed his face of its bloom and left it much sallower, if more interesting than once it had been. For in a way there was interest about the face; also a certain charm. It was a good and honest face with a rather eager, rather puzzled look, that of a man who has imagination and ideas and who searches for the truth but fails to find it. As for the charm, it lay for the most part in the pleasant, open smile and in the frank but rather round brown eyes overhung by a somewhat massive forehead which projected a little, or perhaps the severe illness already alluded to had caused the rest of the face to sink. Though thin, the man was bigly built, with broad shoulders and well-developed limbs, measuring a trifle under six feet in height.

Such was the outward appearance of Alan Vernon. As for his mind, it was able enough in certain fashions, for instance those of engineering, and the soldier-like faculties to which it had been trained; frank and kindly also, but in other respects not quick, perhaps from its unsuspiciousness. Alan Vernon was a man slow to discover ill and slower still to believe in it even when it seemed to be discovered, a weakness that may have gone far to account for his presence in the office of those eminent and brilliant financiers, Messrs. Aylward & Champers-Haswell. Just now he looked a little worried, like a fish out of water, or rather a fish which has begun to suspect the quality of the water, something in its smell or taste.

"Jeffreys tells me that you want to see me, Sir Robert," he said in his low and pleasant voice, looking at the baronet rather anxiously.

"Yes, my dear Vernon, I wish to ask you to do something, if you kindly will, although it is not quite in your line. Old Jackson, the editor of The Judge, is a friend of yours, isn't he?"

"He was a friend of my father's, and I used to know him slightly."

"Well, that's near enough. As I daresay you have heard, he is an unreasonable old beggar, and has taken a dislike to our Sahara scheme. Someone has set him against it and he refuses to receive advertisements, threatens criticisms, etc. Now the opposition of The Judge or any other paper won't kill us, and if necessary we can fight, but at the same time it is always wise to agree with your enemy while he is in the way, and in short—would you mind going down and explaining his mistake to him?"

Before answering Major Vernon walked to the window leisurely and looked out.

"I don't like asking favours from family friends," he replied at length, "and, as you said, I think it isn't quite my line. Though of course if it has anything to do with the engineering possibilities, I shall be most happy to see him," he added, brightening.

"I don't know what it has to do with; that is what I shall be obliged if you will find out," answered Sir Robert with some asperity. "One can't divide a matter of this sort into watertight compartments. It is true that in so important a concern each of us has charge of his own division, but the fact remains that we are jointly and severally responsible for the whole. I am not sure that you bear this sufficiently in mind, my dear Vernon," he added with slow emphasis.

His partner moved quickly; it might almost have been said that he shivered, though whether the movement, or the shiver, was produced by the argument of joint and several liability or by the familiarity of the "my dear Vernon," remains uncertain. Perhaps it was the latter, since although the elder man was a baronet and the younger only a retired Major of Engineers, the gulf between them, as any one of discernment could see, was wide. They were born, lived, and moved in different spheres unbridged by any common element or impulse.

"I think that I do bear it in mind, especially of late, Sir Robert," answered Alan Vernon slowly.

His partner threw a searching glance on him, for he felt that there was meaning in the words, but only said:

"That's all right. My motor is outside and will take you to Fleet Street in no time. Meanwhile you might tell them to telephone that you are coming, and perhaps you will just look in when you get back. I haven't got to go to the House to-night, so shall be here till dinner time, and so, I think, will your cousin Haswell. Muzzle that old bulldog, Jackson, somehow. No doubt he has his price like the rest of them, in meal or malt, and you needn't stick at the figure. We don't want him hanging on our throat for the next week or two."

Ten minutes later the splendid, two-thousand guinea motor brougham drew up at the offices of the Judge and the obsequious motor-footman bowed Major Vernon through its rather grimy doorway. Within, a small boy in a kind of box asked his business, and when he heard his name, said that the "Guvnor" had sent down word that he was go up at once—third floor, first to the right and second to the left. So up he went, and when he reached the indicated locality was taken possession of by a worried-looking clerk who had evidently been waiting for him, and almost thrust through a door to find himself in a big, worn, untidy room. At a huge desk in this room sat an elderly man, also big, worn, and untidy-looking, who waved a long slip of galley-proof in his hand, and was engaged in scolding a sub-editor.

"Who is that?" he said, wheeling round. "I'm busy, can't see anyone."

"I beg your pardon," answered the Major with humility, "your people told me to come up. My name is Alan Vernon."

"Oh! I remember. Sit down for a moment, will you, and—Mr. Thomas, oblige me by taking away this rot and rewriting it entirely in the sense I have outlined."

Mr. Thomas snatched his rejected copy and vanished through another door, whereon his chief remarked in an audible voice:

"That man is a perfect fool. Lucky I thought to look at his stuff. Well, he is no worse than the rest, in this weary world," and he burst into a hearty laugh and swung his chair round, adding, "Now then, Alan, what is it? I have a quarter of an hour at your service. Why, bless me! I was forgetting that it's more than a dozen years since we met; you were still a boy then, and now you have left the army with a D.S.O. and gratuity, and turned financier, which I think wouldn't have pleased your old father. Come, sit down here and let us talk."

"I didn't leave the army, Mr. Jackson," answered his visitor; "it left me; I was invalided out. They said I should never get my health back after that last go of fever, but I did."

"Ah! bad luck, very bad luck, just at the beginning of what should have been a big career, for I know they thought highly of you at the War Office, that is, if they can think. Well, you have grown into a fine-looking fellow, like your father, very, and someone else too," and he sighed, running his fingers through his grizzled hair. "But you don't remember her; she was before your time. Now let us get to business; there's no time for reminiscences in this office. What is it, Alan, for like other people I suppose that you want something?"

"It is about that Sahara flotation, Mr. Jackson," he began rather doubtfully.

The old editor's face darkened. "The Sahara flotation! That accursed—" and he ceased abruptly. "What have you, of all people in the world, got to do with it? Oh! I remember. Someone told me that you had gone into partnership with Aylward the company promoter, and that little beast, Champers-Haswell, who really is the clever one. Well, set it out, set it out."

"It seems, Mr. Jackson, that The Judge has refused not only our article, but also the advertisement of the company. I don't know much about this side of the affair myself, but Sir Robert asked me if I would come round and see if things couldn't be arranged."

"You mean that the man sent you to try and work on me because he knew that I used to be intimate with your family. Well, it is a poor errand and will have a poor end. You can't—no one on earth can, while I sit in this chair, not even my proprietors."

There was silence broken at last by Alan, who remarked awkwardly:

"If that is so, I must not take up your time any longer."

"I said that I would give you a quarter of an hour, and you have only been here four minutes. Now, Alan Vernon, tell me as your father's old friend, why you have gone to herd with these gilded swine?"

There was something so earnest about the man's question that it did not even occur to his visitor to resent its roughness.

"Of course it is not original," he answered, "but I had this idea about flooding the Desert; I spent a furlough up there a few years ago and employed my time in making some rough surveys. Then I was obliged to leave the Service and went down to Yarleys after my father's death—it's mine now, you know, but worth nothing except a shooting rent, which just pays for the repairs. There I met Champers-Haswell, who lives near and is a kind of distant cousin of mine—my mother was a Champers—and happened to mention the thing to him. He took it up at once and introduced me to Aylward, and the end of it was, that they offered me a partnership with a small share in the business, because they said I was just the man they wanted."

"Just the man they wanted," repeated the editor after him. "Yes, the last of the Vernons, an engineer with an old name in his county, a clean record and plenty of ability. Yes, you would be just the man they wanted. And you accepted?"

"Yes. I was on my beam ends with nothing to do; I wanted to make some money. You see Yarleys has been in the family for over five hundred years, and it seemed hard to have to sell it. Also—also—" and he paused.

"Ever meet Barbara Champers?" asked Mr. Jackson inconsequently. "I did once. Wonderfully nice girl, and very good-looking too. But of course you know her, and she is her uncle's ward, and their place isn't far off Yarleys, you say. Must be a connection of yours also."

Major Vernon started a little at the name and his face seemed to redden.

"Yes," he said, "I have met her and she is a connection."

"Will be a big heiress one day, I think," went on Mr. Jackson, "unless old Haswell makes off with her money. I think Aylward knows that; at any rate he was hanging about when I saw her."

Vernon started again, this time very perceptibly.

"Very natural—your going into the business, I mean, under all the circumstances," went on Mr. Jackson. "But now, if you will take my advice, you'll go out of it as soon as you can."

"Why?"

"Because, Alan Vernon, I am sure you don't want to see your name dragged in the dirt, any more than I do." He fumbled in a drawer and produced a typewritten document. "Take that," he said, "and study it at your leisure. It's a sketch of the financial career of Messrs. Aylward and Champers-Haswell, also of the companies which they have promoted and been connected with, and what has happened to them and to those who invested in them. A man got it out for me yesterday and I'm going to use it. As regards this Sahara business, you think it all right, and so it may be from an engineering point of view, but you will never live to sail upon that sea which the British public is going to be asked to find so many millions to make. Look here. We have only three minutes more, so I will come to the point at once. It's Turkish territory, isn't it, and putting aside everything else, the security for the whole thing is a Firman from the Sultan?"

"Yes, Sir Robert Aylward and Haswell procured it in Constantinople. I have seen the document."

"Indeed, and are you well acquainted with the Sultan's signature? I know when they were there last autumn that potentate was very ill—"

"You mean—" said Major Vernon, looking up.

"I mean, Alan, that I like not the security. I won't say any more, as there is a law of libel in this land. But The Judge has certain sources of information. It may be that no protest will be made at once, for baksheesh can stop it for a while, but sooner or later the protest or repudiation will come, and perhaps some international bother; also much scandal. As to the scheme itself, it is shamelessly over-capitalized for the benefit of the promoters—of whom, remember, Alan, you will appear as one. Now time's up. Perhaps you will take my advice, and perhaps you won't, but there it is for what it's worth as that of a man of the world and an old friend of your family. As for your puff article and your prospectus, I wouldn't put them in The Judge if you paid me a thousand pounds, which I daresay your friend, Aylward, would be quite ready to do. Good-bye. Come and see me again sometime, and tell me what has happened—and, I say"—this last was shouted through the closing door,—"give my kind regards to Miss Barbara, for wherever she happens to live, she is an honest woman."

CHAPTER II

THE YELLOW GOD

Alan Vernon walked thoughtfully down the lead-covered stairs, hustled by eager gentlemen hurrying up to see the great editor, whose bell was already ringing furiously, and was duly ushered by the obsequious assistant-chauffeur back into the luxurious motor. There was an electric lamp in this motor, and by the light of it, his mind being perplexed, he began to read the typewritten document given to him by Mr. Jackson, which he still held in his hand.

As it chanced they were blocked for a quarter of an hour near the Mansion House, so that he found time, if not to master it, at least to gather enough of its contents to make him open his brown eyes very wide before the motor pulled up at the granite doorway of his office. Alan descended from the machine, which departed silently, and stood for a moment wondering what he should do. His impulse was to jump into a bus and go straight to his rooms or his club, to which Sir Robert did not belong, but being no coward, he dismissed it from his mind.

His fate hung in the balance, of that he was well aware. Either he must disregard Mr. Jackson's warning, confirmed as it was by many secret fears and instincts of his own, and say nothing except that he had failed in his mission, or he must take the bull by the horns and break with the firm. To do the latter meant not only a good deal of moral courage, but practical ruin, whereas if he chose the former course, probably within a fortnight he would find himself a rich man. Whatever Jackson and a few others might say in its depreciation, he was certain that the Sahara flotation would go through, for it was underwritten, of course upon terms, by responsible people, moreover the unissued preferred shares had already been dealt in at a heavy premium. Now to say nothing of the allotment to which he was entitled upon his holding in the parent Syndicate, the proportion of cash due to him as a partner, would amount to quite a hundred thousand pounds. In other words, he, who had so many reasons for desiring money, would be wealthy. After working so hard and undergoing so much that he felt to be humiliating and even degrading, why should he not take his reward and clear out afterwards?

This he remembered he could do, since probably by some oversight of Aylward's, who left such matters to his lawyers, his deed of partnership did not bind him to a fixed term. It could be broken at any moment. To this argument there was only one possible answer, that of his conscience. If once he were convinced that things were not right, it would be dishonest to participate in their profits. And he was convinced. Mr. Jackson's arguments and his damning document had thrown a flood of light upon many matters which he had suspected but never quite understood. He was the partner of, well, adventurers, and the money which he received would in fact be filched from the pockets of unsuspecting persons. He would vouch for that of which he was doubtful and receive the price of sharp practice. In other words he, Alan Vernon, who had never uttered a wilful untruth or taken a halfpenny that was not his own, would before the tribunal of his own mind, stand convicted as a liar and a thief. The thing was not to be borne. At whatever cost it must be ended. If he were fated to be a beggar, at least he would be an honest beggar.

With a firm step and a high head he walked straight into Sir Robert's room, without even going through the formality of knocking, to find Mr. Champers-Haswell seated at the ebony desk by his partner's side examining some document through a reading-glass, which on his appearance, was folded over and presently thrust away into a drawer. It seemed, Alan noticed, to be of an unusual shape and written in some strange character.

Mr. Haswell, a stout, jovial-looking, little man with a florid complexion and white hair, rose at once to greet him.

"How do you do, Alan," he said in a cheerful voice, for as a cousin by marriage he called him by his Christian name. "I am just this minute back from Paris, and you will be glad to learn that they are going to support us very well there; in fact I may say that the Government has taken up the scheme, of course under the rose. You know the French have possessions all along that coast and they won't be sorry to find an opportunity of stretching out their hand a little further. Our difficulties as to capital are at an end, for a full third of it is guaranteed in Paris, and I expect that small investors and speculators for the rise will gobble a lot more. We shall plant £10,000,000 worth of Sahara scrip in sunny France, my boy, and foggy England has underwritten the rest. It will be a case of 'letters of Allotment and regret,' and regret, Alan, financially the most successful issue of the last dozen years. What do you say to that?" and in his elation the little man puffed out his chest and pursing up his lips, blew through them, making a sound like that of wind among wires.

"I don't know, Mr. Haswell. If we are all alive I would prefer to answer the question twelve months hence, or later, when we see whether the company is going to be a practical success as well, or not."

Again Mr. Haswell made the sound of wind among wires, only this time there was a shriller note in it; its mellowness was gone, it was as though the air had suddenly been filled with frost.

"A practical success!" he repeated after him. "That is scarcely our affair, is it? Promoters should not bother themselves with long views, Alan. These may be left to the investing public, the speculative parson and the maiden lady who likes a flutter—those props of modern enterprise. But what do you mean? You originated this idea and always said that the profits should be great."

"Yes, Mr. Haswell, on a moderate capitalization and provided that we are sure of the co-operation of the Porte."

Mr. Haswell looked at him very searchingly and Sir Robert, who had been listening, said in his cold voice:

"I think that we thrashed out these points long ago, and to tell you the truth I am rather tired of them, especially as it is too late to change anything. How did you get on with Jackson, Vernon?"

"I did not get on at all, Sir Robert. He will not touch the thing on any terms, and indeed means to oppose it tooth and nail."

"Then he will find himself in a minority when the articles come out to-morrow. Of course it is a bore, but we are strong enough to snap our fingers at him. You see they don't read The Judge in France, and no one has ever heard of it in Constantinople. Therefore we have nothing to fear—so long as we stick together," he added meaningly.

Alan felt that the crisis had come. He must speak now or for ever hold his peace; indeed Aylward was already looking round for his hat.

"Sir Robert and Mr. Haswell," he broke in rather nervously, "I have something to say to you, something unpleasant," and he paused.

"Then please say it at once, Vernon. I want to dress for dinner, I am going to the theatre to-night and must dine early," replied Aylward in a voice of the utmost unconcern.

"It is, Sir Robert," went on Alan with a rush, "that I do not like the lines upon which this business is being worked, and I wish to give up my interest in it and retire from the firm, as I have a right to do under our deed of partnership."

"Have you?" said Aylward. "Really, I forget. But, my dear fellow, do not think that we should wish to keep you for one moment against your will. Only, might I ask, has that old puritan, Jackson, hypnotized you, or is it a case of sudden madness after influenza?"

"Neither," answered Alan sternly, for although he might be diffident on matters that he did not thoroughly understand, he was not a man to brook trifling or impertinence. "It is what I have said, no more nor less. I am not satisfied either as to the capitalization or as to the guarantee that the enterprise can be really carried out. Further"—and he paused,—"Further, I should like what I have never yet been able to obtain, more information as to that Firman under which the concession is granted."

For one moment a sort of tremor passed over Sir Robert's impassive countenance, while Mr. Haswell uttered his windy whistle, this time in a tone of plaintive remonstrance.

"As you have formally resigned your membership of the firm, I do not see that any useful purpose can be served by discussing such matters. The fullest explanations, of course, we should have been willing to give—"

"My dear Alan," broke in Mr. Champers-Haswell, who was quite upset, "I do implore you to reflect for one moment, for your own sake. In a single week you would have been a wealthy man; do you really mean to throw away everything for a whim?"

"Perhaps Vernon remembers that he holds over 1700 of the Syndicate shares which we have worked up to £18, and thinks it wiser to capture the profit in sight, generally speaking a very sound principle," interrupted Aylward sarcastically.

"You are mistaken, Sir Robert," replied Alan, flushing. "The way that those shares have been artificially put up is one of the things to which I most object. I shall only ask for mine the face value which I paid for them."

Now notwithstanding their experience, both of the senior partners did for a moment look rather scared. Such folly, or such honesty, was absolutely incredible to them. They felt that there must be much behind. Sir Robert, however, recovered instantly.

"Very well," he said; "it is not for us to dictate to you; you must make your own bed and lie on it. To argue or remonstrate would only be rude." He put out his hand and pushed the button of an electric bell, adding as he did so, "Of course we understand one thing, Vernon, namely, that as a gentleman and a man of honour you will make no public use of the information which you have acquired during your stay in this office, either to our detriment, personal or financial, or to your own advantage."

"Certainly you may understand that," replied Vernon. "Unless my character is attacked and it becomes necessary for me to defend myself, my lips are sealed."

"That will never happen—why should it?" said Sir Robert with a polite bow.

The door opened and the head clerk, Jeffreys, appeared.

"Mr. Jeffreys," said Sir Robert, "please find us the deed of partnership between Major Vernon and ourselves, and bring it here. One moment. Please make out also a transfer of Major Vernon's parcel of Sahara Syndicate shares to Mr. Champers-Haswell and myself at par value, and fill in a cheque for the amount. Please remove also Major Vernon's name wherever it appears in the proof prospectus, and—yes—one thing more. Telephone to Specton—the Right Honourable the Earl of Specton, I mean, and say that after all I have been able to arrange that he shall have a seat on the Board and a block of shares at a very moderate figure, and that if he will wire his assent, his name shall be put into the prospectus. You approve, don't you, Haswell?—yes—then that is all, I think, Jeffreys, only please be as quick as you can, for I want to get away."

Jeffreys, the immaculate and the impassive, bowed, and casting one swift glance at Vernon out of the corner of his eye, departed.

What is called an awkward pause ensued; in fact it was a very awkward pause. The die was cast, the matter ended, and what were the principals to do until the ratifications had been exchanged or, a better simile perhaps, the decree nisi pronounced absolute. Mr. Champers-Haswell remarked that the weather was very cold for April, and Alan agreed with him, while Sir Robert found his hat and brushed it with his sleeve. Then Mr. Haswell, in desperation, for in minor matters he was a kindly sort of man who disliked scenes and unpleasantness, muttered something as to seeing him—Alan—at his house, The Court, in Hertfordshire, from Saturday to Monday.

"That was the arrangement," answered Alan bluntly, "but possibly after what has happened you will not wish that it should be kept."

"Oh! why not, why not?" said Mr. Haswell. "Sunday is a day of rest when we make it a rule not to talk business, and if we did, perhaps we might all change our minds about these matters. Sir Robert is coming, and I am sure that your cousin Barbara will be very disappointed if you do not turn up, for she understands nothing about these city things which are Greek to her."

At the mention of the name of Barbara Sir Robert Aylward looked up from the papers which he affected to be tidying, and Alan thought that there was a kind of challenge in his eyes. A moment before he had made up his mind that no power on earth would induce him to spend a Sunday with his late partners at The Court. Now, acting upon some instinct or impulse, he reversed his opinion.

"Thanks," he said, "if that is understood, I shall be happy to come. I will drive over from Yarleys in time for dinner to-morrow. Perhaps you will say so to Barbara."

"She will be glad, I am sure," answered Mr. Haswell, "for she told me the other day that she wants to consult you about some outdoor theatricals that she means to get up in July."

"In July!" answered Alan with a little laugh. "I wonder where I shall be in July."

Then came another pause, which seemed to affect even Sir Robert's nerves, for abandoning the papers, he walked down the room till he came to the golden object that has been described, and for the second time that day stood there contemplating it.

"This thing is yours, Vernon," he said, "and now that our relations are at an end, I suppose that you will want to take it away. What is its history? You never told me."

"Oh! that's a long story," answered Alan in an absent voice. "My uncle, who was a missionary, brought it from West Africa. I rather forget the facts, but Jeekie, my negro servant, knows them all, for as a lad my uncle saved him from sacrifice, or something, in a place where they worship these things, and he has been with us ever since. It is a fetish with magical powers and all the rest of it. I believe they call it the Swimming Head and other names. If you look at it, you will see that it seems to swim between the shoulders, doesn't it?"

"Yes," said Sir Robert, "and I admire the beautiful beast. She is cruel and artistic, like—like finance. Look here, Vernon, we have quarrelled, and of course henceforth are enemies, for it is no use mincing matters, only fools do that. But in a way you are being hardly treated. You could get £10 apiece to-day for those shares of yours in a block on the market, and I am paying you £1. I understand your scruples, but there is no reason why we should not square things. This fetish of yours has brought me luck, so let's do a deal. Leave it here, and instead of a check for £1700, I will make you one out for £17,000."

"That's a very liberal offer," said Vernon. "Give me a moment to think it over."

Then he also walked into the corner of the room and contemplated the golden mask that seemed to float between the frog-like shoulders. The shimmering eyes drew his eyes, though what he saw in them does not matter. Indeed he could never remember. Only when he straightened himself again there was left on his mind a determination that not for seventeen or for seventy thousand pounds would he part with his ownership in this very unique fetish.

"No, thank you," he said presently. "I don't think I will sell the Yellow God, as Jeekie calls it. Perhaps you will kindly keep her here for a week or so, until I make up my mind where to stow her."

Again Mr. Champers-Haswell uttered his windy whistle. That a man should refuse £17,000 for a bit of African gold worth £100 or so, struck him as miraculous. But Sir Robert did not seem in the least surprised, only very disappointed.

"I quite understand your dislike to selling," he said. "Thank you for leaving it here for the present to see us through the flotation," and he laughed.

At that moment Jeffreys entered the room with the documents. Sir Robert handed the deed of partnership to Alan, and when he had identified it, took it from him again and threw it on the fire, saying that of course the formal letter of release would be posted and the dissolution notified in the Gazette. Then the transfer was signed and the cheque delivered.

"Well, good-bye till Saturday," said Alan when he had received the latter, and nodding to them both, he turned and left the room.

The passage ran past the little room in which Mr. Jeffreys, the head clerk, sat alone. Catching sight of him through the open door, Alan entered, shutting it behind him. Finding his key ring he removed from it the keys of his desk and of the office strongroom, and handed them to the clerk who, methodical in everything, proceeded to write a formal receipt.

"You are leaving us, Major Vernon?" he said interrogatively as he signed the paper.

"Yes, Jeffreys," answered Alan, then prompted by some impulse, added, "Are you sorry?"

Mr. Jeffreys looked up and there were traces of unwonted emotion upon his hard, regulated face.

"For myself, yes, Major—for you, on the whole, no."

"What do you mean, Jeffreys? I do not quite understand."

"I mean, Major, that I am sorry because you have never tried to shuffle off any shady business on to my back and leave me to bear the brunt of it; also because you have always treated me as a gentleman should, not as a machine to be used until a better can be found, and kicked aside when it goes out of order."

"It is very kind of you to say so, Jeffreys, but I can't remember having done anything particular."

"No, Major, you can't remember what comes natural to you. But I and the others remember, and that's why I am sorry. But for yourself I am glad, since although Aylward and Haswell have put a big thing through and are going to make a pot of money, this is no place for the likes of you, and now that you are going I will make bold to tell you that I always wondered what you were doing here. By and by, Major, the row will come, as it has come more than once in the past, before your time."

"And then?" said Alan, for he was anxious to get to the bottom of this man's mind, which hitherto he had always found so secret.

"And then, Major, it won't matter much to Messrs. Aylward and Champers-Haswell, who are used to that kind of thing and will probably dissolve partnership and lie quiet for a bit, and still less to folk like myself, who are only servants. But if you were still here it would have mattered a great deal to you, for it would blacken your name and break your heart, and then what's the good of the money? I tell you, Major," the clerk went on with quiet intensity, "though I am nobody and nothing, if I could afford it I would follow your example. But I can't, for I have a sick wife and a family of delicate children who have to live half the year on the south coast, to say nothing of my old mother, and—I was fool enough to be taken in and back Sir Robert's last little venture, which cost me all I had saved. So you see I must make a bit before the machine is scrapped, Major. But I tell you this, that if I can get £5000 together, as I hope to do out of Saharas before I am a month older, for they had to give me a look-in, as I knew too much, I am off to the country, where I was born, to take a farm there. No more of Messrs. Aylward and Haswell for Thomas Jeffreys. That's my bell. Good-bye, Major, I'll take the liberty to write you a line sometimes, for I know you won't give me away. Good-bye and God bless you, as I am sure He will in the long run," and stretching out his hand, he took that of the astonished Alan and wrung it warmly.

When he was gone Alan went also, noticing that the clerks, whom some rumour of these events seemed to have reached, eyed him curiously through the glass screens behind which they sat at their desks, as he thought not without regret and a kind of admiration. Even the magnificent be-medalled porter at the door emerged from the carved teak box where he dwelt and touching his cap asked if he should call a cab.

"No, thank you, Sergeant," answered Alan, "I will take a bus, and, Sergeant, I think I forgot to give you a present last Xmas. Will you accept this?—I wish I could make it more," and he presented him with ten shillings.

The Sergeant drew himself up and saluted.

"Thank you kindly, Major," he said. "I'd rather take that from you than £10 from the other gentlemen. But, Major, I wish we were out on the West Coast again together. It's a stinking, barbarous hole, but not so bad as this 'ere city."

For once these two had served as comrades, and it was through Alan that the sergeant obtained his present lucrative but somewhat uncongenial post.

He was outside at last. The massive granite portal vanished behind him in the evening mists, much as a nightmare vanishes. He, Alan Vernon, who for a year or more had been in bondage, was a free man again. All his dreams of wealth had departed; indeed if anything, save in experience, he was poorer than when first the shadow of yonder doorway fell upon him. But at least he was safe, safe. The deed of partnership which had been as a chain about his neck, was now white ashes; his name was erased from that fearful prospectus of Sahara Limited, wherein millions which someone would provide were spoken of like silver in the days of Solomon, as things of no account. The bitterest critic could not say that he had made a halfpenny out of the venture, in fact, if trouble came, his voluntary abandonment of the profits due to him must go to his credit. He had plunged into the icy waters of renunciation and come up clean if naked. Never since he was a boy could Alan remember feeling so utterly light-hearted and free from anxiety. Not for a million pounds would he have returned to gather gold in that mausoleum of reputations. As for the future, he did not in the least care what happened. There was no one dependent on him, and in this way or in that he could always earn a crust, a nice, honest crust.

He ran down the street and danced for joy like a child, yes, and presented a crossing-sweeper against whom he butted with a whole sixpence in compensation. Thus he reached the Mansion House, not unsuspected of inebriety by the police, and clambered to the top of a bus crowded with weary and anxious-looking City clerks returning home after a long day's labour at starvation wage. In that cold company and a chilling atmosphere some of his enthusiasm evaporated. He remembered that this step of his meant that sooner or later, within a year or two at most, Yarleys, where his family had dwelt for centuries, must go to the hammer. Why had he not accepted Aylward's offer and sold that old fetish to him for £17,000? There was no question of share-dealing there, and if a very wealthy man chose to give a fancy price for a curiosity, he could take it without doubt or shame. At least it would have sufficed to save Yarleys, which after all was only mortgaged for £20,000. For the life of him he could not tell. He had acted on impulse, a very curious impulse, and there was an end of it perhaps; it might be because his uncle had told him as a boy that the thing was unique, or perhaps because old Jeekie, his negro servant, venerated it so much and swore that it was "lucky." At any rate he had declined and there was an end.

But another and a graver matter remained. He had desired wealth to save Yarleys, but he desired it still more for a different purpose. Above everything on earth he loved Barbara, his distant cousin and the niece of Mr. Champers-Haswell, who until an hour ago had been his partner. Now she was a great heiress, and without fortune he could not marry her, even if she would marry him, which remained in doubt. For one thing her uncle and guardian Haswell, under her father's will, had absolute discretion in this matter until she reached the age of twenty-five, and for another he was too proud. Therefore it would seem that in abandoning his business, he had abandoned his chance of Barbara also, which was a truly dreadful thought.

Well, it was in order that he might see her, that he had agreed to visit The Court on the morrow, even though it meant a meeting with his late partners, who were the last people with whom he desired to foregather again so soon. Then and there he made up his mind that before he bade Barbara farewell, he would tell her the whole story, so that she might not misjudge him. After that he would go off somewhere—to Africa perhaps. Meanwhile he was quite tired out, as tired as though he had lain a week in the grip of fever. He must eat some food and get to bed. Sufficient unto the day was the evil thereof, yet on the whole he blessed the name of Jackson, editor of The Judge and his father's old friend.

When Alan had left the office Sir Robert turned to Mr. Champers-Haswell and asked him abruptly, "What the devil does this mean?"

Mr. Haswell looked up at the ceiling and whistled in his own peculiar fashion, then answered:

"I cannot say for certain, but our young friend's strange conduct seems to suggest that he has smelt a rat, possibly even that Jackson, the old beast, has shown him a rat—of a large Turkish breed."

Sir Robert nodded.

"Vernon is a fellow who doesn't like rats; they seem to haunt his sleep," he said; "but do you think that having seen it, he will keep it in the bag?"

"Oh! certainly, certainly," answered Mr. Haswell with cheerfulness; "the man is the soul of honour; he will never give us away. Look how he behaved about those shares. Still, I think that perhaps we are well rid of him. Too much honour, like too much zeal, is a very dangerous quality in any business."

"I don't know that I agree with you," answered Sir Robert. "I am not sure that in the long run we should not do better for a little more of the article. For my part, although it will not hurt us publicly, for the thing will never be noticed, I am sorry that we have lost Vernon, very sorry indeed. I don't think him a fool, and awkward as they may be, I respect his qualities."

"So do I, so do I," answered Mr. Haswell, "and of course we have acted against his advice throughout, which must have been annoying to him. The scheme as he suggested it was a fair business proposition that might have paid ten per cent. on a small capital, but what is the good of ten per cent. to you and me? We want millions and we are going to get them. Well, he is coming to The Court to-morrow, and perhaps after all we shall be able to arrange matters. I'll give Barbara a hint; she has great influence with him, and you might do the same, Aylward."

"Miss Champers has great influence with everyone who is fortunate enough to know her," answered Sir Robert courteously. "But even if she chooses to use it, I doubt if it will avail in this case. Vernon has been making up his mind for a long while. I have watched him and am sure of that. To-night he determined to take the plunge and I do not think that we shall see any more of him in this office. Haswell," he added with sudden energy, "I tell you that of late our luck has been too good to last. The boom, the real boom, came in with Vernon, and with Vernon I think that it will go."

"At any rate it must leave something pretty substantial behind it this time, Aylward, my friend. Whatever happens, within a week we shall be rich, really rich for life."

"For life, Haswell, yes, for life. But what is life? A bubble that any pin may prick. Oh! I know that you do not like the subject, but it is as well to look it in the face sometimes. I'm no church-goer, but if I remember right we were taught to pray the good Lord to deliver us especially 'in all times of our wealth,' which is followed by something about tribulation and sudden death, for when they wrote that prayer the wheel of human fortune went round just as it does to-day. There, let's get out of this before I grow superstitious, as men who believe in nothing sometimes do, because after all they must believe in something, I suppose. Got your hat and coat? So have I, come on," and he switched off the light, so that the room was left in darkness except for the faint glimmering of the fire.

His partner grumbled audibly, for in turning he had knocked his hand against the desk.

"Leave me my only economy, Haswell," he answered with a hard little laugh. "Electricity is strength and I hate to see strength burning to waste. Why do you mind?" he went on as he stepped towards the door. "Is it the contrast? In all times of our wealth, in all times of our tribulation, from sickness and from sudden death—"

"Good Lord deliver us," chimed in Mr. Haswell in a shaking voice behind him. "What the devil's that?"

Sir Robert looked round and saw, or thought that he saw, something very strange. From the pillar on which it stood the golden fetish with a woman's face, appeared to have floated. The firelight showed it gliding towards them across, but a few inches above the floor of the great room. It came very slowly, but it came. Now it reached them and paused, and now it rose into the air until it attained the height of Mr. Champers-Haswell and stayed there, staring into his face and not a hand's breadth away, just as though it were a real woman glaring at him.

He uttered a sound, half whistle and half groan, and fell back, as it chanced on to a morocco-covered seat behind him. For a moment or two the gleaming, golden mask floated in the air. Then it turned very deliberately, rose a little way, and moving sidelong to where Sir Robert stood, hung in front of his face.

Presently Aylward staggered to the mantelpiece and began to fumble for the switch; in the silence his nails scratching at the panelling made a sound like to that of a gnawing mouse. He found it at last, and next instant the office broke into a blaze of light, showing Mr. Haswell, his rubicund face quite pale, his hat and umbrella on the floor, gasping like a dying man upon the couch, and Sir Robert himself clinging to the mantel-shelf as a person might do who had received a mortal wound, while the golden fetish reposed calmly on its pillar, to all appearance as immovable and undisturbed as the antique Venus which matched it at the other end of the room. For a while there was silence. Then Sir Robert, recovering himself, asked:

"Did you notice anything unusual just now, Haswell?"

"Yes," whispered his partner. "I thought that hideous African thing which Vernon brought here, came sliding across the floor and stared into my face with its glittering eyes, and in the eyes—"

"Well, what was in the eyes?"

"I can't remember. It was a kind of picture and the meaning of it was Sudden Death—oh Lord! Sudden Death. Tell me it was a fancy bred of that ill-omened talk of yours?"

"I can't tell you anything of the sort," answered Aylward in a hollow voice, "for I saw something also."

"What?" asked his partner.

"Death that wasn't sudden, and other things."

Again the silence fell till it was broken by Aylward.

"Come," he said, "we have been over-working—too much strain, and now the reaction. Keep this rubbish to yourself, or they will lock you up in an asylum."

"Certainly, Aylward, certainly. But can't you get rid of that beastly image?"

"Not on any account, Haswell, even if it haunts us all day. Here it shall stop until the Saharas are floated on Monday, if I have to lock it in the strongroom and throw the keys into the Thames. Afterwards Vernon can take it, as he has a right to do, and I am sure that with it will go our luck."

"Then the sooner our luck goes, the better," replied Haswell, with a mere ghost of his former whistle. "Life is better than luck, and—Aylward, that Yellow God you are so fond of means to murder us. We are being fatted for the sacrifice, that is all. I remember now, that was one of the things I saw written in its eyes!"

CHAPTER III

JEEKIE TELLS A TALE

The Court, Mr. Champers-Haswell's place, was a very fine house indeed, of a sort. That is, it contained twenty-nine bedrooms, each of them with a bathroom attached, a large number of sitting-rooms, ample garages, stables, and offices, the whole surrounded by several acres of newly-planted gardens. Incidentally it may be mentioned that it was built in the most atrocious taste and looked like a suburban villa seen through a magnifying glass.

It was in this matter of taste that it differed from Sir Robert Aylward's home, Old Hall, a few miles away. Not that this was old either, for the original house had fallen down or been burnt a hundred years before. But Sir Robert, being gifted with artistic perception, had reared up in place of it a smaller but really beautiful dwelling of soft grey stone, long and low, and built in the Tudor style with many gables.

This house, charming as it was, could not of course compare with Yarleys, the ancient seat of the Vernons in the same neighbourhood. Yarleys was pure Elizabethan, although it contained an oak-roofed hall which was said to date back to the time of King John, a remnant of a former house. There was no electric light or other modern convenience at Yarleys, yet it was a place that everyone went to see because of its exceeding beauty and its historical associations. The moat by which it was surrounded, the grass court within, for it was built on three sides of a square, the mullioned windows, the towered gateway of red brick, the low-panelled rooms hung with the portraits of departed Vernons, the sloping park and the splendid oaks that stood about, singly or in groups, were all of them perfect in their way. It was one of the most lovely of English homes, and oddly enough its neglected gardens and the air of decay that pervaded it, added to rather than decreased its charm.

But it is with The Court that we have to do at present, not with Yarleys. Mr. Champers-Haswell had a week-end party. There were ten guests, all men, and with the exception of Alan, who it will be remembered was one of them, all rich and in business. They included two French bankers and three Jews, everyone a prop of the original Sahara Syndicate and deeply interested in the forthcoming flotation. To describe them is unnecessary, for they have no part in our story, being only financiers of a certain class, remarkable for the riches they had acquired by means that for the most part would not bear examination. The riches were evident enough. Ever since the morning the owners of this wealth had arrived by ones or twos in their costly motorcars, attended by smart chauffeurs and valets. Their fur coats, their jewelled studs and rings, something in their very faces suggested money, which indeed was the bond that brought and held them together.

Alan did not come until it was time to dress for dinner, for he knew that Barbara would not appear before that meal, and it was her society he sought, not that of his host or fellow guests. Accompanied by his negro servant, Jeekie, for in a house like this it was necessary to have someone to wait upon him, he drove over from Yarleys, a distance of ten miles, arriving about eight o'clock.

"Mr. Haswell as gone up to dress, Major, and so have the other gentlemen," said the head butler, Mr. Smith, "but Miss Champers told me to give you this note and to say that dinner is at half-past eight."

Alan took the note and asked to be shown to his room. Once there, although he had only five and twenty minutes, he opened it eagerly, while Jeekie unpacked his bag.

"Dear Alan," it ran: "Don't be late for dinner, or I may not be able to keep a place next to me. Of course Sir Robert takes me in. They are a worse lot than usual this time, odious—odious!—and I can't stand one on the left hand as well as on the right. Yours,

"B.

"P.S. What have you been doing? Our distinguished guests, to say nothing of my uncle, seem to be in a great fuss about you. I overheard them talking when I was pretending to arrange some flowers. One of them called you a sanctimonious prig and an obstinate donkey, and another answered—I think it was Sir

Robert —'No doubt, but obstinate donkeys can kick and have been known to upset other people's applecarts ere now.' Is the Sahara Syndicate the applecart? If so, I'll forgive you.

"P.P.S. Remember that we will walk to church together to-morrow, but come down to breakfast in knickerbockers or something to put them off, and I'll do the same—I mean I'll dress as if I were going to golf. We can turn into Christians later. If we don't—dress like that, I mean—they'll guess and all want to come to church, except the Jews, which would bring the judgment of Heaven on us.

"P.P.P.S. Don't be careless and leave this note lying about, for the under-footman who waits upon you reads all the letters. He steams them over a kettle. Smith the butler is the only respectable man in this house."

Alan laughed outright as he finished this peculiar and outspoken epistle, which somehow revived his spirits, that since the previous day had been low enough. It refreshed him. It was like a breath of frosty air from an open window blowing clean and cold into a scented, overheated room. He would have liked to keep it, but remembering Barbara's injunctions and the under-footman, threw it onto the fire and watched it burn. Jeekie coughed to intimate that it was time for his master to dress, and Alan turned and looked at him in an absent-minded fashion.

He was worth looking at, was Jeekie. Let the reader imagine a very tall and powerfully-built negro with a skin as black as a well-polished boot, woolly hair as white as snow, a little tufted beard also white, a hand like a leg of mutton, but with long delicate fingers and pink, filbert-shaped nails, an immovable countenance, but set in it beneath a massive brow, two extraordinary humorous and eloquent black eyes which expressed every emotion passing through the brain behind them, that is when their owner chose to allow them to do so. Such was Jeekie.

"Shall I unlace your boots, Major?" he said in his full, melodious voice and speaking the most perfect English. "I expect that the gong will sound in nine and a half minutes."

"Then let it sound and be hanged to it," answered Alan; "no, I forgot—I must hurry. Jeekie, put that fire out and open all the windows as soon as I go down. This room is like a hot-house."

"Yes, Major, the fire shall be extinguished and the sleeping-chamber ventilated. The other boot, if you please, Major."

"Jeekie," said Alan, "who is stopping in this place? Have you heard?"

"I collected some names on my way upstairs, Major. Three of the gentlemen you have never met before, but," he added suddenly breaking away from his high-flown book-learned English, as was his custom when in earnest, "Jeekie think they just black niggers like the rest, thief people. There ain't a white man in this house, except you and Miss Barbara and me, Major. Jeekie learnt all that in servant's hall palaver. No, not now, other time. Everyone tell everything to Jeekie, poor old African fool, and he look up an answer, 'O law! you don't say so?' but keep his eyes and ears open all the same."

"I'll be bound you do, Jeekie," replied Alan, laughing again. "Well, go on keeping them open, and give me those trousers."

"Yes, Major," answered Jeekie, reassuming his grand manner, "I shall continue to collect information which may prove to your advantage, but personally I wish that you were clear of the whole caboodle, except Miss Barbara."

"Hear, hear," ejaculated Alan, "there goes the gong. Mind you come in and help to wait," and hurrying into his coat he departed downstairs.

The guests were gathered in the hall drinking sherry and bitters, a proceeding that to Alan's mind set a stamp upon the house. His host, Mr. Champers-Haswell, came forward and greeted him with much affectionate enthusiasm, and Alan noticed that he looked very pale, also that his thoughts seemed to be wandering, for he introduced a French banker to him as a noted Jew, and the noted Jew as the French banker, although the distinction between them was obvious and the gentlemen concerned evidently resented the mistake. Sir Robert Aylward, catching sight of him, came across the hall in his usual, direct fashion, and shook him by the hand.

"Glad to see you, Vernon," he said, fixing his piercing eyes upon Alan as though he were trying to read his thoughts. "Pleasant change this from the City and all that eternal business, isn't it? Ah! you are thinking that one is not quite clear of business after all," and he glanced round at the company. "That's one of your cousin Haswell's faults; he can never shake himself free of the thing, never get any real recreation. I'd bet you a sovereign that he has a stenographer waiting by a telephone in the next room, just in case any opportunity should arise in the course of conversation. That is magnificent, but it is not wise. His heart can't stand it; it will wear him out before his time. Listen, they are all talking about the Sahara. I wish I were there; it must be quiet at any rate. The sands beneath, the eternal stars above. Yes, I wish I were there," he repeated with a sigh, and Alan noted that although his face could not be more pallid than its natural colour, it looked quite worn and old.

"So do I," he answered with enthusiasm.

Then a French gentleman on his left, having discovered that he was the engineer who had formulated the great flooding scheme, began to address him as "Cher maitre," speaking so rapidly his own language that Alan, whose French was none of the best, struggled after him in vain. Whilst he was trying to answer a question which he did not understand, the door at the end of the hall opened, and through it appeared Barbara Champers.

It was a large hall and she was a long way off, which caused her to look small, who indeed was only of middle height. Yet even at that distance it was impossible to mistake the dignity of her appearance. A slim woman with brown hair, cheerful brown eyes, a well-modelled face, a rounded figure and an excellent complexion, such was Barbara. Ten thousand young ladies could be found as good, or even better looking, yet something about her differentiated her from the majority of her sex. There was determination in her step, and overflowing health and vigour in her every movement. Her eyes had a trick of looking straight into any other eyes they met, not boldly, but with a kind of virginal fearlessness and enterprise that people often found embarrassing. Indeed she was extremely virginal and devoid of the usual fringe of feminine airs and graces, a nymph of the woods and waters, who although she was three and twenty, as yet recked little of men save as companions whom she liked or disliked according to her instincts. For the rest she was sweetly dressed in a white robe with silver on it, and wore no ornaments save a row of small pearls about her throat and some lilies of the valley at her breast.

Barbara came straight onwards, looking neither to the right or to the left, till she reached her uncle, to whom she nodded. Then she walked to Alan and, offering him her hand, said:

"How do you do! Why did you not come over at lunch time? I wanted to play a round of golf with you this afternoon."

Alan answered something about being busy at Yarleys.

"Yarleys!" she replied. "I thought that you lived in the City now, making money out of speculations, like everyone else that I know."

"Why, Miss Champers," broke in Sir Robert reproachfully, "I asked you to play a round of golf before tea and you would not."

"No," she answered, "because I was waiting for my cousin. We are better matched, Sir Robert."

There was something in her voice, usually so soft and pleasant, as she spoke these words, something of steeliness and defiance that caused Alan to feel at once happy and uncomfortable. Apparently also it caused Aylward to feel angry, for he flashed a glance at Alan over her head of which the purport could not be mistaken, though his pale face remained as immovable as ever. "We are enemies. I hate you," said that glance. Probably Barbara saw it; at any rate before either of them could speak again, she said:

"Thank goodness, there is dinner at last. Sir Robert, will you take me in, and, Alan, will you sit on the other side of me? My uncle will show the rest their places."

The meal was long and magnificent; the price of each dish of it would have kept a poor family for a month, and on the cost of the exquisite wines they might have lived for a year or two. Also the last were well patronized by everyone except Barbara, who drank water, and Alan, who since his severe fever took nothing but weak whiskey and soda and a little claret. Even Aylward, a temperate person, absorbed a good deal of champagne. As a consequence the conversation grew animated, and under cover of it, while Sir Robert was arguing with his neighbour on the left, Barbara asked in a low voice:

"What is the row, Alan? Tell me, I can't wait any longer."

"I have quarrelled with them," he answered, staring at his mutton as though he were criticizing it. "I mean, I have left the firm and have nothing more to do with the business."

Barbara's eyes lit up as she whispered back:

"Glad of it. Best news I have heard for many a day. But then, may I ask why you are here?"

"I came to see you," he replied humbly—"thought perhaps you wouldn't mind," and in his confusion he let his knife fall into the mutton, whence it rebounded, staining his shirt front.

Barbara laughed, that happy, delightful little laugh of hers, presumably at the accident with the knife. Whether or no she "minded" did not appear, only she handed her handkerchief, a costly, lace-fringed trifle, to Alan to wipe the gravy off his shirt, which he took thinking it was a napkin, and as she did so, touched his hand with a little caressing movement of her fingers. Whether this was done by chance or on purpose did not appear either. At least it made Alan feel extremely happy. Also when he discovered what it was, he kept that gravy-stained handkerchief, nor did she ever ask for it back again. Only once in after days when she happened to come across it stuffed away in the corner of a despatch-box, she blushed all over, and said that she had no idea that any man could be so foolish out of a book.

"Now that you are really clear of it, I am going for them," she said presently when the wiping process was finished. "I have only restrained myself for your sake," and leaning back in her chair she stared at the ceiling, lost in meditation.

Presently there came one of those silences which will fall upon dinner-parties at times, however excellent and plentiful the champagne.

"Sir Robert Aylward," said Barbara in that clear, carrying voice of hers, "will you, as an expert, instruct a very ignorant person? I want a little information."

"Miss Champers," he answered, "am I not always at your service?" and all listened to hear upon what point their hostess desired to be enlightened.

"Sir Robert," she went on calmly, "everyone here is, I believe, what is called a financier, that is except myself and Major Vernon, who only tries to be and will, I am sure, fail, since Nature made him something else, a soldier and—what else did Nature make you, Alan?"

As he vouchsafed no answer to question, although Sir Robert muttered an uncomplimentary one between his lips which Barbara heard, or read, she continued:

"And you are all very rich and successful, are you not, and are going to be much richer and much more successful—next week. Now what I want to ask you is—how is it done?"

"Accepting the premises for the sake of argument, Miss Champers," replied Sir Robert, who felt that he could not refuse the challenge, "the answer is that it is done by finance."

"I am still in the dark," she said. "Finance, as I have heard of it, means floating companies, and companies are floated to earn money for those who invest in them. Now this afternoon as I was dull, I got hold of a book called the Directory of Directors, and looked up all your names in it, except those of the gentlemen from Paris, and the companies that you direct—I found out about those in another book. Well, I could not make out that any of these companies have ever earned any money, a dividend, don't you call it? Therefore how do you all grow so rich, and why do people invest in them?"

Now Sir Robert frowned, Alan coloured, two or three of the company laughed outright, and one of the French gentlemen who understood English and had already drunk as much as was good for him, remarked loudly to his neighbour, "Ah! she is charming. She do touch the spot, like that ointment you give me to-day. How do we grow rich and why do the people invest? Mon Dieu! why do they invest? That is the great mystery. I say that cette belle demoiselle, votre nièce, est ravissante. Elle a d'esprit, mon ami Haswell."

Apparently her uncle did not share these sentiments, for he turned as red as any turkey-cock, and said across the great round table:

"My dear Barbara, I wish that you would leave matters which you do not understand alone. We are here to dine, not to talk about finance."

"Certainly, Uncle," she answered sweetly. "I stand, or rather sit, reproved. I suppose that I have put my foot into it as usual, and the worst of it is," she added, turning to Sir Robert, "that I am just as ignorant as I was before."

"If you want to master these matters, Miss Champers," said Aylward with a rather forced laugh, "you must go into training and worship at the shrine of"—he meant to say Mammon, then thinking that the word sounded unpleasant, substituted—"the Yellow God as we do."

At these words Alan, who had been studying his plate, looked up quickly, and her uncle's face turned from red to white. But the irrepressible Barbara seized upon them.

"The Yellow God," she repeated. "Do you mean money or that fetish thing of Major Vernon's with the terrible woman's face that I saw at the office in the City. Well, to change the subject, tell us, Alan, what is that yellow god of yours and where did it come from?"

"My uncle Austin, who was my mother's brother and a missionary, brought it from West Africa a great many years ago. He was the first to visit the tribe who worship it; in fact I do not think that anyone has ever visited them since. But really I do not know all the story. Jeekie can tell you about it if you want to know, for he is one of that people and escaped with my uncle."

Now Jeekie having left the room, some of the guests wished to send for him, but Mr. Champers-Haswell objected. The end of it was that a compromise was effected, Alan undertaking to produce his retainer afterwards when they went to play billiards or cards.

Dinner was over at length and the diners, who had dined well, were gathered in the billiard room to smoke and amuse themselves as they wished. It was a very large room, sixty feet long indeed, with a wide space in the centre between the two tables, which was furnished as a lounge. When the gentlemen entered it they found Barbara standing by the great fireplace in this central space, a little shape of white and silver in its emptiness.

"Forgive me for intruding on you," she said, "and please do not stop smoking, for I like the smell. I have sat up expressly to hear Jeekie's story of the Yellow God. Alan, produce Jeekie, or I shall go to bed at once."

Her uncle made a movement as though to interfere, but Sir Robert said something to him which appeared to cause him to change his mind, while the rest in some way or another signified an enthusiastic assent. All of them were anxious to see this Jeekie and hear his tale, if he had one to tell. So Jeekie was sent for and presently arrived clad in the dress clothes which are common to all classes in England and America. There he stood before them white-headed, ebony-faced, gigantic, imperturbable. There is no doubt that his appearance produced an effect, for it was unusual and indeed striking.

"You sent for me, Major?" he said, addressing his master, to whom he gave a military salute, for he had been Alan's servant when he was in the Army.

"Yes, Jeekie. Miss Barbara here and these gentlemen, wish you to tell them all that you know about the Yellow God."

The negro started and rolled his round eyes upwards till the whites of them showed, then began in his school-book English:

"That is a private subject, Major, upon which I should prefer not to discourse before this very public company."

A chorus of remonstrance arose and one of the Jewish gentlemen approaching Jeekie, slipped a couple of sovereigns into his great hand, which he promptly transferred to his pocket without seeming to notice them.

"Jeekie," said Barbara, "don't disappoint me."

"Very well, miss, I fall in with your wishes. The Yellow God that all these gentlemen worship, quite another god to that of which you desire that I should tell you. You know all about him. My god is of female sex."

At this statement his audience burst into laughter while Jeekie rolled his eyes again and waited till they had finished. "My god," he went on presently, "I mean, gentlemen, the god I used to pray to, for I am a good Christian now, has so much gold that she does not care for any more," and he paused.

"Then what does she care for?" asked someone.

"Blood," answered Jeekie. "She is god of Death. Her name is Little Bonsa or Small Swimming Head; she is wife of Big Bonsa or Great Swimming Head."

Again there was laughter, though less general—for instance, neither Sir Robert nor Mr. Champers-Haswell laughed. This merriment seemed to excite Jeekie. At any rate it caused him to cease his stilted talk and relapse into the strange vernacular that is common to all negroes, tinctured with a racy slang that was all his own.

"You want to hear Yellow God palaver?" he said rapidly. "Very well, I tell you, you cocksure white men who think you know everything, but know nothing at all. My people, people of the Asiki, that mean people of Spirits, what you call ghosts and say you no believe in, but always look for behind door, they worship Yellow God, Bonsa Big and Bonsa Little, worship both and call them one; only Little Bonsa on trip to this country just now and sit and think in City office. Yellow God live long way up a great river, then turn to the left and walk six days through big forest where dwarf people shoot you with poisoned arrow. Then turn to the right, walk up stream where many wild beasts. Then turn to the left again and go in canoe through swamp where you die of fever, and across lake. Then walk over grassland and mountains. Then in kloof of the mountains where big black trees make a roof and river fall like thunder, find Asiki and gold house of the Yellow God. All that mountain gold, full of gold and beneath gold house Yellow God afloat in water. She what you call Queen, priestess, live there also, always there, very beautiful woman called Asika with face like Yellow God, cruel, cruel. She take a husband every year, and every year he die because she always hunt for right man but never find him."

"Does she kill him then?" asked Barbara.

"Oh! no, she no kill him, Miss, he kill himself at end of year, glad to get away from Asika and go to spirits. While he live he have a very good time, plenty to eat, plenty wives, fine house, much gold as he like, only nothing to spend it on, pretty necklace, nice paint for face. But Asika, little bit by little bit she eat up his spirit. He see too many ghosts. The house where he sleep with dead men who once have his billet, full of ghosts and every night there come more and sit with him, sit all round him, look at him with great eyes, just like you look at me, till at last when Asika finish eating up his spirit, he go crazy, he howl like man in hell, he throw away all the gold they give him, and then, sometimes after one week, sometimes after one month, sometimes after one year if he be strong but never more, he run out at night and jump into canal where Yellow God float and god get him, while Asika sit on the bank and laugh, 'cause she hungry for new man to eat up his spirit too."

Jeekie's big voice died away to a whisper and ceased. There was a silence in the room, for even in the shine of the electric light and through the fumes of champagne, in more than one imagination there rose a vision of that haunted water in which floated the great Yellow God, and of some mad being casting himself to his death beneath the moon, while his beautiful witch wife who was "hungry for more spirits" sat upon its edge and laughed. Although his language was now commonplace enough, even ludicrous at times, the negro had undoubtedly the art of narration. His auditors felt that he spoke of what he knew, or had seen, that the very recollection of it frightened him, therefore he frightened them.

Again Barbara broke the silence which she felt to be awkward.

"Why do more ghosts come very night to sit with the queen's husband, Jeekie?" she asked. "Where do they come from?"

"Out of the dead, miss, dead husbands of Asika from beginning of the world; what they call Munganas. Also always they make sacrifice to Yellow God. From far, far away them poor niggers send people to be sacrifice that their house or tribe get luck. Sometimes they send kings, sometimes great men, sometimes doctors, sometimes women what have twin babies. Also the Asiki bring people what is witches, or have drunk poison stuff which blacks call muavi and have not been sick, or perhaps son they love best to take curse off their roof. All these come to Yellow God. Then Asiki doctor, they have Death-palaver. On night of full moon they beat drum, and drum go Wow! Wow! Wow! and doctors pick out those to die that month. Once they pick out Jeekie, oh! good Lord, they pick out me," and as he said the words he gasped and with his great hand wiped off the sweat that started from his brow. "But Yellow God no take Jeekie that time, no want him and I escape."

"How?" asked Sir Robert.

"With my master, Major's uncle, Reverend Austin, he who come try to make Asiki Christian. He snap his fingers, put on small mask of Yellow God which he prig, Little Bonsa herself, that same face which sit in your office now," and he pointed to Sir Robert, "like one toad upon a stone. Priests think that god make herself into man, want holiday, take me out into forest to kill me and eat my life. So they let us go by and we go just as though devil kick us—fast, fast, and never see the Asiki any more. But Little Bonsa I bring with me for luck, tell truth I no dare leave her behind, she not stand that; and now she sit in your office and think and think and make magic there. That why you grow rich, because she know you worship her."

"That's a nice way for a baptized Christian to talk," said Barbara, adding, "But Jeekie, what do you mean when you say that the god did not take you?"

"I mean this, miss; when victim offered to Big Yellow God, priest-men bring him to edge of canal where the great god float. Then if Yellow God want him, it turn and swim across water."

"Swim across water! I thought you said it was only a mask of gold?"

"I don't know, miss, perhaps man inside the mask, perhaps spirit. I say it swim across water in the night, always in the night, and lift itself up and look in victim's face. Then priest take him and kill him, sometimes one way—sometimes another. Or if he escape and they not kill him, all same for that Johnnie, he die in about one year, always die, no one ever live long if Yellow God swim to him in dark and rise up and smile in his face. No matter if it Big Bonsa or Little Bonsa, for they man and wife joined in holy matrimony and either do trick."

As these words left Jeekie's lips Alan became aware of some unusual movement on his left and looking round, saw that Mr. Champers-Haswell, who stood by him, had dropped the cigar which he held and, white as a sheet, was swaying to and fro. Indeed in another instant he would have fallen had not Alan caught him in his arms and supported him till others came to his assistance, when between them they carried him to a sofa. On their way they passed a table where spirits and soda water were set out, and to his astonishment Alan noticed that Sir Robert Aylward, looking little if at all better than his partner, had helped himself to half a tumbler of cognac, which he was swallowing in great gulps. Then there was confusion and someone went to telephone the doctor, while the deep voice of Jeekie was heard exclaiming:

"That Yellow God at work—oh yes, Little Bonsa on the job. Jeekie Christian man but no doubt she very powerful fetish and can do anything she like to them that worship her, and you see, she sit in office of these gentlemen. 'Spect she make Reverend Austin and me bring her to England because she got eye on firm of Messrs. Aylward & Haswell, London, E.C. Oh, shouldn't wonder at all, for Bonsa know everything."

"Oh, confound you and your fetish! Be off, you old donkey," almost shouted Alan.

"Major," replied the offended Jeekie, assuming his grand manner and language, "it was not I who wished to narrate this history of blood-stained superstitions of poor African. Mustn't blame old Jeekie if they make Christian gents sick as Channel steamer."

"Be off," repeated Alan, stamping his foot.

So Jeekie went, but outside the door, as it chanced, he encountered one of the Jew gentlemen who also appeared to be a little "sick." An idea striking him, he touched his white hair with his finger and said:

"You like Jeekie's pretty story, sir? Well, Jeekie think that if you make little present to him, like your brother in there, it please Yellow God very much, and bring you plenty luck."

Then acting upon some unaccustomed impulse, that Jew became exceedingly generous. In his pocket was a handful of sovereigns which he had been prepared to stake at bridge. He grasped them all and thrust them into Jeekie's outstretched palm, where they seemed to melt.

"Thank you, sir," said Jeekie. "Now I sure you have plenty luck, just like your grandpa Jacob in Book when he do his brudder in eye."

CHAPTER IV

ALAN AND BARBARA

There was no bridge or billiards at the Court that night, where ordinarily the play ran high enough. After Mr. Haswell had been carried to his room, some of the guests, among them Sir Robert Aylward, went to bed, remarking that they could do no good by sitting up, while others, more concerned, waited to hear the verdict of the doctor, who must drive from six miles away. He came, and half an hour later Barbara entered the billiard room and told Alan, who was sitting there smoking, that her uncle had recovered from his faint, and that the doctor, who was to stay all night, said that he was in no danger, only suffering from a heart attack brought on apparently by over-work or excitement.

When Alan woke next morning the first thing that he heard through his open window was the sound of the doctor's departing dogcart. Then Jeekie appeared and told him that Mr. Haswell was all right again, but that all night he had shaken "like one jelly." Alan asked what had been the matter with him, but Jeekie only shrugged his shoulders and said that he did not know—"perhaps Yellow God touch him up."

At breakfast, as in her note she had said she would, Barbara appeared wearing a short skirt. Sir Robert, who was there, also looked extremely pale even for him and with black rims round his eyes, asked her if she were going to golf, to which she answered that she would think it over. It was a somewhat melancholy meal, and as though by common consent no mention was made of Jeekie's tale of the Yellow God, and beyond the usual polite inquiries, very little of their host's seizure.

As Barbara went out she whispered to Alan, who opened the door for her, "Meet me at half-past ten in the kitchen garden."

Accordingly, having changed his clothes surreptitiously, Alan, avoiding the others, made his way by a circuitous route to this kitchen garden, which after the fashion of modern places was hidden behind a belt of trees nearly a quarter of a mile from the house. Here he wandered about till presently he heard Barbara's pleasant voice behind him saying:

"Don't dawdle so, we shall be late for church."

So they started, somewhat furtively like runaway children. As they went Alan asked how her uncle was.

"All right now," she answered, "but he has had a bad shake. It was that Yellow God story which did it. I know, for I was there when he was coming to, with Sir Robert. He kept talking about it in a confused manner, saying that it was swimming to him across the floor, till at last Sir Robert bent over him and told him to be quiet quite sternly. Do you know, Alan, I believe that your pet fetish has been manifesting itself in some unpleasant fashion up there in the office?"

"Indeed. If so, it must be since I left, for I never heard of anything of the sort, nor are Aylward and your uncle likely people to see ghosts. In fact Sir Robert wished to give me about £17,000 for the thing only the day before yesterday, which doesn't look as though it had been frightening him."

"Well, he won't repeat the offer, Alan, for I heard him promise my uncle only this morning that it should be sent back to Yarleys at once. But why did he want to buy it for such a lot of money? Tell me quickly, Alan, I am dying to hear the whole story."

So he began and told her, omitting nothing, while she listened eagerly to every word, hardly interrupting him at all. As he finished his tale they reached the door of the quaint old village church just as the clock was striking eleven.

"Come in, Alan," she said gently, "and thank Heaven for all its mercies, for you should be a grateful man to-day."

Then without giving him time to answer she entered the church and they took their places in the great square pew that for generations had been occupied by the owners of the ancient house which Mr. Haswell pulled down when he built The Court. There were their monuments upon the wall and their gravestones in the chancel floor. But now no one except Barbara ever sat in their pew; even the benches set aside for the servants were empty, for those who frequented The Court were not church-goers and "like master, like man." Indeed the gentle-faced old clergyman looked quite pleased and surprised when he saw two inhabitants of that palatial residence amongst his congregation, although it is true that Barbara was his friend and helper.

The simple service went on; the first lesson was read. It cried woe upon them that joined house to house and field to field, that draw iniquity with cords of vanity and sin as it were with a cart rope; that call evil good and good evil, that put darkness for light and light for darkness, that justify the wicked for reward; that feast full but regard not the work of the Lord, neither consider the operation of His hand, for of such it prophesied that their houses great and fair should be without inhabitant and desolate.

It was very well read, and Alan, listening, thought that the denunciations of the old seer of thousands of years ago were not inappropriate to the dwellers in some houses great and fair of his own day, who, whatever they did or left undone, regarded not the work of the Lord, neither considered the operation of His hand. Perhaps Barbara thought so too; at any rate a rather sad little smile appeared once or twice upon her sweet, firm face as the immortal poem echoed down the aisle.

The peace that passeth understanding was invoked upon their heads, and rising with the rest of the scanty congregation they went away.

"Shall we walk home by the woods, Alan?" asked Barbara. "It is three miles round, but we don't lunch till two."

He nodded, and presently they were alone in those woods, the beautiful woods through which the breath of spring was breathing, treading upon carpets of bluebells, violet and primrose; quite alone, unaccompanied save by the wild things that stole across their path, undisturbed save by the sound of the singing birds and of the wind among the trees.

"What did you mean, Barbara, when you said that I should be a grateful man to-day?" asked Alan presently.

Barbara looked him in the eyes in that open, virginal fashion of hers and answered in the words of the lesson, "'Woe unto them that draw iniquity with the cords of vanity and sin as it were with a cart-rope, that lay house to house,'" and through an opening in the woods she pointed to the roof of The Court standing on one hill, and to the roof of Old Hall standing upon another—"'and field to field,'" and with a sweep of her hand she indicated all the country round, "'for many houses great and fair that have music in their feasts shall be left desolate.'" Then turning she said:

"Do you understand now, Alan?"

"I think so," he answered. "You mean that I have been in bad company."

"Very bad, Alan. One of them is my own uncle, but the truth remains the truth. Alan, they are no better than thieves; all this wealth is stolen, and I thank God that you have found it out in time before you became one of them in heart as well as in name."

"If you refer to the Sahara Syndicate," he said, "the idea is sound enough; indeed, I am responsible for it. The thing can be done, great benefits would result, too long to go into."

"Yes, yes, Alan, but you know that they never mean to do it, they only mean to get the millions from the public. I have lived with my uncle for ten years, ever since my poor father died, and I know the backstairs of the business. There have been half a dozen schemes like this, and although they have had their bad times, very bad times, he and Sir Robert have grown richer and richer. But what has happened to those who have invested in them? Oh! let us drop the subject, it is unpleasant. For myself it doesn't matter, because although it isn't under my control, I have money of my own. You know we are a plebeian lot on the male side, my grandfather was a draper in a large way of business, my father was a coal-merchant who made a great fortune. His brother, my uncle, in whom my father always believed implicitly, took to what is called Finance, and when my father died he left me, his only child, in his guardianship. Until I am five and twenty I cannot even marry or touch a halfpenny without his consent; in fact if I should marry against his will the most of my money goes to him."

"I expect that he has got it already," said Alan.

"No, I think not. I found out that, although it is not mine, it is not his. He can't draw it without my signature, and I steadily refuse to sign anything. Again and again they have brought me documents, and I have always said that I would consider them at five and twenty, when I came of age under my father's will. I went on the sly to a lawyer in Kingswell and paid him a guinea for his advice, and he put me up to that. 'Sign nothing,' he said, and I have signed nothing, so, except by forgery nothing can have gone. Still for all that it may have gone. For anything I know I am not worth more than the clothes I stand in, although my father was a very rich man."

"If so, we are about in the same boat, Barbara," Alan answered with a laugh, "for my present possessions are Yarleys, which brings in about £100 a year less than the interest on its mortgages and cost of upkeep, and the £1700 that Aylward paid me back on Friday for my shares. If I had stuck to them I understand that in a week or two I should have been worth £100,000, and now you see, here I am, over thirty years of age without a profession, invalided out of the army and having failed in finance, a mere bit of driftwood without hope and without a trade."

Barbara's brown eyes grew soft with sympathy, or was it tears?

"You are a curious creature, Alan," she said. "Why didn't you take the £17,000 for that fetish of yours? It would have been a fair deal and have set you on your legs."

"I don't know," he answered dejectedly. "It went against the grain, so what is the use of talking about it? I think my old uncle Austin told me it wasn't to be parted with—no, perhaps it was Jeekie. Bother the Yellow God! it is always cropping up."

"Yes," replied Barbara, "the Yellow God is always cropping up, especially in this neighbourhood."

They walked on a while in silence, till suddenly Barbara sat down upon a bole of felled oak and began to cry.

"What is the matter with you?" asked Alan.

"I don't know," she answered. "Everything goes wrong. I live in a kind of gilded hell. I don't like my uncle and I loath the men he brings about the place. I have no friends, I scarcely know a woman intimately, I have troubles I can't tell you and—I am wretched. You are the only creature I have left to talk to, and I suppose that after this row you must go away too to make your living."

Alan looked at her there weeping on the log and his heart swelled within him, for he had loved this girl for years.

"Barbara," he gasped, "please don't cry, it upsets me. You know you are a great heiress—"

"That remains to be proved," she answered. "But anyway, what has it to do with the case?"

"It has everything to do with it, at least so far as I am concerned. If it hadn't been for that I should have asked you to marry me a long while ago, because I love you, as I would now, but of course it is impossible."

Barbara ceased her weeping, wiped her eyes with the back of her hand, and looked up at him.

"Alan," she said, "I think that you are the biggest fool I ever knew—not but that a fool is rather refreshing when one lives among knaves."

"I know I am a fool," he answered. "If I wasn't I should not have mentioned my misfortune to you, but sometimes things are too much for one. Forget it and forgive me."

"Oh! yes," she said; "I forgive you; a woman can generally forgive a man for being fond of her. Whatever she may be, she is ready to take a lenient view of his human weakness. But as to forgetting, that is a different matter. I don't exactly see why I should be so anxious to forget, who haven't many people to care about me," and she looked at him in quite a new fashion, one indeed which gave him something of a shock, for he had not thought the nymph-like Barbara capable of such a look as that. She and any sort of passion had always seemed so far apart.

Now after all Alan was very much a man, if a modest one, with all a man's instincts, and therefore there are appearances of the female face which even such as he could not entirely misinterpret.

"You—don't—mean," he said doubtfully, "you don't really mean—" and he stood hesitating before her.

"If you would put your question a little more clearly, Alan, I might be able to give you an answer," she replied, that quaint little smile of hers creeping to the corners of her mouth like sunshine through a mist of rain.

"You don't really mean," he went on, "that you care anything about me, like, like I have cared for you for years?"

"Oh! Alan," she said, laughing outright, "why in the name of goodness shouldn't I care about you? I didn't say that I do, mind, but why shouldn't I? What is the gulf between us?"

"The old one," he answered, "that between Dives and Lazarus—that between the rich and the poor."

"Alan," said Barbara, looking down, "I don't know what has come over me, but for some unexplained and inexplicable reason I am inclined to give Lazarus a lead—across that gulf, the first one, I mean, not the second!"

Like the glance which preceded it, this was a saying that even Alan could not misunderstand. He sat himself on the log beside her, while she, still looking down, watched him out of the corners of her eyes. He went red, he went white, his heart beat very violently. Then he stretched out his big brown hand and took her small white one, and as this familiarity produced no remonstrance, let it fall, and passing his arm about her, drew her to him and embraced her, not once, but often, with such vigour that a squirrel which had been watching these proceedings from a neighbouring tree, bolted round it scandalized and was seen no more.

"I love you, I love you," he said huskily.

"So I gather," she answered in a feeble voice.

"Do you care for me?" he asked.

"It would seem that I must, Alan, otherwise I should scarcely—oh! you foolish Alan," and heedless of her Sunday hat, which never recovered from this encounter, but was kept as a holy relic, she let her head fall upon his shoulder and began to cry again, this time for very happiness.

He kissed her tears away, then as he could think of nothing else to say, asked her if she would marry him.

"It is the general sequel to this kind of thing, I believe," she answered; "or at any rate it ought to be. But if you want a direct answer—yes, I will, if my uncle will let me, which he won't, as you have quarrelled with him, or at any rate two years hence, when I am five and twenty and my own mistress; that is if we have anything to marry on, for one must eat. At present our worldly possessions seem to consist chiefly of a large store of mutual affection, a good stock of clothes and one Yellow God, which after what happened last night, I do not think you will get another chance of turning into cash."

"I must make money somehow," he said.

"Yes, Alan, but I am afraid it is not easy to do—honestly. Nobody wants people without capital whose only stock in trade is a brief but distinguished military career, and a large experience of African fever."

Alan groaned at this veracious but discouraging remark, and she went on quickly:

"I mean to spend another guinea upon my friend the lawyer at Kingswell. Perhaps he can raise the wind, by a post-obit, or something," she added vaguely, "I mean a post-uncle-obit."

"If he does, Barbara, I can't live on your money alone, it isn't right."

"Oh! don't you trouble about that, Alan. If once I can get hold of those dim thousands you will soon be able to make more, for unto him that hath shall be given. But at present they are very dim, and for all I know may be represented by stock in deceased companies. In short, the financial position is extraordinarily depressed, as they say in the Market Intelligence in The Times. But that's no reason why we should be depressed also."

"No, Barbara, for at any rate we have got each other."

"Yes," she answered, springing up, "we have got each other, dear, until Death do us part, and somehow I don't think he'll do that yet awhile; it comes into my heart that he won't do that, Alan, that you and I are going to live out our days. So what does the rest matter? In two years I shall be a free woman. In fact, if the worst comes to the worst, I'll defy them all," and she set her little mouth like a rock, "and marry you straight away, as being over age, I can do, even if it costs me every halfpenny that I've got."

"No, no," he said, "it would be wrong, wrong to yourself and wrong to your descendants."

"Very well, Alan, then, we will wait, or perhaps luck will come our way—why shouldn't it? At any rate for my part I never felt so happy in my life; for, dear Alan, we have found what we were born to find, found it once and for always, and the rest is mere etceteras. What would be the use of all the gold of the Asiki people that Jeekie was talking about last night, to either of us, if we had not each other? We can get on without the wealth, but we couldn't get on apart, or at least I couldn't and I don't mind saying so."

"No, my darling, no," he answered, turning white at the very thought, "we couldn't get on apart—now. In fact I don't know how I have done so so long already, except that I was always hoping that a time would come when we shouldn't be apart. That is why I went into that infernal business, to make enough money to be able to ask you to marry me. And now I have gone out of the business and asked you just when I shouldn't."

"Yes, so you see you might as well have done it a year or two ago when perhaps things would have been simpler. Well, it is a fine example of the vanity of human plans, and, Alan, we must be going home to lunch. If we don't, Sir Robert will be organizing a search party to look for us; in fact, I shouldn't wonder if he is doing that already, in the wrong direction."

The mention of Sir Robert Aylward's name fell on them both like a blast of cold wind in summer, and for a while they walked in silence.

"You are afraid of that man, Barbara," said Alan presently, guessing her thoughts.

"A little," she answered, "so far as I can be afraid of anything any more. And you?"

"A little also. I think that he will give us trouble. He can be very malevolent and resourceful."

"Resourceful, Alan; well, so can I. I'll back my wits against his any day. He shan't separate us by anything short of murder, which he won't go in for. Men like that don't like to break the law; they have too much to lose. But no doubt he will make things uncomfortable for you, if he can, for several reasons."

Again they walked on lost in reflections, when Barbara suddenly saw her lover's face brighten.

"What is it, Alan?" she asked.

"Something that is rare enough with me, Barbara—an idea. You remember speaking about that Asiki gold just now. Well, why shouldn't I go and get it?"

She stared at him.

"It sounds a little speculative," she said; "something like one of my uncle's companies."

"Not half so speculative as you think. I have no doubt it is there and Jeekie knows the way. Also I seem to remember that there is a map and an account of the whole thing in Uncle Austin's diaries, though to tell you the truth the old fellow wrote such a fearful hand, that I have never taken the trouble to read it. You see," he went on with enthusiasm, "it is the kind of business that I can do. I am thoroughly salted to fever, I know the West Coast, where I spent three years on that Boundary Commission, I have studied the natives and can talk several of their dialects. Of course there would be a risk, but there are risks in everything, and like you I am not afraid about that, for I believe that we have got our lives before us."

"Read up those diaries, Alan, and we will talk the thing over again. I'll pump Jeekie, who will tell me anything by coaxing, and try to get at the truth. Meanwhile what are you going to do about my uncle?"

"Speak to him, of course, and have the row over."

"Yes," she answered, "that is the best and the most honest. Of course he can turn you out, but he can't prevent my seeing you. If he does, go home to Yarleys and I'll come over and call. Here we are, let us go in by the back door," and she pointed to her crushed hat, and laughed.

CHAPTER V

BARBARA MAKES A SPEECH

While Alan and Barbara, on the most momentous occasion of their lives, were seated upon the fallen oak in the woods that thrilled with the breath of spring, another interview was taking place in Mr. Champers-Haswell's private suite at The Court, the decorations of which, as he was wont to inform his visitors, had cost nearly £2000. Sir Robert, whose taste at any rate was good, thought them so appalling that while waiting for his host and partner, whom he had come to see, he took a seat in the bow window of the sitting-room and studied the view that nobody had been able to spoil. Presently Mr. Haswell emerged from his bedroom, wrapped in a dressing gown and looking very pale and shaky.

"Delighted to see you all right again," said Sir Robert as he wheeled up a chair into which Mr. Haswell sank.

"I am not all right, Aylward," he answered; "I am not all right at all. Never had such an upset in my life; thought I was going to die when that accursed savage told his beastly tale. Aylward, you are a man of the world, tell me, what is the meaning of the thing? You remember what we thought we saw in the office, and then—that story."

"I don't know," he answered; "frankly I don't know. I am a man who has never believed in anything I cannot see and test, one who utterly lacks faith. In my leisure I have examined into the various religious systems and found them to be rubbish. I am convinced that we are but highly-developed mammals born by chance, and when our day is done, departing into the black nothingness out of which we came. Everything else, that is, what is called the higher and spiritual part, I attribute to the superstitions incident to the terror of the hideous position in which we find ourselves, that of gods of a sort hemmed in by a few years of fearful and tormented life. But you know the old arguments, so why should I enter on them? And now I am confronted with an experience which I cannot explain. I certainly thought that in the office on Friday evening I saw that gold mask to which I had taken so strange a fancy that I offered to give Vernon £17,000 for it because I thought that it brought us luck, swim across the floor of our room and look first into your face and then into mine. Well, the next night that negro tells his story. What am I to make of it?"

"Can't tell you," answered Mr. Champers-Haswell with a groan. "All I know is that it nearly made a corpse of me. I am not like you, Aylward, I was brought up as an Evangelical, and although I haven't given much thought to these matters of late years—well, we don't shake them off in a hurry. I daresay there is something somewhere, and when the black man was speaking, that something seemed uncommonly near. It got up and gripped me by the throat, shaking the mortal breath out of me, and upon my word, Aylward, I have been wishing all the morning that I had led a different kind of life, as my old parents and my brother John, Barbara's father, who was a very religious kind of man, did before me."

"It is rather late to think of all that now, Haswell," said Sir Robert, shrugging his shoulders. "One takes one's line and there's an end. Personally I believe that we are overstrained with the fearful and anxious work of this flotation, and have been the victims of an hallucination and a coincidence. Although I confess that I came to look upon the thing as a kind of mascot, I put no trust in any fetish. How can a bit of gold move, and how can it know the future? Well, I have written to them to clear it out of the office to-morrow, so it won't trouble us any more. And now I have come to speak to you on another matter."

"Not business," said Mr. Haswell with a sigh. "We have that all the week and there will be enough of it on Monday."

"No," he answered, "something more important. About your niece Barbara."

Mr. Haswell glanced at him with those little eyes of his which were so sharp that they seemed to bore like gimlets.

"Barbara?" he said. "What of Barbara?"

"Can't you guess, Haswell? You are pretty good at it, generally. Well, it is no use beating about the bush; I want to marry her."

At this sudden announcement his partner became exceedingly interested. Leaning back in the chair he stared at the decorated ceiling, and uttered his favourite wind-in-the-wires whistle.

"Indeed," he said. "I never knew that matrimony was in your line, Aylward, any more than it has been in mine, especially as you are always preaching against it. Well, has the young lady given her consent?"

"No, I have not spoken to her. I meant to do so this morning, but she has slipped off somewhere, with Vernon, I suppose."

Mr. Haswell whistled again, but on a new note.

"Pray do stop that noise," said Sir Robert; "it gets upon my nerves, which are shaky this morning. Listen: It is a curious thing, one less to be understood even than the coincidence of the Yellow God, but at my present age of forty-four, for the first time in my life I have committed the folly of what is called falling in love. It is not the case of a successful, middle-aged man wishing to ranger himself and settle down with a desirable partie, but of sheer, stark infatuation. I adore Barbara; the worse she treats me the more I adore her. I had rather that the Sahara flotation should fail than that she should refuse me. I would rather lose three-quarters of my fortune than lose her. Do you understand?"

His partner looked at him, pursed up his lips to whistle, then remembered and shook his head instead.

"No," he answered. "Barbara is a nice girl, but I should not have imagined her capable of inspiring such sentiments in a man almost old enough to be her father. I think that you are the victim of a kind of mania, which I have heard of but never experienced. Venus—or is it Cupid?—has netted you, my dear Aylward."

"Oh! pray leave gods and goddesses out of it, we have had enough of them already," he answered, exasperated. "That is my case at any rate, and what I want to know now is if I have your support in my suit. Remember, I have something to offer, Haswell, for instance, a large fortune of which I will settle half—it is a good thing to do in our business,—and a baronetcy that will be a peerage before long."

"A peerage! Have you squared that?"

"I think so. There will be a General Election within the next three months, and on such occasions a couple of hundred thousand in cool cash come in useful to a Party that is short of ready money. I think I may say that it is settled. She will be the Lady Aylward, or any other name she may fancy, and one of the richest women in England. Now have I your support?"

"Yes, my dear friend, why not, though Barbara does not want money, for she has plenty of her own, in first-class securities that I could never persuade her to vary, for she is shrewd in that way and steadily refuses to sign anything. Also she will probably be my heiress—and, Aylward," here a sickly look of alarm spread itself over his face, "I don't know how long I have to live. That infernal doctor examined my heart this morning and told me that it was weak. Weak was his word, but from the tone in which he said it, I believe that he meant more. Aylward, I gather that I may die any day."

"Nonsense, Haswell, so may we all," he replied, with an affectation of cheerfulness which failed to carry conviction.

Presently Mr. Haswell, who had hidden his face in his hand, looked up with a sigh and said:

"Oh! yes, of course you have my support, for after all she is my only relation and I should be glad to see her safely married. Also, as it happens, she can't marry anyone without my consent, at any rate until she is five and twenty, for if she does, under her father's will all her property goes away, most of it to charities, except a beggarly £200 a year. You see my brother John had a great horror of imprudent marriages and a still greater belief in me, which as it chances, is a good thing for you."

"Had he?" said Sir Robert. "And pray why is it a good thing for me?"

"Because, my dear Aylward, unless my observation is at fault, there is another Richard in the field, our late partner, Vernon, of whom, by the way, Barbara is extremely fond, though it may only be in a friendly fashion. At any rate she pays more attention to his wishes and opinions than to mine and yours put together."

At the mention of Alan's name Aylward started violently.

"I feared it," he said, "and he is more than ten years my junior and a soldier, not a man of business. Also there is no use disguising the truth, although I am a baronet and shall be a peer and he is nothing but a beggarly country gentleman with a D.S.O. tacked on to his name, he belongs to a different class to us, as she does too on her mother's side. Well, I can smash him up, for you remember I took over that mortgage on Yarleys, and I'll do it if necessary. Practically our friend has not a shilling that he can call his own. Therefore, Haswell, unless you play me false, which I don't think you will, for I can be a nasty enemy," he added with a threat in his voice, "Alan Vernon hasn't much chance in that direction."

"I don't know, Aylward, I don't know," replied Haswell, shaking his white head. "Barbara is a strong-willed woman and she might choose to take the man and let the money go, and then—who can stop her? Also I don't like your idea of smashing Vernon. It isn't right, and it may come back on our own heads, especially yours. I am sorry that he has left us, as you were on Friday night, for somehow he was a good, honest stick to lean on, and we want such a stick. But I am tired now, I really can't talk any more. The doctor warned me against excitement. Get the girl's consent, Aylward, and we'll see. Ah! here comes my soup. Good-bye for the present."

When Sir Robert came down to luncheon he found Barbara looking particularly radiant and charming, already presiding at that meal and conversing in her best French to the foreign gentlemen, who were paying her compliments.

"Forgive me for being late," he said; "first of all I have been talking to your uncle, and afterwards skimming through the articles in yesterday's papers on our little venture which comes out to-morrow. A cheerful occupation on the whole, for with one or two exceptions they are all favourable."

"Mon Dieu," said the French gentlemen on the right, "seeing what they did cost, that is not strange. Your English papers they are so expensive; in Paris we have done it for half the money."

Barbara and some of the guests laughed outright, finding this frankness charming.

"But where have you been, Miss Champers? I thought that we were going to have a round of golf together. The caddies were there, I was there, the greens had been specially rolled this morning, but there was no You."

"No," she answered, "because Major Vernon and I walked to church and heard a very good sermon upon the observance of the Sabbath."

"You are severe," he said. "Do you think it wrong for men who work hard all the week to play a harmless game on Sunday?"

"Not at all, Sir Robert." Then she looked at him and, coming to a sudden decision, added, "If you like I will play you nine holes this afternoon and give you a stroke a hole, or would you prefer a foursome?"

"No, let us fight alone and let the best player win."

"Very well, Sir Robert; but you mustn't forget that I am handicapped."

"Don't look angry," she whispered to Alan as they strolled out into the garden after lunch, "I must clear things up and know what we have to face. I'll be back by tea-time, and we will have it out with my uncle."

The nine holes had been played, and by a single stroke Barbara had won the match, which pleased her very much, for she had done her best, and with such heavy odds in his favour Sir Robert, who had also done his best, was no mean opponent, even for a player of her skill. Indeed the fight had been quite earnest, for each party knew that it was but a prelude to another and more serious fight, and looked upon the result as in some sense an omen.

"I am conquered," he said in a voice in which vexation struggled with a laugh, "and by a woman over whom I had an advantage. It is humiliating, for I confess I do not like being beaten."

"Don't you think that women generally win if they mean to?" asked Barbara. "I believe that when they fail, which is often enough, it is because they don't care, or can't make up their minds. A woman in earnest is a dangerous antagonist."

"Yes," he answered, "or the best of allies." Then he gave the clubs and half-a-crown to the caddies, and when they were out of hearing, added, "Miss Champers, I have been wondering for some time whether it is possible that you would become such an ally to me."

"I know nothing of business, Sir Robert; my tastes do not lie that way."

"You know well that I was not speaking of business, Miss Champers. I was speaking of another kind of partnership, that which Nature has ordained between men and women—marriage. Will you accept me as a husband?"

She opened her lips to speak, but he lifted his hand and went on. "Listen before you give that ready answer which it is so hard to recall, or smooth away. I know all my disadvantages, my years, which to you may seem many; my modest origin; my trade, which, not altogether without reason, you despise and dislike. Well, the first two cannot be changed except for the worse; the second can be, and already is, buried beneath the gold and ermine of wealth and titles. What does it matter if I am the son of a City clerk who never earned more than £2 a week and was born in a tenement at Battersea, when I am one of the rich men of this rich land and shall die a peer in a palace, leaving millions and honours to my children? As for the third, my occupation, I am prepared to give it up. It has served my turn, and after next week I shall have earned the amount that years ago I determined to earn. Thenceforth, set above the accidents of fortune, I propose to devote myself to higher aims, those of legitimate ambition. So far as my time would allow I have already taken some share in politics as a worker; I intend to continue in them as a ruler which I still have the health and ability to do. I mean to be one of the first men in this Empire, to ride to power over the heads of all the nonentities whose only claim upon the confidence of their countrymen is that they were born in a certain class, with money in their pockets and without the need to spend the best of their manhood in work. With you at my side I can do all these things and more, and such is the future that I have to offer you."

Again she would have broken in upon his speech and again he stopped her, reading the unspoken answer on her lips.

"Listen: I have not told you all. Perhaps I have put first what should have come last. I have not told you that I love you earnestly and sincerely, with the settled, unalterable love that sometimes comes to men in middle-age who have never turned their thought that way before. I will not attempt the rhapsodies of passion which at my time of life might sound foolish or out of place; yet it is true that I am filled with this passion which has descended on me and taken possession of me. I who often have laughed at such things in other men, adore you. You are a joy to my eyes. If you are not in the room, for me it is empty. I admire the uprightness of your character, and even your prejudices, and to your standard I desire to approximate my own. I think that no man can ever love you quite so well as I do, Barbara Champers. Now speak. I am ready to meet the best or the worst."

After her fashion Barbara looked him straight in the face with her steady eyes, and answered gently enough, for the man's method of presenting his case, elaborate and prepared though it evidently was, had touched her.

"I fear it is the worst, Sir Robert. There are hundreds of women superior to myself in every way who would be glad to give you the help and companionship you ask, with their hearts thrown in. Choose one of them, for I cannot do so."

He heard and for the first time his face broke, as it were. All this while it had remained masklike and immovable, even when he spoke of his love, but now it broke as ice breaks at the pressure of a sudden flood beneath, and she saw the depths and eddies of his nature and understood their strength. Not that he revealed them in speech, angry or pleading, for that remained calm and measured enough. She did not hear, she saw, and even then it was marvellous to her that a mere change in a man's expression could explain so much.

"Those are very cruel words," he said. "Are they unalterable?"

"Quite. I do not play in such matters, it would be wicked."

"May I ask you one question, for if the answer is in the negative, I shall still continue to hope? Do you care for any other man?"

Again she looked at him with her fearless eyes and answered:

"Yes, I am engaged to another man."

"To Alan Vernon?"

She nodded.

"When did that happen? Some years ago?"

"No, this morning."

"Great Heavens!" he muttered in a hoarse voice turning his head away, "this morning. Then last night it might not have been too late, and last night I should have spoken to you, I had arranged it all. Yes, if it had not been for the story of that accursed fetish and your uncle's illness, I should have spoken to you, and perhaps succeeded."

"I think not," she said.

He turned upon her and notwithstanding the tears in his eyes they burned like fire.

"You think—you think," he gasped, "but I know. Of course after this morning it was impossible. But, Barbara, I say that I will win you yet. I have never failed in any object that I set before myself, and do not suppose that I shall fail in this. Although in a way I liked and respected him, I have always felt that Vernon was my enemy, one destined to bring grief and loss upon me, even if he did not intend to do so. Now I understand why, and he shall learn that I am stronger than he. God help him! I say."

"I think He will," Barbara answered, calmly. "You are speaking wildly, and I understand the reason and hope that you will forget your words, but whether you forget or remember, do not suppose that you frighten me. You men who have made money," she went on with swelling indignation, "who have made money somehow, and have bought honours with the moneys somehow, think yourselves great, and in your little day, your little, little day that will end with three lines in small type in The Times, you are great in this vulgar land. You can buy what you want and people creep round you and ask you for doles and favours, and railway porters call you 'my Lord' at every other step. But you forget your limitations in this world, and that which lives above you. You say you will do this and that. You should study a book which few of you ever read, where it tells you that you do not know what you will be on the morrow; that your life is even as a vapour appearing for a little time and then vanishing away. You think that you can crush the man to whom I have given my heart because he is honest and you are dishonest, because you are rich and he is poor, and because he chances to have succeeded where you have not. Well, for myself and for him I defy you. Do your worst and fail, and when you have failed, in the hour of your extremity remember my words to-day. If I have given you pain by refusing you it is not my fault and I am sorry, but when you threaten the man who has honoured me with his love and whom I honour above every creature upon the earth, then I threaten back, and may the Power that made us all judge between you and me, as judge it will," and bursting into tears she turned and left him.

Sir Robert watched her go.

"What a woman!" he said meditatively, "what a woman—to have lost. Well she has set the stakes and we will play out the game. The cards all seem to be in my hands, but it would not in the least surprise me if she won the rubber, for the element that I call Chance and she would call something else, may come in. Still, I never refused a challenge yet and we will play the game out without pity to the loser."

That night the first trick was played. When he got back to The Court Sir Robert ordered his motorcar and departed on urgent business, either to his own place, Old Hall, or to London, saying only that he had been summoned away by telegram. As the 70-horse-power Mercedes glided out of the gates a pencilled note was put into Mr. Haswell's hand.

It ran: "I have tried and failed—for the present. By ill-luck A.V. had been before me, only this morning. If I had not missed my chance last night owing to your illness, it would have been different. I do not, however, in the least abandon my plan, in which of course I rely on and expect your support. Keep V. in the office or let him go as you like. Perhaps it would be better if you could prevail upon him to stop there until after the flotation. But whatever you say at the moment, I trust to you to absolutely veto any engagement between him and your niece, and to that end to use all your powers and authority as her guardian. Burn this note.

"R.A."

CHAPTER VI

MR. HASWELL LOSES HIS TEMPER

Alan and Barbara sat in Mr. Champers-Haswell's private sitting-room with the awful decorations, and before them by the fire Mr. Champers-Haswell reclined upon his couch. Alan in a few, brief, soldier-like words had just informed him of his engagement to Barbara. During the recital of this interesting fact Barbara said nothing, but Mr. Haswell had whistled several times. Now at length he spoke, in that tone of forced geniality which he generally adopted towards his cousin.

"You are asking for the hand of a considerable heiress, Alan my boy," he said, "but you have neglected to inform me of your own position."

"Where is the use of telling you what you know already, Mr. Haswell? I have left the firm, therefore I have practically nothing."

"You have practically nothing, and yet—Well, in my young days men were more delicate, they did not like being called fortune-hunters, but of course times have changed."

Alan bit his lip and Barbara sat up quite straight in her chair, observing which indications, Mr. Haswell went on hurriedly:

"Now if you had stopped in the firm and earned the very handsome competence in a small way which would have become due to you this week, instead of throwing us over at the last moment for some quixotic reasons of your own, it might have been a different matter. I do not say it would have been, I say it might have been, and you may remember a proverb about winks and nods and blind horses. So I ask you whether you are inclined to withdraw that resignation of yours and bring up this question again let us say, next Sunday?"

Alan thought a while before he answered. As he understood Mr. Haswell practically was promising to assent to the engagement upon these terms. The temptation was enormously great, the fiercest that he had ever been called upon to face. He looked at Barbara. She had closed her eyes and made absolutely no sign. For some reason of her own she had elected that he should determine this vital point without the slightest assistance from her. And it must be determined at once; procrastination was impossible. For a moment he hesitated. On the one side was Barbara, on the other his conscience. After long doubts he had come to a certain conclusion which he quite understood to be inconvenient to his partners. Should he throw it over now? Should he even try to make a sure and certain bargain as the price of his surrender? Probably he would not suffer if he did. The flotation was underwritten and bound to go through; the scandal would come afterwards, months or years hence, long before which he might get out, as most of the others meant to do. No, he could not. His conscience was too much for him.

"I do not see any use in reconsidering that question, Mr. Haswell," he said quietly; "we settled it on Friday night."

Barbara reopened her brown eyes and stared amiably at the painted ceiling, and Mr. Haswell whistled.

"Then I am afraid," he said, "that I do not see any use in discussing your kind proposal for my niece's hand. Listen—I will be quite open with you. I have other views for Barbara, and as it happens I have the power to enforce them, or at any rate to prevent their frustration by you. If Barbara marries against my will before she is five and twenty, that is within the next two years, her entire fortune, with the exception of a pittance, goes elsewhere. This I am sure is a fact that will influence you, who have nothing and even if it did not, I presume that you are scarcely so selfish as to wish to beggar her."

"No," answered Alan, "you need not fear that, for it would be wrong. I understand that you absolutely refuse to sanction my suit on the ground of my poverty, which under the circumstances is perhaps not wonderful. Well, the only thing to do is to wait for two years, a long time, but not endless, and meanwhile I can try to better my position."

"Do what you will, Alan," said Mr. Haswell harshly, for now all his faux bonhomme manner had gone, leaving him revealed in his true character of an unscrupulous tradesman with dark ends of his own to serve. "Do what you will, but understand that I forbid all communication between you and my niece, and that the sooner you cease to trespass upon a hospitality which you have abused, the better I shall be pleased."

"I will go at once," said Alan, rising, "before my temper gets the better of me and I tell you some truths that I might regret, for after all you are Barbara's uncle. But on your part I ask you to understand that I refuse to cut off from my cousin, who is of full age and has promised to be my wife," and he turned to go.

"Stop a minute, Alan," said Barbara, who all this while had sat silent. "I have something to say which I wish you to hear. You told us just now, uncle, that you have other views for me, by which you meant that you wish me to marry Sir Robert Aylward, whom, as you are probably aware, I refused definitely this afternoon. Now I wish to make it clear at once that no earthly power will induce me to take as a husband a man whom I dislike, and whose wealth, of which you think so much, has in my opinion been dishonestly acquired."

"What are you saying?" broke in her uncle furiously. "He has been my partner for years, you are reflecting upon me."

"I am sorry, uncle, but I withdraw nothing. Even if Alan here were dead, I would not marry that man, and perhaps you will make him understand this," she added with emphasis. "Indeed I had sooner die myself. You told us also that if I marry against your will, you can take away all the property that my father left to me. Uncle, I shall not give you that satisfaction. I shall wait until I am twenty-five and do what I please with myself and my fortune. Lastly, you said that you forbade us to see each other or to correspond. I answer that I shall both write to and see Alan as often as I like. If you attempt to prevent me from doing so, I shall go to the Court of Chancery, lay all the facts before it, as I have been advised that I can do—not by Alan—please remember, all the facts, and ask for its protection and for a separate maintenance out of my estate until I am twenty-five. I am sure that the Court would grant me this and would declare that considering his distinguished family and record Alan is a perfectly proper person to be my affianced husband. I think that is all I have to say."

"All you have to say!" gasped Mr. Haswell, "all you have to say, you impertinent and ungrateful minx!" Then he fell into a furious fit of rage and in language that need not be repeated, poured a stream of threats and abuse upon Alan and herself. Barbara waited until he ceased from exhaustion.

"Uncle," she said, "you should remember that your heart is weak and you must not overexcite yourself, also when you are calmer, that if you speak to me like that again, I shall go to the Court at once, for I will not be sworn at by you or by any other man. I apologize to you, Alan; I am afraid I have brought you into strange company. Come, my dear, we will go and order your dogcart," and putting her arm affectionately through his, she went with him from the room.

"I wonder who put her up to all this?" gasped Haswell, as the door closed behind them. "Some infernal lawyer, I'll be bound. Well, she has got the whip hand of me, and I can't face an investigation in Chancery, especially as the only thing against Vernon is that the value of his land has fallen. But I swear that she shall never marry him while I live," he ended in a kind of shout and the domed and painted ceiling echoed back his words—"while I live" after which the room was silent, save for the heavy thumping of his heart.

When Alan reached home that night after his ten-mile drive he sent Jeekie to tell the housekeeper to find him some food. In his mysterious African fashion the negro had already collected much intelligence as to the events of the day, mostly in the servants' hall, and more particularly from the two golf-caddies, sons of one of the gardeners, who it seemed instead of retiring with the clubs, had taken shelter in some tall whins and thence followed the interview between Barbara and Sir Robert with the intensest interest. Reflecting that this was not the time to satisfy his burning curiosity, Jeekie went and in due course returned with some cold mutton and a bottle of claret. Then came his chance, for Alan could scarcely touch the mutton and demanded toast and butter.

"Very inferior chop"—that was his West African word for food—"for a gentleman, Major," he said, shaking his white head sympathetically and pointing to the mutton,—"specially when he has unexpectedly departed from magnificent eating of The Court. Why did you not wait till after dinner, Major, before retiring?"

Alan laughed at the man's inflated English, and answered in a more nervous and colloquial style:

"Because I was kicked out, Jeekie."

"Ah! I gathered that kicking was in the wind, Major. Sir Robert Aylward, Bart., he also was kicked out, but by smaller toe."

Again Alan laughed and, as it was a relief to talk even to Jeekie, asked him:

"How do you know that?"

"I gathered it out of atmosphere, Major; from Sir Robert's gentleman, from two youths who watch Sir Robert and Miss Barbara talking upon golf green No. 9, from the machine driver of Sir Robert whose eyes he damn in public, and last but not least from his own noble countenance."

"I see that you are observant, Jeekie."

"Observation, Major, it is art of life. I see Miss Barbara's eyes red like morning sky and I deduct. I see you shot out and gloomy like evening cloud, and I deduct. I listen at door of Mr. Haswell's room, I hear him curse and swear like holy saint in Book, and you and Miss Barbara answer him not like saint, though what you speak I cannot hear, and I deduct. Jeekie deduct this—that you make love to Miss Barbara in proper gentlemanlike, 'nogamous, Christian fashion such as your late Reverend Uncle approve, and Miss Barbara, she make love to you with ten per cent. compound interest, but old gent with whistle, he not approve; he say, 'Where corresponding cash!' He say 'Noble Sir Robert have much cash and interested in identical business. I prefer Sir Robert. Get out, you Cashless.' Often I see this same thing when boy in West Africa, very common wherever sun shine. I note all these matters and I deduct—that Jeekie's way and Jeekie seldom wrong."

Alan laughed for the third time, until the tears ran down his face indeed.

"Jeekie," he said, "you are a great rascal—"

"Yes, yes," interrupted Jeekie, "great rascal. Best thing to be in this world, Major. Honourable Sir Robert, Bart., M.P., and Mr. Champers-Haswell, D.L., J.P., they find that out long ago and sit on top of tree of opulent renown. Jeekie great rascal and therefore have Savings Bank account—go on, Major."

"Well, Jeekie, because if you are a rascal you are kind-hearted and because I believe that you care for me—"

"Oh! Major," broke in Jeekie again, "that most 'utterably true. Honour bright I love you, Major, better than anyone on earth, except my late old woman, now happily dead, gone and forgotten in best oak coffin, £4 10 without fittings but polished, and perhaps your holy uncle, Reverend Mr. Austin, also coffined and departed, who saved me from early extinction in a dark place. Major, I no like graves, I see too much of them, and can't tell what lie on other side. Though everyone say they know, Jeekie not quite sure. May be all light and crowns of glory, may be damp black hole and no way out. But this at least true, that I love you better, yes, better than Miss Barbara, for love of woman very poor, uncertain thing, quick come, quick go. Jeekie find that out—often. Yes, if need be, though death most nasty, if need be I say I die for you, which great unpleasant sacrifice," and Jeekie in the genuine enthusiasm of his warm heart, throwing himself upon his knees after the African fashion, seized his master's hand and kissed it.

"Thanks, Jeekie," said Alan, "very kind of you, I am sure. But we haven't come to that yet, though no one knows what may happen later on. Now sit upon that chair and take a little whisky—not too much—for I am going to ask your advice."

"Major," said Jeekie, "I obey," and seizing the whisky bottle in a casual manner, he poured out half a tumbler full, for Jeekie was fond of whisky. Indeed before now this taste had brought him into conflict with the local magistrates.

"Put back three parts of that," said Alan, and Jeekie did so. "Now," he went on, "listen: this is the case, Miss Barbara and I are—" and he hesitated.

"Oh! I know; like me and Mrs. Jeekie once," said Jeekie, gulping down some of the neat whisky. "Go on, Major."

"And Sir Robert Aylward is—"

"Same thing, Major. Continue."

"And Mr. Haswell has—"

"Those facts all ascertained, Major," said Jeekie, contemplating his glass with a mournful eye. "Now come to the point, Major."

"Well, the point is, Jeekie, that I am what you called just now cashless, and therefore—"

"Therefore," interrupted Jeekie again, "stick fast in honourable intention towards Miss Barbara owing to obstinate opposition of Mr. Haswell, legal uncle with control of property fomented by noble Sir Robert who desire same girl."

"Quite right, Jeekie, but if you would talk a little less and let me talk a little more, we might get on better."

"I henceforth silent, Major," and lifting his empty tumbler Jeekie looked through it as if it were a telescope, a hint that Alan ignored.

"Jeekie, you infernal old fool, I want money."

"Yes, Major, I understand, Major. Forgive me for breaking conspiracy of silence, but if £500 in Savings Bank any use, very much at your service, Major; also £20 more extracted last night from terror of wealthy Jew who fear fetish."

"Jeekie, you old donkey, I don't want your £500; I want a great deal more, £50,000 or £500,000. Tell me how to get it."

"City best place, Major. But you chuck City, too much honest man, great mistake to be honest in this terrestrial sphere. Often notice that in West Africa."

"Perhaps, Jeekie, but I have done with the City. As you would say, for me it is 'wipe out, finish.'"

"Yes, Major, too much pickpocket, too much dirt. Bottom always drop out of bucket shop at last. I understand, end in police court and severe magistrate, or perhaps even 'Gentlemen of Jury'; etcetera."

"Well, Jeekie, then what remains? Now last night when you told us that amazing yarn of yours, you said something about a mountain full of gold, and houses full of gold, among your people. Jeekie, do you think—" and he paused, looking at him.

Jeekie rolled his black eyes round the room and in a fit of absentmindedness helped himself to some more whisky.

"Do I think, Major, that this useless lucre could be converted into coin of gracious King Edward? Not at all, Major, by no one, Major, by no one whatsoever, except possibly by Major Alan Vernon, D.S.O., and by one, Jeekie, Christian surname Smith."

"Proceed, Jeekie," said Alan, removing the whisky bottle, "proceed and explain."

"Major, thus: The Asiki tribe care nothing about all that gold, it no good to them. Dead people who live long, long ago, no one know when, dig it up and store it there and make the great fetish which they call Bonsa to keep away enemy who want to steal. Also old custom when any one in country round find big nugget, or pretty stone, like ladies wear on bosom, to bring it as offering to Bonsa, so that there now great plenty of all this stuff. But no one use it for anything except to set on walls of house of Asiki, or to make basin, stool, table and pot to cook with. Once Arab come there and I see the priests give him weight in gold for iron hoe, though afterwards they murder him, not for the gold, but lest he go away and tell their secret."

"One might trade with them then, Jeekie?"

He shook his white head doubtfully.

"Yes, perhaps, if you can find anything they want buy and can carry it there. But I think there only one thing they want, and you got that, Major."

"I, Jeekie! What have I got?"

The negro leant forward and tapped his master on the knee, saying in a portentous whisper:

"You got Little Bonsa, which much more holy than anything, even than Big Bonsa her husband, I mean greater, more powerful devil. That Little Bonsa sit in front room Asika's house, and when she want see things, she put it in big basin of gold, but I no tell you what it float in. Also once or twice every year they take out Little Bonsa; Asika wear it on head as mask, and whoever they meet they kill as offering to Little Bonsa, so that spirit come back to world to be priest of Bonsa. I tell you, Major, that Yellow God see many thousand of people die."

"Indeed," said Alan. "A pleasing fetish truly. I should think that the Asiki must be glad it is gone."

"No, not glad, very sorry. No luck for them when Little Bonsa go away, but plenty luck for those who got her. That why firm Aylward & Haswell make so much money when you join them and bring her to office. She drop green in eye of public so they no smell rat. That why you so lucky, not die of blackwater fever when you should; get safe out of den of thieves in City with good name; win love of sweet maiden, Miss Barbara. Little Bonsa do all those things for you, and by and by do plenty more, as Little Bonsa bring my old master, your holy uncle, safe out of that country because all the Asiki run away when they see him wear her on head, for they think she come sacrifice them after she eat up my life."

"I don't wonder that they ran," said Alan, laughing, for the vision of a missionary with Little Bonsa on his head caught his fancy. "But come to the point, you old heathen. What do you mean that I should do?"

"Jeekie not heathen now, Major, but plenty other things true in this world, besides Christian religion. I no want you do anything, but I say this—you go back to Asiki wearing Little Bonsa on head and dressed like Reverend uncle whom you very like, for he just your age then thirty years ago, and they give you all the gold you want, if you give them back Little Bonsa whom they love and worship for ever and ever, for Little Bonsa very, very old."

Alan sat up in his chair and stared at Jeekie, while Jeekie nodded his head at him.

"There is something in it," he said slowly, speaking more to himself than to the negro, "and perhaps that is why I would not sell the fetish, for as you say, there are plenty of true things in the world besides those which we believe. But, Jeekie, how should I find the way?"

"No trouble, Major, Little Bonsa find way, want to get back home, very hungry by now, much need sacrifice. Think it good thing kill pig to Little Bonsa—or even lamb. She know you do your best, since human being not to be come at in Christian land, and say 'thank you for life of pig.'"

"Stop that rubbish," said Alan. "I want a guide; if I go, will you come with me?"

At this suggestion the negro looked exceedingly uncomfortable.

"Not like to, not like to at all," he said, rolling his eyes. "Asiki-land very funny place for native-born. But," he added sadly, "if you go Jeekie must, for I servant of Little Bonsa and if I stay behind, she angry and kill me because I not attend her where she walk. But perhaps if I go and take her to Gold House again, she pleased and let me off. Also I able help you there. Yes, if you and Little Bonsa go, think I go too."

After this announcement Jeekie rose and walked down the room, carrying the cold mutton in his hand. Then he returned, replaced it on the table and standing in front of Alan, said earnestly:

"Major, I tell you all truth, just this once. Jeekie believe he got go with you to Asiki-land. Jeekie have plenty bad dream lately, Little Bonsa come in middle of the night and sit on his stomach and scratch his face with her gold leg, and say, 'Jeekie, Jeekie, you son of Bonsa, you get up quick and take me back Bonsa Town, for I darned tired of City fog and finished all I come here to do. Now I want jolly good sacrifice and got plenty business attend to there at home, things you not understand just yet. You take me back sharp, or I make you sit up, Jeekie, my boy;'" and he paused.

"Indeed," said Alan; "and did she tell you anything else in her midnight visitations?"

"Yes, Major. She say, 'You take that white master of yours along also, for I want come back Asiki-land on his head, and someone wish see him there, old pal, what he forget but what not forget him. You tell him Little Bonsa got score she wants settle with that party and wish use him to square account. You tell him too that she pay him well for trip; he lose nothing if he play her game 'cause she got no score against him. But if he not go, that another matter, then he look out, for Little Bonsa very nasty customer if she riled, as his late partners find out one day.'"

"Oh! shut up, Jeekie. What's the use of wasting time telling me your nightmares?"

"Very well, Major, just as you like, Major. But I got other reasons why I willing go. Jeekie want see his ma."

"Your ma? I never heard you had a ma. Besides she must be dead long ago."

"No, Major, 'cause she turn up in dream too, very much alive, swear at me 'cause I bag her blanket. Also she tough old woman, take lot kill her."

"Perhaps you have a pa too," suggested Alan.

"Think not, Major, my ma always say she forget him. What she mean, she not like talk about him, he such a swell. Why Jeekie so strong, so clever and with such beautiful face? No doubt because he is son of very great man. All this true reason why he want to go with you, Major. Still, p'raps poor old Jeekie make mistake, p'raps he dream 'cause he eat too much supper, p'raps his ma dead, after all. If so, p'raps better stay at home—not know."

"No," answered Alan, "not know. What between Little Bonsa and one thing and another my head is swimming—like Little Bonsa in the water."

"Big Bonsa swim in water," interrupted Jeekie. "Little Bonsa swim in gold tub."

"Well, Big Bonsa, or Little Bonsa, I don't care which. I'm going to bed and you had better clear away these things and do the same. But, Jeekie, if you say a word of our talk to anyone, I shall be very angry. Do you understand?"

"Yes, Major, I understand. I understand that if I tell secrets of Little Bonsa to anyone except you with whom she live in strange land far away from home, Little Bonsa come at me like one lion, and cut my throat. No fear Jeekie split on Little Bonsa, oh! no fear at all," and still shaking his head solemnly, for the second time he seized the cold mutton and vanished from the room.

"A farrago of superstitious nonsense," thought Alan to himself when he had gone. "But still there may be something to be made out of it. Evidently there is lots of gold in this Asiki country, if only one can persuade the people to deal."

Then weary of Jeekie and his tribal gods, Alan lit his pipe and sat a while thinking of Barbara and all the events of that tumultuous day. Notwithstanding his rebuff at the hands of Mr. Haswell and the difficulties and dangers which threatened, he felt even then that it had been a happy and a fortunate day. For had he not discovered that Barbara loved him with all her heart and soul as he loved Barbara? And as this was so, he did not care a—Little Bonsa about anything else. The future must look to itself, sufficient to the day was the abiding joy thereof.

So he went to bed and for a while to sleep, but he did not sleep very long, for presently he fell to dreaming, something about Big Bonsa and Little Bonsa which sat, or rather floated on either side of his couch and held an interminable conversation over him, while Jeekie and Sir Robert Aylward, perched respectively at its head and its foot, like the symbols of the good and evil genii on a Mahommedan tomb, acted as a kind of insane chorus. He struck his repeater, it was only one o'clock, so he tried to go to sleep again, but failed utterly. Never had he been more painfully awake.

For an hour or more Alan persevered, then at last in despair he jumped out of bed wondering what he could do to occupy his mind. Suddenly he remembered the diary of his uncle, the Rev. Mr. Austin, which he had inherited with the Yellow God and a few other possessions, but never examined. They had been put away in a box in the library about fifteen years before, just at the time he entered the army, and there doubtless they remained. Well, as he could not sleep, why should he not examine them now, and thus get through some of this weary night?

He lit a candle and went down to the library, an ancient and beautiful apartment with black oak panelling between the bookcases, set there in the time of Elizabeth. In this panelling there were cupboards, and in one of the cupboards was the box he sought, made of teak wood. On its lid was painted, "The Reverend Henry Austin. Passenger to Acra," showing that it had once been his uncle's cabin box. The key hung from the handle, and having lit more candles, Alan drew it out and unlocked it, to be greeted by a smell of musty documents done up in great bundles. One by one he placed them on the floor. It was a dreary occupation alone there in that great, silent room at the dead of night, one indeed with which he was soon satisfied, for somehow it reminded him of rifling coffins in a vault. Before him so carefully put away lay the records of a good if not a distinguished life, and until this moment he had never found the energy even to look through them.

At length he came to the end of the bundles and saw that beneath lay a number of manuscript books packed closely with their backs upwards, marked—"Journal"—and with the year and sometimes the place of the author's residence. As he glanced at them in dismay, for they were many, his eye caught the title of one inscribed—as were several others—"West Africa," and written in brackets beneath—"This vol. contains all that is left of the notes of my escape with Jeekie from the Asiki Devil-worshippers."

Alan drew it out, and having refilled and closed the box, bore it off to his room, where he proceeded to read it in bed. As a matter of fact he found that there was not very much to read, for the reason that most of the closely-written volume had been so damaged by water, that the pencilled writing had run and become utterly illegible. The centre pages, however, not having been soaked, could still be deciphered, at any rate in part, also there was a large manuscript map, executed in ink, apparently at a later date, on the back of which was written: "I purpose, D.V., to re-write at some convenient time all the history of my visit to the unknown Asiki people, as my original notes were practically destroyed when the canoe overset in the rapids and most of our few possessions were lost, except this book and the gold fetish mask which is called Little Bonsa or Small Swimming Head. This I think I can do with the aid of Jeekie from memory, but as the matter has only a personal and no religious interest, seeing that I was not able even to preach the Word among those benighted and blood-thirsty savages in whose country, as I verily believe, the Devil has one of his principal habitations, it must stand over till a convenient season, such as the time of old age or sickness. H.A."

"P.S. I ought to add with gratitude that even out of this hell fire I was enabled to snatch one brand from the burning, namely, the negro lad, Jeekie, to whose extraordinary resource and faithfulness I owe my escape. After a long hesitation I have been able to baptize him, although I fear that the taint of heathenism still clings to him. Thus not six months ago I caught him sacrificing a white cock to the image, Little Bonsa, in gratitude, as to my horror he explained, for my having been appointed an Honorary Canon of the Cathedral. I have told him to take that ugly mask which has been so often soaked in human blood, and melt it down over the kitchen stove, after picking out the gems in the eyes, that the proceeds may be given to the poor. Note. I had better see to this myself, as where Little Bonsa is concerned, Jeekie is not to be trusted. He says (with some excuse) that it has magic, and that if he melts it down, he will melt down too, and so shall I. How dark and ridiculous are the superstitions of the heathen! Perhaps, however, instead of destroying the thing, which is certainly unique, I might sell it to a museum, and thus spare the feelings of that weak vessel, Jeekie, who otherwise would very likely take it into his head to waste away and die, as these Africans do when their nerves are affected by terror of their fetish."

CHAPTER VII

THE DIARY

Reflecting that time evidently had made little change in Jeekie, Alan studied this route map with care, and found that it started from Old Calabar, in the Bight of Biafra, on the west coast of Africa, whence it ran up to the Great Qua River, which it followed for a long way. Then it struck across country marked "dense forest," northwards, and came to a river called Katsena, along the banks of which the route went eastwards. Thence it turned northward again through swamps, and ended in mountains called Shaku. In the middle of these mountains was written "Asiki People live here on Raaba River."

The map was roughly drawn to scale, and Alan, who was an engineer accustomed to such things, easily calculated that the distance of this Raaba River from Old Calabar was about 350 miles as the crow flies, though probably the actual route to be travelled was nearer five hundred miles.

Having mastered the map, he opened the water-soaked diary. Turning page after page, only here and there could he make out a sentence, such as "so I defied that beautiful but terrific woman. I, a Christian minister, the husband of a heathen priestess! Perish the thought. Sooner would I be sacrificed to Bonsa."

Then came more illegible pages and again a paragraph that could be read—"They gave me 'The Bean' in a gold cup, and knowing its deadly nature I prepared myself for death. But happily for me my stomach, always delicate, rejected it at once, though I felt queer for days afterwards. Whereon they clapped their hands and said I was evidently innocent and a great medicine man."

And again, further on—"never did I see so much gold whether in dust, nuggets, or worked articles. I imagine it must be worth millions, but at that time gold was the last thing with which I wished to trouble myself."

After this entry many pages were utterly effaced.

The last legible passage ran as follows—"So guided by the lad Jeekie, and wearing the gold mask, Little Bonsa, on my head, I ran through them all, holding him by the hand as though I were dragging him away. A strange spectacle I must have been with my old black clergyman's coat buttoned about me, my naked legs and the gold mask, as pretending to be a devil such as they worship, I rushed through them in the moonlight, blowing the whistle in the mask and bellowing like a bull. . . . Such was the beginning of my dreadful six months' journey to the coast. Setting aside the mercy of Providence that preserved me for its own purposes, I could never have lived to reach it had it not been for Little Bonsa, since curiously enough I found this fetish known and dreaded for hundreds of miles, and that by people who had never seen it, yes, even by the wild cannibals. Whenever it was produced food, bearers, canoes, or whatever else I might want were forthcoming as though by magic. Great is the fame of Big and Little Bonsa in all that part of West Africa, although, strange as it may seem, the outlying tribes seldom mention them by name. If they must speak of either of these images which are supposed to be man and wife, they call it the 'Yellow-God-who-lives-yonder.'"

Not another word of all this strange history could Alan decipher, so with aching eyes he shut up the stained and tattered volume, and at last, just as the day was breaking, fell asleep.

At eleven o'clock on that same morning, for he had slept late, Alan rose from his breakfast and went to smoke his pipe at the open door of the beautiful old hall in Yarleys that was clad with brown Elizabethan oak for which any dealer would have given hundreds of pounds. It was a charming morning, one of those that comes to us sometimes in an English April when the air is soft like that of Italy and the smell of the earth rises like that of incense, and little clouds float idly across a sky of tender blue. Standing thus he looked out upon the park where the elms already showed a tinge of green and the ash-buds were coal black. Only the walnuts and the great oaks, some of them pollards of a thousand years of age, remained stark and stern in their winter dress.

Alan was in a reflective mood and involuntarily began to wonder how many of his forefathers had stood in that same spot upon such April mornings and looked out upon those identical trees wakening in the breath of spring. Only the trees and the landscape knew, those trees which had seen every one of them borne to baptism, to bridal and to burial. The men and women themselves were forgotten. Their portraits, each in the garb of his or her generation, hung here and there upon the walls of the ancient house which once they had owned or inhabited, but who remembered anything of them to-day? In many cases their names even were lost, for believing that they, so important in their time, could never sink into oblivion, they had not thought it necessary to record them upon their pictures.

And now the thing was coming to an end. Unless in this way or in that he could save it, what remained of the old place, for the outlying lands had long since been sold, must go to the hammer and become the property of some pushing and successful person who desired to found a family, and perhaps in days to be would claim these very pictures that hung upon the walls as those of his own ancestors, declaring that he had brought in the estate because he was a relative of the ancient and ruined race.

Well, it was the way of the world, and perhaps it must be so, but the thought of it made Alan Vernon sad. If he could have continued that business, it might have been otherwise. By this hour his late partners, Sir Robert Aylward and Mr. Champers-Haswell, were doubtless sitting in their granite office in the City, probably in consultation with Lord Specton, who had taken his place upon the Board of the great Company which was being subscribed that day. No doubt applications for shares were pouring in by the early posts and by telegram, and from time to time Mr. Jeffreys respectfully reported their number and amount, while Sir Robert looked unconcerned and Mr. Haswell rubbed his hands and whistled cheerfully. Almost he could envy them, these men who were realizing great fortunes amidst the bustle and excitement of that fierce financial life, whilst he stood penniless and stared at the trees and the ewes which wandered among them with their lambs, he who, after all his work, was but a failure. With a sigh he turned away to fetch his cap and go out walking—there was a tenant whom he must see, a shifty, new-fangled kind of man who was always clamouring for fresh buildings and reductions in his rent. How was he to pay for more buildings? He must put him off, or let him go.

Just then a sharp sound caught his ear, that of an electric bell. It came from the telephone which, since he had been a member of a City firm, he had caused to be put into Yarleys at considerable expense in order that he might be able to communicate with the office in London. "Were they calling him up from force of habit?" he wondered. He went to the instrument which was fixed in a little room he used as a study, and took down the receiver.

"Who is it?" he asked. "I am Yarleys. Alan Vernon."

"And I am Barbara," came the answer. "How are you, dear? Did you sleep well?"

"No, very badly."

"Nerves—Alan, you have got nerves. Now although I had a worse day than you did, I went to bed at nine, and protected by a perfect conscience, slumbered till nine this morning, exactly twelve hours. Isn't it clever of me to think of this telephone, which is more than you would ever have done? My uncle has departed to London vowing that no letter from you shall enter this house, but he forgot that there is a telephone in every room, and in fact at this moment I am speaking round by his office within a yard or two of his head. However, he can't hear, so that doesn't matter. My blessing be on the man who invented telephones, which hitherto I have always thought an awful nuisance. Are you feeling cheerful, Alan?"

"Very much the reverse," he answered; "never was more gloomy in my life, not even when I thought I had to die within six hours of blackwater fever. Also I have lots that I want to talk to you about and I can't do it at the end of this confounded wire that your uncle may be tapping."

"I thought it might be so," answered Barbara, "so I just rang you up to wish you good-morning and to say that I am coming over in the motor to lunch with my maid Snell as chaperone. All right, don't remonstrate, I am coming over to lunch—I can't hear you—never mind what people will say. I am coming over to lunch at one o'clock, mind you are in. Good-bye, I don't want much to eat, but have something for Snell and the chauffeur. Good-bye."

Then the wire went dead, nor could all Alan's "Hello's" and "Are you there's?" extract another syllable.

Having ordered the best luncheon that his old housekeeper could provide Alan went off for his walk in much better spirits, which were further improved by his success in persuading the tenant to do without the new buildings for another year. In a year, he reflected, anything might happen. Then he returned by the wood where a number of new-felled oaks lay ready for barking. This was not a cheerful sight; it seemed so cruel to kill the great trees just as they were pushing their buds for another summer of life. But he consoled himself by recalling that they had been too crowded and that the timber was really needed on the estate. As he reached the house again carrying a bunch of white violets which he had plucked in a sheltered place for Barbara, he perceived a motor travelling at much more than the legal speed up the walnut avenue which was the pride of the place. In it sat that young lady herself, and her maid, Snell, a middle-aged woman with whom, as it chanced, he was on very good terms, as once, at some trouble to himself, he had been able to do her a kindness.

The motor pulled up at the front door and out of it sprang Barbara, laughing pleasantly and looking fresh and charming as the spring itself.

"There will be a row over this, dear," said Alan, shaking his head doubtfully when at last they were alone together in the hall.

"Of course, there'll be a row," she answered. "I mean that there should be a row. I mean to have a row every day if necessary, until they leave me alone to follow my own road, and if they won't, as I said, to go to the Court of Chancery for protection. Oh! by the way, I have brought you a copy of The Judge. There's a most awful article in it about that Sahara flotation, and among other things it announces that you have left the firm and congratulates you upon having done so."

"They'll think I have put it in," groaned Alan as he glanced at the head lines, which were almost libellous in their vigour, and the summaries of the financial careers of Sir Robert Aylward and Mr. Champers-Haswell. "It will make them hate me more than ever, and I say, Barbara, we can't live in an atmosphere of perpetual warfare for the next two years."

"I can, if need be," answered that determined young woman. "But I admit that it would be trying for you, if you stay here."

"That's just the point, Barbara. I must not stay here, I must go away, the further the better, until you are your own mistress."

"Where to, Alan?"

"To West Africa, I think."

"To West Africa?" repeated Barbara, her voice trembling a little. "After that treasure, Alan?"

"Yes, Barbara. But first come and have your lunch, then we will talk. I have got lots to tell and show you."

So they lunched, speaking of indifferent things, for the servant was there waiting on them. Just as they were finishing their meal Jeekie entered the room carrying a box and a large envelope addressed to his master, which he said had been sent by special messenger from the office in London.

"What's in the box?" asked Alan, looking somewhat nervously at the envelope, which was addressed in a writing that he knew.

"Don't know for certain, Major," answered Jeekie, "but think Little Bonsa; think I smell her through wood."

"Well, look and see," replied Alan, while he broke the seal of the envelope and drew out its contents. They proved to be sundry documents sent by the firm's lawyers, among which were a notice of the formal dissolution of partnership to be approved by him before it appeared in the Gazette, a second notice calling in a mortgage for fifteen thousand and odd pounds on Yarleys, which as a matter of business had been taken over by the firm while he was a partner; a cash account showing a small balance against him, and finally a receipt for him to sign acknowledging the return of the gold image that was his property.

"You see," said Alan with a sigh, pushing over the papers to Barbara, who read them carefully one by one.

"I see," she answered presently. "It is war to the knife. Alan, I hate the idea of it, but perhaps you had better go away. While you are here they will harass the life out of you."

Meanwhile with the aid of a big jack-knife and the dining-room poker, Jeekie had prized off the lid of the box. Chancing to look round Barbara saw him on his knees muttering something in a strange tongue, and bowing his white head until it touched an object that lay within the box.

"What are you doing, Jeekie?" she asked.

"Make bow to Little Bonsa, Miss Barbara, tell her how glad I am see her come back from town. She like feel welcome. Now you come bow too, Little Bonsa take that as compliment."

"I won't bow, but I will look, Jeekie, for although I have heard so much about it I have never really examined this Yellow God."

"Very good, you come look, miss," and Jeekie propped up the case upon the end of the dining-room table. As from its height and position she could not see its contents very well whilst standing above it, Barbara knelt down to get a better view of it.

"My goodness!" she exclaimed, "what a terrible face, beautiful too in its way."

Hardly had the words left her lips when for some reason unexplained that probably had to do with the shifting of the centre of gravity, Little Bonsa appeared to glide or fall out of her box with a startling suddenness, and project herself straight at Barbara, who, with a faint scream, fearing lest the precious thing should be injured, caught it in her arms and for a moment hugged it to her breast.

"Saved!" she exclaimed, recovering herself and placing it on the table, whereon Jeekie, to their astonishment, began to execute a kind of war dance.

"Oh! yes," he said, "saved, very much saved. All saved, most magnificent omen. Lady kneel to Little Bonsa and Little Bonsa nip out of box, make bow and jump in lady's arms. That splendid, first-class luck, for miss and everybody. When Little Bonsa do that need fear nothing no more. All come right as rain."

"Nonsense," said Barbara, laughing. Then from a cautious distance she continued her examination of the fetish.

"See," said Jeekie, pointing to the misshapen little gold legs which were yet so designed that it could be stood up upon them, "when anyone wear Little Bonsa, tie her on head behind by these legs; look, here same old leather string. Now I put her on, for she like to be worn again," and with a quick movement he clapped the mask on to his face, manipulated the greasy black leather thongs and made them fast. Thus adorned the great negro looked no less than terrific.

"I see you, miss," he said, turning the fixed eyes of opal-like stone, bloodshot with little rubites, upon Barbara, "I see you, though you no see me, for these eyes made very cunning. But listen, you hear me," and suddenly from the mask, produced by some contrivance set within it, there proceeded an awful, howling sound that made her shiver.

"Take that thing off, Jeekie," said Alan, "we don't want any banshees here."

"Banshees? Not know him, he poor English fetish p'raps," said Jeekie, as he removed the mask. "This real African god, howl banshee and all that sort into middle of next week. This Little Bonsa and no mistake, ten thousand years old and more, eat up lives, so many that no one can count them, and go on eating for ever, yes unto the third and fourth generation, as Ten Commandments lay it down for benefit of Christian man, like me. Look at her again, Miss Barbara."

Miss Barbara took the hateful, ancient thing in her hands and studied it. No one could doubt its antiquity, for the gold plate of which it was made was literally worn away wherever it had touched the foreheads of the high priests or priestesses who donned it upon festive occasions or days of sacrifice, showing that hundreds and hundreds of them must have used it thus in succession. So was the vocal apparatus within the mouth, and so were the little toad-like feet upon which it was stood up. Also the substance of the gold itself as here and there pitted as though with acid or salts, though what those salts were she did not inquire. And yet, so consummate was the art with which it had originally been fashioned, that the battered beautiful face of Little Bonsa still peered at them with the same devilish smile that it had worn when it left the hands of its maker, perhaps before Mohammed preached his holy war, or even earlier.

"What is all that writing on the back of it?" asked Barbara, pointing to the long lines of rune-like characters which were inscribed within it.

"Not know, miss, think they dead tongue cut in the beginning when black men could write. But Asiki priests swear they remember every one of them, and that why no one can copy Little Bonsa, for they look inside and see if marks all right. They say they names of those who died for Little Bonsa, and when they all done, Little Bonsa begin again, for Little Bonsa never die. But p'raps priests lie."

"I daresay," said Barbara, "but take Little Bonsa away, for however lucky she may be, she makes me feel sick."

"Where I put her, Major?" asked Jeekie of Alan. "In box in library where she used to live, or in plate-safe with spoons? Or under your bed where she always keep eye on you?"

"Oh! put her with the spoons," said Alan angrily, and Jeekie departed with his treasure.

"I think, dear," remarked Barbara as the door closed behind him, "that if I come to lunch here any more, I shall bring my own christening present with me, for I can't eat off silver that has been shut up with that thing. Now let us get to business—show me the diary and the map."

"Dearest Alan," wrote Barbara from The Court two days later, "I have been thinking everything over, and since you are so set upon it, I suppose that you had better go. To me the whole adventure seems perfectly mad, but at the same time I believe in our luck, or rather in the Providence which watches over us, and I don't believe that you, or I either, will come to any harm. If you stop here, you will only eat your heart out and communication between us must become increasingly difficult. My uncle is furious with you, and since he discovered that we were talking over the telephone, to his own great inconvenience he has had the wires cut outside the house. That horrid letter of his to you saying that you had 'compromised' me in pursuance of a 'mercenary scheme' is all part and parcel of the same thing. How are you to stop here and submit to such insults? I went to see my friend the lawyer, and he tells me that of course we can marry if we like, but in that case my father's will, which he has consulted at Somerset House, is absolutely definite, and if I do so in opposition to my uncle's wishes, I must lose everything except £200 a year. Now I am no money-grubber, but I will not give my uncle the satisfaction of robbing me of my fortune, which may be useful to both of us by and by. The lawyer says also that he does not think that the Court of Chancery would interfere, having no power to do so as far as the will is concerned, and not being able to make a ward of a person like myself who is over age and has the protection of the common law of the country. So it seems to me that the only thing to do is to be patient, and wait until time unties the knot.

"Meanwhile, if you can make some money in Africa, so much the better. So go, Alan, go as soon as you like, for I do not wish to prolong this agony, or to see you exposed daily to all you have to bear. Whenever you return you will find me waiting for you, and if you do not return, still I shall wait, as you in like circumstances will wait for me. But I think you will return."

Then followed much that need not be written, and at the end a postscript which ran:

"I am glad to hear that you have succeeded in shifting the mortgage on Yarleys, although the interest is so high. Write to me whenever you get a chance, to the care of the lawyer, for then the letters will reach me, but never to this house, or they may be stopped. I will do the same to you to the address you give. Good-bye, dearest Alan, my true and only lover. I wonder where and when we shall meet again. God be with us both and enable us to bear our trial.

"P.P.S. I hear that the Sahara flotation was really a success, notwithstanding the Judge attacks. Sir Robert and my uncle have made millions. I wonder how long they will keep them."

A week after he received this letter Alan was on the seas heading for the shores of Western Africa.

CHAPTER VIII

THE DWARF FOLK

It was dawn at last. All night it had rained as it can rain in West Africa, falling on the wide river with a hissing splash, sullen and continuous. Now, towards morning, the rain had ceased and everywhere rose a soft and pearly mist that clung to the face of the waters and seemed to entangle itself like strands of wool among the branches of the bordering trees. On the bank of the river at a spot that had been cleared of bush, stood a tent, and out of this tent emerged a white man wearing a sun helmet and grey flannel shirt and trousers. It was Alan Vernon, who in these surroundings looked larger and more commanding than he had done at the London office, or even in his own house of Yarleys. Perhaps the moustache and short brown beard which he had grown, or his skin, already altered and tanned by the tropics, had changed his appearance for the better. At any rate it was changed. So were his manner and bearing, whereof all the diffidence had gone. Now they were those of a man accustomed to command who found himself in his right place.

"Jeekie," he called, "wake up those fellows and come and light the oil-stove. I want my coffee."

Thereon a deep voice was heard speaking in some native tongue and saying:

"Cease your snoring, you black dogs, and arouse yourselves, for your lord calls you," an invocation that was followed by the sound of kicks, thumps, and muttered curses.

A minute or two later Jeekie himself appeared, and he also was much changed in appearance, for now instead of his smart, European clothes, he wore a white robe and sandals that gave him an air at once dignified and patriarchal.

"Good-morning, Major," he said cheerfully. "I hope you sleep well, Major, in this low-lying and accursed situation, which is more than we do in boat that half full of water, to say nothing of smell of black man and prevalent mosquito. But the rain it over and gone, and presently the sun shine out, so might be much worse, no cause at all complain."

"I don't know," answered Alan, with a shiver. "I believe that I am fever proof, but otherwise I should have caught it last night, and—just give me the quinine, I will take five grains for luck."

"Yes, yes, for luck," answered Jeekie as he opened the medicine chest and found the quinine, at the same time glancing anxiously out of the corner of his eye at his master's face, for he knew that the spot where they had slept was deadly to white men at this season of the year. "You not catch fever, Little Bonsa," here he dropped his voice and looked down at the box which had served Alan for a pillow, "see to that. But quinine give you appetite for breakfast. Very good chop this morning. Which you like best? Cold ven'son, or fish, or one of them ducks you shoot yesterday?"

"Oh! some of the cold meat, I think. Give the ducks to the boatmen, I don't fancy them in this hot place. By the way, Jeekie, we leave the Qua River here, don't we?"

"Yes, yes, Major, just here. I 'member spot well, for your uncle he pray on it one whole hour; I pretend pray too, but in heart give thanks to Little Bonsa, for heathen in those days, quite different now. This morning we begin walk through forest where it rather dark and cool and comfortable, that is if we no see dwarf people from whom good Lord deliver us," and he bowed towards the box containing Little Bonsa.

"Will those four porters come with us through the forest, Jeekie, as they promised?"

"Yes, yes, they come. Last night they say they not come, too much afraid of dwarf. But I settle their hash. I tell them I save up bits of their hair and toe nails when they no thinking, and I mix it with medicine, and if they not come, they die every one before they get home. They think me great doctor and they believe. Perhaps they die if they go on. If so, I tell them that because they want show white feather, and they think me greater doctor still. Oh! they come, they come, no fear, or else Jeekie know reason why. Now, here coffee, Major. Drink him hot before you go take tub, but keep in shallow water, because crocodile he very early riser."

Alan laughed, and departed to "take tub." Notwithstanding the mosquitoes that buzzed round him in clouds, the water was cool and pleasant by comparison with the hot, sticky air, and the feel of it seemed to rid him of the languor resulting from his disturbed night.

A month had passed since he had left Old Calabar, and owing to the incessant rains the journeying had been hard. Indeed the white men there thought that he was mad to attempt to go up the river at this season. Of course he had said nothing to them of the objects of his expedition, hinting only that he wished to explore and shoot, and perhaps prospect for mines. But knowing as they did, that he was an Engineer officer with a good record and much African experience, they soon made up their minds that he had been sent by Government upon some secret mission that for reasons of his own he preferred to keep to himself. This conclusion, which Jeekie zealously fostered behind his back, in fact did Alan a good turn, since owing to it he obtained boatmen and servants at a season when, had he been supposed to be but a private person, these would scarcely have been forthcoming at any price. Hitherto his journey had been one long record of mud, mosquitoes, and misery, but otherwise devoid of incident, except the eating of one of his boatmen by a crocodile which was a particularly "early riser," for it had pulled the poor fellow out of the canoe in which he lay asleep at night. Now, however, the real dangers were about to begin, since at this spot he left the great river and started forward through the forest on foot with Jeekie and the four bearers whom he had paid highly to accompany him.

He could not conceal from himself that the undertaking seemed somewhat desperate. But of this he said nothing in the long letter he had written to Barbara on the previous night, sighing as he sealed it, at the thought that it might well be the last which would ever reach her from him, even if the boatmen got safely back to Calabar and remembered to put it in the post. The enterprise had been begun and must be carried through, until it ended in success—or death.

An hour later they started. First walked Alan as leader of the expedition, carrying a double-barrelled gun that could be used either for ball or shot, about fifty cartridges with brass cases to protect them from the damp, a revolver, a hunting-knife, a cloth mackintosh, and lastly, strapped upon his back like a knapsack, a tin box containing the fetish, Little Bonsa, which was too precious to be trusted to anyone else. It was quite a sufficient load for any white man in that climate, but being very wiry, Alan did not feel its weight, at any rate at first.

After him in single file came the four porters, laden with a small tent, some tinned provisions and brandy, ammunition, a box containing beads, watches, etc. for presents, blankets, spare clothing and so forth. These were stalwart fellows enough, who knew the forest, but their dejected air showed that now they had come face to face with its dangers, they heartily wished themselves anywhere else. Indeed, notwithstanding their terror of Jeekie's medicine, at the last moment they threw down their loads intending to make a wild rush for the departing boat, only to be met by Jeekie himself who, anticipating some such move, was waiting for them on the bank with a shotgun. Here he remained until the canoe was too far out in the stream for them to reach it by swimming. Then he asked them if they wished to sit and starve there with the devils he would leave them for company, of if they would carry out their bargain like honest men?

The end of it was they took up their loads again and marched, while behind them walked the terrible and gigantic Jeekie, the barrels of the shotgun which he carried at full cock and occasionally used to prod them, pointing directly at their backs. A strange object he looked truly, for in addition to the weapons with which he bristled, several cooking-pots were slung about him, to say nothing of a cork mattress and a mackintosh sheet tied in a flat bundle to his shoulders, a box containing medicines and food which he carried on his head, and fastened to the top of it with string like a helmet on a coffin, an enormous solar-tope stuffed full of mosquito netting, of which the ends fell about him like a green veil. When Alan remonstrated with him as to the cork mattress, suggesting that it should be thrown away as too hot to wear, Jeekie replied that he had been cold for thirty years, and wished to get warm again. Guessing that his real reason for declining to part with the article, was that his master should have something to lie on, other than the damp ground, Alan said no more at the time, which, as will be seen, was fortunate enough for Jeekie.

For a mile or more their road ran through fantastic-looking mangrove trees rooted in the mud, that in the mist resembled, Alan thought, many-legged arboreal octopi feeling for their food, and tall reeds on the tops of which sat crowds of chattering finches. Then just as the sun broke out, strongly, cheering them with its warmth and sucking up the vapours, they entered sparse bush with palms and great cotton trees growing here and there, and so at length came to the borders of the mighty forest.

Oh! dark, dark was that forest; he who entered it from the cheerful sunshine felt as though suddenly and without preparation he had wandered out of the light we know into some dim Hades such as the old Greek fancy painted, where strengthless ghosts flit aimlessly, mourning the lost light. Everywhere the giant boles of trees shooting the height of a church tower into the air without a branch; great rib-rooted trees, and beneath them a fierce and hungry growth of creepers. Where a tree had fallen within the last century or so, these creepers ramped upwards in luxuriance, their stems thick as the body of a man, drinking the shaft of light that pierced downwards, drinking it with eagerness ere the boughs above met again and starved them. Where no tree had fallen the creepers were thin and weak; from year to year they lived on feebly, biding their time, but still they lived, knowing that some day it would come. And always it was coming to those expectant parasites, since from minute to minute, somewhere in the vast depths, miles and miles away perhaps, a great crash echoed in the stillness, the crash of a tree that, sown when the Saxons ruled in England, or perhaps before Cleopatra bewitched Anthony, came to its end at last.

On the second day of their march in the forest Alan chanced to see such a tree fall, and the sight was one that he never could forget. As it happened, owing to the vast spread of its branches which had killed out all rivals beneath, for in its day it had been a very successful tree embued with an excellent constitution by its parent, it stood somewhat alone, so that from several hundred yards away as these six human beings crept towards it like ants towards a sapling in a cornfield, its mighty girth and bulk set upon a little mound and the luxuriant greenness of its far-reaching boughs made a kind of landmark. Then in the hot noon when no breath of wind stirred, suddenly the end came. Suddenly that mighty bole seemed to crumble; suddenly those far-reaching arms were thrown together as their support failed, gripping at each other like living things, flogging the air, screaming in their last agony, and with an awful wailing groan sinking, a tumbled ruin, to the earth.

Silence again, and in the midst of the silence Jeekie's cheerful voice.

"Old tree go flop! Glad he no flop on us, thanks be to Little Bonsa. Get on, you lazy nigger dog. Who pay you stand there and snivel? Get on or I blow out your stupid skull," and he brought the muzzle of the full-cocked, double-barrelled gun into sharp contact with that part of the terrified porter's anatomy.

Such was the forest. Of their march through it for the first four days, there is nothing to tell. Its depths seemed to be devoid of life, although occasionally they heard the screaming of parrots in the treetops a couple of hundred feet above, or caught sight of the dim shapes of monkeys swinging themselves from bough to bough. That was in the daytime, when, although they could not see it, they knew that the sun was shining somewhere. But at night they heard nothing, since beasts of prey do not come where there is no food. What puzzled Alan was that all through these impenetrable recesses there ran a distinct road which they followed. To the right and left rose a wall of creepers, but between them ran this road, an ancient road, for nothing grew on it, and it only turned aside to avoid the biggest of the trees which must have stood there from time immemorial, such a tree as that which he had seen fall; indeed it was one of those round which the road ran.

He asked Jeekie who made the road.

"People who come out Noah's Ark," answered Jeekie, "I think they run up here to get out of way of water, and sent them two elephants ahead to make path. Or perhaps dwarf people make it. Or perhaps those who go up to Asiki-land to do sacrifice like old Jews."

"You mean you don't know," said Alan.

"No, of course don't know. Who know about forest path made before beginning of world. You ask question, Major, I answer. More lively answer than to shake head and roll eyes like them silly fool porters."

It was on the fourth night that the trouble began. As usual they had lit a huge fire made of the fallen boughs and rotting tree trunks that lay about in plenty. There was no reason why the fire should be so large, since they had little to cook and the air was hot, but they made it so for the same reason that Jeekie answered questions, for the sake of cheerfulness. At least it gave light in the darkness, leaping up in red tongues of flame twenty or thirty feet high, and its roar and crackle were welcome in the primeval silence.

Alan lay upon the cork mattress in the open, for here there was no need to pitch the tent; if any rain fell above, the canopy of leaves absorbed it. He was amusing himself while he smoked his pipe with watching the reflection of the fire-light against a patch of darkness caused probably by some bush about twenty yards away, and by picturing in his own mind the face of Barbara, that strong, pleasant English face, as it might appear on such a background. Suddenly there, on the identical spot he did see a face, though one of a very different character. It was round and small and hideous, resembling in its general outline that of a bloated child. At this distance he could not distinguish the features, except the lips, which were large and pendulous, and between them the flash of white teeth.

"Look here," he whispered to Jeekie in English, and Jeekie looked, then without saying a word, lifted the shotgun that lay at his side and fired straight at the bush. Instantly there arose a squeaking noise, such as might be made by a wounded animal, and the four porters sprang up in alarm.

"Sit down," said Jeekie to them in their own tongue, "a leopard was stalking us and I fired to frighten it away. Don't go near the place, as it may be wounded and angry, but drag up some boughs and make a fence round the fire, for fear of others."

The men who dreaded leopards, looking on these animals, indeed, with superstitious reverence, obeyed readily enough, and as there was plenty of wood lying within a few yards, soon constructed a boma fence that, rough as it was, would serve for protection.

"Jeekie," said Alan presently as they laboured at the fence, "that was not a leopard, it was a man."

"No, no, Major, not man, little dwarf devil, him that have poisoned arrow. I shoot at once to make him sit up. Think he no come back to-night, too much afraid of shot fetish. But to-morrow, can't say. Not tell those fellows anything," and he nodded towards the porters, "or perhaps they bolt."

"I think you would have done better to leave the dwarf alone," said Alan, "and they might have left us alone. Now they will have a blood feud against us."

"Not agree, Major, only chance for us put him in blue funk. If I not shoot, presently he shoot," and he made a sound that resembled the whistling of an arrow, then added, "Now you go sleep. I not tired, I watch, my eyes see in dark better than yours. Only two more days of this damn forest, then open land with tree here and there, where dwarf no come because he afraid of lion and cannibal man, who like eat him."

As there was nothing else to be done Alan took Jeekie's advice and in time fell fast asleep, nor did he wake again till the faint light which for the want of a better name they called dawn, was filtering down to them through the canopy of boughs.

"Been to look," said Jeekie as he handed him his coffee. "Hit that dwarf man, see his blood, but think others carry him away. Jeekie very good shot, stone, spear, arrow, or gun, all same to him. Now get off as quick as we can before porters smell a rat. You eat chop, Major, I pack."

Presently they started on their trudge through those endless trees, with Fear for a companion. Even the porters, who had been told nothing, seemed more afraid than usual, though whether this was because they "smell rat," as Jeekie called it, or owing to the progressive breakdown of their nervous systems, Alan did not know. About midday they stopped to eat because the men were too tired to walk further without rest. For an hour or more they had been looking for a comparatively open place, but as it chanced could find none, so were obliged to halt in dense forest. Just as they had finished their meal and were preparing to proceed, that which they had feared, happened, since from somewhere behind the tree boles came a volley of reed arrows. One struck a porter in the neck, one fixed itself in Alan's helmet without touching him, and no less than three hit Jeekie on the back and stuck there, providentially enough in the substance of the cork mattress that he still carried on his shoulders, which the feeble shafts had not the strength to pierce.

Everybody sprang up and with a curious fascination instead of attempting to do anything, watched the porter who had been hit in the neck somewhere in the region of the jugular vein. The poor man rose to his feet with great deliberation, reminding Alan in some grotesque way of a speaker who has suddenly been called on to address a meeting and seeks to gain time for the gathering of his thoughts. Then he turned towards that vast audience of the trees, stretched out his hand with a declamatory gesture, said something in a composed voice, and fell upon his face stone dead! The swift poison had reached his heart and done its work.

His three companions looked at him for a moment and the next with a yell of terror, rushed off into the forest, hurling down their loads as they ran. What became of them Alan never learned, for he saw them no more, and the dwarf people keep their secrets. At the time indeed he scarcely noticed their departure, for he was otherwise engaged.

One of their hideous little assailants, made bold by success, ventured to run across an open space between two trees, showing himself for a moment. Alan had a gun in his hand, and mad with rage at what had happened, he raised it and swung on him as he would upon a rabbit. He was a quick and practised shot and his skill did not fail him now, for just as the dwarf was vanishing behind a tree, the bullet caught him and next instant he was seen rolling over and over upon its further side.

"That very nice," said Jeekie reflectively, "very nice indeed, but I think we best move out of this."

"Aren't you hurt?" gasped Alan. "Your back is full of arrows."

"Don't feel nothing, Major," he answered, "best cork mattress, 25/3 at Stores, very good for poisoned arrow, but leave him behind now, because perhaps points work through as I run, one scratch do trick," and as he spoke Jeekie untied a string or several strings, letting the little mattress fall to the ground.

"Great pity leave all those goods," said Jeekie, surveying the loads that the porters had cast away, "but what says Book? Life more than raiment. Also take no thought for morrow. Dwarf people do that for us. Come, Major, make tracks," and dashing at a bag of cartridges which he cast about his neck, a trifling addition to his other impedimenta, and a small case of potted meats that he hitched under his arm, he poked his master in the back with the muzzle of his full-cocked gun as a signal that it was time to start.

"Keep that cursed thing off me," said Alan furiously. "How often have I told you never to carry firearms at full cock?"

"About one thousand times, Major," answered Jeekie imperturbably, "but on such occasion forget discreetness. My ma just same, it run in family, but story too long tell you now. Cut, Major, cut like hell. Them dwarfs be back soon, but," he puffed, "I think, I think Little Bonsa come square with them one day."

So Alan "cut" and the huge Jeekie blundered along after him, the paraphernalia with which he was hung about rattling like the hoofs of a galloping giraffe. Nor for all his load did he ever turn a hair. Whether it were fear within or a desire to save his master, or a belief in the virtues of Little Bonsa, or that his foot was, as it were, once more upon his native heath, the fact remained that notwithstanding the fifty years, almost, that had whitened his wool, Jeekie was absolutely inexhaustible. At least at the end of that fearful chase, which lasted all the day, and through the night also, for they dared not camp, he appeared to be nearly as fresh as when he started from Old Calabar, nor did his spirits fail him for one moment.

When the light came on the following morning, however, they perceived by many signs and tokens that the dwarf people were all about them. Some arrows were shot even, but these fell short.

"Pooh!" said Jeekie, "all right now, they much afraid. Still, no time for coffee, we best get on."

So they got on as they could, till towards midday the forest began to thin out. Now as the light grew stronger they could see the dwarfs, of whom there appeared to be several hundred, keeping a parallel course to their own on either side of them at what they thought to be a safe distance.

"Try one shot, I think," said Jeekie, kneeling down and letting fly at a clump of the little men, which scattered like a covey of partridges, leaving one of its number kicking on the ground. "Ah! my boy," shouted Jeekie in derision, "how you like bullet in tummy? You not know Paradox guaranteed flat trajectory 250 yard. You remember that next time, sonny." Then off they went again up a long rise.

"River other side of that rise," said Jeekie. "Think those tree-monkeys no follow us there."

But the "monkeys" appeared to be angry and determined. They would not come any more within the range of the Paradox, but they still marched on either side of the two fugitives, knowing well that at last their strength must fail and they would be able to creep up and murder them. So the chase went on till Alan began to wonder whether it would not be better to face the end at once.

"No, no, if say die, can't change mind to-morrow morning," gasped Jeekie in a hoarse voice. "Here top rise, much nearer than I thought. Oh, my aunt! who those?" and he pointed to a large number of big men armed with spears who were marching up the further side of the hill from the river that ran below.

At the same moment these savages, who were not more than two hundred yards away, caught sight of them and of their pursuers, who just then appeared on the ridge to the right and left. The dwarfs, on perceiving these strangers, uttered a shrill yell of terror, and wheeled about to fly to their fastnesses in the forest, which evidently they regretted ever having left. It was too late. With an answering shout the spearsmen, who were extended in a long line, apparently hunting for game, charged after them at full speed. They were fresh and their legs were long. Therefore very soon they overtook the dwarfs and even got in front of them, heading them off from the forest. The end may be guessed,—save a few whom they reserved alive, they killed them mercilessly, and almost without loss to themselves, since the little forest folk were too terrified and exhausted to shoot at them with their poisoned arrows, and they had no other weapons.

In fact, as Alan discovered afterwards, for generations there had been war between them, since all the other tribes hate the dwarfs, whom they look upon as dangerous human monkeys, and never before had the big men found such a chance of squaring their account.

When Jeekie saw this fearful-looking company, for the first time his spirits seemed to fail him.

"Ogula!" he exclaimed with a groan and sat himself upon a flat rock, pulling Alan down beside him. "Ogula! Know them by hair and spears," he repeated. "Up gum tree now, say good-night."

"Why? Who are they?" gasped Alan.

"Great cannibal, Major, eat man, eat us to-night, or perhaps to-morrow morning when we nice and cool. Say prayers, Major, quick no time waste."

"I think I will shoot an Ogula or two first," said Alan grimly, as he stood up and lifted his gun.

"No, not shoot, no good. Pretend not be afraid, best chance. Let Jeekie think, let Jeekie think," and he slapped his forehead with his large hand.

Apparently the action brought inspiration, for next instant he grabbed his master by the arm and dragged him back behind the shelter of a big boulder which they had just passed. Then with really marvellous swiftness he cut the straps of the tin box that Alan wore upon his back, and since there was no time to find the key and unlock it, seized the little padlock with which it was fastened between his finger and thumb, and putting out his great strength, with a single wrench twisted it off.

"What are you—" began Alan.

"Hold tongue," he answered savagely, "make you god, I priest. Ogula know Little Bonsa. Quick, quick!"

In a minute it was done, the golden mask was clapped on to Alan's head, and the leather thongs were fastened. Moreover, Jeekie himself was arrayed in the solar-tope to which all this while he had clung, allowing streams of green mosquito netting to hang down over his white robe.

"Come out now, Major," he said, "and play god. You whistle, I do palaver."

Then hand in hand they walked from behind the rock. By this time the particular company of the cannibals that was opposite to them, which happened to include their chief, had climbed the steep slope of the hill and arrived within a distance of twenty yards. Having seen the two men and guessed that they had taken refuge behind the rock, their spears were lifted to kill them, since when he beholds anything strange, the first impulse of a savage is to bring it to its death. They looked; they saw. Of a sudden down went the raised spears.

Some of those who held them fell upon their faces, while others turned to fly, appalled by the vision of this strangely clad man with the head of gold. Only their chief, a great yellow-toothed fellow who wore a necklace of baboon claws, remained erect, staring at them with open mouth.

Alan blew the whistle that was set between the lips of the mask, and they shivered. Then Jeekie spoke to them in some tongue which they understood, saying:

"Do you, O Ogula, dare to offer violence to Little Bonsa and her priests? Say now, why should we not strike you dead with the magic of the god which she has borrowed from the white man?" and he tapped the gun he held.

"This is witchcraft," answered the chief. "We saw two men running, hunted by the dwarfs, not three minutes ago, and now we see—what we see," and he put his hand before his eyes, then after a pause went on—"As for Little Bonsa, she left this country in my father's day. He gave her passage upon the head of a white man and the Asiki wizards have mourned her ever since, or so I hear."

"Fool," answered Jeekie, "as she went, so she returns, on the head of a white man. Yonder I see an elder with grey hair who doubtless knew of Little Bonsa in his youth. Let him come up and look and say whether or no this is the god."

"Yes, yes," exclaimed the chief, "go up, old man, go up," and he jabbed at him with his spear until, unwillingly enough, he went.

The elder arrived, making obeisance, and when he was near, Alan blew the whistle in his face, whereon he fell to his knees.

"It is Little Bonsa," he said in a trembling voice, "Little Bonsa without a doubt. I should know, as my father and my elder brother were sacrificed to her, and I only escaped because she rejected me. Down on your face, Chief, and do honour to the Yellow God before she slay you."

Instantly every man within hearing prostrated himself and lay still. Then Jeekie strode up and down among them shouting out:

"Little Bonsa has come back and brought to you, Man-eaters, a fat offering, an offering of the dwarf-people whom you hate, of the treacherous dwarf-people who when you walk the ancient forest path, murder you with their poisoned arrows. Praise Little Bonsa who delivers you from your foes, and hearken to her bidding. Send on messengers to the Asiki saying that Little Bonsa comes home again from across the Black Water bringing the White Preacher, whom she led away in the day of their fathers. Say to them that the Asiki must send out a company that Little Bonsa and the Magician with whom she ran away, may be escorted back to her house with the state which has been hers from the beginning of time. Say to them also that they must prepare a great offering of pure gold out of their store, as much gold as fifty strong men can carry, not one handful less, to be given to the White Magician who brings back Small Swimming Head, for if they withhold such an offering, he and Little Bonsa will vanish never to be seen again, and curses and desolation will fall upon their land. Rise and obey, Chief of the Ogula."

Then the man scrambled to his feet and answered:

"It shall be done, O Priest of the Yellow God. To-morrow at the dawn swift messengers will start for the Gold House of the Asiki. To-night they cannot leave, as we are all very hungry and must eat."

"What must you eat?" asked Jeekie suspiciously.

"O Priest," answered the chief with a deprecatory gesture, "when first we saw you we hoped that it would be the white man and yourself, for we have never tasted white man. But now we fear that you will not consent to this, and as you are holy and the guardian of the god, we cannot eat you without your own consent. Therefore fat dwarf must be our food, of which, however, there will be plenty for you as well as us."

"You dog!" exclaimed Jeekie in a voice of furious indignation. "Do you think that white men and their high-born companions, such as myself, were made to fill your vile stomachs? I tell you that a meal of the deadly Bean would agree better with you, for if you dare so much as to look on us, or on any of the white race with hunger, agony shall seize your vitals and you and all your tribe shall die as though by poison. Moreover, we do not touch the flesh of men, nor will we see it eaten. It is our 'orunda,' it is consecrate to us, it must not pass our lips, nor may our eyes behold it. Therefore we will camp apart from you further up the stream and find our own food. But to-morrow at the dawn the messengers must leave as we have commanded. Also you shall provide strong men and a large canoe to bear Little Bonsa forward towards her own home until she finds her people coming out to greet her.

"It shall be done," answered the chief humbly, "Everything shall be done according to the will of Little Bonsa spoken by her priest, that she may leave a blessing and not a curse upon the heads of the tribe of the Ogula. Say where you wish to camp and men shall run to build a house of reeds for the god to dwell in."

CHAPTER IX

THE DAWN

Jeekie looked up and down the river and saw that in the centre of it about half a mile away, there was an island on which grew some trees.

"Little Bonsa will camp yonder," he said. "Go, make her house ready, light fire and bring canoe to paddle us across. Now leave us, all of you, for if you look too long upon the face of the Yellow God she will ask a sacrifice, and it is not lawful that you should see where she hides herself away."

At this saying the cannibals departed as one man, and at top speed, some of the canoes and others to warn their fellows who were engaged in the congenial work of hunting and killing the dwarfs, not to dare to approach the white man and his companion. A third party ran to the bank of the river that was opposite to the island to make ready as they had been bidden, so that presently Alan and Jeekie were left quite alone.

"Ah!" said Jeekie, with a gasp of satisfaction, "that all right, everything arranged quite comfortable. Thought Little Bonsa come out top somehow and score off dirty dwarf monkeys. They never get home to tea anyway—stay and dine with Ogula."

"Stop chattering, Jeekie, and untie this infernal mask, I am almost choked," broke in Alan in a hollow voice.

"Not say 'infernal mask,' Major, say 'face of angel.' Little Bonsa woman and like it better, also true, if on this occasion only, for she save our skins," said Jeekie as he unknotted the thongs and reverently replaced the fetish in its tin box. "My!" he added, contemplating his master's perspiring countenance, "you blush like garden carrot; well, gold hot wear in afternoon sun beneath Tropic of Cancer. Now we walk on quietly and I tell you all I arrange for night's lodging and future progress of joint expedition."

So gathering together what remained of their few possessions, they started leisurely down the slope towards the island, and as they went Jeekie explained all that had happened, since Ogula was not one of the African languages with which Alan was acquainted and he had only been able to understand a word here and there.

"Look," said Jeekie when he had finished, and turning, he pointed to the cannibals who were driving the few survivors of the dwarfs before them to the spot where their canoes were beached. "Those dwarfs done for; capital business, forest road quite safe to travel home by; Ogula best friends in world; very remarkable escape from delicate situation."

"Very remarkable indeed," said Alan; "I shall soon begin to believe in the luck of Little Bonsa."

"Yes, Major, you see she anxious to get home and make path clear. But," he added gloomily, "how she behave when she reach there, can't say."

"Nor can I, Jeekie, but meanwhile I hope she will provide us with some dinner, for I am faint for want of food and all the tinned meat is lost."

"Food," repeated Jeekie. "Yes, necessity for human stomach, which unhappily built that way, so Ogula find out, and so dwarfs find out presently." Then he looked about him and in a kind of aimless manner lifted his gun and fired. "There we are," he said, "Little Bonsa understand bodily needs," and he pointed to a fat buck of the sort that in South Africa is called Duiker, which his keen eyes had discovered in its form against a stone where it now lay shot through the head and dying. "No further trouble on score of grub for next three day," he added. "Come on to camp, Major. I send one savage skin and bring that buck."

So on they went to the river bank, Alan so tired now that the excitement was over, that he was not sorry to lean upon Jeekie's arm. Reaching the stream they drank deep of its water, and finding that it was shallow at this spot, waded through it to the island without waiting for a canoe to ferry them over. Here they found a party of the cannibals already at work clearing reeds with their large, curved knives, in order to make a site for the hut. Another party under the command of their chief himself had gone to the top end of the island, to cut the stems of a willow-like shrub to serve as uprights. These people stared at Alan, which was not strange, as they had never before seen the face of a white man and were wondering, doubtless, what had become of the ancient and terrible fetish that he had worn. Without entering into explanations Jeekie in a great voice ordered two of them to fetch the buck, which the white man, whom he described as "husband of the goddess," had "slain by thunder." When these had departed upon their errand, leaving Jeekie to superintend the building operations, Alan sat down upon a fallen tree, watching one of the savages making fire with a pointed stick and some tinder.

Just then from the head of the island where the willows were being cut, rose the sound of loud roarings and of men crying out in affright. Seizing his gun Alan ran towards the spot whence the noise came. Forcing his way through a brake of reeds, he saw a curious sight. The Ogula in cutting the willows which grew about some tumbled rocks, had disturbed a lioness that had her lair there, and being fearless savages, had tried to kill her with their spears. The brute, rendered desperate by wounds, and the impossibility of escape, for here the surrounding water was deep, had charged them boldly, and as it chanced, felled to the ground their chief, that yellow-toothed man to whom Jeekie gave his orders. Now she was standing over him looking round her royally, her great paw upon his breast, which it seemed almost to cover, while the Ogula ran round and round shouting, for they feared that if they tried to attack her, she would kill the chief. This indeed she seemed about to do, for just as Alan arrived she dropped her head as though to tear out the man's throat. Instantly he fired. It was a snap shot, but as it chanced a good one, for the bullet struck the lioness in the back of the neck just forward of and between the shoulders, severing the spine so that without a sound or any further movement she sank stone dead upon the prostrate cannibal. For a while his followers stood astonished. They might have heard of guns from the coast people, but living as they did in the interior where white folk did not dare to travel, they had never seen their terrible effects.

"Magic!" they cried. "Magic!"

"Of course," exclaimed Jeekie, who by now had arrived upon the scene. "What else did you expect from the husband of Little Bonsa? Magic, the greatest of magic. Go, roll that beast away before your chief is crushed to death."

They obeyed, and the man sat up, a fearful spectacle, for he was smothered with the blood of the lion and somewhat cut by her claws, though otherwise unhurt. Then feeling that the life was still whole in him, he crept on his hands and knees to where Alan stood, and kissed his feet.

"Aha!" said Jeekie, "Little Bonsa score again. Cannibal tribe our slave henceforth for evermore. Yes, till kingdom come. Come on, Major, and cook supper in perfect peace."

The supper was cooked and eaten with gratitude, for seldom had two men needed a square meal more, and never did venison taste better. By the time that it was finished darkness had fallen, and before they turned in to sleep in the neat reed hut that the Ogula had built, Alan and Jeekie walked up the island to see if the lioness had been skinned, as they directed. This they found was done; even the carcase itself had been removed to serve as meat for these foul-feeding people. They climbed on to the pile of rocks in which the beast had made her lair, and looked down the river to where, two hundred yards away, the Ogula were encamped. From this camp there rose a sound of revelry, and by the light of the great fires that burned there, they perceived that the hungry savages were busy feasting, for some of them sat in circles, whilst others, their naked forms looking at that distance like those of imps in the infernal regions, flitted to and fro against the glowing background of the fires, bearing strange-looking joints on prongs of wood.

"I suppose they are eating the lioness," said Alan doubtfully.

"No, no, Major, not lioness; eat dwarf by dozen—just like oysters at seaside. But for Little Bonsa we sit on those forks now and look uncommon small."

"Beasts!" said Alan in disgust; "they make me feel uncommon sick. Let us go to bed. I suppose they won't murder us in our sleep, will they?"

"Not they, Major, too much afraid. Also we their blood-brothers now, because we bring them first-class dinner and save chief from lion's fury. No blame them too much, Major, good fellows really with gentle heart, but grub like that from generation to generation. Every mother's son of them have many men inside, that why they so big and strong. Ogula people cover great multitude like Charity in Book. No doubt sent by Providence to keep down extra pop'lation. Not right to think too hard of poor fellows who, as I say, very kind and gentle at heart and most loving in family relation, except to old women whom they eat also, so that they no get bored with too long life."

Weary and disgusted by this abominable sight though he was, Alan burst out laughing at his retainer's apology for the sweet-natured Ogula, who struck him as the most repulsive blackguards that he had ever met or heard of in all his experience of African savages. Then wishing to see and hear no more of them that night, he retreated rapidly to the hut and was soon fast asleep with his head pillowed on the box that hid the charms of Little Bonsa. When he awoke it was broad daylight. Rising he went down to the river to wash, and never had a bath been more welcome, for during all their journey through the forest no such thing was obtainable. On his return he found his garments well brushed with dry reeds and set upon a rock in the hot sun to air, while Jeekie in a cheerful mood, was engaged cooking breakfast in the frying-pan, to which he had clung through all the vicissitudes of their flight.

"No coffee, Major," he said regretfully, "that stop in forest. But never mind, hot water better for nerve. Ogula messengers gone in little canoe to Asiki at break of day. Travel slow till they work off dwarf, but afterwards go quick. I send lion skin with them as present from you to great high-priestess Asika, also claws for necklace. No lions there and she think much of that. Also it make her love mighty man who can kill fierce lion like Samson in Book. Love of head woman very valuable ally among beastly savage peoples."

"I am sure I hope it won't," said Alan with earnestness, "but no doubt it is as well to keep on the soft side of the good lady if we can. What time do we start?"

"In one hour, Major. I been to camp already, chosen best canoe and finest men for rowers. Chief—he called Fanny—so grateful that he come with them himself."

"Indeed. That is very kind of him, but I say, Jeekie, what are these fellows going to live on? I can't stand what you call their 'favourite chop.'"

"No, no, Major, that all right. I tell them that when they travel with Little Bonsa, they must keep Lent like pious Roman Catholic family that live near Yarleys. They catch plenty fish in river, and perhaps we shoot game, or rich 'potamus, which they like 'cause he fat."

Evidently the Ogula chief, Fahni by name, not Fanny, as Jeekie called him, was a man of his word, for before the hour was up he appeared at the island in command of a large canoe manned by twelve splendid-looking savages. Springing to land, he prostrated himself before Alan, kissing his feet as he had done on the previous night, and making a long speech.

"That very good spirit," exclaimed Jeekie. "Like to see heathen in his darkness lick white gentleman's boot. He say you his lord and great magician who save his life, and know all Little Bonsa's secrets, which many and unrepeatable. He say he die for you twice a day if need be, and go on dying to-morrow and all next year. He say he take you safe till you meet Asiki and for your sake, though he hungry, eat no man for one whole month, or perhaps longer. Now we start at once."

So they started up the river that was called Katsena, Alan and Jeekie seated in a lordly fashion near the stern of the canoe beneath an awning made out of some sticks and a grass mat. In truth after their severe toil and adventures in the forest, this method of journeying proved quite luxurious. Except for a rapid here and there over or round which the canoe must be dragged, the river was broad and the scenery on its banks park-like and beautiful. Moreover the country, perhaps owing to the appetites of the Ogula, appeared to be practically uninhabited except by vast herds of every sort of game.

All day they sat in the canoe which the stalwart rowers propelled, in silence for the most part, since they were terribly afraid of the white man, and still more so of the renowned fetish which they knew he carried with him. Then when evening came they moored their craft to the bank and camped till the following morning. Nor did they lack for food, since game being so plentiful, it was only necessary for Alan to walk a few hundred yards and shoot a fat eland, or hartebeest, or other buck which in its ignorance of guns would allow him to approach quite close. Elephants, rhinoceros, and buffalo were also common, while great herds of giraffe might be seen wandering between the scattered trees, but as they were not upon a hunting trip and their ammunition was very limited, with these they did not interfere.

Having their daily fill of meat which their souls loved, the Ogula oarsmen remained in an excellent mood, indeed the chief, Fahni, informed Alan that if only they had such magic tubes wherewith to slaughter game, he and his tribe would gladly give up cannibalism—except on feast days. He added sadly that soon they would be obliged to do so, or die, since in those parts there were now few people left to eat, and they hated vegetables. Moreover, they kept no cattle, it was not the custom of that tribe, except a very few for milk. Alan advised them to increase their herds, since, as he pointed out to them, "dog should not eat dog" or the human being his own kind.

The chief answered that there was a great deal in what he said, which on his return he would lay before his head men. Indeed Alan, to his astonishment, discovered that Jeekie had been quite right when he alleged that these people, so terrible in their mode of life, were yet "kind and gentle at heart." They preyed upon mankind because for centuries it had been their custom so to do, but if anyone had been there to show them a better way, he grew sure that they would follow it gladly. At least they were brave and loyal and even after their first fear of the white man had worn off, fulfilled their promises without a murmur. Once, indeed, when he chanced to have gone for a walk unarmed and to be charged by a bull elephant, these Ogula ran at the brute with their spears and drove it away, a rescue in which one of them lost his life, for the "rogue" caught and killed him.

So the days went on while they paddled leisurely up the river, Alan employing the time by taking lessons in the Asiki tongue from Jeekie, a language which he had been studying ever since he left England. The task was not easy, as he had no books and Jeekie himself after some thirty years of absence, was doubtful as to many of its details. Still being a linguist by nature and education and finding in the tongue similarities to other African dialects which he knew, he was now able to speak it a little, in a halting fashion.

On the fifth day of their ascent of the river, they came to a tributary that flowed into it from the north, up which the Ogula said they must proceed to reach Asiki-land. The stream was narrow and sluggish, widening out here and there into great swamps through which it was not easy to find a channel. Also the district was so unhealthy that even several of the Ogula contracted fever, of which Alan cured them by heavy doses of quinine, for fortunately his travelling medicine chest remained to him. These cures were effected after their chief suggested that they should be thrown overboard, or left to die in the swamp as useless, with the result that the white man's magical powers were thenceforth established beyond doubt or cavil. Indeed the poor Ogula now looked on him as a god superior even to Little Bonsa, whose familiar he was supposed to be.

The journey through that swamp was very trying, since in this wet season often they could find no place on which to sleep at night, but must stay in the canoe tormented by mosquitoes, and in constant danger of being upset by the hippopotami that lived there. Moreover, as no game was now available, they were obliged to live on these beasts, fish when they could catch them, and wildfowl, which sometimes they were unable to cook for lack of fuel. This did not trouble the Ogula, who ate them raw, as did Jeekie when he was hungry. But Alan was obliged to starve until they could make a fire. This it was only possible to do when they found drift or other wood, since at that season the rank vegetation was in full growth. Also the fearful thunderstorms which broke continually and in a few minutes half filled their canoe with water, made the reeds and the soil on which they grew, sodden with wet. As Jeekie said:

"This time of year only fit for duck and crocodile. Human should remember uncontrollable forces of nature and wait till winter come in due course, when quagmire bear sole of his foot."

This elaborate remark he made to Alan during the progress of a particularly fearful tempest. The lightning blazed in the black sky and seemed to strike all about them like stabbing swords of fire, the thunder crashed and bellowed as it may be supposed that it will do on that day when the great earth, worn out at last, shall reel and stagger to its doom. The rain fell in a straight and solid sheet; the tall reeds waved confusedly like millions of dim arms and while they waved, uttered a vast and groaning noise; the scared wildfowl in their terror, with screams and the sough of wings, rushed past them in flocks a thousand strong, now seen and now lost in the vapours. To keep their canoe afloat the poor, naked Ogula oarsmen, shivering with cold and fear, baled furiously with their hands, or bowls of hollowed wood, and called back to Alan to save them as though he were the master of the elements. Even Jeekie was depressed and appeared to be offering up petitions, though whether these were directed to Little Bonsa or elsewhere it was impossible to know.

As for Alan, the heart was out of him. It is true that so far he had escaped fever or other sickness, which in itself was wonderful, but he was chilled through and through and practically had eaten nothing for two days, and very little for a week, since his stomach turned from half-cooked hippopotamus fat and wildfowl. Moreover, they had lost the channel and seemed to be wandering aimlessly through a wilderness of reeds broken here and there by lines of deeper water.

According the Ogula they should have reached the confines of the great lake several days before and landed on healthful rising ground that was part of the Asiki territory. But this had not happened, and now he doubted whether it ever would happen. It was more likely that they would come to their deaths, there in the marsh, especially as the few ball and shot cartridges which they had saved in their flight were now exhausted. Not one was left; nothing was left except their revolvers with some charges, which of course were quite useless for the killing of game. Therefore they were in a fair way to die of hunger, for here if fish existed, they refused to be caught and nought remained for them to fill themselves with except water slugs, and snails which the boatmen were already gathering and crunching up in their great teeth. Or, perhaps the Ogula, forgetting friendship under the pressure of necessity, would murder them as they slept and—revert to their usual diet.

Jeekie was right, he should have remembered the "uncontrollable forces of Nature." Only a madman would have undertaken such an expedition in the rains. No wonder that the Asiki remained a secret and hidden people when their frontier was protected by such a marsh as this upon the one side and, as he understood, by impassable mountains upon the other.

There came a lull in the tempest and the boatmen began to get the better of the water, which now was up to their knees. Alan asked Jeekie if he thought it was over, but that worthy shook his white head mournfully, causing the spray to fly as from a twirling mop, and replied:

"Can't say, cats and dogs not tumble so many for present, only pups and kitties left, so to speak, but think there plenty more up there," and he nodded at the portentous fire-laced cloud which seemed to be spreading over them, its black edges visible even through the gloom.

"Bad business, I am afraid, Jeekie. Shouldn't have brought you here, or those poor beggars either," and he looked at the scared, frozen Ogula. "I begin to wonder—"

"Never wonder, Major," broke in Jeekie in alarm. "If wonder, not live, if wonder, not be born, too much wonder about everywhere. Can't understand nothing, so give it up. Say, 'Right-O and devil hindermost!' Very good motto for biped in tight place. Better drown here than in City bucket shop. But no drown. Should be dead long ago, but Little Bonsa play the game, she not want to sink in stinking swamp when so near her happy home. Come out all right somehow, as from dwarf. Every cloud have silver lining, Major, even that black chap up there. Oh! my golly!"

This last exclamation was wrung from Jeekie's lips by a sudden development of "forces of Nature" which astonished even him. Instead of a silver lining the "black chap" exhibited one of gold. In an instant it seemed to turn to acres of flame; it was as though the heavens had taken fire. A flash or a thunderbolt struck the water within ten yards of their canoe, causing the boatmen to throw themselves upon their faces through shock or terror. Then came the hurricane, which fortunately was so strong that it permitted no more rain to fall. The tall reeds were beaten flat beneath its breath; the canoe was seized in its grip and whirled round and round, then driven forward like an arrow. Only the weight of the men and the water in it prevented it from oversetting. Dense darkness fell upon them and although they could see no star, they knew that it must be night. On they rushed, driven by that shrieking gale, and all about and around them this wall of darkness. No one spoke, for hope was abandoned, and if they had, their voices could not have been heard. The last thing that Alan remembered was feeling Jeekie dragging a grass mat over him to protect him a little if he could. Then his senses wavered, as does a dying lamp. He thought that he was back in what Jeekie had rudely called "City bucket shop," bargaining across the telephone wire, upon which came all the sounds of the infernal regions, with a financial paper for an article on a Little Bonsa Syndicate that he proposed to float. He thought he was in The Court woods with Barbara, only the birds in the trees sang so unnaturally loud that he could not hear her voice, and she wore Little Bonsa on her head as a bonnet. Then she departed in flame, leaving him and Death alone.

Alan awoke. Above the sun shone hotly, warming him back to life, but in front was a thick wall of mist and rising beyond it in the distance he saw the rugged swelling forms of mountains. Doubtless these had been visible before, but the tall reeds through which they travelled had hid the sight of them. He looked behind him and there in a heap lay the Ogula around their chief, insensible or sleeping. He counted them and found that two were gone, lost in the tempest, how or where no man ever learned. He looked forward and saw a peculiar sight, for in the prow of the drifting canoe stood Jeekie clad in the remains of his white robe and wearing on his head the battered helmet and about his shoulders the torn fragments of green mosquito net. While Alan was wondering strangely why he had adopted this ceremonial garb, from out of the mist there came a sound of singing, of wild and solemn singing. Jeekie seemed to listen to it; then he lifted up his great musical voice and sang as though in answer. What he sang Alan could not understand, but he recognized that the language which he used was that of the Asiki people.

A pause and a confused murmuring, and now again the wild song rose and again Jeekie answered.

"What the deuce are you doing? Where are we?" asked Alan faintly.

Jeekie turned and beamed upon him; although his teeth were chattering and his face was hollow, still he beamed.

"You awake, Major?" he said. "Thought good old sun do trick. Feel your heart now and find it beat. Pulse, too, strong, though temp'rature not normal. Well, good news this morning. Little Bonsa come out top as usual. Asiki priests on bank there. Can't see them, but know their song and answer. Same old game as thirty years ago. Asiki never change, which good business when you been away long while."

"Hang the Asiki," said Alan feebly, "I think all these poor beggars are dead, and he pointed to the rowers.

"Look like it, Major, but what that matter now since you and I alive? Plenty more where they come from. Not dead though, think only sleep, no like cold, like dormouse. But never mind cannibal pig. They serve our turn, if they live, live; if they die, die and God have mercy on souls, if cannibal have soul. Ah! here we are," and from beneath six inches of water he dragged up the tin box containing Little Bonsa, from which he extracted the fetish, wet but uninjured.

"Put her on now, Major. Put her on at once and come sit in prow of canoe. Must reach Asiki-land in proper style. Priests think it your reverend uncle come back again, just as he leave. Make very good impression."

"I can't," said Alan feebly. "I am played out, Jeekie."

"Oh! buck up, Major, buck up!" he replied imploringly. "One kick more and you win race, mustn't spoil ship for ha'porth of tar. You just wear fetish, whistle once on land, and then go to sleep for whole week if you like. I do rest, say it all magic, and so forth—that you been dead and just come out of grave, or anything you like. No matter if you turn up as announced on bill and God bless hurricane that blow us here when we expect die. Come, Major, quick, quick! mist melt and soon they see you." Then without waiting for an answer Jeekie clapped the wet mask on his master's head, tied the thongs and led Alan to the prow of the canoe, where he set him down on a little cross bench, stood behind supporting him and again began to sing in a great triumphant voice.

The mist cleared away, rolling up like a curtain and revealing on the shore a number of men and women clad in white robes, who were martialled in ranks there, chanting and staring out at the dim waters of the lagoon. Yonder upon the waters, driven forward by the gentle breeze, floated a canoe and lo! in the prow of that canoe sat a white man and on his head the god which they had lost a whole generation gone. On the head of a white man it had departed; on the head of a white man it returned. They saw and fell upon their knees.

"Blow, Major, blow!" whispered Jeekie, and Alan blew a feeble note through the whistle in the mouth of the mask. It was enough, they knew it. They sprang into the water and dragged the canoe to land. They set Alan on the shore and worshipped him. They haled up a lad as though for sacrifice, for a priest flourished a great knife above his head, but Jeekie said something that caused them to let him go. Alan thought it was to the effect that Little Bonsa had changed her habits across the Black Water, and wanted no blood, only food. Then he remembered no more; again the darkness fell upon him.

CHAPTER X

BONSA TOWN

When consciousness returned to Alan, the first thing of which he became dimly aware was the slow, swaying motion of a litter. He raised himself, for he was lying at full length, and in so doing felt that there was something over his face.

"That confounded Little Bonsa," he thought. "Am I expected to spend the rest of my life with it on my head like the man in the iron mask?"

Then he put up his hand and felt the thing, to find that it was not Little Bonsa, but something made apparently of thin, fine linen, fitted to the shape of his face, for there was a nose on it, and eyeholes through which he could see, yes, and a mouth whereof the lips by some ingenious contrivance could be moved up and down.

"Little Bonsa's undress uniform, I expect," he muttered, and tried to drag it off. This, however, proved to be impossible, for it was fitted tightly to his head and laced or fastened at the back of his neck so securely that he could not undo it. Being still weak, soon he gave up the attempt and began to look about him.

He was in a litter, a very fine litter hung round with beautifully woven and coloured grass mats, inside of which were a kind of couch and cushions of soft wool or hair, so arranged that he could either sit up or lie down. He peeped between two of these mats and saw that they were travelling in a mountainous country over a well-beaten road or trail, and that his litter was borne upon the shoulders of a double line of white-robed men, while all around him marched numbers of other men. They seemed to be soldiers, for they were arranged in companies and carried large spears and shields. Also some of them wore torques and bracelets of yellow metal that might be either brass or gold. Turning himself about he found an eyehole in the back of the litter so contrived that its occupant could see without being seen, and perceived that his escort amounted to a veritable army of splendid-looking, but sombre-faced savages of a somewhat Semitic cast of countenance. Indeed many of them had aquiline features and hair that, although crisped, was long and carefully arranged in something like the old Egyptian fashion. Also he saw that about thirty yards behind and separated from him by a bodyguard, was borne a second litter. By means of a similar aperture in front he discovered yet more soldiers, and beyond them, at the head of the procession, was what appeared to be a body of white-robed men and women bearing strange emblems and banners. These he took to be priests and priestesses.

Having examined everything that was within reach of his eye, Alan sank back upon his cushions and began to realize that he was very faint and hungry. It was just then that the sound of a familiar voice reached his ears. It was the voice of Jeekie, and he did not speak, he chanted in English to a melody which Alan at once recognized as a Gregorian tone, apparently from the second litter.

"Oh, Major," he sang, "have you yet awoke from refre-e-eshing sleep? If so, please answer me in same tone of voice, for remember that you de-e-evil of a swell, Lord of the Little Bonsa, and must not speak like co-o-ommon cad."

Feeble as he was Alan nearly burst out laughing, then remembering that probably he was expected not to laugh, chanted his answer as directed, which having a good tenor voice, he did with some effect, to the evident awe and delight of all the escort within hearing.

"I am awake, most excellent Jee-e-ekie, and feel the need of food, if you have such a thing abou-ou-out you and it is lawful for the Lord of Little Bonsa to take nu-tri-ment."

Instantly Jeekie's deep voice rose in reply.

"That good tidings upon the mountain tops, Ma-ajor. Can't come out to bring you chop because too i-i-infra dig, for now I also biggish bug, the little bird what sit upon the rose, as poet sa-a-ays. I tell these Johnnies bring you grub, which you eat without qualm, for Asiki Al coo-o-ook."

Then followed loud orders issued by Jeekie to his immediate entourage, and some confusion.

As a result presently Alan's litter was halted, the curtains were opened and kneeling women thrust through them platters of wood upon which, wrapped up in leaves, were the dismembered limbs of a bird which he took to be chicken or guinea-fowl, and a gold cup containing water pleasantly flavoured with some essence. This cup interested him very much both on account of its shape and workmanship, which if rude, was striking in design, resembling those drinking vessels that have been found in Mycenian graves. Also it proved to him that Jeekie's stories of the abundance of the precious metal among the Asiki had not been exaggerated. If it were not very plentiful, they would scarcely, he thought, make their travelling cups of gold. Evidently there was wealth in the land.

After the food had been handed to him the litter went on again, and seated upon his cushions, he ate and drank heartily enough, for now that the worst of his fatigue had passed away, his hunger was great. In some absurd fashion this meal reminded him of that which a traveller makes out of a luncheon basket upon a railway line in Europe or America. Only there the cups are not of gold and among the Asiki were no paper napkins, no salt and mustard, and no three and sixpence or dollar to pay. Further, until he got used to it, luncheon in a linen mask with a moveable mouth was not easy. This difficulty he overcame at last by propping the imitation lips apart with a piece of bone, after which things were easier.

When he had finished he threw the platter and the remains out of the litter, retaining the cup for further examination, and recommenced his intoned and poetical converse with Jeekie.

To set it out at length would be wearisome, but in the course of an hour or so he collected a good deal of information. Thus he learned that they were due to arrive at the Asiki city, which was called Bonsa Town, by nightfall, or a little after. Also he was informed that the mask he wore was, as he had guessed, a kind of undress uniform without which he must never appear, since for anyone except the Asika herself to look upon the naked countenance of an individual so mysteriously mixed up with Little Bonsa, was sacrilege of the worst sort. Indeed Jeekie assured him that the priests who had put on the headdress when he was insensible were first blindfolded.

This news depressed Alan very much, since the prospect of living in a linen mask for an indefinite period was not cheerful. Recovering, he chanted a query as to the fate of the Ogula crew and their chief Fahni.

"Not de-ad," intoned Jeekie in reply, "and not gone back. A-all alive-O, somewhere behind there. Fanny very sick about it, for he think Asiki bring them along for sacrifice, poo-or beg-gars."

Finally he inquired where Little Bonsa was and was answered that he himself as its lawful guardian, was sitting on the fetish in its tin box, tidings that he was able to verify by groping beneath the cushions.

After this his voice gave out, though Jeekie continued to sing items of interesting news from time to time. Indeed there were other things that absorbed Alan's attention. Looking through the peepholes and cracks in the curtains, he saw that at last they had reached the crest of a ridge up which they had been climbing for hours. Before them lay a vast and fertile valley, much of which seemed to be under cultivation, and down it flowed a broad and placid river. Opposite to him and facing west a great tongue of land ran up to a wall of mountains with stark precipices of black rock that seemed to be hundreds, or even thousands, of feet high, and at the tip of this tongue a mighty waterfall rushed over the precipice, looking at that distance like a cascade of smoke. This torrent, which he remembered was called Raaba, fell into a great pool and there divided itself into two rushing branches that enclosed an ellipse of ground, surrounded on all sides by water, for on its westernmost extremity the branches met again and after flowing a while as one river, divided once more and wound away quietly to north and south further than the eye could reach. On the island thus formed, which may have been three miles long by two in breadth, stood thousands of straw-roofed, square-built huts with verandas, neatly arranged in blocks and lines and having between them streets that were edged with palms.

On the hither side of the pool was what looked like a park, for here grew great, black trees, which from their flat shape Alan took to be some variety of cedar, and standing alone in the midst of this park where no other habitations could be discovered, was a large, low building with dark-coloured walls and gabled roofs that flashed like fire.

"The Gold House!" said Alan to himself with a gasp. "So it is not a dream or a lie."

The details at that distance he could not discover, nor did he try to do so, for the general glory of the scene held him in its grip. At this evening hour, for a little while, the level rays of the setting sun poured straight up the huge, water-hollowed kloof. They struck upon the face of the fall, staining it and the clouds of mist that hung above, to a hundred glorious hues; indeed the substance of the foaming water seemed to be interlaced with rainbows whereof the arch reached their crest and the feet were lost in the sullen blackness of the pool beneath. Beautiful too was the valley, glowing in the quiet light of evening, and even the native town thus gilded and glorified, looked like some happy home of peace.

The sun was sinking rapidly, and before the litter reached the foot of the hill and began to cross the rich valley, all the glory had departed and only the cataract showed white and ghost-like through the gloom. But still the light, which seemed to gather to itself, gleamed upon that golden roof amid the cedar trees; then the moon rose and the gold was turned to silver. Alan lay back upon his cushions full of wonder, almost of awe. It was a marvellous thing that he should have lived to reach this secret place hidden in the heart of Africa and defended by swamps, mountains and savages to which, so far as he knew, only one white man had ever penetrated. And to think of it! That white man, his own uncle, had never even held it worth while to make public any account of its wonders, which apparently had seemed to him of no importance. Or perhaps he thought that if he did he would not be believed. Well, there they were before and about him, and now the question was, what would be his fate in this Gold House where the great fetish dwelt with its priestess?

Ah! that priestess! Somehow he shivered a little when he thought of her; it was as though her influence were over him already. Next moment he forgot her for a while, for they had come to the river brink and the litter was being carried on to a barge or ferry, about which were gathered many armed men. Evidently the Gold House was well defended both by Nature and otherwise. The ferry was pulled or rowed across the river, he could not see which, and they passed through a gateway into the town and up a broad street where hundreds of people watched his advent. They did not seem to speak, or if they spoke their voices were lost in the sound of the thunder of the great cataract which dominated the place with its sullen, continuous roar. It took Alan days to become accustomed to that roar, but by the inhabitants of Asiki-land apparently it was not noticed; their ears and voices were attuned to overcome its volume which their fathers had known from the beginning.

Presently they were through the town and a wooden gate in an inner wall which surrounded the park where the cedars grew. At this spot Alan noted that everybody left them except the bearers and a few men whom he took to be priests. On they stole like ghosts beneath the mighty trees, from whose limbs hung long festoons of moss. It was very dark there, only in places where a bough was broken the moonlight lay in white gules upon the ground. Another wall and another gate, and suddenly the litter was set down. Its curtains opened, torches flashed, women appeared clad in white robes, veiled and mysterious, who bowed before him, then half led and half lifted him from his litter. He could feel their eyes on him through their veils, but he could not see their faces. He could see nothing except their naked, copper-coloured arms and long thin hands stretched out to assist him.

Alan descended from the litter as slowly as he could, for somehow he shrank from the quaint, carved portal which he saw before him. He did not wish to pass it; its aspect filled him with reluctance. The women drew him on, their hands pulled at his arms, their shoulders pressed him from behind. Still he hung back, looking about him, till to his delight he saw the other litter arrive and out of it emerge Jeekie, still wearing his sun-helmet with its fringe of tattered mosquito curtain.

"Here we are, Major," he said in his cheerful voice, "turned up all right like a bad ha'penny, but in odd situation."

"Very odd," echoed Alan. "Could you persuade these ladies to let go of me?"

"Don't know," answered Jeekie. "'Spect they doubtfully your wives; 'spect you have lots of wives here; don't get white man every day, so make most of him. Best thing you do, kick out and teach them place. Rub nose in dirt at once and make them good, that first-class plan with female. I no like interfere in such delicate matter."

Terrified by this information, Alan put out his strength and shook the women off him, whereon without seeming to take any offence they drew back to a little distance and began to bow, like automata. Then Jeekie addressed them in their own language, asking them what they meant by defiling this mighty lord, born of the Heavens, with the touch of their hands, whereat they went on bowing more humbly than before. Next he threw aside the cushions of the litter and finding the tin box containing Little Bonsa, held it before him in both hands and bade the women lead on.

The march began, a bewildering march. It was like a nightmare. Veiled women with torches before and behind, Jeekie stalking ahead carrying the battered tin box, long passages lined with gold, a vision of black water edged with a wide promenade, and finally a large lamp-lit room whereof the roof was supported by gilded columns, and in the room couches of cushions, wooden stools inlaid with ivory, vessels of water, great basins made of some black, hard wood, and in the centre a block of stone that looked like an altar.

Jeekie set down the tin box upon the altar-like stone, then he turned to the crowd of women and said, "Bring food." Instantly they departed, closing the door of the room behind them.

"Now for a wash," said Alan, "unlace this confounded mask, Jeekie."

"Mustn't, Major, mustn't. Priests tell me that. If those girls see you without mask, perhaps they kill them. Wait till they gone after supper, then take it off. No one allowed see you without mask except Asika herself."

Alan stepped to one of the wooden bowls full of water which stood under a lamp, and gazed at his own reflection. The mask was gilded; the sham lips were painted red and round the eye-holes were black lines.

"Why, it is horrible," he exclaimed, starting back. "I look like a devil crossed with Guy Fawkes. Do you mean to tell me that I have got to live in this thing?"

"Afraid so, Major, upon all public occasion. At least they say that. You holy, not lawful see your sacred face."

"Who do the Asiki think I am, then, Jeekie?"

"They think you your reverend uncle come back after many, many year. You see, Major, they not believe uncle run away with Little Bonsa; they believe Little Bonsa run away with uncle just for change of air and so on, and that now, when she tired of strange land, she bring him back again. That why you so holy, favourite of Little Bonsa who live with you all this time and keep you just same age, bloom of youth."

"In Heaven's name," asked Alan, exasperated, "what is Little Bonsa, beyond an ancient and ugly gold fetish?"

"Hush," said Jeekie, "mustn't call her names here in her own house. Little Bonsa much more than fetish, Little Bonsa alive, or so," he added doubtfully, "these silly niggers say. She wife of Big Bonsa, you see, to-morrow p'raps. But their story this, that she get dead sick of Big Bonsa and bolt with white Medicine man, who dare preach she nothing but heathen idol. She want show him whether or no she only idol. That the yarn, priests tell it me to-day. They always watch for her there by the edge of the lake. They always sure Little Bonsa come back. Not at all surprised, but as she love you once, you stop holy; and I holy also, thank goodness, because she take me too as servant. Therefore we sleep in peace, for they not cut out throats, at any rate at present, though I think," he added mournfully, "they not let us go either."

Alan sat down on a stool and groaned at the appalling prospect suggested by this information.

"Cheer up, Major," said Jeekie sympathetically. "Perhaps manage hook it somehow, and meanwhile make best of bad business and have high old time. You see you want to come Asiki-land, though I tell you it rum place, and," he added with certitude and a circular sweep of his hand, "by Jingo! you here now and I daresay they give you all the gold you want."

"What's the good of gold unless one can get away with it? What's the good of anything if we are prisoners among these devils?"

"Perhaps time show, Major. Hush! here come dinner. You sit still on stool and look holy."

The door opened and through it appeared four of the women bearing dishes and cups full of drink, fashioned of gold like that which had been given to Alan in the litter. He noticed at once that they had removed their veils and outer garments, if indeed they were the same women, and now, like many other Africans, were but lightly clad in linen capes open in front that hung over their shoulders, short petticoats or skirts about their middles, and sandals. Such was their attire which, scanty as it might be, was yet becoming enough and extremely rich. Thus the cape was fastened with a brooch of worked gold, so were the sandal straps, while the petticoat was adorned with beads of gold that jingled as they walked, and amongst them strings of other beads of various and beautiful colours, that might be glass or might be precious stones. Moreover, these women were young and handsome, having splendid figures and well-cut features, soft, dark eyes and rather long hair worn in the formal and attractive fashion that has been described.

Advancing to Alan two of them knelt before him, holding out the trays upon which was the food. So they remained while he ate, like bronze statues, nor would they consent to change their posture even when he told them in their language to be pleased to go away. On hearing themselves addressed in the Asiki language, they seemed surprised, for their faces changed a little, but go they would not. The result was that Alan grew extremely nervous and ate and drank so rapidly that he scarcely noted what he was putting into his mouth. Then before Jeekie, to whom the women did not kneel, had half finished his dinner, Alan rose and walked away, whereon two of the women gathered up everything, including the dishes that had been given to Jeekie, and in spite of his remonstrances carried them out of the room.

"I say, Major," said Jeekie, "if you gobble chop so fast you go ill inside. Poor nigger like me can't keep up with you and sleep hungry to-night."

"I am sorry, Jeekie," said Alan with a little laugh, "but I can't eat off living tables, especially when they stare at one like that. You tell them that to-morrow we will breakfast alone."

"Oh, yes, I tell them, Major, but I don't know if they listen. They mean it great compliment and only think you not like those girls and send others."

"Look here, Jeekie," exclaimed Alan, turning his masked face towards the two who remained, "let us come to an understanding at once. Clear them out. Tell them I am so holy that Little Bonsa is enough for me. Say I can't bear the sight of females, and that if they stop here I will sacrifice them. Say anything you like, only get rid of them and lock the door."

Thus adjured, Jeekie began to reason with the women, and as they treated his remarks with lofty disdain, at last seized first one and then the other by the elbows and literally ran them out of the room.

"There," he said, "baggage gone since you make such fuss about it, though I 'spect they try to give me Bean for this job" (here he spoke not in figurative English slang, but of the Calabar bean, which is a favourite native poison). "Well, dinner gone and girls gone, and we tired, so best go to bed. Think we all private here now, though in Gold House never can be sure," and he looked round him suspiciously, adding, "rummy place, Gold House, full of all sort of holes made by old fellows thousand year ago, which no one know but Bonsa priests. Still, best risk it and take off your face so that you have decent wash," and he began to unlace the mask on his master's head.

Never has a City clerk dressed up for a fancy ball in the armour of a Norman knight, been more glad to get rid of his costume than was Alan of that hateful head-dress. At length it was gone with his other garments and the much-needed wash accomplished, after which he clothed himself in a kind of linen gown which apparently had been provided for him, and lay down on one of the couches, placing his revolver by his side.

"Will those lamps burn all night, Jeekie?" he asked.

"Hope so, Major, as we haven't got no match. Not fond of dark in Gold House," answered Jeekie sleepily. Then he began to snore.

Alan fell asleep, but was too excited and tired to rest very soundly. All sorts of dreams came to him, one of which he remembered on awakening, perhaps because it was the last. He dreamed that he heard some noise and opened his eyes, to see that they were no longer alone in the room. The oil lamps had burned quite low, indeed some of them were out, but by the light of those that remained he saw a tall figure which seemed to appear at the edge of the surrounding blackness, a woman's figure. It walked forward to the altar-like stone upon which lay the tin box containing Little Bonsa, and after several rather awkward attempts, succeeded in opening it, thereby making a noise which, in his dream, finally awoke Alan. For a while the figure gazed at the fetish. Then it shut the box, glided to his bed and bent down as though to study him. Out of the corners of his eyes he peered up at it, pretending all the while to be fast asleep.

It was that of a woman wonderfully clad in gold-spangled, veil-like garments with round bosses shaped to the breast, covered with thin plates of gold fashioned like the scales of a fish which showed off the extraordinary elegance of her lithe form. The low lamp-light shone upon her face and the coronet of gold set upon her dark hair. What a face it was! Never in all his days had he seen its like for evil loveliness. The great, languid, oblong eyes, the rich red lips bent like a bow, the cruel smile of the mouth, the broad forehead on which the hair grew low, the delicately arched eyebrows and the long curving lashes of the heavy lids beneath them, the rounded cheeks, smooth as a ripe fruit, the firm, shapely chin, the snake-like poise of the head, the long bending neck, and the feline smile; all of these combined made such a dream-vision as he had never seen before, and to tell the truth, notwithstanding its beauty, for that could not be doubted, never wished to see again. Somehow he felt that if Satan should happen to have a copper-coloured wife, the exact picture of that lady had projected itself upon his sleeping senses.

She seemed to study him very earnestly, with a kind of passionate eagerness, indeed, moving a little now and again to let the light fall upon some part that was in shadow. Once even she stretched out her rounded arm and just lifted the edge of the blanket so as to expose his hand, the left. As it chanced on the little finger of this hand Alan wore a plain gold ring which Barbara had given him; once it had been her grandfather's signet. This ring, which had a coat of arms cut upon its bezel seemed to interest her very much as she examined it for a long while. Then she drew off from her own finger another ring of gold fashioned of two snakes curiously intertwined, and gently, so gently that in his sleep he scarcely felt it, slipped it on to his finger above Barbara's ring.

After this she seemed to vanish away, and Alan slept soundly until the morning, when he awoke to find the light of the sun pouring into the room through the high-set latticed window places.

CHAPTER XI

Alan rose and stretched himself, and hearing him, Jeekie, who had a dog's faculty of instantly awaking from what seemed to be the deepest sleep, sat up also.

"You rest well, Major? No dream, eh?" he asked curiously.

"Not very," answered Alan, "and I had a dream, of a woman who stood over me and vanished away, as dreams do."

"Ah!" said Jeekie. "But where you find that new ring on finger, Major?"

Alan stared at his hand and started, for there set on it above that of Barbara, was the little circlet formed of twisted snakes which he had seen in his sleep.

"Then it must have been true," he said in a low and rather frightened voice. "But how did she come and go?"

"Funny place, Gold House. I tell you that yesterday, Major. People come up through hole, like rat. Never quite sure you alone in Gold House. But what this lady like?"

Alan described his visitor to the best of his ability.

"Ah!" said Jeekie, "pretty girl. Big eyes, gold crown, gold stays which fit tight in front, very nice and decent; sort of night-shirt with little stars all over—by Jingo! I think that Asika herself. If so—great compliment."

"Confound the compliment, I think it great cheek," answered Alan angrily. "What does she mean by poking about here at night and putting rings on my finger?"

"Don't know, Major, but p'raps she wish make you understand that she like cut of your jib. Find out by and by. Meanwhile you wear ring, for while that on finger no one do you any harm."

"You told me that this Asika is a married woman, did you not?" remarked Alan gloomily.

"Oh, yes, Major, always married; one down, other come on, you see. But she not always like her husband, and then she make him sit up, poor devil, and he die double quick. Great honour to be Asika's husband, but soon all finished. P'raps—"

Then he checked himself and suggested that Alan should have a bath while he cleaned his clothes, an attention that they needed.

Scarcely had Alan finished his toilet, donned the Arab-looking linen robe over his own fragmentary flannels, and above it the hateful mask which Jeekie insisted he must wear, when there came a knocking on the door. Motioning to Alan to take his seat upon a stool, Jeekie undid the bars, and as before women appeared with food and waited while they ate, which this time, having overcome his nervousness, Alan did more leisurely. Their meal done, one of the women asked Jeekie, for to his master they did not seem to dare to speak, whether the white lord did not wish to walk in the garden. Without waiting for an answer she led him to the end of the large room and, unbarring another door that they had not noticed, revealed a passage, beyond which appeared trees and flowers. Then she and her companions went away with the fragments of the meal.

"Come on," said Alan, taking up the box containing Little Bonsa, which he did not dare to leave behind, "and let us get into the air."

So they went down the passage and at the end of it through gates of copper or gold, they knew not which, that had evidently been left open for them, into the garden. It was a large place, a good many acres in extent indeed, and kept with some care, for there were paths in it and flowers that seemed to have been planted. Also here grew certain of the mighty cedar trees that they had seen from far off, beneath those spreading boughs twilight reigned, while beyond, not more than half a mile away, the splendid river-fall thundered down the precipice. For the rest they could find no exit to that garden which on one side was enclosed by a sheer cliff of living rock, and on the others with steep stone walls beyond which ran a torrent, and by the buildings of the Gold House itself.

For a while they walked up and down the rough paths, till at last Jeekie, wearying of this occupation, remarked:

"Melancholy hole this, Major. Remind me of Westminster Abbey in London fog, where your uncle of blessed mem'ry often take me pray and look at fusty tomb of king. S'pose we go back Gold House and see what happen. Anything better than stand about under cursed old cedar tree."

"All right," said Alan, who through the eyeholes of his mask had been studying the walls to seek a spot in them that could be climbed if necessary, and found none.

So they returned to the room, which had been swept and garnished in their absence. No sooner had they entered it than the door opened and through it came long lines of Asiki priests, each of whom staggered beneath the weight of a hide bag that he bore upon his shoulder, which bags they piled up about the stone altar. Then, as though at some signal, each priest opened the mouth of his bag and Alan saw that they wee filled with gold, gold in dust, gold in nuggets, gold in vessels perfect or broken; more gold than Alan had ever seen before.

"Why do they bring all this stuff here?" he asked, and Jeekie translated his question.

"It is an offering to the lord of Little Bonsa," answered the head priest, bowing, "a gift from the Asika. The heaven-born white man sent word by his Ogula messengers that he desired gold. Here is the gold that he desired."

Alan stared at the treasure, which after all was what he had come to seek. If only he had it safe in England, he would be a rich man and his troubles ended. But how could he get it to England? Here it was worthless as mud.

"I thank the Asika," he said. "I ask for porters to bear her gift back to my own country, since it is too heavy for me and my servant to carry alone."

At these words the priest smiled a little, then said that the Asika desired to see the white lord and to receive from him Little Bonsa in return for the gold, and that he could proffer his request to her.

"Good," replied Alan, "lead me to the Asika."

Then they started, Alan bearing the box containing Little Bonsa, and Jeekie following after him. They went down passages and through sundry doors till at length they came to a long and narrow hall that seemed to be lined with plates of gold. At the end of this hall was a large chair of black wood and ivory placed upon a dais, and sitting in this chair with the light pouring on her from some opening above, was the woman of Alan's dream, beautiful to look on in her crown and glittering garments. Upon a stool at the foot of the dais sat a man, a handsome and melancholy man. His hair was tied behind his head in a pigtail and gilded, his face was painted red, white and yellow; he wore ropes of bright-coloured stones about his neck, middle, arms and ankles, and held a kind of sceptre in his hand.

"Who is that creature?" asked Alan over his shoulder to Jeekie. "The Court fool?"

"That husband of Asika, Major. He not fool, very big gun, but look a little low now because his time soon up. Come on, Major, Asika beckon us. Get on stomach and crawl; that custom here," he added, going down on to his hands and knees, as did all the priests who followed them.

"I'll see her hanged first," answered Alan in English.

Then accompanied by the creeping Jeekie and the train of prostrate priests, he marched up the long hall to the edge of the dais and there stood still and bowed to the woman in the chair.

"Greeting, white man," she said in a low voice when she had studied him for a while. "Do you understand my tongue?"

"A little," he answered in Asiki, "moreover, my servant here knows it well and can translate."

"I am glad," she said. "Tell me then, in your country do not people go on to their knees before their queen, and if not, how do they greet her?"

"No," answered Alan with the help of Jeekie. "They greet her by raising their head-dress or kissing her hand."

"Ah!" she said. "Well, you have no head-dress, so kiss my hand," and she stretched it out towards him, at the same time prodding the man whom Jackie had said was her husband, in the back with her foot, apparently to make him get out of the way.

Not knowing what to do, Alan stepped on to the dais, the painted man scowling at him as he passed. Then he halted and said:

"How can I kiss your hand through this mask, Asika?"

"True," she answered, then considered a little and added, "White man, you have brought back Little Bonsa, have you not, Little Bonsa who ran away with you a great many years ago?"

"I have," he said, ignoring the rest of the question.

"Your messengers said that you required a present of gold in return for Little Bonsa. I have sent you one, is it sufficient? If not, you can have more."

"I cannot say, O Asika, I have not examined it. But I thank you for the present and desire porters to enable me to carry it away."

"You desire porters," she repeated meditatively. "We will talk of that when you have rested here a moon or two. Meanwhile, give me Little Bonsa that she may be restored to her own place."

Alan opened the tin box and lifting out the fetish, gave it to the priestess, who took it and with a serpentine movement of extraordinary grace glided from her chair on to her knees, holding the mask above her head in both hands, then thrice covered her face with it. This done, she called to the priests, bidding them take Little Bonsa to her own place and give notice throughout the land that she was back again. She added that the ancient Feast of Little Bonsa would be held on the night of the full moon within three days, and that all preparations must be made for it as she had commanded.

Then the head medicine-man, raising himself upon his knees, crept on to the dais, took the fetish from her hands, and breaking into a wild song of triumph, he and his companions crawled down the hall and vanished through the door, leaving them alone save for the Asika's husband.

When they had gone the Asika looked at this man in a reflective way, and Alan looked at him also through the eyeholes of his mask, finding him well worth studying. As has been said, notwithstanding his paint and grotesque decorations, he was very good-looking for a native, with well-cut features of an Arab type. Also he was tall and muscular and not more than thirty years of age. What struck Alan most, however, was none of these things, nor his jewelled chains, nor even his gilded pigtail, but his eyes, which were full of terrors. Seeing them, Alan remembered Jeekie's story, which he had told to Mr. Haswell's guests at The Court, of how the husband of the Asika was driven mad by ghosts.

Just then she spoke to the man, addressing him by name and saying:

"Leave us alone, Mungana, I wish to speak with this white lord."

He did not seem to hear her words, but continued to stare at Alan.

"Hearken!" she exclaimed in a voice of ice. "Do my bidding and begone, or you shall sleep alone to-night in a certain chamber that you know of."

Then Mungana rose, looked at her as a dog sometimes does at a cruel master who is about to beat it, yes, with just that same expression, put his hands before his eyes for a little while, and turning, left the hall by a side door which closed behind him. The Asika watched him go, laughed musically and said:

"It is a very dull thing to be married,—but how are you named, white man?"

"Vernon," he answered.

"Vernoon, Vernoon," she repeated, for she could not pronounce the O as we do. "Are you married, Vernoon?"

He shook his head.

"Have you been married?"

"No," he answered, "never, but I am going to be."

"Yes," she repeated, "you are going to be. You remember that you were near to it many years ago, when Little Bonsa got jealous and ran away with you. Well, she won't do that again, for doubtless she is tired of you now, and besides," she added with a flash of ferocity, "I'd melt her with fire first and set her spirit free."

While Jeekie was trying to explain this mysterious speech to Alan, the Asika broke in, asking:

"Do you always want to wear that mask?"

He answered, "Certainly not," whereon she bade Jeekie take it off, which he did.

"Understand me," she said, fixing her great languid eyes upon his in a fashion that made him exceedingly uncomfortable, "understand, Vernoon, that if you go out anywhere, it must be in your mask, which you can only put off when you are alone with me?"

"Why?"

"Because, Vernoon, I do not choose that any other woman should see your face. If a woman looks upon your uncovered face, remember that she dies—not nicely."

Alan stared at her blankly, being unable to find appropriate Asiki words in which to reply to this threat. But the Asika only leaned back in her chair and laughed at his evident confusion and dismay, till a new thought struck her.

"Your lips are free now," she said; "kiss my hand after the fashion of your own country," and she stretched it out to Alan, leaving him no choice but to obey her.

"Why," she went on mischievously, taking his hand and in turn touching it with her red lips, "why, are you a thief, Vernoon? That ring was mine and you have stolen it. How did you steal that ring?"

"I don't know," he answered, through Jeekie, "I found it on my finger. I cannot understand how it came there. I understand nothing of all this talk."

"Well, well, keep it, Vernoon, only give me that other ring of yours in exchange."

"I cannot," he replied, colouring. "I promised to wear it always."

"Whom did you promise?" she asked with a flash of rage. "Was it a woman? Nay, I see, it is a man's ring, and that is well, for otherwise I would bring a curse on her, however far off she may be dwelling. Say no more and forgive my anger. A vow is a vow—keep your ring. But where is that one you used to wear in bygone days? I recall that it had a cross upon it, not this star and figure of an eagle."

Now Alan remembered that his uncle owned such a ring with a cross upon it, and was frightened, for how did this woman know these things?

"Jeekie," he said, "ask the Asika if I am mad, or if she is. How can she know what I used to wear, seeing that I was never in this place till yesterday, and certainly I have not met her anywhere else."

"She mean when you your reverend uncle," said Jeekie, wagging his great head, "she think you identical man."

"What troubles you, Vernoon," the Asika asked softly, then added anything but softly to Jeekie, "Translate, you dog, and be swift."

So Jeekie translated in a great hurry, telling her what Alan had said, and adding on his own account that he, silly white man that he was, could not understand how, as she was quite a young woman, she could have seen him before she was born. If that were so, she would be old and ugly now, not beautiful as she was.

"I never saw you before, and you never saw me, Lady, yet you talk as though we had been friends," broke in Alan in his halting Asiki.

"So we were in the spirit, Vernoon. It was she who went before me who loved that white man whose face was as your face is, but her ghost lives on in me and tells me the tale. There have been many Asikas, for thousands of years they have ruled in this land, yet but one spirit belongs to them all; it is the string upon which the beads of their lives are threaded. White man, I, whom you think young, know everything back to the beginning of the world, back to the time when I was a monkey woman sitting in those cedar trees, and if you wish, I can tell it you."

"I should like to hear it very much indeed," answered Alan, when he had mastered her meaning, "though it is strange that none of the rest of us remember such things. Meanwhile, O Asika, I will tell you that I desire to return to my own land, taking with me that gift of gold that you have given me. When will it please you to allow me to return?"

"Not yet a while, I think," she said, smiling at him weirdly, for no other word will describe that smile. "My spirit remembers that it was always thus. Those wanderers who came hither always wished to return again to their own country, like the birds in spring. Once there was a white man among them, that was more than twenty hundred years ago; he was a native of a country called Roma, and wore a helmet. He wished to return, but my mother of that day, she kept him and by and by I will show him to you if you like. Before that there was a brown man who came from a land where a great river overflows its banks every year. He was a prince of his own country, who had fled from his king and the desert folk made a slave of him, and so he drifted hither. He wished to return also, for my mother of that day, or my spirit that dwelt in her, showed to him that if he could but be there they would make him king in his own land. But my mother of that day, she would not let him go, and by and by I will show him to you, if you wish."

Bewildered, amazed, Alan listened to her. Evidently the woman was mad, or else she played some mystical part for reasons of her own.

"When will you let me go, O Asika?" he repeated.

"Not yet a while, I think," she said again. "You are too comely and I like you," and she smiled at him. There was nothing coarse in the smile, indeed it had a certain spiritual quality which thrilled him. "I like you," she went on in her dreamy voice, "I would keep you with me until your spirit is drawn up into my spirit, making it strong and rich as all the spirits that went before have done, those spirits that my mothers loved from the beginning, which dwell in me to-day."

Now Alan grew alarmed, desperate even.

"Queen," he said, "but just now your husband sat here, is it right then that you should talk to me thus?"

"My husband," she answered, laughing. "Why, that man is but a slave who plays the part of husband to satisfy an ancient law. Never has he so much as kissed my finger tips; my women—those who waited on you last night—are his wives, not I,—or may be, if he will. Soon he will die of love for me, and then when he is dead, though not before, I may take another husband, any husband that I choose, and I think that no black man shall be my lord, who have other, purer blood in me. Vernoon, five centuries have gone by since an Asika was really wed to a foreign man who wore a green turban and called himself a son of the Prophet, a man with a hooked nose and flashing eyes, who reviled our gods until they slew him, even though he was the beloved of their priestess. She who went before me also would have married that white man whose face was like your face, but he fled with Little Bonsa, or rather Little Bonsa fled with him. So she passed away unwed, and in her place I came."

"How did you come, if she whom you call your mother was not your mother?" asked Alan.

"What is that to you, white man?" she replied haughtily. "I am here, as my spirit has been here from the first. Oh! I see you think I lie to you, come then, come, and I will show you those who from the beginning have been the husbands of the Asika," and rising from her chair she took him by the hand.

They went through doors and by long, half-lit passages till they came to great gates guarded by old priests armed with spears. As they drew near to these priests the Asika loosed a scarf that she wore over her breast-plate of gold fish scales, and threw the star-spangled thing over Alan's head, that even these priests should not see his face. Then she spoke a word to them and they opened the gates. Here Jeekie evinced a disposition to remain, remarking to his master that he thought that place, into which he had never entered, "much too holy for poor nigger like him."

The Asika asked him what he had said and he explained his sense of unworthiness in her own tongue.

"Come, fellow," she exclaimed, "to translate my words and to bear witness that no trick is played upon your lord."

Still Jeekie lingered bashfully, whereon at a sign from her one of the priests pricked him behind with his great spear, and uttering a low howl he sprang forward.

The Asika led the way down a passage, which they saw ended in a big hall lit with lamps. Now they were in it and Alan became aware that they had entered the treasure house of the Asiki, since here were piled up great heaps of gold, gold in ingots, gold in nuggets, in stone jars filled with dust, in vessels plain or embossed with monstrous shapes in fetishes and in little squares and discs that looked as though they had served as coins. Never had he seen so much gold before.

"You are rich here, Lady," he said, gazing at the piles astonished.

She shrugged her shoulders. "Yes, as I have heard that some people count wealth. These are the offerings brought to our gods from the beginning; also all the gold found in the mountains belongs to the gods, and there is much of it there. The gift I sent to you was taken from this heap, but in truth it is but a poor gift, seeing that although this stuff is bright and serves for cups and other things, it has no use at all and is only offered to the gods because it is harder to come by than other metals. Look, these are prettier than the gold," and from a stone table she picked up at hazard a long necklace of large, uncut stones, red and white in colour and set alternatively, that Alan judged to be crystals and spinels.

"Take it," she said, "and examine it at your leisure. It is very old. For hundreds of years no more of these necklaces have been made," and with a careless movement she threw the chain over his head so that it hung upon his shoulders.

Alan thanked her, then remembered that the man called Mungana, who was the husband, real or official, of this priestess, had been somewhat similarly adorned, and shivered a little as though at a presage of advancing fate. Still he did not return the thing, fearing lest he should give offence.

At this moment his attention was taken from the treasure by the sound of a groan behind him. Turning round he perceived Jeekie, his great eyes rolling as though in an extremity of fear.

"Oh my golly! Major," he ejaculated, pointing to the wall, "look there."

Alan looked, but at first in that dim light could only discover long rows of gleaming objects which reached from the floor to the roof.

"Come and see," said the Asika, and taking a lamp from that table on which lay the gems, she led him past the piles of gold to one side of the vault or hall. Then he saw, and although he did not show it, like Jeekie he was afraid.

For there, each in his own niche and standing one above the other, were what looked like hundreds of golden men with gleaming eyes. At first until the utter stillness undeceived him, he thought that they must be men. Then he understood that this was what they had been; now they were corpses wrapped in sheets of thin gold and wearing golden masks with eyes of crystal, each mask being beaten out to a hideous representation of the man in life.

"All these are the husbands of my spirit," said the priestess, waving the lamp in front of the lowest row of them, "Munganas who were married to the Asikas in the past. Look, here is he who said that he ought to be king of that rich land where year after year the river overflows its banks," and going to one of the first of the figures in the bottom row, she drew out a fastening and suffered the gold mask to fall forward on a hinge, exposing the face within.

Although it had evidently been treated with some preservative, this head now was little more than a skull still covered with dark hair, but set upon its brow appeared an object that Alan recognized at once, a simple band of plain gold, and rising from it the head of an asp. Without doubt it was the uraeus, that symbol which only the royalties of Old Egypt dared to wear. Without doubt also either this man had brought it with him from the Nile, or in memory of his rank and home he had fashioned it of the gold that was so plentiful in the place of his captivity. So this woman's story was true, an ancient Egyptian had once been husband to the Asika of his day.

Meanwhile his guide had passed a long way down the line and halting in front of another gold-wrapped figure, opened its mask.

"This is that man," she said, "who told us he came from a land called Roma. Look, the helmet still rests upon his head, though time has eaten into it, and that ring upon your hand was taken from his finger. I have a head-dress made upon the model of that helmet which I wear sometimes in memory of this man who, my soul remembers, was brave and pleasant and a gallant lover."

"Indeed," answered Alan, looking at the sunken face above which a rim of curls appeared beneath the rusting helmet. "Well, he doesn't look very gallant now, does he?" Then he peered down between the body and its gold casing and saw that in his body hand the man still held a short Roman sword, lifted as though in salute. So she had not lied in this matter either.

Meanwhile the Asika had glided on to the end of the hall behind the heaps of treasure.

"There is one more white man," she said, "though we know little of him, for he was fierce and barbarous and died without learning our tongue, after killing a great number of the priests of that day because they would not let him go; yes, died cutting them down with a battle-axe and singing some wild song of his own country. Come hither, slave, and bend yourself so, resting your hands upon the ground."

Jeekie obeyed, and actively as a cat the priestess leaped on to his back, and reaching up opened the mask of a corpse in the second row and held her lamp before its face.

It was better preserved than the others, so that its features remained comparatively perfect, and about them hung a tangle of golden hair. Moreover, a broad battle-axe appeared resting on the shoulder.

"A viking," thought Alan. "I wonder how he came here."

When he had looked the Asika leaped from Jeekie's back to the ground and waving her arm around her, began to talk so rapidly that Alan could understand nothing of her words, and asked Jeekie to translate them.

"She say," explained Jeekie between his chattering teeth, "that all rest these Johnnies very poor crew, natives and that lot except one who worship false Prophet and cut throat of Asika of that time, because she infidel and he teach her better; also eat his dinner out of Little Bonsa and chuck her into water. Very wild man, that Arab, but priests catch him at last and fill him with hot gold before Little Bonsa because he no care a damn for ghosts. So he die saying Hip, hip, hurrah! for houri and green field of Prophet and to hell with Asika and Bonsa, Big and Little! Now he sit up there and at night time worst ghost of all the crowd, always come to finish off Mungana. That all she say, and quite enough too. Come on quick, she want you and no like wait."

By now the Asika had passed almost round the hall, and was standing opposite to an empty niche beyond and above which there were perhaps a score of bodies gold-plated in the usual fashion.

"That is your place, Vernoon," she said gently, contemplating him with her soft and heavy eyes, "for it was prepared for the white man with whom Little Bonsa fled away, and since then, as you see, there have been many Munganas, some of whom belong to me; indeed, that one," and she touched a corpse on which the gold looked very fresh, "only left me last year. But we always knew that Little Bonsa would bring you back again, and so you see, we have kept your place empty."

"Indeed," remarked Alan, "that is very kind of you," and feeling that he would faint if he stayed longer in this horrible and haunted vault, he pushed past her with little ceremony and walked out through the gates into the passage beyond.

CHAPTER XII

THE GOLD HOUSE

"How you like Asiki-land, Major?" asked Jeekie, who had followed him and was now leaning against a wall fanning himself feebly with his great hand. "Funny place, isn't it, Major? I tell you so before you come, but you no believe me."

"Very funny," answered Alan, "so funny that I want to get out."

"Ah! Major, that what eel say in trap where he go after lob-worm, but he only get out into frying pan after cook skin him alive-o. Ah! here come cook—I mean Asika. She only stop shut up those stiff 'uns, who all love lob-worm one day. Very pretty woman, Asika, but thank God she not set cap at me, who like to be buried in open like Christian man."

"If you don't stop it, Jeekie," replied Alan in a concentrated rage, "I'll see that you are buried just where you are."

"No offence, Major, no offence, my heart full and bubble up. I wonder what Miss Barbara say if she see you mooing and cooing with dark-eyed girl in gold snake skin?"

Just then the Asika arrived and by way of excuse for his flight, Alan remarked to her that the treasure-hall was hot.

"I did not notice it," she answered, "but he who is called my husband, Mungana, says the same. The Mungana is guardian of the dead," she explained, "and when he is required so to do, he sleeps in the Place of the Treasure and gathers wisdom from the spirits of those Munganas who were before him."

"Indeed. And does he like that bed-chamber?"

"The Mungana likes what I like, not what he likes," she replied haughtily. "Where I send him to sleep, there he sleeps. But come, Vernoon, and I will show you the Holy Water where Big Bonsa dwells; also the house in which I have my home, where you shall visit me when you please."

"Who built this place?" asked Alan as she led him through more dark and tortuous passages. "It is very great."

"My spirit does not remember when it was built, Vernoon, so old is it, but I think that the Asiki were once a big and famous people who traded to the water upon the west, and even to the water on the east, and that was how those white men became their slaves and the Munganas of their queens. Now they are small and live only by the might and fame of Big and Little Bonsa, not half filling the rich land which is theirs. But," she added reflectively and looking at him, "I think also that this is because in the past fools have been thrust upon my spirit as Munganas. What it needs is the wisdom of the white man, such wisdom as yours, Vernoon. If that were added to my magic, then the Asiki would grow great again, seeing that they have in such plenty the gold which you have shown me the white man loves. Yes, they would grow great and from coast to coast the people should bow at the name of Bonsa and send him their sons for sacrifice. Perhaps you will live to see that day, Vernoon. Slave," she added, addressing Jeekie, "set the mask upon your lord's head, for we come where women are."

Alan objected, but she stamped her foot and said it must be so, having once worn Little Bonsa, as her people told her he had done, his naked face might not be seen. So Alan submitted to the hideous head-dress and they entered the Asika's house by some back entrance.

It was a place with many rooms in it, but they were all remarkable for extreme simplicity. With a single exception no gilding or gold was to be seen, although the food vessels were made of this material here as everywhere. The chambers, including those in which the Asika lived and slept, were panelled, or rather boarded with cedar wood that was almost black with age, and their scanty furniture was mostly made of ebony. They were very insufficiently lighted, like his own room, by means of barred openings set high in the wall. Indeed gloom and mystery were the keynotes of this place, amongst the shadows of which handsome, half-naked servants or priestesses flitted to and fro at their tasks, or peered at them out of dark corners. The atmosphere seemed heavy with secret sin; Alan felt that in those rooms unnameable crimes and cruelties had been committed for hundreds or perhaps thousands of years, and that the place was yet haunted by the ghosts of them. At any rate it struck a chill to his healthy blood, more even than had that Hall of the Dead and of heaped-up golden treasure.

"Does my house please you?" the Asika asked of him.

"Not altogether," he answered, "I think it is dark."

"From the beginning my spirit has ever loved the dark, Vernoon. I think that it was shaped in some black midnight."

They passed through the chief entrance of the house which had pillars of woodwork grotesquely carved, down some steps into a walled and roofed-in yard where the shadows were even more dense than in the house they had left. Only at one spot was there light flowing down through a hole in the roof, as it did apparently in that hall where Alan had found the Asika sitting in state. The light fell on to a pedestal or column made of gold which was placed behind an object like a large Saxon font, also made of gold. The shape of this column reminded Alan of something, namely of a very similar column, although fashioned of a different material which stood in the granite-built office of Messrs. Aylward & Haswell in the City of London. Nor did this seem wonderful to him, since on top of it, squatting on its dwarf legs, stood a horrid but familiar thing, namely Little Bonsa herself come home at last. There she sat smiling cruelly, as she had smiled from the beginning, forgetful doubtless of her wanderings in strange lands, while round her stood a band of priests armed with spears.

Followed by the Asika and Jeekie, Alan walked up and looked her in the face and to his excited imagination she appeared to grin at him in answer. Then while the priests prostrated themselves, he examined the golden basin or laver, and saw that at the further side of it was a little platform approached by steps. On the top of these golden steps were two depressions such as might have been worn out in the course of ages by persons kneeling there. Also the flat edge of the basin which stood about thirty inches above the level of the topmost step, was scored as though by hundreds of sword cuts which had made deep lines in the pure metal. The basin itself was empty.

Seeing that these things interested him, the Asika volunteered the information through Jeekie, that this was a divining-bowl, and that if those who went before her had wished to learn the future, they caused Little Bonsa to float in it and found out all they wanted to know by her movements. She, however, she added, had other and better methods of learning things that were predestined.

"Where does the water come from?" asked Alan thoughtlessly searching the bowl for some tap or inlet.

"Out of the hearts of men," she answered with a low and dreadful laugh. "These marks are those of swords and every one of them means a life." Then seeing that he looked incredulous she added, "Stay, I will show you. Little Bonsa must be thirsty who has fasted so long, also there are matters that I desire to know. Come hither—you, and you," and she pointed at hazard to the two priests who knelt nearest to her, "and do you bid the executioner bring his axe," she went on to a third.

The dark faces of the men turned ashen, but they made no effort to escape their doom. One of them crept up the steps and laid his neck upon the edge of gold, while the other, uttering no word, threw himself on his face at the foot of them, waiting his turn. Then a door opened and there appeared a great and brutal-looking fellow, naked except for a loin cloth, who bore in his hand a huge weapon, half knife and half axe.

First he looked at the Asika, who nodded almost imperceptibly, then sprang on to a prolongation of the golden steps, bowed to Little Bonsa on her column behind and heaved up his knife.

Now for the first time Alan really understood what was about to happen, and that what he had imagined a stage rehearsal, was to become a hideous murder.

"Stop!" he shouted in English, being unable to remember the native word.

The executioner paused with his axe poised in mid-air; the victim turned his head and looked, as though surprised; the second victim and the priests their companions looked also. Jeekie fell on to his knees and burst into fervent prayer addressed apparently to Little Bonsa. The Asika smiled and did nothing.

Again the weapon was lifted and as he felt that words were no longer of any use, even if he could find them, Alan took refuge in action. Springing on to the other side of the little platform, he hit out with all his strength across the kneeling man. Catching the executioner on the point of the chin, he knocked him straight backwards in such fashion that his head struck upon the floor before any other portion of his body, so that he lay there either dead or stunned. Alan never learned which, since the matter was not thought of sufficient importance to be mentioned.

At this sight the Asika burst into a low laugh, then asked Alan why he had felled the executioner. He answered because he would not stand by and see two innocent men butchered.

"Why not," she said in an astonished voice; "if Little Bonsa, whose priests they are, needs them, and I, who am the Mouth of the gods declare that they should die? Still, she has been in your keeping for a long while and you may know her will, so if you wish it, let them live. Or perhaps you require other victims," and she fixed her eyes upon Jeekie with a glance of suggestive hope.

"Oh my golly!" gasped Jeekie in English, "tell her not for Joe, Major, tell her most improper. Say Yellow God my dearest friend and go mad as hatter if my throat cut—"

Alan stopped his protestations with a secret kick.

"I choose no victims," he broke in, "nor will I see man's blood shed—to me it is orunda—unholy; I may not look on human blood, and if you cause me to do so, Asika, I shall hate you because you make me break my oath."

The Asika reflected for a moment, while Jeekie behind muttered between his chattering teeth:

"Good missionary talk that, Major. Keep up word in season, Major. If she make Christian martyr of Jeekie, who get you out of this confounded hole?"

Then the Asika spoke.

"Be it as you will, for I desire neither that you should hate me, nor that you should look on that which is unlawful for your eyes to see. The feasts and ceremonies you must attend, but if I can help it, no victim shall be slain in your presence, not even that whimpering hound, your servant," she added with a contemptuous glance at Jeekie, "who it seems, fears to give his life for the glory of the god, but who because he is yours, is safe now and always."

"That very satisfactory," said Jeekie, rising from his knees, his face wreathed in smiles, for he knew well that a decree of the Asika could not be broken. Then he began to explain to the priestess that it was not fear of losing his own life that had moved him, but the certainty that this occurrence would disagree morally with Little Bonsa, whose entire confidence he possessed.

Taking no notice of his words, with a slight reverence to the fetish, she passed on, beckoning to Alan. As he went by the two prostrate priests whose lives he had saved, lifted their heads a little and looked at him with heartfelt gratitude in their eyes; indeed one of them kissed the place where his foot had trodden. Jeekie, following, gave him a kick to intimate that he was taking a liberty, but at the same time stooped down and asked the man his name. It occurred to him that these rescued priests might some day be useful.

Alan followed her through a kind of swing door which opened into another of the endless halls, but when he looked for her there she was nowhere to be seen. A priest who was waiting beyond the door bowed and informed him that the Asika had gone to her own place, and would see him that evening. Then bowing again he led them back by various passages to the room where they had slept.

"Jeekie," said Alan after their food had been brought to them, this time, he observed, by men, for it was now past midday, "you were born in Asiki-land; tell me the truth of this business. What does that woman mean when she talks about her spirit having been here from the beginning."

"She mean, Major, that every time she die her soul go into someone else, whom priests find out by marks. Also Asika always die young, they never let her become old woman, but how she die and where they bury her, no one know 'cept priests. Sometimes she have girl child who become Asika after her, but if they have boy child, they kill him. I think this Asika daughter of her who make love to your reverend uncle. All that story 'bout her mother not being married, lies, and all her story lies too, she often marry."

"But how about the spirit coming back, Jeekie?"

"'Spect that lie too, Major, though she think it solemn fact. Priests teach her all those old things. Still," he added doubtfully, "Asika great medicine-woman and know a lot we don't know, can't say how. Very awkward customer, Major."

"Quite so, Jeekie, I agree with you. But to come to the point, what is her game with me?"

"Oh! Major," he answered with a grin, "that simple enough. She tired of black man, want change, mean to marry you according to law, that is when Mungana dies, and he die jolly quick now. She mustn't kill him, but polish him off all the same, stick him to sleep with those dead uns, till he go like drunk man and see things and drown himself. Then she marry you. But till he dead, you all right, she only talk and make eyes, 'cause of Asiki law, not 'cause she want to stop there."

"Indeed, Jeekie, and how long do you think that Mungana will last?"

"Perhaps three months, Major, and perhaps two. Think not more than two. Strong man, but he look devilish dicky this morning. Think he begin see snakes."

"Very well, Jeekie. Now listen to me—you've got to get us out of Asiki-land by this day two months. If you don't, that lady will do anything to oblige me and no doubt there are more executioners left."

"Oh! Major, don't talk like silly fool. Jeekie always hate fools and suffer them badly—like holy first missionary bishop. You know very well this no place for ultra-Christian man like Jeekie, who only come here to please you. Both in same bag, Major, if I die, you die and leave Miss Barbara up gum tree. I get you out if I can. But this stuff the trouble," and he pointed to the bags of gold. "Not want to leave all that behind after such arduous walk. No, no, I try get you out, meanwhile you play game."

"The game! What game, Jeekie?"

"What game? Why, Asika-game of course. If she sigh, you sigh; if she look at you, you look at her; if she squeeze hand, you squeeze hand; if she kiss, you kiss."

"I am hanged if I do, Jeekie."

"Must, Major; must or never get out of Asiki-land. What all that matter?" he added confidentially. "Miss Barbara never know. Jeekie doesn't split, also quite necessary in situation, and you can't be married till that Mungana dead. All matter business, Major; make time pass pleasant as well. Asika jolly enough if you stroke her fur right way, but if you put her back up—oh Lor! No trouble, sit and smile and say, 'Oh, ducky, how beautiful you are!' that not hurt anybody."

In spite of himself Alan burst out laughing.

"But how about the Mungana?" he asked.

"Mungana, he got take that with rest. Also I try make friends with that poor devil. Tell him it all my eye. Perhaps he believe me—not sure. If he me, I no believe him. Mungana," he added oracularly, "Mungana take his chance. What matter? In two months' time he nothing but gold figure, No. 2403; just like one mummy in museum. Now I try catch my ma. I hear she alive somewhere. They tell me she used keep lodging house for Bonsa pilgrim, but steal grub, say it cat, all that sort of thing, and get run in as thief. Afraid my ma come down very much in world, not society lady now, shut up long way off in suburb. Still p'raps she useful so best send her message by p'liceman, say how much I love her; say her dear little Jeekie turn up again just to see her sweet face. Only don't know if she swallow that or if they let her out prison unless I pay for all she prig."

CHAPTER XIII

THE FEAST OF LITTLE BONSA

It was the night of full moon and of the great feast of the return of Little Bonsa. Alan sat in his chamber waiting to be summoned to take part in this ceremony and listening the while to that Wow! Wow! Wow! of the death drums, whereof Jeekie had once spoken in England, which could be clearly heard even above the perpetual boom of the cataract tumbling down its cliff behind the town. By now he had recovered from the fatigue of his journey and his health was good, but the same could not be said of his spirits, for never in his life had he felt more downhearted, not even when he was sickening for blackwater fever, or lay in bondage in the City, expecting every morning to wake up and find his reputation blasted. He was a prisoner in this dreadful, gloomy place where he must live like a second Man in the Iron Mask, without recreation or exercise other than he could find in the walled garden where grew the black cedar trees, and, so far as he could see, a prisoner without hope of escape.

Moreover, he could no longer disguise from himself the truth; Jeekie was right. The Asika had fallen in love with him, or at any rate made up her mind that he should be her next husband. He hated the sight of the woman and her sinuous, evil beauty, but to be free of her was impossible, and to offend her, death. All day long she kept him about her, and from his sleep he would wake up and as on the night of his arrival, distinguish her leaning over him studying his face by the light of the faintly-burning lamps, as a snake studies the bird it is about to strike. He dared not stir or give the slightest sign that he saw her. Nor indeed did he always see her, for he kept his eyes closely shut. But even in his heaviest slumber some warning sense told him of her presence, and then above Jeekie's snores (for on these occasions Jeekie always snored his loudest) he would hear a soft footfall, as cat-like, she crept towards him, or the sweep of her spangled robe, or the tinkling of the scales of her golden breastplate. For a long while she would stand there, examining him greedily and even the few little belongings that remained to him, and then with a hungry sigh glide away and vanish in the shadows. How she came or how she vanished Alan could not discover. Clearly she did not use the door, and he could find no other entrance to the room. Indeed at times he thought he must be suffering from delusion, but Jeekie shook his great head and did not agree with him.

"She there right enough," he said. "She walk over me as though I log and I smell stuff she put on hair, but I think she come and go by magic. Asika do that if she please."

"Then I wish she would teach me the secret, Jeekie. I should soon be out of Asiki-land, I can tell you."

All that day Alan had been in her company, answering her endless questions about his past, the lands that he had visited, and especially the women that he had known. He had the tact to tell her that none of these were half so beautiful as she was, which was true in a sense and pleased her very much, for in whatever respects she differed from them, in common with the rest of her sex she loved a compliment. Emboldened by her good humour, he had ventured to suggest that being rested and having restored Little Bonsa, he would be glad to return with her gifts to his own country. Next instant he was sorry, for as soon as she understood his meaning she grew almost white with rage.

"What!" she said; "you desire to leave me? Know, Vernoon, that I will see you dead first and myself also, for then we shall be born again together and can never more be separated."

Nor was this all, for she burst into weeping, threw her arms about him, drew him to her, kissed him on the forehead, and then thrust him away, saying:

"Curses on the priests' law that makes us wait so long, and curses on that Mungana who will not die and may not be killed. Well, he shall pay for it and within two months, Vernoon, oh! within two months—" and she stretched out her arms with a gesture of infinite passion, then turned and left him.

"My!" said Jeekie afterwards, for he had watched all this scene open-mouthed, "my! but she mean business. Mrs. Jeekie never kiss me like that, nor any other female either. She dead nuts on you, Major. Very great compliment! 'Spect when you Mungana, she keep you alive a long time, four or five years perhaps, if no other white man come this way. Pity you can't take it on a bit, Major," he added insidiously, "because then she grow careless and make you chief and we get chance scoop out that gold house and bolt with bally lot. Miss Barbara sensible woman, when she see all that cash she not mind, she say 'Bravo, old boy, quite right spoil Lady Potiphar in land of bondage, but Jeekie must have ten per cent. because he show you how do it.'"

Alan was so depressed, and indeed terrified by this demonstration on the part of his fearful hostess, that he could neither laugh at Jeekie, nor swear at him. He only sat still and groaned, feeling that bad as things were they were bound to become worse.

Above the perpetual booming of the death drums rose a sound of wild music. The door burst open, and through it came a number of priests, their nearly naked bodies hideously painted and on their heads the most devilish-looking masks. Some of them clashed cymbals, some blew horns and some beat little drums all to time which was given to them by a bandmaster with a golden rod. In front of them with painted face and decked in his gorgeous apparel, walked the Mungana himself.

"They come to take us to Bonsa worship," explained Jeekie. "Cheer up, Major, very exciting business, no go to sleep there, as in English church. See the god all time and no sermon."

Alan, who wore a linen robe over the remains of his European garments, and whose mask was already on his head, rose listlessly and bowed to the gorgeous Mungana who, poor man, answered him with a stare of hate, knowing that this wanderer was destined to fill his place. Then they started, Jeekie accompanying them, and walked a long way through various halls and passages, bearing first to the left and then to the right again, till suddenly through some side door they emerged upon a marvellous scene. The first impressions that reached Alan's mind were those of a long stretch of water, very black and still and not more than eighty feet in width. On the hither edge of this canal, seated upon a raised dais in the midst of a great open space of polished rock, was the Asika, or so he gathered from her gold breastplate and sparkling garments, for her fierce and beautiful features were hid beneath an object familiar enough to him, the yellow, crystal-eyed mask of Little Bonsa. Arranged in companies about and behind her were hundreds of people, male and female, clad in hideous costumes to resemble demons, with masks to match. Some of these masks were semi-human and some of them bore a likeness to the heads of animals and had horns on them, while their wearers were adorned with skins and tails. To describe them in their infinite variety would be impossible; indeed the recollection that Alan carried away was one of a mediæval hell as it is occasionally to be found portrayed upon "Doom pictures" in old churches.

On the further side of the water the entire Asiki people seemed to be gathered, at least there were thousands of them seated upon a rising rocky slope as in an amphitheatre, clad only in the ordinary costume of the Western African native, and in some instances in linen cloaks. This great amphitheatre was surrounded by a high wall with gates, but in the moonlight he found it difficult to discern its exact limits.

Jeekie nudged Alan and pointed to the centre of the canal or pool. He looked and saw floating there a huge and hideous golden head, twenty times as large as life perhaps, with great prominent eyes that glared up to the sky. Its appearance was quite unlike anything else in the world, more loathsome, more horrible, man, fish and animal, all seemed to have their part in it, human mouth and teeth, fish-like eyes and snout, bestial expression.

"Big Bonsa," whispered Jeekie. "Just the same as when I sweet little boy.—He live here for thousand of years."

Preceded by the Mungana and followed by Jeekie and the priests, the band bringing up the rear, Alan was marched down a lane left open for him till he came to some steps leading to the dais, upon which in addition to that occupied by the Asika, stood two empty chairs. These steps the Mungana motioned him to mount, but when Jeekie tried to follow him he turned and struck him contemptuously in the face. At once the Asika, who was watching Vernon's approach through the eye-holes in the Little Bonsa mask, said fiercely:

"Who bade you strike the servant of my guest, O Mungana? Let him come also that he may stand behind us and interpret."

Her wretched husband, who knew that this public slight was put upon him purposely, but did not dare to protest against it, bowed his head. Then all three of them climbed to the dais, the priests and the musicians remaining below.

"Welcome, Vernoon," said the Asika through the lips of the mask, which to Alan, notwithstanding the dreadful cruelty of its expression, looked less hateful than the lovely, tigerish face it hid. "Welcome and be seated here on my left hand, since on my right you may not sit—as yet."

He bowed and took the chair to which she pointed, while her husband placed himself in the other chair upon her right, and Jeekie stood behind, his great shape towering above them all.

"This is a festival of my people, Vernoon," she went on, "such a festival as has not been seen for years, celebrated because Little Bonsa has come back to them."

"What is to happen?" he asked uneasily. "I have told you, Lady, that blood is orunda to me. I must not witness it."

"I know, be not afraid," she answered. "Sacrifice there must be, since it is the custom and we may not defraud the gods, but you shall not see the deed. Judge from this, Vernoon, how greatly I desire to please you."

Now Alan, looking about him, saw that immediately beneath the dais and between them and the edge of the water, were gathered his cannibal friends, the Ogula, and Fahni their chief who had rowed him to Asiki-land, and with them the messengers whom they had sent on ahead. Also he saw that their arms were tied behind them and that they were guarded by men dressed like devils and armed with spears.

"Ask Fahni why he and his people are bound, Jeekie," said Alan, "and why have they not returned to their own country."

Jeekie obeyed, putting the question in the Ogula language, whereon the poor men turned and began to implore Alan to save their lives, Fahni adding that he had been told they were to be killed that night.

"Why are these men to be slain?" asked Alan of the Asika.

"Because I have learned that they attacked you in their own country, Vernoon," she answered, "and would have killed you had it not been for Little Bonsa. It is therefore right that they should die as an offering to you."

"I refuse the offering since afterwards they dealt well with me. Set them free and let them return to their own land, Asika."

"That cannot be," she replied coldly. "Here they are and here they remain. Still, their lives are yours to take or to spare, so keep them as your servants if you will," and bending down she issued a command which was instantly obeyed, for the men dressed like devils cut the bonds of the Ogula and brought them round to the back of the dais, where they stood blessing Alan loudly in their own tongue.

Then the ceremonies began with a kind of infernal ballet. On the smooth space between them and the water's edge appeared male and female bands of dancers who emerged from the shadows. For the most part they were dressed up like animals and imitated the cries of the beasts that they represented, although some of them wore little or no clothing. To the sound of wild music of horns and drums these creatures danced a kind of insane quadrille which seemed to suggest everything that is cruel and vile upon the earth. They danced and danced in the moonlight till the madness spread from them to the thousands who were gathered upon the farther side of the water, for presently all of these began to dance also. Nor did it stop there, since at length the Asika rose from her chair upon the dais and joined in the performance with the Mungana her husband. Even Jeekie began to prance and shout behind, so that at last Alan and the Ogula alone remained still and silent in the midst of a scene and a noise which might have been that of hell let loose.

Leaving go of her husband, the Asika bounded up to Alan and tried to drag him from his chair, thrusting her gold mask against his mask. He refused to move and after a while she left him and returned to Mungana. Louder and louder brayed the music and beat the drums, wilder and wilder grew the shrieks. Individuals fell exhausted and were thrown into the water where they sank or floated away on the slow moving stream, as part of some inexplicable play that was being enacted.

Then suddenly the Asika stood still and threw up her arms and they fell upon their faces and lay as though they were dead. A third time she threw up her arms and they rose and remained so silent that the only sound to be heard was that of their thick breathing. Then she spoke, or rather screamed, saying:

"Little Bonsa has come back again, bringing with her the white man whom she led away," and all the audience answered, "Little Bonsa has come back again. Once more we see her on the head of the Asika as our fathers did. Give her a sacrifice. Give her the white man."

"Nay," she screamed back, "the white man is mine. I name him as the next Mungana."

"Oho!" roared the audience, "Oho! she names him as the next Mungana. Good-bye, old Mungana! Greeting, new Mungana! When will be the marriage feast?"

"Tell us, Mungana, tell us," cried the Asika, patting her wretched husband on the cheek. "Tell us when you mean to die, as you are bound to do."

"On the night of the second full moon from now," he answered with a terrible groan that seemed to be wrung out of his heavy heart; "on that night my soul will be eaten up and my day done. But till then I am lord of the Asika, and if she forgets it, death shall be her portion, according to the ancient law."

"Yes, yes," shouted the multitude, "death shall be her portion, and her lover we will sacrifice. Die in honour, Mungana, as all those died that went before you."

"Thank Heaven!" muttered Alan to himself, "I am safe from that witch for the next two months," and through the eye-holes of his mask he contemplated her with loathing and alarm.

At the moment, indeed, she was not a pleasing spectacle, for in the heat and excitement of her mad dance she had cast off her gold breast-plate or stomacher, leaving herself naked except for her kirtle and the thin, gold-spangled robe upon her shoulders over which streamed her black, disordered hair. Contrasting strangely in the silver moonlight with her glistening, copper-coloured body, the mask of Little Bonsa on her head glared round with its fixed crystal eyes and fiendish smile as she turned her long neck from side to side. Seen thus she scarcely looked human, and Alan's heart was filled with pity for the poor bedizened wretch she named her husband, who had just been forced to announce the date of his own suicide.

Soon, however, he forgot it, for a new act in the drama had begun. Two priests clad in horns and tails leapt on to the dais and at a signal unlaced the mask of Little Bonsa. Now the Asika lifted it from her streaming face and held it on high, then she lowered it to the level of her breast, and holding it in both hands, walked to the edge of the dais, whereon priests, disguised as fiends, began to leap at it, striving to reach it with their fingers and snatch it from her grasp. One by one they leapt with the most desperate energy, each man being allowed to make three attempts, and Alan noted that this novel jumping competition was watched with the deepest interest by all the audience, at the time he knew not why.

The first two were evidently elderly men who failed to come anywhere near the mark. Their failure was received with shouts of derision. They sank exhausted to the ground and from the motion of his body Alan could see that one of them was weeping, while the other remained sullenly silent. Then a younger man advanced and at the third try almost grasped the fetish. Indeed he would have grasped it had he not met with foul play, for the Asika, seeing that he was about to succeed, lifted it an inch or two, so that he also missed and with a groan joined the band of the defeated. Next appeared a fourth priest, even more horribly arrayed than those before him, but Alan noticed that his mask was of the lightest, and that his garments consisted chiefly of paint, the main idea of his make-up being that of a skeleton. He was a thin active fellow, and all the watching thousands greeted him with a shout. For a few seconds he stood back gazing at the mask as a wolf might at an unapproachable bone. Then suddenly he ran forward and sprang into the air. Such an amazing jump Alan had never seen before. So high was it indeed that his head came level with that of the fetish, which he snatched with both hands tearing it from Asika's grasp. Coming to the ground again with a thud, he began to caper to and fro, kissing the mask, while the audience shouted:

"Little Bonsa has chosen. What fate for the fallen? Ask her, priest?"

The man stopped his capering and held the mouth of Little Bonsa to his ear, nodding from time to time as though she were speaking to him and he heard what she said. Then he passed round the dais where Alan could not see him, and presently reappeared holding Little Bonsa in his right hand and in his left a great gold cup. A silence fell upon the place. He advanced to the first man who had jumped and offered him the cup. He turned his head away, but a thousand voices thundered "Drink!" Then he took it and drank, passing it to a companion in misfortune, who in turn drank also and gave it to the third priest, he who would have snatched the mask had not the Asika lifted it out of his reach.

This man drained it to the dregs, and with an exclamation of rage dashed the empty vessel into the face of the chosen priest with such fury that the man rolled upon the ground and for a while lay there stunned. Now he who had drunk first began to spring about in a ludicrous fashion, and presently was joined in his dance by the other two. So absurd were their motions and tumblings and clownlike grimaces, for they had dragged off their masks, that roars of brutal laughter rose from the audience, in which the Asika joined.

At first Alan thought that the thing was a joke, and that the men had merely been made mad drunk, till catching sight of their eyes in the moonlight, he perceived that they were in great pain and turned indignantly to remonstrate with the Asika.

"Be silent, Vernoon," she said savagely, "blood is your orunda and I respect it. Therefore by decree of the god these die of poison," and again she fell to laughing at the contortions of the victims.

Alan shut his eyes, and when at length, drawn by some fearful fascination, he opened them once more, it was to see that the three poor creatures had thrown themselves into the water, where they rolled over and over like wounded porpoises, till presently they sank and vanished there.

This farce, for so they considered it, being ended and the stage, so to speak, cleared, the audience having laughed itself hoarse, set itself to watch the proceedings of the newly chosen high-priest of Little Bonsa, who by now had recovered from the blow dealt to him by one of the murdered men. With the help of some other priests he was engaged in binding the fetish on to a little raft of reeds. This done he laid himself flat upon a broad plank which had been made ready for him at the edge of the water, placing the mask in front of him and with a few strokes of his feet that hung over the sides of the plank, paddled himself out to the centre of the canal where the god called Big Bonsa floated, or was anchored. Having reached it he pushed the little raft off the plank into the water, and in some way that Alan could not see, made it fast to Big Bonsa, so that now the two of them floated one behind the other. Then while the people cheered, shouting out that husband and wife had come together again at last, he paddled his plank back to the water's edge, sat down and waited.

Meanwhile, at a sign from the Asika, all the scores of priests and priestesses who were dressed as devils had filed off to right and left, and vanished, presumably to cross the water by bridges or boats that were out of sight. At any rate now they began to appear upon its further side and to wind their way singly among the thousands of the Asiki people who were gathered upon the rocky slope beyond in order to witness this fearsome entertainment. Alan observed that the spectators did not appear to appreciate the arrival amongst them of these priests, from whom they seemed to edge away. Indeed many of them rose and tried to depart altogether, only to be driven back to their places by a double line of soldiers armed with spears, who now for the first time became visible, ringing in the audience. Also other soldiers and with them bodies of men who looked like executioners, showed themselves upon the further brink of the water and then marched off, disappearing to left and right.

"What's the matter now?" Alan asked of Jeekie over his shoulder.

"All in blue funk," whispered Jeekie back, "joke done. Get to business now. Silly fools forget that when they laugh so much. Both Bonsas very hungry and Asika want wipe out old scores. Presently you see."

Presently Alan did see, for at some preconcerted signal the devil priests, each of them, jumped with a yell at a person near to them, gripping him or her by the hair, whereon assistants rushed in and dragged them down to the bank of the canal. Here to the number of a hundred or more, a wailing, struggling mass, they were confined in a pen like sheep. Then a bar was lifted and one of them allowed to escape, only to find himself in a kind of gangway which ran down into shallow water. Being forced along this he came to an open space of water exactly opposite to the floating fetishes, and there was kept a while by men armed with spears. As nothing happened they lifted their spears and the man bolted up an incline and was lost among the thousands of spectators.

The next one, evidently a person of rank, was not so fortunate. Jumping into the pool off the gangway, he stood there like a sheep about to be washed, the water reaching up to his middle. Then Alan saw a terrifying thing, for suddenly the horrid, golden head of Big Bonsa, towing Little Bonsa behind it, began to swim with a deliberate motion across the stream until, reaching the man, it seemed to rear itself up and poke him with its snout in the chest as a turtle might do. Then it sank again into the water and slowly floated back to its station, directed by some agency or power that Alan could not discover.

At the touch of the fetish the man screamed like a horse in pain or terror, and soldiers leaping on him with a savage shout, dragged him up another gangway opposite to that by which he had descended, whereon, to all appearances more dead than alive, he departed into the shadows. The horns and drums set up a bray of triumph, the Asika clapped her hands approvingly, the spectators cheered, and another victim was bundled down the gangway and submitted to the judgment of the Bonsas, which came at him like a hungry pike at a frog. Then followed more and more, some being chosen and some let go, till at last, growing weary, the priests directed the soldiers to drive the prisoners down in batches until the pen in the water was full as though with huddled sheep. If the horrible golden masks swam at them and touched one of their number, they were all dragged away; if these remained quiescent they were let go.

So the thing went on until at length Alan could bear no more of it.

"Lady," he said to the Asika when she paused for a moment from her hand-clapping, "I am weary, I would sleep."

"What!" she exclaimed, "do you wish to sleep on such a glorious night when so many evil doers are coming to their just doom? Well, well, go if you will, for then my promise is off me and I can hasten this business and deal with the wicked before the people according to our custom. Good-night to you, Vernoon, to-morrow we will meet," and she called to some priests to lead him away, and with him the Ogula cannibals whom she had given to him as servants.

Alan went thankfully enough. As he plunged into one of the passages the sound of frightful yelling reached his ears, followed by loud, triumphant shouts.

"Now you gone they kill those who Bonsa smell out," said Jeekie. "Why you no wait and see? Very interesting sight."

"Hold your tongue," answered Alan savagely. "Did you think so years ago when you were put into that pen to be butchered?"

"No, Major," replied the unabashed Jeekie, "not think at all then, too far gone. But see other people in there and know it not you, quite different matter."

They reached their room. At the door of it Fahni and his followers were led off to some quarters near by, blessing Alan as they went because he had saved their lives.

"Jeekie," he said when they were alone, "tell me, what makes that hellish idol swim about in the water picking out some people and leaving others alone?"

"Major, I not know, no one know except top priest and Asika. Perhaps there man underneath, perhaps they pull string, or perhaps fetish alive and he do what he like. Please don't call him names, Major, or he remember and come after us one time, and that bad job," and Jeekie shivered visibly.

"Bosh!" answered Alan, but all the same he shivered also. "Jeekie," he asked again, "what happens to those people whom the Bonsas smell out?"

"Case of good-bye, Major. Sometimes they chop off nut, sometimes they spifflicate in gold tub, sometimes priest-man make hole in what white doctor call diagram—and shake hands with heart.—All matter of taste, Major, just as Asika please. If she like victim or they old friends, chop off head; if she not like him—do worse things."

More than satisfied with his information Alan went to bed. For hour after hour that night he lay tossing and turning, haunted by the recollections of the dreadful sights that he had seen and of the horrible Asika, horrible and half-naked, glaring at him amorously through the crystal eyes of Little Bonsa. When at last he fell asleep it was to dream that he was alone in the water with the god which pursued him as a shark pursues a shipwrecked sailor. Never did he experience a nightmare that was half so awful. Only one thing could be more awful, the reality itself.

CHAPTER XIV

THE MOTHER OF JEEKIE

"Jeekie," said Alan next morning, "I tell you again that I have had enough of this place, I want to get out."

"Yes, Major, that just what mouse say when he finish cheese in trap, but missus come along, call him 'Pretty, pretty,' and drown him all the same," and he nodded in the direction of the Asika's house.

"Jeekie, it has got to be done—do you hear me? I had rather die trying to get away than stop here till the next two months are up. If I am here on the night of the next full moon but one, I shall shoot that Asika and then shoot myself, and you must take your chance. Do you understand?"

"Understand that foolish game and poor lookout for Jeekie, Major, but can't think of any plan." Then he rubbed his big nose reflectively and added, "Fahni and his people your slaves now, 'spose we have talk with him. I tell priests to bring him along when they come with breakfast. Leave it to me, Major."

Alan did leave it to him, with the result that after long argument the priests consented or obtained permission to produce Fahni and his followers, and a little while after the great men arrived looking very dejected, and saluted Alan humbly. Bidding the rest of them be seated, he called Fahni to the end of the room and asked him through Jeekie if he and his men did not wish to return home.

"Indeed we do, white lord," answered the old chief, "but how can we? The Asika has a grudge against our tribe and but for you would have killed every one of us last night. We are snared and must stop here till we die."

"Would not your people help you if they knew, Fahni?"

"Yes, lord, I think so. But how can I tell them who doubtless believe us dead? Nor can I send a messenger, for this place is guarded and he would be killed at once. We came here for your sake because you had Little Bonsa, a god that is known in the east and the west, in the north and the south, and because you saved me from the lion, and here, alas! we must perish."

"Jeekie," said Alan, "can you not find a messenger? Have you, who were born of this people, no friend among them at all?"

Jeekie shook his white head and rolled his eyes. Then suddenly an idea struck him.

"Yes," he said, "I think one, p'raps. I mean my ma."

"Your ma!" said Alan. "Oh! I remember. Have you heard anything more about her?"

"Yes, Major. Very old girl now, but strong on leg, so they say. Believe she glad go anywhere, because she public nuisance; they tired of her in prison and there no workhouse here, so they want turn her out starve, which of course break my heart. Perhaps she take message. Some use that way. Only think she afraid go Ogula-land because they nasty cannibal and eat old woman."

When all this was translated to Fahni he assured Jeekie with earnestness that nothing would induce the Ogula people to eat his mother; moreover, that for her sake they would never look carnivorously on another old woman, fat or thin.

"Well," said Jeekie, "I try again to get hold of old lady and we see. I pray priests, whom you save other day, let her out of chokey as I sick to fall upon bosom, which quite true, only so much to think of that no time to attend to domestic relation till now."

That very afternoon, on returning to his room from walking in the dismal cedar garden, Alan's ears were greeted by a sound of shrill quarrelling. Looking up he saw an extraordinary sight. A tall, gaunt, withered female who might have been of any age between sixty and a hundred, had got Jeekie's ear in one hand, and with the other was slapping him in the face while she exclaimed:

"O thief, whom by the curse of Bonsa I brought into the world, what have you done with my blanket? Was it not enough that you, my only son, should leave me to earn my own living? Must you also take my best blanket with you, for which reason I have been cold ever since. Where is it, thief, where is it?"

"Worn out, my mother, worn out," he answered, trying to free himself. "You forget, honourable mother, that I grow old and you should have been dead years ago. How can you expect a blanket to last so long? Leave go of my ear, beloved mother, and I will give you another. I have travelled across the world to find you and I want to hear news of your husband."

"My husband, thief, which husband? Do you mean your father, the one with the broken nose, who was sacrificed because you ran away with the white man whom Bonsa loved? Well, you look out for him when you get into the world of ghosts, for he said that he was going to wait for you there with the biggest stick that he could find. Why I haven't thought of him for years, but then I have had three other husbands since his time, bad enough, but better than he was, so who would? And now Bonsa has got the lot, and I have no children alive, and they say I am to be driven out of the prison to starve next week as they won't feed me any longer, I who can still work against any one of them, and—you've got my blanket, you ugly old rascal," and collapsing beneath the weight of her recited woes, the hag burst into a melancholy howl.

"Peace, my mother," said Jeekie, patting her on the head. "Do what I tell you and you shall have more blankets than you can wear and, as you are still so handsome, another husband too if you like, and a garden and slaves to work for you and plenty to eat."

"How shall I get all these things, my son?" asked the old woman, looking up. "Will you take me to your home and support me, or will that white lord marry me? They told me that the Asika had named him as the Mungana, and she is very jealous, the most jealous Asika that I have ever known."

"No, mother, he would like to, but he dare not, and I cannot support you as I should wish, as here I have no house or property. You will get all this by taking a walk and holding your tongue. You see this man here, he is Fahni, king of a great tribe, the Ogula. He wants you to carry a message for him, and by and by he will marry you, won't you, Fahni?"

"Oh! yes, yes," said Fahni; "I will do anything she likes. No one shall be so rich and honoured in my country, and for her sake we will never eat another old woman, whereas if she stays here she will be driven to the mountains to starve in a week."

"Set out the matter," said the mother of Jeekie, who was by no means so foolish as she seemed.

So they told her what she must do, namely, travel down to the Ogula and tell them of the plight of their chief, bidding them muster all their fighting men and when the swamps were dry enough, advance as near as they dared to the Asiki country and, if they could not attack it, wait till they had further news.

The end of it was that the mother of Jeekie, who knew her case to be desperate at home, where she was in no good repute, promised to attempt the journey in consideration of advantages to be received. Since she was to be turned adrift to meet her fate with as much food as she could carry, this she could do without exciting any suspicion, for who would trouble about the movements of a useless old thief? Meanwhile Jeekie gave her one of the robes which the Asika had provided for Alan, also various articles which she desired and, having learned Fahni's message by heart and announced that she considered herself his affianced bride, the gaunt old creature departed happy enough after exchanging embraces with her long lost son.

"She will tell somebody all about it and we shall only get our throats cut," said Alan wearily, for the whole thing seemed to him a foolish farce.

"No, no, Major. I make her swear not split on ghosts of all her husbands and by Big Bonsa hisself. She sit tight as wax, because she think they haunt her if she don't and I too by and by when I dead. P'raps she get to Ogula country and p'raps not. If she don't, can't help it and no harm done. Break my heart, but only one old woman less. Anyhow she hold tongue, that main point, and I really very glad find my ma, who never hoped to see again. Heaven very kind to Jeekie, give him back to family bosom," he added, unctuously.

That day there were no excitements, and to Alan's intense relief he saw nothing of the Asika. After its orgy of witchcraft and bloodshed on the previous night, weariness and silence seemed to have fallen upon the town. At any rate no sound came from it that could be heard above the low, constant thunder of the great waterfall rushing down its precipice, and in the cedar-shadowed garden where Alan walked till he was weary, attended by Jeekie and the Ogula savages, not a soul was to be seen.

On the following morning, when he was sitting moodily in his room, two priests came to conduct him to the Asika. Having no choice, followed by Jeekie, he accompanied them to her house, masked as usual, for without this hateful disguise he was not allowed to stir. He found her lying upon a pile of cushions in a small room that he had never seen before, which was better lighted than most in that melancholy abode, and seemed to serve as her private chamber. In front of her lay the skin of the lion that he had sent as a present, and about her throat hung a necklace made of its claws, heavily set in gold, with which she was playing idly.

At the opening of the door she looked up with a swift smile that turned to a frown when she saw that he was followed by Jeekie.

"Say, Vernoon," she asked in her languorous voice, "can you not stir a yard without that ugly black dog at your heels? Do you bring him to protect your back? If so, what is the need? Have I not sworn that you are safe in my land?"

Alan made Jeekie interpret this speech, then answered that the reason was that he knew but little of her tongue.

"Can I not teach it to you alone, then, without this low fellow hearing all my words? Well, it will not be for long," and she looked at Jeekie in a way that made him feel very uncomfortable. "Get behind us, dog, and you, Vernoon, come sit on these cushions at my side. Nay, not there, I said upon the cushions—so. Now I will take off that ugly mask of yours, for I would look into your eyes. I find them pleasant, Vernoon," and without waiting for his permission, she sat up and did so. "Ah!" she went on, "we shall be happy when we are married, shall we not? Do not be afraid, Vernoon, I will not eat out your heart as I have those of the men that went before you. We will live together until we are old, and die together at last, and together be born again, and so on and on till the end which even I cannot foresee. Why do you not smile, Vernoon, and say that you are pleased, and that you will be happy with me who loved you from the moment that my eyes fell upon you in sleep? Speak, Vernoon, lest I should grow angry with you."

"I don't know what to say," answered Alan despairingly through Jeekie, "the honour is too great for me, who am but a wandering trader who came here to barter Little Bonsa against the gold I need"—to support my wife and family, he was about to add, then remembering that this statement might not be well received, substituted, "to support my old parents and eight brothers and sisters who are dependent upon me, and remain hungry until I return to them."

"Then I think they will remain hungry a long time, Vernoon, for while I live you shall never return. Much as I love you I would kill you first," and her eyes glittered as she said the words. "Still," she added, noting the fall in his face, "if it is gold that they need, you shall send it them. Yes, my people shall take all that I gave you down to the coast, and there it can be put in a big canoe and carried across the water. See to the packing of the stuff, you black dog," she said to Jeekie over her shoulder, "and when it is ready I will send it hence."

Alan began to thank her, though he thought it more than probable that even if she kept her word, this bullion would never get to Old Calabar, and much less to England. But she waived the matter aside as one in which she was not interested.

"Tell me," she asked; "would you have me other than I am? First, do you think me beautiful?"

"Yes," answered Alan honestly, "very beautiful when you are quiet as now, not when you are dancing as you did the other night without your robes."

When she understood what he meant the Asika actually blushed a little.

"I am sorry," she answered in a voice that for her was quite humble. "I forget that it might seem strange in your eyes. It has always been the custom for the Asika to do as I did at feasts and sacrifices, but perhaps that is not the fashion among your women; perhaps they always remain veiled, as I have heard the worshippers of the Prophet do, and therefore you thought me immodest. I am very, very sorry, Vernoon. I pray you to forgive me who am ignorant and only do what I have been taught."

"Yes, they always remain veiled," stammered Alan, though he was not referring to their faces, and as the words passed his lips he wondered what the Asika would think if she could see a ballet at a London music-hall.

"Is there anything else wrong?" she went on gently. "If so, tell me that I may set it right."

"I do not like cruelty or sacrifices, O Asika. I have told you that bloodshed is orunda to me, and at the feast those men were poisoned and you mocked them in their pain; also many others were taken away to be killed for no crime."

She opened her beautiful eyes and stared at him, answering:

"But, Vernoon, all this is not my fault; they were sacrifices to the gods, and if I did not sacrifice, I should be sacrificed by the priests and wizards who live to sacrifice. Yes, myself I should be made to drink the poison and be mocked at while I died like a snake with a broken back. Or even if I escaped the vengeance of the people, the gods themselves would kill me and raise up another in my place. Do they not sacrifice in your country, Vernoon?"

"No, Asika, they fight if necessary and kill those who commit murder. But they have no fetish that asks for blood, and the law they have from heaven is a law of mercy."

She stared at him again.

"All this is strange to me," she said. "I was taught otherwise. Gods are devils and must be appeased, lest they bring misfortune on us; men must be ruled by terror, or they would rebel and pull down the great House; doctors must learn magic, or how could they avert spells? wizards must be killed, or the people would perish in their net. May not we who live in a hell, strive to beat back its flame with the wisdom our forefathers have handed on to us? Tell me, Vernoon, for I would know."

"You make your own hell," answered Alan when with the help of Jeekie he understood her talk.

She pondered over his words for a while, then said:

"I must think. The thing is big. I wander in blackness; I will speak with you again. Say now, what else is wrong with me?"

Now Alan thought that he saw opportunity for a word in season and made a great mistake.

"I think that you treat your husband, that man whom you call Mungana, very badly. Why should you drive him to his death?"

At these words the Asika leapt up in a rage, and seeking something to vent her temper on, violently boxed Jeekie's ears and kicked him with her sandalled foot.

"The Mungana!" she exclaimed, "that beast! What have I to do with him? I hate him, as I hated the others. The priests thrust him on me. He has had his day, let him go. In your country do they make women live with men whom they loathe? I love you, Bonsa himself knows why? Perhaps because you have a white skin and white thoughts. But I hate that man. What is the use of being Asika if I cannot take what I love and reject what I hate? Go away, Vernoon, go away, you have angered me, and if it were not for what you have said about that new law of mercy, I think that I would cut your throat," and again she boxed Jeekie's ears and kicked him in the shins.

Alan rose and bowed himself towards the door while she stood with her back towards him, sobbing. As he was about to pass it she wheeled round, wiping the tears from her eyes with her hand, and said:

"I forgot, I sent for you to thank you for your presents; that," and she pointed to the lion skin, "which they tell me you killed with some kind of thunder to save the life of that old cannibal, and this," and she pulled off the necklace of claws, then added, "as I am too bad to wear it, you had better take it back again," and she threw it with all her strength straight into Jeekie's face.

Fearing worse things, the much maltreated Jeekie uttered a howl and bolted through the door, while Alan, picking up the necklace, returned it to her with a bow. She took it.

"Stop," she said. "You are leaving the room without your mask and my women are outside. Come here," and she tied the thing upon his head, setting it all awry, then pushed him from the place.

"Very poor joke, Major, very poor indeed," said Jeekie when they had reached their own apartment. "Lady make love to you; you play prig and lecture lady about holy customs of her country and she box my ear till head sing, also kick me all over and throw sharp claws in face. Please you do it no more. The next time, who knows? she stick knife in my gizzard, then kiss you afterward and say she so sorry and hope she no hurt you. But how that help poor departed Jeekie who get all kicks, while you have ha'pence?"

"Oh! be quiet," said Alan; "you are welcome to the halfpence if you would only leave me the kicks. The question is, how am I to get out of this mess? While she was a beautiful savage devil, one could deal with the thing, but if she is going to become human it is another matter."

Jeekie looked at him with pity in his eyes.

"Always thought white man mad at bottom," he said, shaking his big head. "To benighted black nigger thing so very simple. All you got to do, make love and cut when you get chance. Then she pleased as Punch, everything go smooth and Jeekie get no more kicks. Christian religion business very good, but won't wash in Asiki-land. Your reverend uncle find out that."

Not wishing to pursue the argument, Alan changed the subject by asking his indignant retainer if he thought that the Asika had meant what she said when she offered to send the gold down to the coast.

"Why not, Major? That good lady always mean what she say, and what she do too," and he dabbed wrathfully at the scratches made by the lion's claws on his face, then added, "She know her own mind, not like shilly-shally, see-saw white woman, who get up one thing and go to bed another. If she love she love, if she hate she hate. If she say she send gold, she send it, though pity to part with all that cash, because 'spect someone bag it."

Alan reflected a while.

"Don't you see, Jeekie, that here is a chance, if a very small one, of getting a message to the coast. Also it is quite clear that if we are ever able to escape, it will be impossible for us to carry this heavy stuff, whereas if we send it on ahead, perhaps some of it might get through. We will pack it up, Jeekie, at any rate it will be something to do. Go now and send a message to the Asika, and ask her to let us have some carpenters, and a lot of well-seasoned wood."

The message was sent and an hour later a dozen of the native craftsmen arrived with their rude tools and a supply of planks cut from a kind of iron-wood or ebony tree. They prostrated themselves to Alan, then the master of them rising, instantly began to measure Jeekie with a marked reed. That worthy sprang back and asked what in the name of Bonsa, Big and Little, they were doing, whereon the man explained with humility that the Asika had said that she thought the white lord wanted the wood to make a box to bury his servant in, as he, the said servant, had offended her that morning, and doubtless the white lord wished to kill him on that account, or perhaps to put him away under ground alive.

"Oh, my golly!" said Jeekie, shaking till his great knees knocked together, "oh! my golly! here pretty go. She think you want bury me all alive. That mean she want to be rid of Jeekie, because he got sit there and play gooseberry when she wish talk alone with you. Oh, yes! I see her little game."

"Well, Jeekie," said Alan, bursting into such a roar of laughter that he nearly shook off his mask, "you had better be careful, for you just told me that the Asika is not like a see-saw white woman and never changes her mind. Say to this man that he must tell the Asika there is a mistake, and that however much I should like to oblige her, I can't bury you because it has been prophesied to me that on the day you are buried, I shall be buried also, and that therefore you must be kept alive."

"Capital notion that, Major," said Jeekie, much relieved. "She not want bury you just at present; next year perhaps, but not now. I tell him." And he did with much vigour.

This slight misconception having been disposed of, they explained to the carpenters what was wanted. First, all the gold was emptied out of the sacks in which it remained as the priests had brought it, and divided into heaps, each of which weighed about forty pounds, a weight that with its box Alan considered would be a good load for a porter. Of these heaps there proved to be fifty-three, their total value, Alan reckoned, amounting to about £100,000 sterling. Then the carpenters were set to work to make a model box, which they did quickly enough and with great ingenuity, cutting the wood with their native saws, dovetailing it as a civilized craftsman would do, and finally securing it everywhere with ebony pegs, driven into holes which they bored with a hot iron. The result was a box that would stand any amount of rough usage and when finally pegged down, one that could only be opened with a hammer and a cold chisel.

This box-making went on for two whole days. As each of them was filled and pegged down, the gold within being packed in sawdust to keep it from rattling, Alan amused himself in adding an address with a feather brush and a supply of red paint such as the Asiki priests used to decorate their bodies. At first he was puzzled to know what address to put, but finally decided upon the following:

Major A. Vernon, care of Miss Champers, The Court, near Kingswell, England. Adding in the corner, From A. V., Asiki Land, Africa.

It was all childish enough, he knew, yet when it was done he regarded his handiwork with a sort of satisfaction. For, reflected Alan, if but one of those boxes should chance to get through to England, it would tell Barbara a great deal, and if it were addressed to himself, her uncle could scarcely dare to take possession of it.

Then he bethought him of sending a letter, but was obliged to abandon the idea, as he had neither pen, pencil, ink, nor paper left to him. Whatever arts remained to them, that of any form of writing was now totally unknown to the Asiki, although marks that might be writing, it will be remembered, did appear on the inner side of the Little Bonsa mask, an evidence of its great antiquity. Even in the days when they had wrapped up the Egyptian, the Roman, and other early Munganas in sheets of gold and set them in their treasure-house, apparently they had no knowledge of it, for not even an hieroglyph or a rune appeared upon the imperishable metal shrouds. Since that time they had evidently decreased, not advanced, in learning till at the present day, except for these relics and some dim and meaningless survival of rites that once had been religious and were still offered to the same ancient idols, there was little to distinguish them from other tribes of Central African savages. Still Alan did something, for obtaining a piece of white wood, which he smoothed as well as he was able with a knife, he painted on it this message:

"Messrs. Aston, Old Calabar. Please forward accompanying fifty-three packages, or as many as arrive, and cable as follows (all costs will be remitted): Miss Champers, Kingswell, England. Prisoner among Asiki. No present prospect of escape, but hope for best. Jeekie and I well. Allowed send this, but perhaps no future message possible. Good-bye. Alan."

As it happened just as Alan was finishing this scrawl with a sad heart, he heard a movement and glancing up, perceived standing at his side the Asika, of whom he had seen nothing since the interview when she had beaten Jeekie:

"What are those marks that you make upon the board, Vernoon?" she asked suspiciously.

With the assistance of Jeekie, who kept at a respectful distance, he informed her that they were a message in writing to tell the white men at the coast to forward the gold to his starving family.

"Oh!" she said, "I never heard of writing. You shall teach it me. It will serve to pass the time till we are married, though it will not be of much use afterwards, as we shall never be separated any more and words are better than marks upon a board. But," she added cheerfully, "I can send away this black dog of yours," and she looked at Jeekie, "and he can write to us. No, I cannot, for an accident might happen to him, and they tell me you say that if he dies, you die also, so he must stop here always. What have you in those little boxes?"

"The gold you gave me, Asika, packed in loads."

"A small gift enough," she answered contemptuously; "would you not like more, since you value that stuff? Well, another time you shall send all you want. Meanwhile the porters are waiting, fifty men and three, as you sent me word, and ten spare ones to take the place of any who die. But how they will find their way, I know not, since none of them have ever been to the coast."

An idea occurred to Alan, who had small faith in Jeekie's "ma" as a messenger.

"The Ogula prisoners could show them," he said; "at any rate as far as the forest, and after that they could find out. May they not go, Asika?"

"If you will," she answered carelessly. "Let them be ready to start to-morrow at the dawn, all except their chief, Fahni, who must stop here as a hostage. I do not trust those Ogula, who more than once have threatened to make war upon us," she added, then turned and bade the priests bring in the bearers to receive their instructions.

Presently they came, picked men all of them, under the command of an Asiki captain, and with them the Ogula, whom she summoned also.

"Go where the white lord sends you," she said in an indifferent voice, "carrying with you these packages. I do not know where it is, but these man-eaters will show you some of the way, and if you fail in the business but live to come back again, you shall be sacrificed to Bonsa at the next feast; if you run away then your wives and children will be sacrificed. Food shall be given you for your journey, and gold to buy more when it is gone. Now, Vernoon, tell them what they have to do."

So Alan, or rather Jeekie, told them, and these directions were so long and minute, that before they were finished the Asika grew tired of listening and went away, saying as she passed the captain of the company:

"Remember my words, man, succeed or die, but of your land and its secrets say nothing."

"I hear," answered the captain, prostrating himself.

That night Alan summoned the Ogula and spoke to them through Jeekie in their own language. At first they declared that they would not leave their chief, preferring to stay and die with him.

"Not so," said Fahni; "go, my children, that I may live. Go and gather the tribe, all the thousands of them who are men and can fight, and bring them up to attack Asiki-land, to rescue me if I still live, or to avenge me if I am dead. As for these bearers, do them no harm, but send them on to the coast with the white man's goods."

So in the end the Ogula said that they would go, and when Alan woke up on the following morning, he was informed that they and the Asiki porters had already departed upon their journey. Then he dismissed the matter from his mind, for to tell the truth he never expected to hear of them any more.

CHAPTER XV

ALAN FALLS ILL

After the departure of the messengers a deep melancholy fell upon Alan, who was sure that he had now no further hope of communicating with the outside world. Bitterly did he reproach himself for his folly in having ever journeyed to this hateful place in order to secure—what? About £100,000 worth of gold which of course he never could secure, as it would certainly vanish or be stolen on its way to the coast.

For this gold he had become involved in a dreadful complication which must cost him much misery, and sooner or later life itself, since he could not marry that beautiful savage Asika, and if he refused her she would certainly kill him in her outraged pride and fury.

Day by day she sent for him, and when he came, assumed a new character, that of a woman humbled by a sense of her own ignorance, which she was anxious to amend. So he must play the role of tutor to her, telling her of civilized peoples, their laws, customs and religions, and instructing her how to write and read. She listened and learned submissively enough, but all the while Alan felt as one might who is called upon to teach tricks to a drugged panther. The drug in this case was her passion for him, which appeared to be very genuine. But when it passed off, or when he was obliged to refuse her, what, he wondered, would happen then?

Anxiety and confinement told on him far more than all the hardships of his journey. His health ran down, he began to fall ill. Then as bad luck would have it, walking in that damp, unwholesome cedar garden, out of which he might not stray, he contracted the germ of some kind of fever which in autumn was very common in this poisonous climate. Three days later he became delirious, and for a week after that hung between life and death. Well was it for him that his medicine-chest still remained intact, and that recognizing his own symptoms before his head gave way, he was able to instruct Jeekie what drugs to give him at the different stages of the disease.

For the rest his memories of that dreadful illness always remained very vague. He had visions of Jeekie and of a robed woman whom he knew to be the Asika, bending over him continually. Also it seemed to him that from time to time he was talking with Barbara, which even then he knew must be absurd, for how could they talk across thousands of miles of land and sea.

At length his mind cleared suddenly, and he awoke as from a nightmare to find himself lying in the hall or room where he had always been, feeling quite cool and without pain, but so weak that it was an effort to him to lift his hand. He stared about him and was astonished to see the white head of Jeekie rolling uneasily to and fro upon the cushions of another bed near by.

"Jeekie," he said, "are you ill too, Jeekie?"

At the sound of that voice his retainer started up violently.

"What, Major, you awake?" he said. "Thanks be to all gods, white and black, yes, and yellow too, for I thought your goose cooked. No, no, Major, I not ill, only Asika say so. You go to bed, so she make me go to bed. You get worse, she treat me cruel; you seem better, she stuff me with food till I burst. All because you tell her that you and I die same day. Oh, Lord! poor Jeekie think his end very near just now, for he know quite well that she not let him breathe ten minutes after you peg out. Jeekie never pray so hard for anyone before as he pray this week for you, and by Jingo! I think he do the trick, he and that medicine stuff which make him feel very bad in stomach," and he groaned under the weight of his many miseries.

Weak as he was Alan began to laugh, and that laugh seemed to do him more good than anything that he could remember, for after it he was sure that he would recover.

Just then an agonized whisper reached him from Jeekie.

"Look out!" it said, "here come Asika. Go sleep and seem better, Major, please, or I catch it hot."

So Alan almost shut his eyes and lay still. In another moment she was standing over him and he noticed that her hair was dishevelled and her eyes were red as though with weeping. She scanned him intently for a little while, then passed round to where Jeekie lay and appeared to pinch his ear so hard that he wriggled and uttered a stifled groan.

"How is your lord, dog?" she whispered.

"Better, O Asika, I think that last medicine do us good, though it make me very sick inside. Just now he spoke to me and said that he hoped that your heart was not sad because of him and that all this time in his dreams he had seen and thought of nobody but you, O Asika."

"Did he?" asked that lady, becoming intensely interested. "Then tell me, dog, why is he ever calling upon one Bar-bar-a? Surely that is a woman's name?"

"Yes, O Asika, that is the name of his mother, also of one of his sisters, whom, after you, he loves best of anyone in the whole world. When you are here he talks of them, but when you are not here he talks of no one but you. Although he is so sick he remembers white man's custom, which tells him that it is very wrong to say sweet things to lady's face till he is quite married to her. After that they say them always."

She looked at him suspiciously and muttering, "Here it is otherwise. For your own sake, man, I trust that you do not lie," left him, and drawing a stool up beside Alan's bed, sat herself down and examined him carefully, touching his face and hands with her long thin fingers. Then noting how white and wasted he was, of a sudden she began to weep, saying between her sobs:

"Oh! if you should die, Vernoon, I will die also and be born again not as Asika, as I have been for so many generations, but as a white woman that I may be with you. Only first," she added, setting her teeth, "I will sacrifice every wizard in this land, for they have brought the sickness on you by their magic, and I will burn Bonsa-town and cast its gods to melt in the flames, and the Mungana with them. And then amid their ashes I will let out my life," and again she began to weep very piteously and to call him by endearing names and pray him that he would not die.

Now Alan thought it time to wake up. He opened his eyes, stared at her vacantly, and asked if it were raining, which indeed it might have been, for her big tears were falling on his face. She uttered a gasp of joy.

"No, no," she answered, "the weather is very fine. It is I—I who have rained because I thought you die." She wiped his forehead with the soft linen of her robe, then went on, "But you will not die; say that you will live, say that you will live for me, Vernoon."

He looked at her, and feeble though he was, the awfulness of the situation sank into his soul.

"I hope that I shall live," he answered. "I am hungry, please give me some food."

Next instant there was a tumult near by, and when Alan looked up again it was to see Jeekie, very lightly clad, flying through the door.

"It will be here presently," she said. "Oh! if you knew what I have suffered, if you only knew. Now you will recover whom I thought dead, for this fever passes quickly and there shall be such a sacrifice—no, I forgot, you hate sacrifices—there shall be no sacrifice, there shall be a thanksgiving, and every woman in the land shall break her bonds to husband or to lover and take him whom she desires without reproach or loss. I will do as I would be done by, that is the law you taught me, is it not?"

This novel interpretation of a sacred doctrine, worthy of Jeekie himself, so paralyzed Alan's enfeebled brain that he could make no answer, nor do anything except wonder what would happen in Asiki-land when the decree of its priestess took effect. Then Jeekie arrived with something to drink which he swallowed with the eagerness of the convalescent and almost immediately went to sleep in good earnest.

Alan's recovery was rapid, since as the Asika had told him, if a patient lives through it, the kind of fever that he had taken did not last long enough to exhaust his vital forces. When she asked him if he needed anything to make him well, he answered:

"Yes, air and exercise."

She replied that he should have both, and next morning his hated mask was put upon his face and he was supported by priests to a door where a litter, or rather litters were waiting, one for himself and another for Jeekie who, although in robust health, was still supposed to be officially ill and not allowed to walk upon his own legs. They entered these litters and were borne off till presently they met a third litter of particularly gorgeous design carried by masked bearers, wherein was the Asika herself, wearing her coronet and a splendid robe.

Into this litter, which was fitted with a second seat, Alan was transferred, the Mungana, for whom it was designed, being placed in that vacated by Alan, which either by accident or otherwise, was no more seen that day. They went up the mountain side and to the edge of the great fall and watched the waters thunder down, though the crest of them they could not reach. Next they wandered off into the huge forests that clothed the slopes of the hills and there halted and ate. Then as the sun sank they returned to the gloomy Bonsa-Town beneath them.

For Alan, notwithstanding his weakness and anxieties, it was a heavenly day. The Asika was passive, some new mood being on her, and scarcely troubled him at all except to call his attention to a tree, a flower, or a prospect of the scenery. Here on the mountain side, too, the air was sweet, and for the rest—well, he who had been so near to death, was escaped for an hour from that gloomy home of bloodshed and superstition, and saw God's sky again.

This journey was the first of many. Every day the litters were waiting and they visited some new place, although into the town itself they never went. Moreover, if they passed through outlying villages, though Alan was forced to wear his mask, their inhabitants had been warned to absent themselves, so that they saw no one. The crops were left untended and the cattle and sheep lowed hungrily in their kraals. On certain days, at Alan's request, they were taken to the spots where the gold was found in the gravel bed of an almost dry stream that during the rains was a torrent.

He descended from the litter and with the help of the Asika and Jeekie, dug a little in this gravel, not without reward, for in it they found several nuggets. Above, too, where they went afterwards, was a huge quartz reef denuded by water, which evidently had been worked in past ages and was still so rich that in it they saw plenty of visible gold. Looking at it Alan bethought him of his City days and of the hundreds of thousands of pounds capital with which this unique proposition might have been floated. Afterwards they were carried to the places where the gems were found, stuck about in the clay, like plums in a pudding, though none ever sought them now. But all these things interested the Asika not at all.

"What is the good of gold," she asked of Alan, "except to make things of, or the bright stones except to play with? What is the good of anything except food to eat and power and wisdom that can open the secret doors of knowledge, of things seen and things unseen, and love that brings the lover joy and forgetfulness of self and takes away the awful loneliness of the soul, if only for a little while?"

Not wishing to drift into discussion on the matter of love, Alan asked the priestess to define her "soul," whence it came and whither she believed it to be going.

"My soul is I, Vernoon," she answered, "and already very, very old. Thus it has ruled amongst this people for thousands of years."

"How is that?" he asked, "seeing that the Asika dies?"

"Oh! no, Vernoon, she does not die; she only changes. The old body dies, the spirit enters into another body which is waiting. Thus until I was fourteen I was but a common girl, the daughter of a headman of that village yonder, at least so they tell me, for of this time I have no memory. Then the Asika died and as I had the secret marks and the beauty that is hers the priests burnt her body before Big Bonsa and suffocated me, the child, in the smoke of the burning. But I awoke again and when I awoke the past was gone and the soul of the Asika filled me, bringing with it its awful memories, its gathered wisdom, its passion of love and hate, and its power to look backward and before."

"Do you ever do these things?" asked Alan.

"Backward, yes, before very little; since you came, not at all, because my heart is a coward and I fear what I might see. Oh! Vernoon, Vernoon, I know you and your thoughts. You think me a beautiful beast who loves like a beast, who loves you because you are white and different from our men. Well, what there is of the beast in me the gods of my people gave, for they are devils and I am their servant. But there is more than that, there is good also which I have won for myself. I knew you would come even before I had seen your face, I knew you would come," she went on passionately, "and that is why I was yours already. But what would befall after you came, that I neither knew, nor know, because I will not seek, who could learn it all."

He looked at her and she saw the doubt in his eyes.

"You do not believe me, Vernoon. Very well, this night you shall see, you and that black dog of yours, that you may know I do not trick you, and he shall tell me what you see, for he being but a low-born pig will speak the truth, not minding if it hurts me, whereas you are gentle and might spare, and myself I have sworn not to search the future by an oath that I may not break."

"What of the past?" asked Alan.

"We will not waste time on it, for I know it all. Vernoon, have you no memories of Asiki-land? Do you think you never visited it before?"

"Never," said Alan; "it was my uncle who came and ran away with Little Bonsa on his head."

"That is news indeed," she replied mockingly. "Did you then think that I believed it to be you, though it is true that she who went before, or my spirit that was in her, fell into error for an hour, and thought that fool-uncle of yours was the Man. When she found her mistake she let him go, and bade the god go with him that it might bring back the appointed Man, as it has done; yes, that Little Bonsa, who knew him of old, might search him out from among all the millions of men, born or unborn, and bring him back to me. Therefore also she chose a young black dog who would live for many years, and bade the god to take him with her, and told him of the wealth of our people that it might be a bait upon the hook. Do you see, Vernoon, that yellow dirt was the bait, that I—I am the hook? Well, you have felt it before, so it should not gall you overmuch."

Now Alan was more frightened than he had been since he set foot in Asiki-land, for of a sudden this woman became terrible to him. He felt that she knew things which were hidden from him. For the first time he believed in her, believed, that she was more than a mere passionate savage set by chance to rule over a bloodthirsty tribe; that she was one who had a part in his destiny.

"Felt the hook?" he muttered. "I do not understand."

"You are very forgetful," she answered. "Vernoon, we have lived and loved before, who were twin souls from the first. That man now, whom I told you lived once on the great river called the Nile, have you no memory of him? Well, well, let it be, I will tell you afterwards. Here we are at the Gold House again, to-night when I am ready I will send for you, and this I promise, you shall leave me wiser than you were."

When they were alone in their room Alan told Jeekie of the expected entertainment of crystal gazing, or whatever it might be, and the part that he was to play in it.

"You say that again, Major," said Jeekie.

Alan repeated the information, giving every detail that he could remember.

"Oh!" said Jeekie, "I see Asika show us things, 'cause she afraid to look at them herself, or take oath, or can't, or something. She no ask you tell her what she see, because you too kind hurt her feeling, if happen to be something beastly. But Jeekie just tell her because he so truthful and not care curse about her feeling. Well, that all right, Jeekie tell her sure enough. Only, Major, don't you interrupt. Quite possible these magic things, I see one show, you see another. So don't you go say, 'Jeekie, that a lie,' and give me away to Asika just because you think you see different, 'cause if so you put me into dirty hole, and of course I catch it afterwards. You promise, Major?"

"Oh! yes, I promise. But, Jeekie, do you really think we are going to see anything?"

"Can't say, Major," and he shook his head gloomily. "P'raps all put up job. But lots of rum things in world, Major, specially among beastly African savage who very curious and always ready pay blood to bad Spirit. Hope Asika not get this into her head, because no one know what happen. P'raps we see too much and scared all our lives; but p'raps all tommy rot."

"That's it—tommy rot," answered Alan, who was not superstitious. "Well, I suppose that we must go through with it. But oh! Jeekie, I wish you would tell me how to get out of this."

"Don't know, Major, p'raps never get out; p'raps learn how to-night. Have to do something soon if want to go. Mungana's time nearly up, and then—oh my eye!"

It was night, about ten o'clock indeed, the hour at which Alan generally went to bed. No message had come and he began to hope that the Asika had forgotten, or changed her mind, and was just going to say so to Jeekie when a light coming from behind him attracted his attention and he turned to see her standing in a corner of the great room, holding a lamp in her hand and looking towards him. Her gold breastplate and crown were gone, with every other ornament, and she was clad, or rather muffled in robes of pure white fitted with a kind of nun's hood which lay back upon her shoulders. Also on her arm she carried a shawl or veil. Standing thus, all undecked, with her long hair fastened in a simple knot, she still looked very beautiful, more so than she had ever been, thought Alan, for the cruelty of her face had faded and was replaced by a mystery very strange to see. She did not seem quite like a natural woman, and that was the reason, perhaps, that Alan for the first time felt attracted by her. Hitherto she had always repelled him, but this night it was otherwise.

"How did you come here?" he asked in a more gentle voice than he generally used towards her.

Noting the change in his tone, she smiled shyly and even coloured a little, then answered:

"This house has many secrets, Vernoon. When you are lord of it you shall learn them all, till then I may not tell them to you. But, come, there are other secrets which I hope you shall see to-night, and, Jeekie, come you also, for you shall be the mouth of your lord, so that you may tell me what perhaps he would hide."

"I will tell you everything, everything, O Asika," answered Jeekie, stretching out his hands and bowing almost to the ground.

Then they started and following many long passages as before, although whether they were the same or others Alan could not tell, came at last to a door which he recognized, that of the Treasure House. As they approached this door it opened and through it, like a hunted thing, ran the bedizened Mungana, husband of the Asika, terror, or madness, shining in his eyes. Catching sight of his wife, who bore the lamp, he threw himself upon his knees and snatching at her robe, addressed some petition to her, speaking so rapidly that Alan could not follow his words.

For a moment she listened, then dragged her dress from his hand and spurned him with her foot. There was something so cruel in the gesture and the action, so full of deadly hate and loathing, that Alan, who witnessed it, experienced a new revulsion of feeling towards the Asika. What kind of a woman must she be, he wondered, who could treat a discarded lover thus in the presence of his successor?

With a groan or a sob, it was difficult to say which, the poor man rose and perceived Alan, whose face he now beheld for the first time, since the Asika had told him not to mask himself as they would meet no one. The sight of it seemed to fill him with jealous fury; at any rate he leapt at his rival, intending, apparently, to catch him by the throat. Alan, who was watching him, stepped aside, so that he came into violent contact with the wall of the passage and, half-stunned by the shock, reeled onwards into the darkness.

"The hog!" said the Asika, or rather she hissed it, "the hog, who dared to touch me and to strike at you. Well, his time is short—would that I could make it shorter! Did you hear what he sought of me?"

Alan, who wished for no confidences, replied by asking what the Mungana was doing in the Treasure House, to which she answered that the spirits who dwelt there were eating up his soul, and when they had devoured it all he would go quite mad and kill himself.

"Does this happen to all Munganas?" inquired Alan.

"Yes, Vernoon, if the Asika hates them, but if she loves them it is otherwise. Come, let us forget the wretch, who would kill you if he could," and she led the way into the hall and up it, passing between the heaps of gold.

On the table where lay the necklaces of gems she set down her lamp, whereof the light, all there was in that great place, flickered feebly upon the mask of Little Bonsa, which had been moved here apparently for some ceremonial purpose, and still more feebly upon the hideous, golden countenances and winding sheets of the ancient, yellow dead who stood around in scores placed one above the other, each in his appointed niche. It was an awesome scene and one that oppressed Jeekie very much, for he murmured to Alan:

"Oh my! Major, family vault child's play to this hole, just like—" here his comparison came to an end, for the Asika cut it short with a single glance.

"Sit here in front of me," she said to Alan, "and you, Jeekie, sit at your lord's side, and be silent till I bid you speak."

Then she crouched down in a heap behind them, threw the cloth or veil she carried over her head, and in some way that they did not see, suddenly extinguished the lamp.

Now they were in deep darkness, the darkness of death, and in utter silence, the silence of the dead. No glimmer of light, and yet to Alan it seemed as though he could feel the flash of the crystal eyes of Little Bonsa, and of all the other eyes set in the masks of those departed men who once had been the husbands of the bloodstained priestess of the Asiki, till one by one, as she wearied of them, they were bewitched to madness and to doom. In that utter quiet he thought even that he could hear them stir within their winding sheets, or it may have been that the Asika had risen and moved among them on some errand of her own. Far away something fell to the floor, a very light object, such as flake of rock or a scale of gold. Yet the noise of it struck his nerves loud as a clap of thunder, and those of Jeekie also, for he felt him start at his side and heard the sudden hammerlike beat of his heart.

What was the woman doing in this dreadful place, he wondered. Well, it was easy to guess. Doubtless she had brought them here to scare and impress them. Presently a voice, that of some hidden priest, would speak to them, and they would be asked to believe it a message from the spirit world, or a spirit itself might be arranged—what could be easier in their mood and these surroundings?

Now the Asika was speaking behind them in a muffled voice. From the tone of it she appeared to be engaged in argument or supplication in some strange tongue. At any rate Alan could not understand a word of what she said. The argument, or prayer, went on for a long while, with pauses as though for answers. Then suddenly it ceased and once more they were plunged into that unfathomable silence.

CHAPTER XVI

WHAT THE ASIKA SHOWED ALAN

It seemed to Alan that he went to sleep and dreamed.

He dreamed that it was late autumn in England. Leaves drifted down from the trees beneath the breath of a strong, damp wind, and ran or floated along the road till they vanished into a ditch, or caught against a pile of stones that had been laid ready for its repair. He knew the road well enough; he even knew the elm tree beneath which he seemed to stand on the crest of a hill. It was that which ran from Mr. Champers-Haswell's splendid house, The Court, to the church; he could see them both, the house to the right, the church to the left, and his eyesight seemed to have improved, since he was able to observe that at either place there was bustle and preparation as though for some big ceremony.

Now the big gates of The Court opened and through them came a funeral. It advanced toward him with unnatural swiftness, as though it floated upon air, the whole melancholy procession of it. In a few seconds it had come and gone and yet during those seconds he suffered agony, for there arose in his mind a horrible terror that this was Barbara's burying. He could not have endured it for another moment; he would have cried out or died, only now the mourners passed him following the coffin, and in the first carriage he saw Barbara seated, looking sad and somewhat troubled, but well. A little further down the line came another carriage, and in it was Sir Robert Aylward, staring before him with cold, impassive face.

In his dream Alan thought to himself that he must have borrowed this carriage, which would not be strange, as he generally used motors, for there was a peer's coronet upon the panels and the silver-mounted harness.

The funeral passed and suddenly vanished into the churchyard gates, leaving Alan wondering why his cousin Haswell was not seated at Barbara's side. Then it occurred to him that it might be because he was in the coffin, and at that moment in his dream he heard the Asika asking Jeekie what he saw; heard Jeekie answering also, "A burying in the country called England."

"Of whom, Jeekie?" Then after some hesitation, the answer:

"Of a lady whom my lord loves very much. They bury her."

"What was her name, Jeekie?"

"Her name was Barbara."

"Bar-bara, why that you told me was the name of his mother and his sister. Which of them is buried?"

"Neither, O Asika. It was another lady who loved him very much and wanted to marry him, and that was why he ran away to Africa. But now she is dead and buried."

"Are all women in England called Barbara, Jeekie?"

"Yes, O Asika, Barbara means woman."

"If your lord loved this Barbara, why then did he run away from her? Well, it matters not since she is dead and buried, for whatever their spirits may feel, no man cares for a woman that is dead until she clothes herself in flesh again. That was a good vision and I will reward you for it."

"I have earned nothing, O Asika," answered Jeekie modestly, "who only tell you what I see as I must. Yet, O Asika," he added with a note of anxiety in his voice, "why do you not read these magic writings for yourself?"

"Because I dare not, or rather because I can not," she answered fiercely. "Be silent, slave, for now the power of the good broods upon my soul."

The dream went on. A great forest appeared, such a forest as they had passed before they met the cannibals, and set beneath one of the trees, a tent and in that tent Barbara, Barbara weeping. Someone began to lift the flap of the tent. She sprang up, snatching at a pistol that lay beside her, turning its muzzle towards her breast. A man entered the tent. Alan saw his face, it was his own. Barbara let fall the pistol and fell backwards as though a bullet from it had pierced her heart. He leapt towards her, but before he came to where she lay everything had vanished and he heard Jeekie droning out his lies to the Asika, telling her that the vision he had seen was one of her and his master seated with their arms about each other in a chamber of the Golden House.

A third time the dream descended on Alan like a cloud. It seemed to him that he was borne beyond the flaming borders of the world. Everything around was new and unfamiliar, vast, changing, lovely, terrible. He stood alone upon a pearly plain and the sky above him was lit with red moons, many and many of them that hung there like lamps. Spirits began to pass him. He could catch something of their splendour as they sped by with incredible swiftness; he could hear the music of their laughter. One rose up at his side. It was the Asika, only a thousand times more splendid; clothed in all the glory of hell. Majestically she bent towards him, her glowing eyes held his, the deadly perfume of her breath beat upon his brow and made him drunken.

She spoke to him and her voice sounded like distant bells.

"Through many a life, through many a life," she said, "bought with much blood, paid for with a million tears, but mine at last, the soul that I have won to comfort my soul in the eternal day. Come to the place I have made ready for you, the hell that shall turn to heaven at your step, come, you by whom I am redeemed, and drive away those gods that torture me because I was their servant that I might win you."

So she spoke, and though all his soul revolted, yet the fearful strength that was in her seemed to draw him onward whither she would go. Then a light shone and that light was the face of Barbara and with a suddenness that was almost awful, the wild dream came to an end.

Alan was in his own room again, though how he got there he did not recollect.

"Jeekie," he said, "what has happened? I seem to have had a very curious dream, there in the Treasure-place, and to have heard you telling the Asika a string of incredible falsehoods."

"Oh! no, Major, Jeekie can't lie, too good Christian; he tell her what he see, or what he think she see if she look, 'cause though p'raps he see nothing, she never believe that. And," he added with a burst of confidence, "what the dickens it matter what he tell her, so long as she swallow same and keep quiet? Nasty things always make women like Asika quite outrageous. Give them sweet to suck, say Jeekie, and if they ill afterwards, that no fault of his. They had sweet."

"Quite so, Jeekie, quite so, only I should advise you not to play too many tricks upon the Asika, lest she should happen to find you out. How did I get back here?"

"Like man that walk in his sleep, Major. She go first, you follow, just as little lamb after Mary in hymn."

"Jeekie, did you really see anything at all?"

"No, Major, nothing partic'lar, except ghost of Mrs. Jeekie and of your reverend uncle, both of them very angry. That magic all stuff, Major. Asika put something in your grub make you drunk, so that you think her very wise. Don't think of it no more, Major, or you go off your chump. If Jeekie see nothing, depend on it there nothing to see."

"Perhaps so, Jeekie, but I wish I could be sure you had seen nothing. Listen to me; we must get out of this place somehow, or as you say, I shall go off my chump. It's haunted, Jeekie, its haunted, and I think that Asika is a devil, not a woman."

"That what priests say, Major, very old devil—part of Bonsa," he answered, looking at his master anxiously. "Well, don't you fret, Jeekie not afraid of devils, Jeekie get you out in good time. Go to bed and leave it all to Jeekie."

Fifteen more days had gone by, and it was the eve of the night of the second full moon when Alan was destined to become the husband of the Asika. She had sent for him that morning and he found her radiant with happiness. Whether or no she believed Jeekie's interpretation of the visions she had called up, it seemed quite certain that her mind was void of fears and doubts. She was sure that Alan was about to become her husband, and had summoned all the people of the Asiki to be present at the ceremony of their marriage, and incidentally of the death of the Mungana who, poor wretch, was to be forced to kill himself upon that occasion.

Before they parted she had spoken to Alan sweetly enough.

"Vernoon," she said, "I know that you do not love me as I love you, but the love will come, since for your sake I will change myself. I will grow gentle; I will shed no more blood; that of the Mungana shall be the last, and even him I would spare if I could, only while he lives I may not marry you; it is the one law that is stronger than I am, and if I broke it I and you would die at once. You shall even teach me your faith, if you will, for what is good to you is henceforth good to me. Ask what you wish of me, and as an earnest I will do it if I can."

Now Alan looked at her. There was one thing that he wished above all others—that she would let him go. But this he did not dare to ask; moreover, it would have been utterly useless. After all, if the Asika's love was terrible, what would be the appearance of her outraged hate? What could he ask? More gold? He hated the very name of the stuff, for it had brought him here. He remembered the old cannibal chief, Fahni, who, like himself, languished a prisoner, daily expecting death. Only that morning he had implored him to obtain his liberty.

"I thank you, Asika," he said. "Now, if your words are true, set Fahni free and let him return to his own country, for if he stays here he will die."

"Surely, Vernoon, that is a small thing," she answered, smiling, "though it is true that when he gets there he will probably make war upon us. Well, let him, let him." Then she clapped her hands and summoned priests, whom she bade go at once and conduct Fahni out of Bonsa-Town. Also she bade them loose certain slaves who were of the Ogula tribe, that they might accompany him laden with provisions, and send on orders to the outposts that Fahni and his party should pass unmolested from the land.

This done, she began to talk to Alan about many matters, however little he might answer her. Indeed it seemed almost as though she feared to let him leave her side; as though some presentiment of loss oppressed her.

At length, to Alan's great relief, the time came when they must part, since it was necessary for her to attend a secret ceremony of preparation or purification that was called "Putting-off-the-Past." Although she had been thrice summoned, still she would not let him go.

"They call you, Asika," said Alan.

"Yes, yes, they call me," she replied, springing up. "Leave me, Vernoon, till we meet to-morrow to part no more. Oh! why is my heart so heavy in me? That black dog of yours read the visions that I summoned but might not look on, and they were good visions. They showed that the woman who loved you is dead; they showed us wedded, and other deeper things. Surely he would not dare to lie to me, knowing that if he did I would flay him living and throw him to the vultures. Why, then, is my heart so heavy in me? Would you escape me, Vernoon? Nay, you are not so cruel, nor could you do it except by death. Moreover, man, know that even in death you cannot escape me, for there be sure I shall follow you and claim you, to whose side my spirit has toiled for ages, and what is there so strong that it can snatch you from my hand?"

She looked at him a moment, and seizing his hand burst into a flood of tears, and seizing his hand threw herself upon her knees and kissed it again and again.

"Go now," she said, "go, and let my love go with you, through lives and deaths, and all the dreams beyond, oh! let my love go with you, as it shall, Vernoon."

So he went, leaving her weeping on her knees.

During the dark hours that followed Alan and madness were not far apart. What could he do? Escape was utterly impossible. For weeks he and Jeekie had considered it in vain. Even if they could win out of the Gold House fortress, what hope had they of making their way through the crowded, tortuous town where, after the African fashion, peopled walked about all night, every one of whom would recognize the white man, whether he were masked or no? Besides, beyond the town were the river and the guarded walls and gates and beyond them open country where they would be cut off or run down. No, to attempt escape was suicide! Suicide! That gave him an idea, why should he not kill himself? It would be easy enough, for he still had his revolver and a few cartridges, and surely it was better than to enter on such a life as awaited him as the plaything of a priestess of a tribe of fetish-worshipping savages.

But if he killed himself, how about Barbara and how about poor old Jeekie, who would certainly be killed also? Besides, it was not the right thing to do, and while there is life there is always hope.

Alan paused in his walk up and down the room and looked at Jeekie, who sat upon the floor with his back resting against the stone altar, reflectively pulling down his thick under-lip and letting it fly back, negro-fashion.

"Jeekie," he said, "time's up. What am I to do?"

"Do, Major?" he replied with affected cheerfulness. "Oh! that quite simple. Jeekie arrange everything. You marry Asika and by and by, when you master here and tired of her, you give her slip. Very interesting experience; no white man ever have such luck before. Asika not half bad, if she fond of you; she like little girl in song, when she good, she very, very good. At any rate, nothing else to do. Marry Asika or spiflicate, which mean, Major, that Jeekie spiflicate too, and," he added, shaking his white head sadly, "he no like that. One or two little things on his mind that no get time to square up yet. Daren't pray like Christian here, 'cause afraid of Bonsas, and Bonsas come even with him by and by, 'cause he been Christian, so poor Jeekie fall down bump between two stools. 'Postles kick him out of heaven and Bonsas kick him out of hell, and where Jeekie go to then?"

"Don't know, I am sure," answered Alan, smiling a little in spite of his sorrow, "but I think the Bonsas might find a corner for you somewhere. Look here, Jeekie, you old scamp, I am sorry for you, for you have been a good friend to me and we are fond of each other. But just understand this, I am not going to marry that woman if I can help it. It's against my principles. So I shall wait till to-morrow and then I shall walk out of this place. If the guards try to stop me I shall shoot them while I have any cartridges. Then I shall go on until they kill me."

"Oh! But Major, they not kill you—never; they chuck blanket over your head and take you back to Asika. It Jeekie they kill, skin him alive-o, and all the rest of it."

"Hope not, Jeekie, because they think we shall die the same day. But if so, I can't help it. To-morrow morning I shall walk out, and now that's settled. I am tired and going to sleep," and he threw himself down upon the bed and, being worn out with weariness and anxiety, soon fell fast asleep.

But Jeekie did not sleep, although he too lay down upon his bed. On the contrary, he remained wide awake and reflected, more deeply perhaps than he had ever done before, being sure the superstition as to the dependence of Alan's life upon his own was now worn very thin, and that his hour was at hand. He thought of making Alan's wild attempt to depart impossible by the simple method of warning the

Asika, but, notwithstanding his native selfishness, was too loyal to let that idea take root in his mind. No, there was nothing to be done; if the Major wished to start, the Major must start, and he, Jeekie, must pay the price. Well, he deserved it, who had been fool enough to listen to the secret promptings of Little Bonsa and conduct him to Asiki-land.

Thus he passed several hours, for the most part in melancholy speculations as to the exact fashion of his end, until at length weariness overcame him also and, shutting his eyes, Jeekie began to doze. Suddenly he grew aware of the presence of some other person in the room, but thinking that it was only the Asika prowling about in her uncanny fashion, or perhaps her spirit, for how her body entered the place he could not guess, he did not stir, but lay breathing heavily and watching out of the corner of his eye.

Presently a figure emerged from the shadows into the faint light thrown by the single lamp that burned above, and though it was wrapped in a dark cloak, Jeekie knew at once that it was not the Asika. Very stealthily the figure crept towards him, as a leopard might creep, and bent down to examine him. The movement caused the cloak to slip a little, and for an instant Jeekie caught sight of the wasted, half-crazed face of the Mungana, and of a long, curved knife that glittered in his hand. Paralyzed with fear, he lay quite still, knowing that should he show the slightest sign of consciousness that knife would pierce his heart.

The Mungana watched him a while, then satisfied that he slept, turned round and, bending himself almost double, glided with infinite precautions towards Alan's bed, which stood some twelve or fourteen feet away. Silently as a snake that uncoils itself, Jeekie slipped from between his blankets and crept after him, his naked feet making no noise upon the mat-strewn floor. So intent was the Mungana upon the deed which he had come to do that he never looked back, and thus it happened that the two of them reached the bed one immediately behind the other.

Alan was lying on his back with his throat exposed, a very easy victim. For a moment the Mungana stared. Then he erected himself like a snake about to strike, and lifted the great curved knife, taking aim at Alan's naked breast. Jeekie erected himself also, and even as the knife began to fall, with one hand he caught the arm that drove it and with the other the murderer's throat. The Mungana fought like a wild-cat, but Jeekie was too strong for him. His fingers held the man's windpipe like a vice. He choked and weakened; the knife fell from his hand. He sank to the ground and lay there helpless, whereon Jeekie knelt upon his chest and, possessing himself of the knife, held it within an inch of his heart.

It was at this juncture that Alan woke up and asked sleepily what was the matter.

"Nothing, Major," answered Jeekie in low and cheerful tones. "Snake just going to bite you and I catch him, that all," and he gave an extra squeeze to the Mungana's throat, who turned black in the face and rolled his eyes.

"Be careful, Jeekie, or you will kill the man," exclaimed Alan, recognizing the Mungana and taking in the situation.

"Why not, Major? He want kill you, and me too afterwards. Good riddance of bad rubbish, as Book say."

"I am not so sure, Jeekie. Give him air and let me think. Tell him that if he makes any noise, he dies."

Jeekie obeyed, and the Mungana's darkening eyes grew bright again as he drew his breath in great sobs.

"Now, friend," said Alan in Asiki, "why did you wish to stab me?"

"Because I hate you," answered the man, "who to-morrow will take my place and the wife I love."

"As a year or two ago you took someone else's place, eh? Well, suppose now that I don't want either your place or your wife."

"What would that matter even it if were true, white man, since she wants you?"

"I am thinking, friend, that there is someone else she will want when she hears of this. How do you suppose that you will die to-morrow? Not so easily as you hope, perhaps."

The Mungana's eyes seemed to sink into his head, and his face to sicken with terror. That shaft had gone home.

"Suppose I make a bargain with you," went on Alan slowly. "Supposing I say: 'Mungana, show me the way out of this place, as you can, now at once. Or if you prefer it, refuse and be given up to the Asika?' Come, you are not too mad to understand. Answer—and quickly."

"Would you kill me afterwards?" he asked.

"Not I. Why should I wish to kill you? You can come with us and go where you will. Or you can stay here and die as the Asika directs."

"I cannot believe you, white man. It is not possible that you should wish to run away from so much love and glory, or to spare one who would have slain you. Also it would be difficult to get you out of Bonsa-town."

"Jeekie," said Alan, "this fellow is mad after all, I think you had better go to the door and shout for the priests."

"No, no, lord," begged the wretched creature, "I will trust you; I will try, though it is you who must be mad."

"Very good. Stand over him, Jeekie, while I put on my things and, yes, give me that mask. If he stirs, kill him at once."

So Alan made himself ready. Then he mounted guard over the Mungana, as did Jeekie, although he shook his head over their prospect of escape.

"No go," he muttered, "no go! If we get past priests, Asika catch us with her magic. When I bolt with your reverend uncle last time, Little Bonsa arrange business because she go abroad fetch you. Now likely as not she bowl you out, and then good-bye Jeekie."

Alan sternly bade him be quiet and stop behind if he did not wish to come.

"No, no, Major," he answered, "I come all right. Asika very prejudiced beggar, and if she find me here alone—oh my! Better die double after all, Two's company, Major. Now, all ready, March!" and he gave the unfortunate Mungana a fearful kick as a hint to proceed.

So utterly crushed was the poor wretch that even this insult did not stir him to resentment.

"Follow me, white man," he said, "and if you desire to live, be silent. Throw your cloaks about your heads."

They did so, and holding their revolvers in their right hands, glided after the Mungana. In the corner of the big room they came to a little stair. How it opened in that place where no stair had been, they could not see or even guess, for it was too dark, only now they knew the means by which the Asika had been able to visit them at night.

The Mungana went first down the stair. Jeekie followed, grasping him by the arm with one hand, while in the other he kept his own knife ready to stab him at the first sign of treachery. Alan brought up the rear, keeping hold of Jeekie's cloak. They passed down twelve steps of stair, then turned to the right along a tunnel, then to the left, then to the right again. In the pitch darkness it was an awful journey, since they knew not whither they were being led, and expected that every moment would be their last. At length, quite of a sudden, they emerged into moonlight.

Alan looked about him and knew the place. It was where the feast had been held two months before, when the priests were poisoned and the Bonsas chose the victims for sacrifice. Already it was prepared for the great festival of to-morrow, when the Mungana should drown himself and Alan be married to the Asika. There on the dais were the gold chairs in which they were to sit, and green branches of trees mixed with curious flags decked the vast amphitheatre beyond. Moreover, there was the broad canal, and floating in the midst of it the hideous gold fetish, Big Bonsa. The moon shone on its glaring, deathly eyes, its fish-like snout and its huge, pale teeth. Alan looked at it and shivered, for the thing was horrid and uncanny, and the utter loneliness in which it lay staring up at the moon, seemed to accentuate the horror.

The Mungana noticed his fear and whispered:

"We must swim the water. If you have a god, white man, pray him to protect you from Bonsa."

"Lead on," answered Alan, "I do not dread a foul fetish, only the look of it. But is there no way round?"

The Mungana shook his head and began to enter the canal. Jeekie, whose teeth were chattering, hung back, but Alan pushed him from behind, so sharply that he stumbled and made a splash. Then Alan followed, and as the cold, black water rose to his chest, looked again at Big Bonsa.

It seemed to him that the thing had turned round and was staring at them. Surely a few seconds ago its snout pointed the other way. No, that must be fancy. He was swimming now, they were all swimming, Alan and Jeekie holding their pistols and little stock of cartridges above their heads to keep them dry. The gold head of Big Bonsa appeared to be lifting itself up in the water, as a reptile might, in order to get a better view of these proceedings, but doubtless it was the ripples that they caused which gave it this appearance. Only why did the ripples make it come towards them, quite gently, like an investigating fish?

It was about ten yards off and they were in the middle of the canal. The Mungana had passed it. It was in a line with Alan's head. Oh Heavens! a sudden smother of foam, a rush like that of a torpedo, and set low down between two curving waves, a flash of gold. Then a gurgling, inhuman laugh and a weight upon his back. Down went Alan, down and down!

CHAPTER XVII

THE END OF THE MUNGANA

The moonlight above vanished. Alan was alone in the depths with this devil, or whatever it might be. He could feel hands and feet gripping and treading on him, but they did not seem to be human, for there were too many of them. Also they were very cold. He gave himself up for dead and thought of Barbara.

Then something flashed into his mind. In his hand he still held the revolver. He pressed it upwards against the thing that was smothering him, and pulled the trigger. Again he pulled it, and again, for it was a self-cocking weapon, and even there deep down in the water he heard the thud of the explosion of the damp-proof copper cartridges. His lungs were bursting, his senses reeled, only enough of them remained to tell him that he was free of that strangling grip and floating upwards. His head rose above the surface, and through the mouth of his mask he drew in the sweet air with quick gasps. Down below him in the clear water he saw the yellow head of Big Bonsa rocking and quivering like a great reflected moon, saw too that it was beginning to rise. Yet he could not swim away from it, the fetish seemed to have hypnotized him. He heard Jeekie calling to him from the shallow water near the further bank, but still he floated there like a log and stared down at Big Bonsa wallowing beneath.

Jeekie plunged back into the canal and with a few strong strokes reached him, gripped him by the arm and began to tow him to the shore. Before they came there Big Bonsa rose like a huge fish and tried to follow them, but could not, or so it seemed. At any rate it only whirled round and round upon the surface, while from it poured a white fluid that turned the black water to the hue of milk. Then it began to scream, making a thin and dreadful sound more like that of an infant in pain than anything they had ever heard, a very sickening sound that Alan never could forget. He staggered to the bank and stood staring at it where it bled, rolled and shrieked, but because of the milky foam could make nothing out in that light.

"What is it, Jeekie?" he said with an idiotic laugh. "What is it?"

"Oh! don't know. Devil and all, perhaps. Come on, Major, before it catch us."

"I don't think it will catch anyone just at present. Devil or not hollow-nosed bullets don't agree with it. Shall I give it another, Jeekie?" and he lifted the pistol.

"No, no, Major, don't play tomfool," and Jeekie grabbed him by the arm and dragged him away.

A few paces further on stood the Mungana like a man transfixed, and even then Alan noticed that he regarded him with something akin to awe.

"Stronger than the god," he muttered, "stronger than the god," and bounded forward.

Following the path that ran beside the canal, they plunged into a tunnel, holding each other as before. In a few minutes they were through it and in a place full of cedar trees outside the wall of the Gold House, under which evidently the tunnel passed, for there it rose behind them. Beneath these cedar trees they flitted like ghosts, now in the moonlight and now in the shadow.

The great fall to the back of the town was on their left, and in front of them lay one of the arms of the river, at this spot a raging torrent not much more than a hundred feet in width, spanned by a narrow suspension bridge which seemed to be supported by two fibre ropes. On the hither side of this bridge stood a guard hut, and to their dismay out of this hut ran three men armed with spears, evidently to cut them off. One of these men sped across the bridge and took his stand at the further end, while the other two posted themselves in their path at the entrance to it.

The Mungana slacked his speed and said one word—"Finished!" and Jeekie also hesitated, then turned and pointed behind them.

Alan looked back and flitting in and out between the cedar trees, saw the white robes of the priests of Bonsa. Then despair seized them all, and they rushed at the bridge. Jeekie reached it first and dodging beneath the spears of the two guards, plunged his knife into the breast of one of them, and butted the other with his great head, so that he fell over the side of the bridge on to the rocks below.

"Cut, Major, cut!" he said to Alan, who pushed past him. "All right now."

They were on the narrow swaying bridge—it was but a single plank—Alan first, then the Mungana, then Jeekie. When they were half way across Alan looked before him and saw a sight he could never forget.

The third guard at the further side was sawing through one of the fibre ropes with his spear. There they were on the middle of the bridge with the torrent raving fifty feet beneath them, and the man had nearly severed the rope! To get over before it parted was impossible; behind were the priests; beneath the roaring river. All three of them stopped as though paralyzed, for all three had seen. Something struck against Alan's leg, it was his pistol that still remained fastened to his wrist by its leather thong. He cocked and lifted it, took aim and fired. The shot missed, which was not wonderful considering the light and the platform on which the shooter stood. It missed, but the man, astonished, for he had never seen or heard such a thing before, stopped his sawing for a moment, and stared at them. Then as he began again Alan fired once more, and this time by good fortune the bullet struck the man somewhere in the body. He fell, and as he fell grasped the nearly separated rope and hung to it.

"Get hold of the other rope and come on," yelled Alan, and once more they bounded forward.

"My God! it's going," he yelled again. "Hold fast, Jeekie, hold fast!"

Next instant the rope parted and the man vanished. The bridge tipped over, and supported by the remaining rope, hung edgeways up. To this rope the three of them clung desperately, resting their feet upon the edge of the swaying plank. For a few seconds they remained thus, afraid to stir, then Jeekie called out:

"Climb on, Major, climb on like one monkey. Look bad, but quite safe really."

As there was nothing else to be done Alan began to climb, shifting his feet along the plank edge and his hands along the rope, which creaked and stretched beneath their threefold weight.

It was a horrible journey, and in his imagination took at least an hour. Yet they accomplished it, for at last they found themselves huddled together but safe upon the further bank. The sweat pouring down from his head almost blinded Alan; a deadly nausea worked within him, sickly tremors shot up and down his spine; his brain swam. Yet he could hear Jeekie, in whom excitement always took the form of speech, saying loudly:

"Think that man no liar what say our great papas was monkeys. Never look down on monkey no more. Wake up, Major, those priests monkey-men too, for we all brothers, you know. Wait a bit, I stop their little game," and springing up with three or four cuts of the big curved knife, he severed the remaining rope just as their pursuers reached the further side of the chasm.

They shouted with rage as the long bridge swung back against the rock, the cut end of it falling into the torrent, and waved their spears threateningly. To this demonstration Jeekie replied with gestures of contempt such as are known to street Arabs. Then he looked at the Mungana, who lay upon the ground a melancholy and dilapidated spectacle, for the perspiration had washed lines of paint off his face and patches of dye from his hair, also his gorgeous robes were water-stained and his gem necklaces broken. Having studied him a while Jeekie kicked him meditatively till he got up, then asked him to set out the exact situation. The Mungana answered that they were safe for a while, since that torrent could only be crossed by the broken bridge and was too rapid to swim. The Asiki, he added, must go a long journey round through the city in order to come at them, though doubtless they would hunt them down in time.

Here Jeekie cut him short, since he knew all that country well and only wished to learn whether any more bridges had been built across the torrent since he was a boy.

"Now, Major," he said, "you get up and follow me, for I know every inch of ground, also by and by good short cut over mountains. You see Jeekie very clever boy, and when he herd sheep and goat he made note of everything and never forget nothing. He pull you out of this hole, never fear."

"Glad to hear it, I am sure," answered Alan as he rose. "But what's to become of the Mungana?"

"Don't know and don't care," said Jeekie; "no more good to us. Can go and see how Big Bonsa feel, if he like," and stretching out his big hand as though in a moment of abstraction, he removed the costly necklaces from their guide's neck and thrust them into the pouch he wore. Also he picked up the gilded linen mask which Alan had removed from his head and placed it in the same receptacle, remarking, that he "always taught that it wicked to waste anything when so many poor in the world."

Then they started, the Mungana following them. Jeekie paused and waved him off, but the poor wretch still came on, whereon Jeekie produced the big, crooked knife, Mungana's own knife.

"What are you going to do," said Alan, awaking to the situation.

"Cut off head of that cocktail man, Major, and so save him lot of trouble. Also we got no grub, and if we find any he want eat a lot. Chop what do for two p'raps, make very short commons for three. Also he might play dirty trick, so much best dead."

"Nonsense," said Alan sternly; "let the poor devil come along if he likes. One good turn deserves another."

"Just so, Major; that hello-swello want cut our throats, so I want cut his—one good turn deserve another, as wise king say in Book, when he give half baby to woman what wouldn't have it. Well, so be, Major, specially as it no matter, for he not stop with us long."

"You mean that he will run away, Jeekie?"

"Oh! no, he not run away, he in too blue funk for that. But something run away with him, because he ought die to-morrow night. Oh! yes, you see, you see, and Jeekie hope that something not run away with you too, Major, because you ought be married at same time."

"Hope not, I am sure," answered Alan, and bethinking him of Big Bonsa wallowing and screaming on the water and bleeding out white blood, he shivered a little.

By this time, advancing at a trot, the Mungana running after them like a dog, they had entered the bush pierced with a few wandering paths. Along these paths they sped for hour after hour, Jeekie leading them without a moment's hesitation. They met no man and heard nothing, except occasional weird sounds which Alan put down to wild beasts, but Jeekie and the Mungana said were produced by ghosts. Indeed it appeared that all this jungle was supposed to be haunted, and no Asiki would enter it at night, or unless he were very bold and protected by many charms, by day either. Therefore it was an excellent place for fugitives who sorely needed a good start.

At length the day began to dawn just as they reached the main road where it crossed the hills, whence on his journey thither Alan had his first view of Bonsa Town. Peering from the edge of the bush, they perceived a fire burning near the road and round it five or six men, who seemed to be asleep. Their first thought was to avoid them, but the Mungana, creeping up to Alan, for Jeekie he would not approach, whispered:

"Not Asiki, Ogula chief and slaves who left Bonsa Town yesterday."

They crept nearer the fire and saw that this was so. Then rejoicing exceedingly, they awoke the old chief, Fahni, who at first thought they must be spirits. But when he recognized Alan, he flung himself on his knees and kissed his hand, because to him he owed his liberty.

"No time for all that, Fahni," said Alan. "Give us food."

Now of this as it chanced there was plenty, since by the Asika's orders the slaves had been laden with as much as they could carry. They ate of it ravenously, and while they ate, told Fahni something of the story of their escape. The old chief listened amazed, but like Jeekie asked Alan why he had not killed the Mungana, who would have killed him.

Alan, who was in no mood for long explanations, answered that he had kept him with them because he might be useful.

"Yes, yes, friend, I see," exclaimed the old cannibal, "although he is so thin he will always make a meal or two at a pinch. Truly white men are wise and provident. Like the ants, you take thought for the morrow."

As soon as they had swallowed their food they started all together, for although Alan pointed out to Fahni that he might be safer apart, the old chief who had a real affection for him, would not be persuaded to leave him.

"Let us live or die together," he said.

Now Jeekie, abandoning the main road, led them up a stream, walking in the water so that their footsteps might leave no trace, and thus away into the barren mountains which rose between them and the great swamp. On the crest of these mountains Alan turned and looked back towards Bonsa Town. There far across the fertile valley was the hateful, river-encircled place. There fell the great cataract in the roar of which he had lived for so many weeks. There were the black cedars and there gleamed the roofs of the Gold House, his prison where dwelt the Asika and the dreadful fetishes of which she was the priestess. To him it was like the vision of a nightmare, he could scarcely think it real. And yet by this time doubtless they sought him far and wide. What mood, he wondered, would the Asika be in when she learned of his escape and the fashion of it, and how would she greet him if he were recaptured and taken back to her? Well, he would not be recaptured. He had still some cartridges and he would fight till they killed him, or failing that, save the last of them for himself. Never, never could he endure to be dragged back to Bonsa Town there to live and die.

They went on across the mountains, till in the afternoon once more they saw the road running beneath them like a ribbon, and at the end of it the lagoon. Now they rested a while and held a consultation while they ate. Across that lagoon they could not escape without a canoe.

"Lord," said the Mungana presently, "yesterday when these cannibals were let go a swift runner was sent forward commanding that a good boat should be provisioned and made ready for them, and by now doubtless this has been done. Let them descend to the road, walk on to the bay and ask for the boat. Look, yonder, far away a tongue of land covered with trees juts out into the lake. We will make our way thither and after nightfall this chief can row back to it and take us into the canoe."

Alan said that the plan was good, but Jeekie shook his head, asking what would happen if Fahni, finding himself safe upon the water, thought it wisest not to come to fetch them.

Alan translated his words to the old chief, whereon Fahni wanted to fight Jeekie because of the slur that he had cast upon his honour. This challenge Jeekie resolutely declined, saying that already there were plenty of ways to die in Asiki-land without adding another to them. Then Fahni swore by his tribal god and by the spirit of every man he had ever eaten, that he would come to that promontory after dark, if he were still alive.

So they separated, Fahni and his men slipping down to the road, which they did without being seen by anyone, while Alan, Jeekie and the Mungana bore away to the right towards the promontory. The road was long and rough and, though by good fortune they met no one, since the few who dwelt in these wild parts had gone up to Bonsa Town to be present at the great feast, the sun was sinking before ever they reached the place. Moreover, this promontory proved to be covered with dense thorn scrub, through which they must force a way in the gathering darkness, not without hurt and difficulty. Still they accomplished it and at length, quite exhausted, crept to the very point, where they hid themselves between some stones at the water's edge.

Here they waited for three long hours, but no boat came.

"All up a gum-tree now, Major," said Jeekie. "Old blackguard, Fanny, bolt and leave us here, and to-morrow morning Asika nobble us. Better have gone down to bay, steal his boat and leave him behind, because Asika no want him."

Alan made no answer. He was too tired, and although he trusted Fahni, it seemed likely enough that Jeekie was right, or perhaps the cannibals had not been able to get the boat. Well, he had done his best, and if Fate overtook them it was no fault of his. He began to doze, for even their imminent peril could not keep his eyes open, then presently awoke with a start, for in his sleep he thought he heard the sounds of paddles beating the quiet water. Yes, there dimly seen through the mist, was a canoe, and seated in the stern of it Fahni. So that danger had gone by also.

He woke his companions, who slept at his side, and very silently they rose, stepping from rock to rock till they reached the canoe and entered it. It was not a large craft, barely big enough to hold them all indeed, but they found room, and then at a sign from Fahni the oarsmen gave way so heartily that within half an hour they had lost sight of the accursed shores of Asiki-land, although presently its mountains showed up clearly beneath the moon.

Meanwhile Fahni had told his tale. It appeared that when he reached the bay he found the Asiki headman who dwelt there, and those under him, in a state of considerable excitement.

Rumours had reached them that someone had escaped from Bonsa Town; they thought it was the Mungana. Fahni asked who had brought the rumour, whereon the headman answered that it came "in a dream," and would say no more. Then he demanded the canoe which had been promised to him and his people, and the headman admitted that it was ready in accordance with orders received from the Asika, but demurred to letting him have it. A long argument followed, in the midst of which Fahni and his men got into the canoe, the headman apparently not daring to use force to prevent him. Just as they were pushing off a messenger arrived from Bonsa Town, reeling with exhaustion and his tongue hanging from his jaws, who called out that it was the white man who had escaped with his servant and the Mungana, and that although they were believed to be still hidden in the holy woods near Bonsa Town, none were to be allowed to leave the bay. So the headman shouted to Fahni to return, but he pretended not to hear and rowed away, nor did anyone attempt to follow him. Still it was only after nightfall that he dared to put the boat about and return to the headland to pick up Alan and the others as he had promised. That was all he had to say.

Alan thanked him heartily for his faithfulness and they paddled on steadily, putting mile after mile of water between them and Asiki-land. He wondered whether he had seen the last of that country and its inhabitants. Something within him answered No. He was sure that the Asika would not allow him to depart in peace without making some desperate effort to recapture him. Far as he was away, it seemed to him that he could feel her fury hanging over him like a cloud, a cloud that would burst in a rain of blood. Doubtless it would have burst already had it not been for the accident that he and his companions were still supposed to be hiding in the woods. But that error must be discovered, and then would come the pursuit.

He looked at the full moon shining upon him and reflected that at this very hour he should have been seated upon the chair of state, wedding, or rather being wedded by the Asika in the presence of Big and Little Bonsa and all the people. His eye fell upon the Mungana, who had also been destined to play a prominent part in that ceremony. At once he saw that there was something wrong with the man. A curious change had come over his emaciated face. It was working like that of a maniac. Foam appeared upon his dyed lips, his haunted eyes rolled, his thin hands gripped the side of the canoe and he began to sing, or rather howl like a dog baying at the stars. Jeekie hit him on the head and bade him be silent, but he took no notice, even when he hit him again more heavily. Presently came the climax. The man sprang up in the canoe, causing it to rock from side to side. He pointed to the full moon above and howled more loudly than before; he pointed to something that he seemed to see in the air near by and gibbered as though in terror. Then his eyes fixed themselves upon the water at which he stared.

Harder and harder he stared, his head sinking lower every moment, till at length without another sound, very quietly and unexpectedly he went over the side of the boat. For a few seconds they saw his bright-coloured garments sinking to the depths, then he vanished.

They waited a while, expecting that he would rise again. But he never rose. A shot-weighted corpse could not have disappeared more finally and completely. The thing was very awful, and for a while there was silence, which as usual was broken by Jeekie.

"That gay dog gone," he said in a reflective voice. "All those old ghosts come to fetch him at proper time. No good run away from ghosts; they travel too quick; one jump, and pop up where you no expect. Well, more place for Jeekie now," and he spread himself out comfortably in the empty seat, adding, "like hello-swello's room much better than company, he go in scent-bath every day and stink too much, all that water never wash him clean."

Thus died the Mungana, and such was the poor wretch's requiem. With a shiver Alan reflected that had it not been for him and his insane jealousy, he too might have been expected to go into that same scent-bath and have his face painted like a chorus girl. Only would he escape the spell that had destroyed his predecessor in the affections of the priestess of the Bonsas? Or would some dim power such as had drawn Mungana to the death drag him back to the arms of the Asika or to the torture pit of "Great Swimming Head." He remembered his dream in the Treasure Hall and shuddered at the very thought of it, for all he had undergone and seen made him superstitious; then bade the men paddle faster, ever faster.

All that night they rowed on, taking turns to rest, except Alan and Jeekie, who slept a good deal and as a consequence awoke at dawn much refreshed. When the sun rose they found themselves across the lagoon, over thirty miles from the borders of Asiki-land, almost at the spot where the river up which they had travelled some months before, flowed out of the lake. Whether by chance or skill Fahni had steered a wonderfully straight course. Now, however, they were face to face with a new trouble, for scarcely had they begun to descend the river when they discovered that at this dry season of the year it was in many places too shallow to allow the canoe to pass over the sand and mud banks. Evidently there was but one thing to be done—abandon it and walk.

So they landed, ate from their store of food and began a terrible and toilsome journey. On either side of the river lay dessicated swamp covered with dead reeds ten or twelve feet high. Doubtless beyond the swamp there was high land, but in order to reach this, if it existed, they would be obliged to force a path through miles of reeds. Therefore they thought it safer to follow the river bank. Their progress was very slow, since continually they must make detours to avoid a quicksand or a creek, also the stones and scrubby growth delayed them so that fifteen or at most twenty miles was a good day's march.

Still they went on steadily, seeing no man, and when their food was exhausted, living on the fish which they caught in plenty in the shallows, and on young flapper ducks that haunted the reeds. So at length they came to the main river into which this tributary flowed, and camped there thankfully, believing that if any pursuit of them had been undertaken, it was abandoned. At least Alan and the rest believed this, but Jeekie did not.

On the following morning, shortly after dawn, Jeekie awoke his master.

"Come here, Major," he said in a solemn voice, "I got something pretty show you," and he led him to the foot of an old willow tree, adding, "now up you go, Major, and look."

So Alan went up and from the topmost fork of that tree saw a sight at which his blood turned cold. For there, not five miles behind them, on either side of the river bank, the light gleaming on their spears, marched two endless columns of men, who from their head-dresses he took to be Asiki. For a minute he looked, then descended the tree and approaching the others, asked what was to be done.

"Hook, scoot, bolt, leg it!" exclaimed Jeekie emphatically; then he licked his finger, held it up to the wind and added, "but first fire reeds and make it hot for Bonsa crowd."

This was a good suggestion and one on which they acted without delay. Taking red embers, they blew them into a flame and lit torches, which they applied to the reeds over a width of several hundred yards. The strong northward wind soon did the rest; indeed with a quarter of an hour a vast sheet of flame twenty or thirty feet in height was rushing towards the Asiki columns. Then they began their advance along the river bank, running at a steady trot, for here the ground was open.

All that day they ran, pausing at intervals to get their breath, and at night rested because they must. When the light came upon the following morning they looked back from a little hill and saw the outposts of the Asiki advancing not a mile behind. Doubtless some of the army had been burned, but the rest, guessing their route, had forced a way through the reeds and cut across country. So they began to run again harder than before, and kept their lead during the morning. But when afternoon came the Asika gained on them. Now they were breasting a long rise, the river running in the cleft beneath, and Jeekie, who seemed to be absolutely untiring, held Alan by the hand, Fahni following close behind. Two of their men had fallen down and been abandoned, and the rest straggled.

"No go, Jeekie," gasped Alan, "they will catch us at the top of the hill."

"Never say die, Major, never say die," puffed Jeekie, "they get blown too and who know what other side of hill?"

Somehow they struggled to the crest and behold! there beneath them was a great army of men.

"Ogula!" yelled Jeekie, "Ogula! Just what I tell you, Major, who know what other side of any hill."

CHAPTER XVIII

In five minutes more Alan and Jeekie were among the Ogula, who, having recognized their chief while he was yet some way off, greeted him with rapturous cheers and the clapping of hands. Then as there was no time for explanation, they retreated across a little stream which ran down the valley, four thousand or more of them, and prepared for battle. That evening, however, there was no fighting, for when the first of the Asiki reached the top of the rise and saw that the fugitives had escaped to the enemy, who were in strength, they halted and finally retired.

Now Alan, and Fahni also, hoped that the pursuit was abandoned, but again Jeekie shook his big head, saying:

"Not at all, Major, I know Asiki and their little ways. While one of them alive, not dare go back to Asika without you, Major."

"Perhaps she is with them herself," suggested Alan, "and we might treat with her."

"No, Major, Asika never leave Bonsa Town, that against law, and if she do so, priests make another Asika and kill her when they catch her."

After this a council of war was held, and it was decided to camp there that night, since the position was good to meet an attack if one should be made, and the Ogula were afraid of being caught on the march with their backs towards the enemy. Alan was glad enough to hear this decision, for he was quite worn out and ready to take any risk for a few hours' rest. At this council he learned also that the Asiki bearers carrying his gold with their Ogula guides had arrived safely among the Ogula, who had mustered in answer to their chief's call and were advancing towards Asiki-land, though the business was one that did not please them. As for these Asiki bearers, it seemed that they had gone on into the forest with the gold, and nothing more had been heard of them.

As they were leaving the council Alan asked Jeekie if he had any tidings of his mother, who had been their first messenger.

"No, Major," he answered gloomily, "can't learn nothing of my ma, don't know where she is. Ogula camp no place for old girl if they short of chop and hungry. But p'raps she never get there; I nose round and find out."

Apparently Jeekie did "nose round" to some purpose, for just as Alan was dropping off to sleep in his bough shelter a most fearful din arose without, through which he recognized the vociferations of Jeekie. Running out of the shelter he discovered his retainer and a great Ogula whom he knew again as the headman who had been imprisoned with him and freed by the Asika to guide the bearers, rolling over and over on the ground, watched by a curious crowd. Just as he arrived Jeekie, who notwithstanding his years was a man of enormous strength, got the better of the Ogula and kneeling on his stomach, was proceeding to throttle him. Rushing at him, Alan dragged him off and asked what was the matter.

"Matter, Major!" yelled the indignant Jeekie. "My ma inside this black villain, that the matter. Dirty cannibal got digestion of one ostrich and eat her up with all his mates, all except one who not like her taste and tell me. They catch poor old lady asleep by road so stop and lunch at once when Asiki bearers not looking. Let me get at him, Major, let me get at him. If I can't bury my ma, as all good son ought to do, I bury him, which next best thing."

"Jeekie, Jeekie," said Alan, "exercise a Christian spirit and let bygones be bygones. If you don't, you will make a quarrel between us and the Ogula, and they will give us up to the Asiki. Perhaps the man did not eat your mother; I understand that he denies it, and when you remember what she was like, it seems incredible. At any rate he has a right to a trial, and I will speak to Fahni about it to-morrow."

So they were separated, but as it chanced that case never came on, for next morning this Ogula was killed in the fighting together with two of his companions, while the others involved in the charge kept themselves out of sight. Whether Jeekie's "ma" was or was not eaten by the Ogula no one ever learned for certain. At least she was never heard of any more.

Alan was sleeping heavily when a sound of rushing feet and of strange, thrilling battle-cries awoke him. He sprang up, snatching at a spear and shield which Jeekie had provided for him, and ran out to find from the position of the moon that dawn was near.

"Come on, Major," said Jeekie, "Asiki make night attack; they always like do everything at night who love darkness, because their eye evil. Come on quick, Major," and he began to drag him off toward the rear.

"But that's the wrong way," said Alan presently. "They are attacking over there."

"Do you think Jeekie fool, Major, that he don't know that? He take you where they not attacking. Plenty Ogula to be killed, but not many white men like you, and in all world only one Jeekie!"

"You cold-blooded old scoundrel!" ejaculated Alan as he turned and bolted back towards the noise of fighting, followed by his reluctant servant.

By the time that he reached the first ranks, which were some way off, the worst of the attack was over. It had been short and sharp, for the Asiki had hoped to find the Ogula unprepared and to take their camp with a rush. But the Ogula, who knew their habits, were waiting for them, so that presently they withdrew, carrying off their wounded and leaving about fifty dead upon the ground. As soon as he was quite sure that the enemy were all gone, Jeekie, armed with a large battle-axe, went off to inspect these fallen soldiers. Alan, who was helping the Ogula wounded, wondered why he took so much interest in them. Half an hour later his curiosity was satisfied, for Jeekie returned with over twenty heavy gold rings, torques, and bracelets slung over his shoulder.

"Where did you get those, Jeekie?" he asked.

"Off poor chaps that peg out just now, Major. Remember Asiki soldiers nearly always wear these things and that they no more use to them. But if ever he get out of this Jeekie want spend his old age in respectable peace. So he fetch them. Hard work, though, for rings all in one bit and Asiki very tough to chop. Don't look cross, Major; you remember what 'postle say, that he who no provide for his own self worse than cannibal."

Just then Fahni came up and announced that the Asiki general had sent a messenger into the camp proposing terms of peace.

"What terms?" asked Alan.

"These, white man: that we should surrender you and your servant and go our way unharmed."

"Indeed, Fahni, and what did you answer?"

"White man, I refused; but I tell you," he added warningly, "that my captains wished to accept. They said that I had come back to them safe and that they fear the Asiki, who are devils, not men, and who will bring the curse of Bonsa on us if we go on fighting with them. Still I refused, saying that if they gave you up I would go with you, who saved my life from the lion and afterwards from the priests of Bonsa. So the messenger went back and, white man, we march at once, and I pray you always to keep close to me that I may watch over you."

Then began that long tramp down the river, which Alan always thought afterwards tried him more than any of the terrible events of his escape. For although there was but little fighting, only rearguard actions indeed, every day the Asiki sent messengers renewing their offers of peace on the sole condition of the surrender of himself and Jeekie. At last one evening they came to that place where Alan first met the Ogula, and once more he camped upon the island on which he had shot the lion. At nightfall, after he had eaten, Fahni visited him here and Alan boded evil from his face.

"White man," he said, "I can protect you no longer. The Asiki messengers have been with us again and they say that unless we give you up to-morrow at the dawn, their army will push on ahead of us and destroy my town, which is two days' march down the river, and all the women and children in it, and that afterwards they will fight a great battle with us. Therefore my people say that I must give you up, or that if I do not they will elect another chief and do so themselves."

"Then you will give up a dead man, Fahni."

"Friend," said the old chief in a low voice, "the night is dark and the forest not so far away. Moreover, I have set no guards on that side of the river, and Jeekie here does not forget a road that he has travelled. Lastly, I have heard it said that there are some other white people with soldiers camped in the edge of the forest. Now, if you were not here in the morning, how could I give you up?"

"I understand, Fahni. You have done your best for me, and now, good-night. Jeekie and I are going to take a walk. Sometimes you will think of the months we spent together in Bonsa-Town, will you not?"

"Yes, and of you also, white man, for so long as I shall live. Walk fast and far, for the Asiki are clever at following a spoor. Good-night, Friend, and to you, Jeekie the cunning, good-night also. I go to tell my captains that I will surrender you at dawn," and without more words he vanished out of their sight and out of their lives.

Meanwhile Jeekie, foreseeing the issue of this talk, was already engaged in doing up their few belongings, including the gold rings, some food, and a native cooking pot, in a bundle surrounded by a couple of bark blankets.

"Come on, Major," he said, handing Alan one spear and taking another himself. "Old cannibal quite right, very nice night for a walk. Come on, Major, river shallow just here. I think this happen and try it before dark. You just follow Jeekie, that all you got to do."

So leaving the fire burning in front of their bough shelter, they waded the stream and started up the opposing slope, meeting no man. Dark as it was, Jeekie seemed to have no difficulty in finding the way, for as Fahni said, a native does not forget the path he has once travelled. All night long they walked rapidly, and when dawn broke found themselves at the edge of the forest.

"Jeekie," said Alan, "what did Fahni mean by that tale about white people?"

"Don't know, Major, think perhaps he lie to let you down easy. My golly! what that?"

As he spoke a distant echo reached their ears, the echo of a rifle shot. "Think Fanny not lie after all," went on Jeekie; "that white man's gun, sharp crack, smokeless powder, but wonder how he come in this place. Well, we soon find out. Come on, Major."

Tired as they were they broke into a run; the prospect of seeing a white face again was too much for them. Half a mile or so further on they caught sight of a figure evidently engaged in stalking game among the trees, or so they judged from his cautious movements.

"White man!" said Jeekie, and Alan nodded.

They crept forward silently and with care, for who knew what this white man might be after, keeping a great tree between them and the man, till at length, passing round its bole, they found themselves face to face with him and not five yards away. Notwithstanding his unaccustomed tropical dress and his face burnt copper colour by the sun, Alan knew the man at once.

"Aylward!" he gasped; "Aylward! You here?"

He started. He stared at Alan. Then his countenance changed. Its habitual calm broke up as it was wont to do in moments of deep emotion. It became very evil, as though some demon of hate and jealousy were at work behind it. The thin lips quivered, the eyes glared, and without spoken word or warning, he lifted the rifle and fired straight at Alan. The bullet missed him, for the aim was high. Passing over Alan's head, it cut a neat groove through the hair of the taller Jeekie who was immediately behind him.

Next instant, with a spring like that of a tiger Jeekie was on Aylward. The weight of his charge knocked him backwards to the ground, and there he lay, pinned fast.

"What for you do that?" exclaimed the indignant Jeekie. "What for you shoot through wool of respectable nigger, Sir Robert Aylward, Bart.? Now I throttle you, you dirty hog-swine. No Magistrates' Court here in Dwarf Forest," and he began to suit the action to the word.

"Let him go, Jeekie. Take his rifle and let him go," exclaimed Alan, who all this while had stood amazed. "There must be some mistake, he cannot have meant to murder me."

"Don't know what he mean, but know his bullet go through my hair, Major, and give me new parting," grumbled Jeekie as he obeyed.

"Of course it was a mistake, Vernon, for I suppose it is Vernon," said Aylward, as he rose. "I do not wonder that your servant is angry, but the truth is that your sudden appearance frightened me out of my wits and I fired automatically. We have been living in some danger here and my nerves are not as strong as they used to be."

"Indeed," answered Alan. "No, Jeekie will carry the rifle for you; yes, and I think that pistol also, every ounce makes a difference walking in a hot climate, and I remember that you always were dangerous with firearms. There, you will be more comfortable so. And now, who do you mean by 'we'?"

"I mean Barbara and myself," he answered slowly.

Alan's jaw dropped, he shook upon his feet.

"Barbara and yourself!" he said. "Do I understand—"

"Don't you understand nothing, Major," broke in Jeekie. "Don't you believe one word what this pig dog say. If Miss Barbara marry him he no want shoot you; he ask you to tea to see the Missus and how much she love him, ducky! We just go on and call on Miss Barbara and hear the news. Walk up, Sir Robert Aylward, Bart., and show us which way."

"I do not choose to receive you and your impertinent servant at my camp," said Aylward, grinding his teeth.

"We quite understand that, Sir Robert Aylward—"

"Lord Aylward, if you please, Major Vernon."

"I beg your pardon—Lord Aylward. I was aware of the contemplated purchase of that title, I did not know that it had been completed. I was about to add that all the same we mean to go to that camp, and that if any violence towards us is attempted as we approach it, you will remember that you are in our hands."

"Yes, my Lord," added Jeekie, bowing, "and that monkeys don't tell no tales, my Lord, and that here there ain't no twelve Good-Trues to sit on noble corpse unhappily deceased, my Lord, and to bring in Crowner's verdict of done to death lawful or unlawful, according as evidence may show when got, my Lord. So march on, for we no breakfast yet. No, not that way, round here to left, where I think I hear kettle sing."

So having no choice, Aylward came, marching between the other two and saying nothing. When they had gone a couple of hundred yards Alan also heard something, and to him it sounded like a man crying out in pain. Then suddenly they passed round some great trees and reached a glade in the forest where there was a spring of water which Alan remembered. In this glade the camp had been built, surrounded by a "boma" or palisade of rough wood, within which stood two tents and some native shelters made of tall grass and boughs. Outside of this camp a curious and unpleasant scene was in progress.

To a small tree that grew there was tied a man, whom from the fashion of his hair Alan knew to belong to the Coast negroes, while two great fellows, evidently of another tribe, flogged him unmercifully with hide whips.

"Ah!" exclaimed Jeekie, "that the kettle I hear sing. Think you better taken him off the fire, my Lord, or he boil over. Also his brothers no seem to like that music," and he pointed to a number of other men who were standing round watching the scene with sullen dissatisfaction.

"A matter of camp discipline," muttered Aylward. "This man has disobeyed orders."

By now Jeekie was shouting something to the natives in an unknown tongue, which they seemed to understand well enough. At any rate the flogging ceased, the two fellows who were inflicting it slunk away, and the other men ran towards them, shouting back as they came.

"All right, Major. You please stop here one minute with my Lord, late Bart. of Bloody Hand. Some of these chaps friends of mine, I meet them Old Calabar while we get ready to march last rains. Now I have little talk with them and find out thing or two."

Aylward began to bluster about interference with his servants and so forth. Jeekie turned on him with a very ugly grin, and showing his white teeth, as was his fashion when he grew fierce.

"Beg pardon, Right Honourable Lord," he said, or rather snarled, "you do what I tell you just to please Jeekie. Jeekie no one in England, but Jeekie damn big Lord too out here, great medicine man, pal of Little Bonsa. You remember Little Bonsa, eh! These chaps think it great honour to meet Jeekie, so, Major, if he stir, please shoot him through head; Jeekie 'sponsible, not you. Or if you not like do it, I come back and see to job myself and don't think those fellows cry very much."

There was something about Jeekie's manner that frightened Aylward, who understood for the first time that beneath all the negro's grotesque talk lay some dreadful, iron purpose, as courage lay under his affected cowardice and under his veneer of selfishness, fidelity. At any rate he halted with Alan, who stood beside him, the revolver of which Aylward had been relieved by Jeekie, in his hand. Meanwhile Jeekie, who held the rifle which he had reloaded, went on and met the natives about twenty yards away.

"We always disliked each other, Vernon, but I must say that I never thought a day would come when you proposed to murder me in my own camp," said Aylward.

"Odd thing," answered Alan, "but a very similar idea was in my mind. I never thought, Lord Aylward, that however unscrupulous you might be—financially—a day would come when you would attempt to shoot down an unarmed man in an African forest. Oh! don't waste breath in lying; I saw you recognize me, aim, and fire, after which Jeekie would have had the other barrel, and who then would have remained to tell the story, Lord Aylward?"

Aylward made no answer, but Alan felt that if wishes could kill him he would not live long. His eye fell upon a long, unmistakable mound of fresh earth, beneath a tree. He calculated its length, and with a thrill of terror noticed that it was too small for a negro.

"Who is buried there?" he asked.

"Find out for yourself," was the sneering answer.

"Don't be afraid, Lord Aylward; I shall find out everything in time."

The conversation between Jeekie and the natives proceeded, their heads were close together; it grew animated. They seemed to be coming to some decision. Presently one of them ran and cut the lashings of the man who had been bound to the tree, and he staggered towards them and joined in the talk, pointing to his wounds. Then the two fellows who had been engaged in flogging him, accompanied by eight companions of the same type—they appeared to be soldiers, for they carried guns—swaggered towards the group who were being addressed by Jeekie, of whom Alan counted twenty-three. As they approached Jeekie made some suggestion which, after one hesitating moment, the others seemed to accept, for they nodded their heads and separated out a little.

Jeekie stepped forward and asked a question of the guards, to which they replied with a derisive shout. Then without a word of warning he lifted Aylward's express rifle which he carried, and fired first one barrel and then the other, shooting the two leading soldiers dead. Their companions halted amazed, but before they could lift their guns, Jeekie and those with him rushed at them and began stabbing them with spears and striking them with sticks. In three minutes it was over without another shot being fired. Most of them were despatched, and the others, throwing down their guns, had fled wounded into the forest.

Now, shouting in jubilation, some of the men began to drag away the dead bodies, while others collected the rifles and the remainder, headed by Jeekie, advanced towards Alan and Aylward, waving their red spears. Alan stood staring, for he did not in the least understand the meaning of what had happened, but Aylward, who had turned very pale, addressed Jeekie, saying:

"I suppose that you have come to murder me also, you black villain."

"No, no, my Lord," answered Jeekie politely, "not at present. Also that wrong word, execute, not murder, just what you do to some of these poor devils," and he pointed to the mob of porters. "Besides, mustn't kill holy white man, poor black chap don't matter, plenty more where he come from. Think we all go see Miss Barbara now. You come too, my Lord Bart., but p'raps best tie your hands behind you first; if you want scratch head, I do it for you. That only fair, you scratch mine this morning."

Then at a word from Jeekie some of the natives sprang on Aylward and tied his hands behind his back.

"Is Miss Barbara alive?" said Alan to Jeekie in an agonized whisper, at the same time nodding towards the grave that was so ominously short.

"Hope so, think so, these cards say so, but God He know alone," answered Jeekie. "Go and look, that best way to find out."

So they advanced into the camp through a narrow gateway made of a V-shaped piece of wood, to where the two tents were placed in its inner division. Of these tents, the first, was open, whereas the second was closed. As the open tent was obviously empty, they went to the second, whereof Jeekie began to loosen the lashings of the flap. It was a long business, for they seemed to have been carefully knotted inside; indeed at last, growing impatient, Jeekie cut the cord, using the curved knife with which the Mungana had tried to kill Alan.

Meanwhile Alan was suffering torments, being convinced that Barbara was dead and buried in that new-made grave beneath the trees. He could not speak, he could scarcely stand, and yet a picture began to form in his numb mind. He saw himself seated in the dark in the Treasure-house at Bonsa-Town; he saw a vision in the air before him.

Lo! the tent door opened and that vision reappeared.

There was the pale Barbara seated, weeping. There again, as he entered she sprang up and snatching the pistol that lay beside her, turned it to her breast. Then she perceived him and the pistol sank downwards till from her relaxed hand it dropped to the ground. She threw up her arms and without a sound fell backwards, or would have fallen, had he not caught her.

CHAPTER XIX

THE LAST OF THE ASIKI

Barbara had recovered. She sat upon her bed in the tent and by her sat Alan, holding her hand, while before them stood Aylward like a prisoner in the dock, and behind him the armed Jeekie.

"Tell me the story, Barbara," said Alan, "and tell it briefly, for I cannot bear much more of this."

She looked at him and began in a slow, even voice:

"After you had gone, dear, things went on as usual for a month or two. Then came the great Sahara Company trouble. First there were rumours and the shares began to go down. My uncle bought them in by tens and hundreds of thousands, to hold up the market, because he was being threatened, but of course he did not know then that Lord Aylward—for I forgot to tell you, he had become a lord somehow—was secretly one of the principal sellers, let him deny it if he can. At last the Ottoman Government, through the English ambassador, published its repudiation of the concession, which it seems was a forgery, actually executed or obtained in Constantinople by my uncle. Well, there was a fearful smash. Writs were taken out against my uncle, but before they could be served, he died suddenly of heart disease. I was with him at the time and he kept saying he saw that gold mask which Jeekie calls Bonsa, the thing you took back to Africa. He had a fine funeral, for what he had done was not publicly known, and when his will was opened I found that he had left me his fortune, but made Lord Aylward there my trustee until I came to the full age of twenty-five under my father's will. Alan, don't force me to tell you what sort of a guardian he was to me; also there was no fortune, it had all gone; also I had very, very little left, for almost all my own money had gone too. In his despair he had forged papers to get it in order to support those Sahara Syndicate shares. Still I managed to borrow about £2000 from that little lawyer out of the £5000 that remain to me, an independent sum which he was unable to touch, and, Alan, with it I came to find you.

"Alan, Lord Aylward followed me; although everybody else was ruined, he remained rich, very very rich, they say, and his fancy was to marry me, also I think it was not comfortable for him in England. It is a long tale, but I got up here with about five-and-twenty servants, and Snell, my maid, whom you remember. Then we were both taken ill with some dreadful fever and had it not been for those good black people, I should have died, for I have been very sick, Alan. But they nursed me and I recovered; it was poor Snell who died, they buried her a few days ago. I thought that she would live, but she had a relapse. Next Lord Aylward appeared with twelve soldiers and some porters who, I believe, have run away now,—oh! you can guess, you can guess. He wanted my people to carry me away somewhere, to the coast, I suppose, but they were faithful to me and would not. Then he set his soldiers on to maltreat them. They shot several of them and flogged them on every opportunity; they were flogging one of them just now, I heard them. Well, the poor men made me understand that they could bear it no longer and must do what he told them.

"And so, Alan, as I was quite hopeless and helpless, I made up my mind to kill myself, hoping that God would forgive me and that I should find you somewhere, perhaps after sleeping a while, for it was better to die than to be given into the power—of that man. I thought that he was coming for me just now and I was about to do it, but it was you instead, Alan, you, and only just in time. That is all the story, and I hope you will not think that I have acted very foolishly, but I did it for the best. If you only knew what I have suffered, Alan, what I have gone through in one way and another, I am sure that you would not judge me harshly; also I kept dreaming that you were in trouble and wanted me to come to you, and of course I knew where you were gone and had that map. Send him away, Alan, for I am still so weak and I cannot bear the sight of his face. If you knew everything, you would understand."

Alan turned on Aylward and in a cold, quiet voice asked him what he had to say to this story.

"I have to say, Major Vernon, that it is a clever mixture of truth and falsehood. It is true that your cousin, Champers-Haswell, has been proved guilty of some very shameful conduct. For instance it appears that he did forge, or rather cause to be forged that Firman from the Sultan, although I knew nothing of this until it was publicly repudiated. It is also true that fearing exposure he entirely lost his head and spent not only his own great fortune but that of Miss Champers also, in trying to support Sahara shares. I admit also that I sold many hundreds of thousands of those shares in the ordinary way, having made up my mind to retire from business when I was raised to the peerage. I admit further, what you knew before, that I was attached to Miss Champers and wished to marry her. Why should I not, especially as I had a good deal to offer to a lady who has been proved to be almost without fortune?

"For the rest she set out secretly on this mad journey to Africa, whither both my duty as her trustee and my affection prompted me to follow her. I found her here recovering from an illness, and since she has dwelt upon the point, in self-defence I must tell you that whatever has taken place between us, has been with her full consent and encouragement. Of course I allude only to those affectionate amenities which are common between people who purpose to marry as soon as opportunity may offer."

At this declaration poor Barbara gasped and leaned back against her pillow. Alan stood silent, though his lips turned white, while Jeekie thrust his big head through the tent opening and stared upwards.

"What are you looking at, Jeekie?" asked Alan irritably.

"Seem to want air, Major, also look to see if clouds tumble. Believe partickler big lie do that sometimes. Please go on, O good Lord, for Jeekie want his breakfast."

"As regards the execution of two of Miss Champers' bearers and the flogging of some others, these punishments were inflicted for mutiny," went on Aylward. "It was obviously necessary that she should be moved back to the coast, but I found out that they were trying to desert her in a body and to tamper with my own servants, and so was obliged to take strong measures."

"Sure those clouds come down now," soliloquized Jeekie, "or least something rummy happen."

"I have only to add, Major Vernon, that unless you make away with me first, as I daresay you will, as soon as we reach civilization again I shall proceed against you and this fellow for the cold-blooded murder of my men, in punishment of which I hope yet to live to see you hanged. Meanwhile, I have much pleasure in releasing Miss Champers from her engagement to me which, whatever she may have said to you in England, she was glad enough to enter on here in Africa, a country of which I have been told the climate frequently deteriorates the moral character."

"Hear, hear!" ejaculated Jeekie, "he say something true at last; by accident, I think, like pig what find pearl in muck-heap."

"Hold your tongue, Jeekie," said Alan. "I do not intend to kill you, Lord Aylward, or to do you any harm—"

"Nor I neither," broke in Jeekie, "all I do to my Lord just for my Lord's good; who Jeekie that he wish to hurt noble British 'ristocrat?"

"But I do intend that it shall be impossible that Miss Champers should be forced to listen to more of your insults," went on Alan, "and to make sure that your gun does not go off again as it did this morning. So, Lord Aylward, until we have settled what we are going to do, I must keep you under arrest. Take him to his tent, Jeekie, and put a guard over him."

"Yes, Major, certainly, Major. Right turn, march! my Lord, and quick, please, since poor, common Jeekie not want dirty his black finger touching you."

Aylward obeyed, but at the door of the tent swung round and favoured Alan with a very evil look.

"Luck is with you for the moment, Major Vernon," he said, "but if you are wise you will remember that you never have been and never will be my match. It will turn again, I have no doubt, and then you may look to yourself, for I warn you I am a bad enemy."

Alan did not answer, but for the first time Barbara sprang to her feet and spoke.

"You mean that you are a bad man, Lord Aylward, and a coward too, or otherwise you would not have tortured me as you have done. Well, when it seemed impossible that I should escape from you except in one way, I was saved by another way of which I never dreamed. Now I tell you that I do not fear you any more. But I think," she added slowly, "that you would do well to fear for yourself. I don't know why, but it comes into my mind that though neither Alan nor I shall lift a finger against you, you have a great deal of which to be afraid. Remember what I said to you months ago when you were angry because I would not marry you. I believe it is all coming true, Lord Aylward."

Then Barbara turned her back upon him, and that was the last time that either she or Alan ever saw his face.

He was gone, and Barbara, her head upon her lover's shoulder and her sweet eyes filled with tears of joy and gratitude, was beginning to tell him everything that had befallen her when suddenly they heard a loud cough outside the tent.

"It's that confounded Jeekie," said Alan, and he called to him to come in.

"What's the matter now?" he asked crossly.

"Breakfast, Major. His lordship got plenty good stores, borrow some from him and give him chit. Coming in one minute—hot coffee, kipper herring, rasher bacon, also butter (best Danish), and Bath Oliver biscuit."

"Very well," said Alan, but Jeekie did not move.

"Very well," repeated Alan.

"No, Major, not very well, very ill. Thought those lies bring down clouds."

"What do you mean, Jeekie?"

"Mean, Major, that Asiki smelling about this camp. Porter-man what go to fetch water see them. Also believe they catch rest of those soldier chaps and polish them, for porter-man hear the row."

Alan sprang up with an exclamation; in his new-found joy he had forgotten all about the Asiki.

"Keep hair on, Major," said Jeekie cheerfully; "don't think they attack yet, plenty of time for breakfast first. When they come we make it very hot for them, lots of rifle and cartridge now."

"Can't we run away?" asked Barbara.

"No, Missy, can't run; must stop here and do best. Camp well built, open all round, don't think they take it. You leave everything to Jeekie, he see you through, but p'raps you like come breakfast outside, where you know all that go on."

Barbara did like, but as it happened they were allowed to consume their meal in peace, since no Asiki appeared. As soon as it was swallowed she returned to her tent, while Alan and Jeekie set to work to strengthen the defences of the little camp as well as they were able, and to make ready and serve out the arms and ammunition.

About midday a man whom they had posted in a tree that grew inside the camp announced that he saw the enemy, and next moment a company of them rushed towards them across the open and were greeted by a volley which killed and wounded several men. At this exhibition of miraculous power, for none of these soldiers had ever heard the report of firearms or seen their effect, they retreated rapidly, uttering shouts of dismay and carrying their dead and wounded with them.

"Do you suppose they have gone, Jeekie?" asked Alan anxiously.

He shook his head.

"Think not, Major, think they frightened, by big bullet magic, and go consult priest. Also only a few of them here, rest of army come later and try rush us to-morrow morning before dawn. That Asiki custom."

"Then what shall we do, Jeekie? Run for it or stop here?"

"Think must stop here, Major. If we bolt, carrying Miss Barbara, who can't walk much, they follow on spoor and catch us. Best stick inside this fence and see what happen. Also once outside p'raps porters desert and leave us."

So as there was nothing else to do they stayed, labouring all day at the strengthening of their fortifications till at length the boma or fence of boughs, supported by earth, was so high and thick that while any were left to fire through the loopholes, it would be very difficult to storm by men armed with spears.

It was a dreadful and arduous day for Alan, who now had Barbara's safety to think of, Barbara with whom as yet he had scarcely found time to exchange a word. By sunset indeed he was so worn out with toil and anxiety that he could scarcely stand upon his feet. Jeekie, who all that afternoon had been strangely quiet and reflective, surveyed him critically, then said:

"You have good drink and go sleep a bit, Major. Very good little shelter there by Miss Barbara's tent, and you hold her hand if you like underneath the canvas, which comforting and all correct. Jeekie never get tired, he keep good lookout and let you know if anything happen, and then you jump up quite fresh and fight like tom-cat in corner."

At first Alan refused to listen, but when Barbara added her entreaties to those of Jeekie he gave way, and ten minutes later was as soundly asleep as he had ever been in his life.

"Keep eye on him, Miss Barbara, and call me if he wake. Now I go give noble lord his supper and see that he quite comfortable. Jeekie seem very busy to-night, just like when Major have dinner-party at Yarleys and old cook get drunk in kitchen."

If Barbara could have followed Jeekie's movements for the next few hours, she would probably have agreed that he was busy. First he went to Aylward's tent, and as he had said he would, gave him his supper, and with it half a bottle of whisky from the stores which he had been carrying about with him for some time, as he said, to prevent the porters from getting at it. Aylward would drink little, though as his arms were tied to the tent-pole, Jeekie sat beside him and fed him like a baby, conversing pleasantly with him all the while, informing him amongst other things that he had better say "big prayer," because the Asiki would probably cut his throat before morning.

Aylward, who was in a state of sullen fury, scarcely replied to this talk, except to say that if so, there was one comfort, they would cut his and his master's also.

"Yes, my Lord," answered Jeekie, "that quite true, so drink to next meeting, though I think you go different place to me, and when you got tail and I wing, you horn and I crown of glory, of course we not talk much together," and he held a mug of whisky and water—a great deal of whisky and a very little water—to his prisoner's mouth.

Aylward drained it, feeling a need for stimulant.

"There," said Jeekie, holding it upside down, "you drink every drop and not offer one to poor old Jeekie. Well, he turned teetotaller, so no matter. Good-night, my Lord, I call you if Asiki come."

"Who are the Asiki?" asked Aylward drowsily.

"Oh! you want to know? I tell you," and he began a long, rambling story.

Before he ever came to the end of it Aylward had fallen on his side and was fast asleep.

"Dear me!" said Jeekie, contemplating him, "that whisky very strong, though bottle say same as they drink in House of Common. That whisky so strong I think I pour away rest of it," and he did to the last drop, even taking the trouble to wash out the bottle with water. "Now you no tempt anyone," he said, addressing the said bottle with a very peculiar smile, "or if you tempt, at least do no harm—like kiss down telephone!" Then he laid down the bottle on its side and left the tent.

Outside of it three of the head porters, who appeared to be friends of his, were waiting for him, and with these men he engaged in low and earnest conversation. Next, after they had arrived at some agreement, which they seemed to ratify by a curious oath that involved their crossing and clasping hands in an odd fashion, and other symbols known to West African secret societies, Jeekie went the round of the camp to see that everyone was at his post. Then he did what most people would have thought a very curious and strange thing, namely climbed the fence and vanished into the forest, where presently a sound was heard as of an owl hooting.

A little while later and another owl began to hoot in the distance, whereat the three head porters nudged each other. Perhaps they had heard such owls hoot before at night, and perhaps they knew that Jeekie, who had "passed Bonsa," could only be harmed by the direct command of Bonsa speaking through the mouth of the Asika herself. Still they might have been interested in the nocturnal conversation of those two owls, which, as is common with such magical fowl in West Africa, had transformed themselves into human shapes, the shape of Jeekie and the shape of an Asiki priest, who was, as it happened, a blood relation of Jeekie.

"Very good, Brother," said Owl No. 1; "all you want is this white man whom the Asika desires for a husband. Well, I have done my best for him, but I must think of myself and others, and he goes to great happiness. I have given him something to make him sleep; do you come presently with eight men, no more, or we shall kill you, to the fence of the camp, and we will hand over the white man, Vernoon, to you to take back to the Asika, who will give you a wonderful reward, such a reward as you have never imagined. Now let me hear your word."

Then Owl No. 2 answered:

"Brother, I make the bargain on behalf of the army, and swear to it by the double Swimming Head of Bonsa. We will come and take the white man, Vernoon, who is to be Mungana, and carry him away. In return we promise not to follow or molest you, or any others in your camp. Indeed, why should we, who do not desire to be killed by the dreadful magic that you have, a magic that makes a noise and pierces through our bodies from afar? What were the words of the Asika? 'Bring back Vernoon, or perish. I care for nothing else, bring back Vernoon to be my husband.'"

"Good," said Owl No. 1, "within the half of an hour Vernoon shall be ready for you."

"Good," answered Owl No. 2, "within half an hour eight of us will be without the east face of your camp to receive him."

"Silently?"

"Silently, my brother in Bonsa. If he cries out we will gag him. Fear not, none shall know your part in this matter."

"Good, my brother in Bonsa. By the way, how is Big Bonsa? I fear that the white man, Vernoon, hurt him very much, and that is why I give him up—because of his sacrilege."

"When I left the god was very sick and all the people mourned, but doubtless he is immortal."

"Doubtless he is immortal, my brother, a little hard magic in his stomach—if he has one—cannot hurt him. Farewell, dear brother in Bonsa, I wish that I were you to get the great reward that the Asika will give to you. Farewell, farewell."

Then the two owls flitted apart again, hooting as they went, till they came to their respective camps.

Jeekie was in the tent performing a strange toilet upon the sleeping Aylward by the light of a single candle. From his pouch he produced the mask of linen painted with gold that Alan used to be forced to wear, and tied it securely over Aylward's face, murmuring:

"You always love gold, my Lord Aylward, and Jeekie promise you see plenty of it now."

Then he proceeded to remove his coat, his waistcoat, his socks, and his boots and to replace these articles of European attire by his own worn Asiki sandals and his own dirty Asiki robe.

"There," he said, "think that do," and he studied him by the light of the candle. "Same height, same colour hair, same dirty clothes, and as Asiki never see Major's face because he always wear mask in public, like as two peas on shovel. Oh my! Jeekie clever chap, Jeekie devilish clever chap. But when Asika pull off that mask to give him true lover kiss, OH MY! wonder that happen then? Think whole of Bonsa-Town bust up; think big waterfall run backwards; think she not quite pleased; think my good Lord find himself in false position; think Jeekie glad to be on coast; think he not go back to Bonsa-Town no more. Oh my aunt! no, he stop in England and go church twice on Sunday," and pressing his big hands on the pit of his stomach he rocked and rolled in fierce, silent laughter.

Then an owl hooted again immediately beneath the fence and Jeekie, blowing out the candle, opened the flap of the tent and tapped the head porter, who stood outside, on the shoulder. He crept in and between them they lifted the senseless Aylward and bore him to the V-shaped entrance of the boma which was immediately opposite to the tent and, oddly enough, half open. Here the two other porters with whom Jeekie had performed some ceremony, chanced to be on guard, the rest of their company being stationed at a distance. Jeekie and the head porter went through the gap like men carrying a corpse to midnight burial, and presently in the darkness without two owls began to hoot.

Now Aylward was laid upon a litter that had been prepared, and eight white-robed Asiki bearers stared at his gold mask in the faint starlight.

"I suppose he is not dead, brother," said Owl No. 2 doubtfully.

"Nay, brother," said Owl No. 1, "feel his heart and his pulse. Not dead, only drunk. He will wake up by daylight, by which time you should be far upon your way. Be good and gentle to the white man Vernoon, who has been my master. Be careful, too, that he does not escape you, brother, for as you know he is very strong and cunning. Say to the Asika that Jeekie her servant makes his reverence to her, and hopes that she will have many, many happy years with the husband that he sends her; also that she will remember him whom she called 'Black Dog,' in her prayers to the gods and spirits of our people."

"It shall be done, brother, but why do you not return with us?"

"Because, brother, I have ties across the Black Water—dear children, almost white—whom I love so much that I cannot leave them. Farewell, brethren, the blessings of the Bonsas be on you, and may you grow fat and prosper in the love and favour of our lady the Asika."

"Farewell," they murmured in answer. "Good fortune be your bedfellow."

Another minute and they had lifted up the litter and vanished at a swinging trot into the shadow of the trees. Jeekie returned to the camp and ordered the three men to re-stop the gateway with thorns, muttering in their ears:

"Remember, brethren, one word of this and you die, all of you, as those die who break the oath."

"Have we not sworn?" they whispered, as they went back to their posts.

Jeekie stood a while in front of the empty tent and if any had been there to note him, they might have seen a shadow as of compunction creep over his powerful black face.

"When he wake up he won't know where he are," he reflected, "and when he get to Bonsa-Town he'll wonder where he is, and when he meet Asika! Well, he very big blackguard; try to murder Major, whom Jeekie nurse as baby, the only thing that Jeekie care for—except—Jeekie; try to make love to Miss Barbara against will when he catch her alone in forest, which not playing game. Jeekie self not such big blackguard as that dirt-born noble Lord; Jeekie never murder no one—not quite; Jeekie never make love to girl what not want him—no need, so many what do that he have to shove them off, like good Christian man. Mrs. Jeekie see to that while she live. Also better that mean white man go call on Bonsas than Major and Missy Barbara and all porters, and Jeekie—specially Jeekie—get throat cut. No, no, Jeekie nothing to be ashamed of, Jeekie do good day's work, though Jeekie keep it tight as wax since white folk such silly people, and when Major in a rage, he very nasty customer and see everything upside down. Now, Jeekie quite tired, so say his prayers and have nap. No, think not in tent, though very comfortable. Major might wake up, poke his nose in there, and if he see black face instead of white one, ask ugly question, which if Jeekie half asleep he no able to answer nice and neat. Still he just arrange things a little so they look all right."

CHAPTER XX

Dawn began to break in the forest and Alan woke in his shelter and stretched himself. He had slept soundly all the night, so soundly that the innocent Jeekie wondered much whether by any chance he also had taken a tot out of that particular whisky bottle, as indeed he had recommended him to do. People who drink whisky after long abstinence from spirits are apt to sleep long, he reflected.

Alan crept out of the shelter and gazed affectionately at the tent in which Barbara slumbered. Thank Heaven she was safe so far, as for some unknown reason, evidently the Asiki had postponed their attack. Just then a clamour arose in the air, and he perceived Jeekie striding towards him waving one arm in an excited fashion, while with the other he dragged along the captain of the porters, who appeared to be praying for mercy.

"Here pretty go, Major," he shouted, "devil and all to pay! That my Lord, he gone and bolted. This silly fool say that three hours ago he hear something break through fence and think it only hyæna what come to steal, so take no notice. Well, that hyæna, you guess who he is. You come look, Major, you come look, and then we tie this fellow up and flog him."

Alan ran to Aylward's tent to find it empty.

"Look," said Jeekie, who had followed, "see how he do business, that jolly clever hyæna," and he pointed to a broken whisky bottle and some severed cords. "You see he manage break bottle and rub rope against cut glass till it come in two. Then he do hyæna dodge and hook it."

Alan inspected the articles, nor did any shadow of doubt enter his mind.

"Certainly he managed very well," he said, "especially for a London-bred man, but, Jeekie, what can have been his object?"

"Oh! who know, Major? Mind of man very strange and various thing; p'raps he no bear to see you and Miss Barbara together; p'raps he bolt coast, get ear of local magistrate before you; p'raps he sit up tree to shoot you; p'raps nasty temper make him mad. But he gone any way, and I hope he no meet Asiki, poor fellow, 'cause if so, who know? P'raps they knock him on head, or if they think him you, they make him prisoner and keep him quite long while before they let him go again."

"Well," said Alan, "he has gone of his own free will, so we have no responsibility in the matter, and I can't pretend that I am sorry to see the last of him, at any rate for the present. Let that poor beggar loose, there seems to have been enough flogging in this place, and after all he isn't much to blame."

Jeekie obeyed, apparently with much reluctance, and just then they saw one of their own people running towards the camp.

"'Fraid he going to tell us Asiki come attack," said Jeekie, shaking his head. "Hope they give us time breakfast first."

"No doubt," answered Alan nervously, for he feared the result of that attack.

Then the man arrived breathless and began to gasp out his news, which filled Alan with delight and caused a look of utter amazement to appear upon the broad face of Jeekie. It was to the effect that he had climbed a high tree as he had been bidden to do, and from the top of that tree by the light of the first rays of the rising sun, miles away on the plain beyond the forest, he had seen the Asiki army in full retreat.

"Thank God!" exclaimed Alan.

"Yes, Major, but that very rum story. Jeekie can't swallow it all at once. Must send out see none of them left behind. P'raps they play trick, but if they really gone, 'spose it 'cause guns frightens them so much. Always think powder very great 'vention, especially when enemy hain't got none, and quite sure of it now. Jeekie very, very seldom wrong. Soon believe," he added with a burst of confidence, "that Jeekie never wrong at all. He look for truth so long that at last he find it always."

Something more than a month had gone by and Major and Mrs. Vernon, the latter fully restored to health and the most sweet and beautiful of brides, stood upon the steamship Benin, and as the sun sank, looked their last upon the coast of Western Africa.

"Yes, dear," Alan was saying to his wife, "from first to last it has been a very queer story, but I really think that our getting that Asiki gold after all was one of the queerest parts of it; also uncommonly convenient, as things have turned out."

"Namely that you have got a little pauper for a wife instead of a great heiress, Alan. But tell me again about the gold. I have had so much to think of during the last few days," and she blushed, "that I never quite took it all in."

"Well, love, there isn't much to tell. When that forwarding agent, Mr. Aston, knew that we were in the town, he came to me and said that he had about fifty cases full of something heavy, as he supposed samples of ore, addressed to me to your care in England which he was proposing to ship on by the Benin. I answered 'Yes, that was all right,' and did not undeceive him about their contents. Then I asked how they had arrived, and if he had not received a letter with them. He replied that one morning before the warehouse was open, some natives had brought them down in a canoe, and dumped them at the door, telling the watchman that they had been paid to deliver them there by some other natives whom they met a long way up the river. Then they went away without leaving any letter or message. Well, I thanked Aston and paid his charges and there's an end of the matter. Those fifty-three cases are now in the hold invoiced as ore samples and, as I inspected them myself and am sure that they have not been tampered with, besides the value of the necklace the Asika gave me we've got £100,000 to begin our married life upon with something over for old Jeekie, and I daresay we shall do very well on that."

"Yes, Alan, very well indeed." Then she reflected a while, for the mention of Jeekie's name seemed to have made her thoughtful, and added, "Alan, what do you think became of Lord Aylward?"

"I am sure I don't know. Jeekie and I and some of the porters went to see the Old Calabar officials and made affidavits as to the circumstances of his disappearance. We couldn't do any more, could we?"

"No, Alan. But do you think that Jeekie quite understands the meaning of an oath? I mean it seems so strange that we should never have found the slightest trace of him, and, Alan, I don't know if you noticed it, but why did Jeekie appear that morning wearing Lord Aylward's socks and boots?"

"He ought to know all about oaths, he has heard enough of them in Magistrates' Courts, but as regards the boots, I am sure I can't say, dear," answered Alan uneasily. "Here he comes, we will ask him," and he did.

"Sock and boot," replied Jeekie, with a surprised air, "why, Mrs. Major, if that good lord go mad and cut off into forest leaving them behind, of course I put them on, as they no more use to him, and I just burn my dirty old Asiki dress and sandal and got nothing to keep jigger out of toe. Don't you sit up here in this damp, cold, Mrs. Major, else you get more fever. You go down and dress dinner, which at half-past six to-night. I just come tell you that."

So Barbara went, leaving the other two talking about various matters, for they were alone together on the deck, all the passengers, of whom there were but few, having gone below.

The short African twilight had come, a kind of soft blue haze that made the ship look mysterious and unnatural. By degrees their conversation died away. They lapsed into a silence, which Alan was the first to break.

"What are you thinking of, Jeekie?" he asked nervously.

"Thinking of Asika, Major," he answered in a scared whisper. "Seem to me that she about somewhere, just as she use pop up in room in Gold House; seem to me I feel her all down my back, likewise in head wool, which stand up."

"It's very odd, Jeekie," replied Alan, "but so do I."

"Well, Major, 'spect she thinking of us, specially of you, and just throw what she think at us, like boy throw stones at bird what fly away out of cage. Asika do all that, you know, she not quite human, full of plenty Bonsa devil, from gen'ration to gen'rations, amen! P'raps she just find out something what make her mad."

"What could she find out after all this time, Jeekie?"

"Oh, don't know. How I know? Jeekie can't guess. Find out you marry Miss Barbara, p'raps. Very sick that she lose you for this time, p'raps. Kill herself that she keep near you, p'raps, while she wait till you come round again, p'raps. Asika can do all these things if she like, Major."

"Stuff and rubbish," answered Alan uneasily, for Jeekie's suggestions were most uncomfortable, "I believe in none of your West Coast superstitions."

"Quite right, Major, nor don't I. Only you 'member, Major, what she show us there in Treasure-place— Mr. Haswell being buried, eh? Miss Barbara in tent, eh? t'other job what hasn't come off yet, eh? Oh!

my golly! Major, just you look behind you and say you see nothing, please," and the eyes of Jeekie grew large as Maltese oranges, while with chattering teeth he pointed over the bulwark of the vessel.

Alan turned and saw.

This was what he saw or seemed to see: The figure of the Asika in her robes and breastplate of gold, standing upon the air, just beyond the ship, as though on it she might set no foot. Her waving black hair hung about her shoulders, but the sharp wind did not seem to stir it nor did her white dress flutter, and on her beautiful face was stamped a look of awful rage and agony, the rage of betrayal, the agony of loss. In her right hand she held a knife, and from a wound in her breast the red blood ran down her golden corselet. She pointed to Jeekie with the knife, she opened her arms to Alan as though in unutterable longing, then slowly raised them upwards towards the fading glory of the sky above—and was gone.

Jeekie sat down upon the deck, mopping his brow with a red handkerchief, while Alan, who felt faint, clung to the bulwarks.

"Tell you, Major, that Asika can do all that kind of thing. Never know where you find her next. 'Spect she come to live with us in England and just call in now and again when it dark. Tell you, she very awkward customer, think p'raps you done better stop there and marry her. Well, she gone now, thank Heaven! seem to drop in sea and hope she stay there."

"Jeekie," said Alan, recovering himself, "listen to me; this is all infernal nonsense; we have gone through a great deal and the nerves of both of us are overstrained. We think we saw what we did not see, and if you dare to say a single word of it to your mistress, I'll break your neck. Do you understand?"

"Yes, Major, think so. All 'fernal nonsense, nerves strained, didn't see what we see, and say nothing of what did see to Mrs. Major, if either do say anything, t'other one break his neck. That all right, quite understand. Anything else, Major?"

"Yes, Jeekie. We have had some wonderful adventures, but they are past and done with and the less we talk or even think about them the better, for there is a lot that would be rather difficult to explain, and that if explained would scarcely be believed."

"Yes, Major, for instance, very difficult explain Mrs. Barbara how Asika so fond of you if you only tell her, 'Go away, go away!' all the time, like old saint-gentleman to pretty girl in picture. P'raps she smell rat."

"Stop your ribald talk," said Alan in a stern voice. "It would be better if instead of making jokes you gave thanks to Providence for bringing both of us alive and well out of very dreadful dangers. Now I am going to dress for dinner," and with an anxious glance seaward into the gathering darkness, he turned and went.

Jeekie stood alone upon the empty deck, wagging his great white head to and fro and soliloquizing thus:

"Wonder if Major see what under lady Asika's feet when she stand out there over nasty deep. Think not or he say something. That noble lord not look nice. No, private view for Jeekie only, free ticket and nothing to pay and me hope it no come back when I go to bed. Major know nothing about it, so he not see, but Jeekie know a lot. Hope that Aylward not write any letters home, or if he write, hope no one post them. Ghost bad enough, but murder, oh my!"

He paused a while, then went on:

"Jeekie do big sacrifice to Bonsa when he reach Yarleys, get lamb in back kitchen at night, or if ghost come any more, calf in wood outside. Not steal it, pay for it himself. Then think Jeekie turn Cath'lic; confess his sins, they say them priest chaps not split, and after they got his sins, they tackle Asika and Bonsas too," and he uttered a series of penitent groans, turning slowly round and round to be sure that nothing was behind him.

Just then the full moon appeared out of a bank of clouds, and as it rose higher, flooding the world with light, Jeekie's spirits rose also.

"Asika never come in moonshine," he said, "that not the game, against rule, and after all, what Jeekie done bad? He very good fellow really. Aylward great villain, serve him jolly well right if Asika spiflicate him, that not Jeekie's fault. What Jeekie do, he do to save master and missus who he love. Care nothing for his self, ready to die any day. Keep it dark to save them too, 'cause they no like the story. If once they know, it always leave taste in mouth, same as bad oyster. Also Jeekie manage very well, take Major safe Asiki-land ('cause Little Bonsa make him), give him very interesting time there, get him plenty gold, nurse him when he sick, nobble Mungana, bring him out again, find Miss Barbara, catch hated rival and bamboozle all Asiki army, bring happy pair to coast and marry them, arrange first-class honeymoon on ship—Jeekie do all these things, and lots more he could tell, if he vain and not poor humble nigger."

Once more he paused a while, lost in the contemplation of his own modesty and virtues, then continued:

"This very ungrateful world. Major there, he not say, 'Thank you, Jeekie, Jeekie, you great, wonderful man. Brave Jeekie, artful Jeekie. Jeekie smart as paint who make all world believe just what he like, and one too many for Asika herself.' No, no, he say nothing like that. He say 'thank Prov'dence,' not 'Jeekie,' as though Prov'dence do all them things. White folk think they clever, but great fools, really, don't know nothing. Prov'dence all very well in his way—p'raps, but Prov'dence not a patch on Jeekie.

"Hullo! moon get behind cloud and there second bell; think Jeekie go down and wait dinner; lonely up here and sure Asika never stand 'lectric light."

H. Rider Haggard – A Short Biography

Sir Henry Rider Haggard, KBE was born on June 22nd 1856 at Bradenham in Norfolk, England.

More familiarly known as H. Rider Haggard, he was the eighth of ten children born to Sir William Meybohm Rider Haggard, a barrister (born, incidentally, in St Petersburg, Russia), and Ella Doveton, an author, poet and daughter of a merchant in the East India Trading Company.

Haggard was initially schooled at Garsington Rectory in Oxfordshire where he studied under the tutelage of Reverend H. J. Graham. His elder brothers, who seemed to find more favour with their father, graduated from various private schools whilst Haggard was sent to Ipswich Grammar School, saving his father a considerable sum in fees.

He failed his army entrance exam, and was therefore sent to a private crammer in London in preparation for the entrance exam to the British Foreign Office, which he appears never to have sat. However, it was during his two years in London that Haggard came into contact with a circle of people interested in the study of psychical phenomena and for which he too now developed a life-long interest together with a series of enduring friendships.

In 1875, Haggard's father used his family's connections to send him to Southern Africa to take up an unpaid position as assistant to the secretary to Sir Henry Bulwer, Lieutenant-Governor of the Colony of Natal. In 1876 he was transferred to the staff of Sir Theophilus Shepstone, Special Commissioner for the Transvaal. It was in this role that Haggard was present in Pretoria in April 1877 for the official announcement of the British annexation of the Boer Republic of the Transvaal. The official who had been nominated to read out the Proclamation lost his voice and Haggard was his replacement. It was a moment in history.

Haggard was to remain in the country for six years, during which time he served as Master of the High Court of the Transvaal and an adjutant of the Pretoria Horse.

It was here that he fell in love with Mary Elizabeth "Lilly" Jackson. He hoped to marry her once he obtained more certainty in his career path.

In 1878 he became Registrar of the High Court in the Transvaal and now the time seemed opportune to write to his father to tell him of his hope to marry. The reply from his father was uncompromising. He forbade it until his son had made a proper career for himself.

The following year, 1879, Lily married Frank Archer, a well-to-do banker.

Haggard returned briefly to England to marry a friend of his sister's, Marianna Louisa Margitson, a 21 year old, in 1880, and the couple travelled to Africa together. Haggard's years in Africa had proved, at least on a writing level, rich and inspirational for him, and while still in Natal he wrote two articles for The Gentleman's Magazine describing his experiences.

Moving back to England in (and accounts here differ as to whether it was 1881 or 1882) the couple settled in Ditchingham, Norfolk, Louisa's ancestral home. Later they moved to Kessingland and established connections with the church in Bungay, Suffolk. The marriage produced four children. A son named Jack (who tragically died at age 10 of measles) and three daughters, Angela, Dorothy and Lilias. (Lilias grew to become an author and her father's biographer.)

In England Law was to be the fulcrum of his career. However, although he studied, writing was growing in its appeal to him. His first book, Cetywayo and His White Neighbours, was an account and study of Britain's policies in South Africa.

From this point his career as a writer began to take substantial hold and with it a dramatic shift to fiction. Two years later he published his first fiction, Dawn followed in 1885 by arguably his most popular novel, King Solomon's Mines—detailing the life of the adventurer Allan Quatermain. This was followed the following year, 1886, by She: A History of Adventure, which introduced the female character Ayesha. Both characters, Quatermain and Ayesha, developed a series of books about their adventures.

The study of Law now fell away entirely. He appeared also to have a keen sense of his commercial appreciation. Rather than sell the copyright of his first best-seller, King Solomon's Mines, for a £100 fee he, instead, accepted a 10% royalty. This book is also generally accepted as the first of the Lost World writing genre.

Haggard obviously thought there were many further adventures to tell and it would be hard to find a publisher who would disagree given the start he had made. Sequels soon followed. Allan Quatermain continued his epic and swash-buckling adventures in Africa whilst the sequel to She entitled Ayesha played out her adventures in Tibet. Interestingly Haggard would later extend his characters adventures around the world with Eric Brighteyes, being the basis for an epic Viking romance.

The Haggard family lived at 69 Gunterstone Road in Hammersmith, London, from mid-1885 to mid-1888. It was here that he wrote his most famous works. His time in Africa had given him the experience and atmosphere as well as several observations and friendships of the people who would so influence his fictional characters. Chief among them were the larger-than-life adventurers Frederick Selous and Frederick Russell Burnham. Both were men of Empire and huge ambition as they helped uncover the great mineral wealth of Africa, as well as the ruins of ancient lost civilisations of the continent, such as Great Zimbabwe.

Three of Haggard's books, The Wizard (1896), Black Heart and White Heart; a Zulu Idyll (1896), and Elissa; the Doom of Zimbabwe (1898), are dedicated to Burnham's daughter Nada, the first white child born in Bulawayo; she had been named after Haggard's 1892 book Nada the Lily.

As is typical of the writing of the time his novels contain many of the stereotypes associated with colonialism, yet they also sympathise, to a degree, with the native populations. Africans often play heroic roles in the novels, although the protagonists are more often than not European. The time around the turn of the century was, after all, the great sprint to Empire by many European countries intent on gaining possessions of land, people and resources.

Three of Haggard's novels were written in collaboration with his friend Andrew Lang who shared his interest in the spiritual realm and paranormal phenomena and who was also a greatly admired editor.

Haggard's stories are still widely read today. Ayesha, the female protagonist of She, has been cited as a prototype by psychoanalysts such as Sigmund Freud (in The Interpretation of Dreams) and Carl Jung. Her epithet is, of course, "She Who Must Be Obeyed" and has for decades been used tongue-in-cheek to describe the presumed balance of influence between the sexes.

As a legacy it is easy to establish Haggard, and his pioneering work, as the author of the Lost World branch of writing and its influence of such other writers as Edgar Rice Burroughs, Robert E. Howard and Talbot Mundy. The Allan Quatermain character influenced many 'serials' in Hollywood during the 30s & 40s and can readily be seen as a template for Indiana Jones, the American archaeologist and explorer and huge box office film character.

Years later, when Haggard was a successful novelist, he was contacted by his former love, Lilly Archer, née Jackson. Lily had been deserted by her husband, who had embezzled funds and fled bankrupt to

Africa. Haggard installed her and her sons in a house and saw to the children's education. Lilly eventually followed her husband to Africa, where he infected her with syphilis before dying of it himself. Lilly returned to England in late 1907, where Haggard again supported her until her death on April 22nd, 1909.

Haggard also wrote about agricultural and social reform, in part inspired by his experiences in Africa, but also based on what he saw in Europe. By the end of his life, he was adamantly opposed to Bolshevism, a position that he shared with his life-long friend Rudyard Kipling. The two had found friendship upon Kipling's arrival at London in 1889 largely on the strength of their shared opinions.

Haggard was extremely interested in the social affairs of the Country and eager to play a more active part in attempting reform. In 1895 he stood unsuccessfully for Parliament as a Conservative candidate for the Eastern division of Norfolk losing by 198 votes.

Also in 1895 he served on a government commission to examine Salvation Army labour colonies. This, and his heavy involvement in agriculture reform, led to him being a member of several further commissions on land use and related affairs, work that involved several trips to the Colonies and Dominions. This work, in part, helped lead to the passage of the 1909 Development Bill.

In 1911 he served on the Royal Commission examining coastal erosion.

He was an absorbed and dedicated writer of letters to The Times, nearly one hundred were published by them and the bibliography attached below reveals much in the range of subjects he wished to bring attention to.

He was made a Knight Bachelor in 1912 and a Knight Commander of the Order of the British Empire in 1919. Haggard was a member of several clubs including the Athenaeum, Savile, and Authors' clubs.

The district of Rider in British Columbia, Canada, was named in his honour.

Henry Rider Haggard died on May 14th, 1925 at the age of 68. His ashes were buried at Ditchingham Church. His papers are held at the Norfolk Record Office.

The first chapter of his book People of the Mist (1894) is credited with inspiring the 1912 motto of the Royal Air Force (formerly the Royal Flying Corps), Per ardua ad astra. "Through adversity to the stars" (or alternately "Through struggle to the stars") it is also used by other Commonwealth air forces such as the RAAF, RCAF, RNZAF, and the SAAF.

H. Rider Haggard – A Concise Bibliography

Novels
Dawn (1884) Published in three volumes
The Witch's Head (1884) Published in three volumes
King Solomon's Mines (1885) Allan Quatermain series
She: A History of Adventure (1886) Ayesha series
Allan Quatermain (1887) Allan Quatermain series

Jess (1887)

A Tale of Three Lions (1887) Allan Quatermain series

Maiwa's Revenge, or the War of the Little Hand (1888) Allan Quatermain series

Colonel Quaritch, VC (1889) Published in three volumes

Cleopatra (1889)

Beatrice (1890)

The World's Desire (1890) Co-written with Andrew Lang

Eric Brighteyes (1891)

Nada the Lily (1892)

An Heroic Effort (1893)

Montezuma's Daughter (1893)

The People of the Mist (1894)

Heart of the World (1895)

Joan Haste (1895)

The Wizard (1896)

Doctor Therne (1898)

Swallow: A Tale of the Great Trek (1899)

Lysbeth (1901)

Pearl Maiden (1903)

Stella Fregelius: A Tale of Three Destinies (1903)

The Brethren (1904)

Ayesha: The Return of She (1905) Ayesha series

The Way of the Spirit (1906)

Benita (1906)

Fair Margaret (1907)

The Ghost Kings(1908)

The Yellow God (1908)

The Lady of Blossholme (1909)

Morning Star (1910)

Queen Sheba's Ring (1910)

Red Eve (1911)

The Mahatma and the Hare (1911)

Marie (1912) Allan Quatermain series

Child of Storm (1913) Allan Quatermain series

The Wanderer's Necklace (1914)

The Holy Flower (1915) Allan Quatermain series

The Ivory Child (1916) Allan Quatermain series

Finished (1917) Allan Quatermain series]

Love Eternal (1918)

Moon of Israel (1918)

When the World Shook (1919)

The Ancient Allan (1920) Allan Quatermain series

She and Allan (1921) Allan Quatermain series / Ayesha series

The Virgin of the Sun (1922)

Wisdom's Daughter (1923) Ayesha series

Heu-Heu (1924) Allan Quatermain series]

Queen of the Dawn (1925)

The Treasure of the Lake (1926) Allan Quatermain series

Allan and the Ice-Gods (1927) Allan Quatermain series
Mary of Marion Isle (1929)
Belshazzar (1930)

Short Story Collections
Allan's Wife and Other Tales (1889)
Black Heart and White Heart: A Zulu Idyll (1900)
Smith and the Pharaohs (1920)

Publications in Periodicals and Newspapers
A Zulu War-Dance (July 1877) The Gentleman's Magazine
A Visit to the Chief (September 1877) The Gentleman's Magazine
Hydrophobia (letter) (3 November 1885) The Times
The Land Question (letter) (28 April 1886) The Times
About Fiction (February 1887) The Contemporary Review
Mr Rider Haggard and His Critics (letter) (27 April 1887) The Times
Our Position in Cyprus (July 1887) The Contemporary Review
American Copyright (letter) (11 October 1887) The Times
On Going Back (November 1887) Longman's Magazine
Delagoa Bay (letter) (17 December 1887) The Times
South African Policy (letter) (27 December 1887) The Times
Suggested Prologue to a Dramatised Version of She (March 1888) Longman's Magazine
Mr. Meeson's Will (18 June 1888) The Illustrated London News
The Wreck of the Copeland (18 August 1888) The Illustrated London News
Cleopatra (3 December 1888) The Illustrated London News
Hydrophobia and Muzzling (letter) (25 October 1889) The Times
The Annals of Natal (23 November 1889) The Saturday Review
Mummy at St Mary/Woolnoth's (letter) (25 December 1889) The Times
Mummies (letter) (27 December 1889) The Times
The Fate of Swaziland (January 1890) The New Review
In Memoriam (17 May 1890) Thompson's Seasons
American Copyright (letter) (5 June 1890) The Times
Mr Herbert Ward and Mr Stanley (10 November 1890) The Times
Nada the Lily (2 January 1892) The Illustrated London News
A New Argument Against Creation (19 December 1892) The Times
My First Book. Dawn. By H. Rider Haggard (April 1893) The Idler
The Tale of Isandlwana and Rorke's Drift (4 October 1893) The True Story Book
Lobengula (letter) (19 October 1893) The Times
The New Sentiment (letter) (6 November 1893) The Times
Wanted—Imagination   (25 December 1893) The Times
The Fate of Captain Patterson's Party (28 December 1893) The Times
The Three Volume Novel (letter) (27 July 1894) The Times
The Adventures of John Gladwyn Jebb (letter) (30 October 1894) The Times
Agriculture in Norfolk (letter) (30 October 1894) The Times
The Nelson Bazaar (letter) (16 February 1895) The Times
Everything is Peaceful (letter) (20 March 1895) The Times

Lord Kimberley in Norfolk (letter) (17 April 1895) The Times
The East Norfolk Election (letter) (23 July 1895) The Times
The East Norfolk Election (letter) (29 July 1895) The Times
Wilson's Last Fight (7 October 1895) The True Story Book
The Crisis in the Transvaal (letter) (2 January 1896) The Times
The Transvaal Crisis (letter) (13 January 1896) The Times
Jameson's Surrender (letter) (14 March 1896) The Times
The Rinderpest in South Africa (letter) (5 November 1896) The Times
Mr Rider Haggard and Dr Neufeld (letter) (9 January 1899) The Times
Shrinkage of Population in Agricultural Districts (letter) (9 May 1899) The Times
The South African Crisis—An Appeal (letter) (1 July 1899) The Times
Commandant-General Joubert and Mr H Rider Haggard (letter) (8 September 1899) The Times
Anglo-African Writers' Club (17 October 1899) The Times
The War (letter) (25 October 1899) The Times
Farming in 1899 (letter) (22 December 1899) The Times
Farming in 1899 (letter) (1 January 1900) The Times
Settlement of Soldiers in South Africa (letter) (5 May 1900) The Times
1881 and 1900 (letter) (2 October 1900) The Times
Farming in 1900 (letter) (1 January 1901) The Times
Central and Associated Chambers of Agriculture (letter) (6 November 1901) The Times
Small Holdings (letter) (8 November 1901) The Times
Rural England (letter) (4 February 1903) The Times
Mr Rider Haggard on Rural Depopulation (3 May 1903) The Times
Agricultural Distress (letter) (11 June 1903) The Times
The Motor Problem (letter) (24 June 1903) The Times
Fiscal Policy and Agriculture (letter) (16 December 1903) The Times
Telepathy Between a Human Being and a Dog (letter) (21 July 1904) The Times
Telepathy Between a Human Being and a Dog (letter) (9 August 1904) The Times
Mr Rider Haggard on Small Holdings (12 September 1904) The Times
Case L.1139 Dream (October 1904) Journal of the Society for Psychical Research
Mr Rider Haggard on Agriculture (22 October 1904) The Times
Mr Rider Haggard on Rural Housing (27 October 1904) The Times
The Deserted Village (letter) (25 August 1905) The Times
Decrease of Population and the Land (letter) (6 January 1906) The Times
Prevention of Cruelty to Children (3 February 1906) The Times
The New Land and Tenure Bill (letter) (12 March 1906) The Times
Garden City Association (17 March 1906) The Times
Mr H. Rider Haggard on the Zulus (19 May 1906) The Illustrated London News
To Be Proof against British Bullets: A Zulu Incantation (19 May 1906) The Illustrated London News
Housing of the Working Classes (26 June 1906) The Times
Mr Rider Haggard on Small Holdings (4 July 1906) The Times
The Unemployed and Waste City Lands (letter) (19 July 1906) The Times
Mr Rider Haggard on the Transvaal Constitution (7 August 1906) The Times
Vanishing East Anglia (1 September 1906) The Saturday Review
The Land Grabbing at Plaistow (5 September 1906) The Times
The Land Tenure Bill (22 November 1906) The Times
Publishers and the Public (letter) (19 February 1907) The Times
The Careless Children (2 March 1907) The Saturday Review

The Government and the Land (letter) (29 April 1907) The Times
Chambers of Agriculture (2 May 1907) The Times
The Government and the Land (letter) (8 May 1907) The Times
Miss Jebb on Small Holdings (15 June 1907) Country Life
Rural Housing and Sanitation Association (27 June 1907) The Times
St Thomas Hospital Medical School (28 June 1907) The Times
The Land Question (4 July 1907) The Times
A Plea for the Sitting Tennant (letter) (12 August 1907) The Times
A Literary Coincidence (letter) (19 October 1907) The Spectator
Town Planning Conference (26 October 1907) The Times
Dr Barnardo's Homes (16 November 1907) The Times
The Proposed Agricultural Party (5 December 1907) The Times
Mr Rider Haggard and Small Holdings (10 January 1908) The Times
Mr Haggard and Children's Legislation (13 March 1908) The Times
The Drink Trade and Common Sense (letter) (2 April 1908) The Times
The Zulus: The Finest Savage Race in the World (June 1908) The Pall Mall Magazine
Sparrows (letter) (18 August 1908) The Times
Sparrows, Rats and Humanity (letter) (5 September 1908) The Times
The Letters of Queen Victoria (letter) (26 November 1908) The Times
The Romance of the World's Greatest Rivers (December 1908) Travel Magazine
Afforestation. Mr Rider Haggard's View (1 March 1909) The Times
The Late Sir Marshal Clarke (letter) (13 April 1909) The Times
Mr Rider Haggard on Agriculture (27 November 1909) The Times
Mr Rider Haggard on South Africa (11 March 1910) The Times
Why? (letter) (25 April 1910) The Times
Mr Rider Haggard on Irish Agriculture (23 May 1910) The Times
Why Not? (letter) (12 July 1910) The Times
Mr Rider Haggard on Agriculture (16 September 1910) The Times
Mr Rider Haggard on Vermin (8 November 1910) The Times
Danish High Schools (21 December 1910) The Times
Sugar Beet Growing in Norfolk (6 March 1911) The Times
Rural Denmark (letter) (22 March 1911) The Times
Rural Denmark (letter) (3 April 1911) The Times
The Copyright Bill (letter) (6 June 1911) The Times
Mr Rider Haggard on Poverty. The Burden of Civilization (15 July 1911) The Times
Mr Rider Haggard and the Public Records (28 July 1911) The Times
The Farmers' Burden (1 December 1911) The Times
Egyptian Date Farm. The Financial Aspect (11 October 1912) The Times
Umslopogaas and Makokel. Sir H. Rider Haggard on Zulu Types (letter) (16 August 1913) The Times
The Death of Mark Haggard (letter) (10 October 1914) The Times
On the Land. Old Problems and New Ways. The War—and After. (15 March 1915) The Times
Soldiers as Settlers. After-War Problem for the Empire (20 August 1915) The Times
Raids by Air. Zeppelins and Zeppelins (letter) (22 October 1915) The Times
Women's Work on the Land. A Palliative in Hard Times (letter) (29 November 1915) The Times
Women on the Land. Town Girls' Unfitness for Farm Work (letter) (9 December 1915) The Times
Soldiers as Settlers. Sir Rider Haggard's Oversea Mission (2 February 1916) The Times
Soldiers as Settlers (letter) (7 February 1916) The Times
Soldier Settlers. The Future of Rural England (letter) (10 February 1916) The Times

Farewell Luncheon to Sir Rider Haggard (March 1916) United Empire
Soldier Settlers for the Empire. Offer from Victoria (18 April 1916) The Times
Sir R Haggard's Tour. Land for Ex-Service Men (22 July 1916) The Times
Sir H. Rider Haggard's Mission. Land for Ex-Soldiers (1 August 1916) The Times
Land for Ex-Soldiers. Outline of Sir R. Haggard's Report   (12 August 1916) The Times
Empire Land Settlement Deputation to the Secretary of State for the Colonies and the President of the Board of Agriculture (September 1916) United Empire
Empire Land Settlement by Sir Rider Haggard (December 1916) United Empire
A Journey through Zululand by Sir H Rider Haggard (December 1916) The Windsor Magazine
Mr Wilson's Note. British Publicity (28 December 1916) The Times
Home Produce (letter) (22 February 1917) The Times
The Milk Supply (letter) (11 April 1917) The Times
Corn Production Bill. A National Measure (letter) (13 June 1917) The Times
A Protest and a Plea. Farmers and Meat (letter) (9 October 1917) The Times
Pig-Breeding. A Subject for Municipal Enterprise (letter) (22 February 1918) The Times
The German Colonies. Interests of the Dominions (letter) (5 November 1918) The Times
Light—More Light! (letter) (19 November 1918) The Times
A Great American. Tributes to the Late Mr Roosevelt (letter) (8 January 1919) The Times
Shut the Door (letter) (10 March 1919) The Times
Population and Housing. Emigration v Birth Control (25 March 1919) The Times
The Ex-Kaiser (letter) (11 April 1919) The Times
Empire Birth-Rate. Sir Rider Haggard on Emigration (17 April 1919) The Times
Ex-Service Men Abroad. Warnings from California (letter) (10 May 1919) The Times
Edith Cavell (letter) (16 May 1919) The Times
The Ex-Kaiser. Uncertainties of Trial (letter) (8 July 1919) The Times
Race Suicide Peril. Western Civilization Threatened (11 October 1919) The Times
The British Cinema. Production of Reputable Films (letter) (5 November 1919) The Times
Horrors on the Film. Limits of Publicity (letter) (19 November 1919) The Times
The British Museum (letter) (24 January 1920) The Times
Air Exploration and Empire (letter) (7 February 1920) The Times
The Liberty League. A Campaign Against Bolshevism (letter) (3 March 1920) The Times
Bolshevist Peril. Counter-Propaganda (4 March 1920) The Times
The Empire's Vacant Lands. Settlers and the Food Supply (14 April 1920) The Times
Films and Happy Endings. The Tyranny of a Convention (letter)   (21 April 1921) The Times
Land and its Burdens. Evil of Grinding Taxation (letter) (8 August 1921) The Times
Boy Emigrants (letter) (31 March 1922) The Times
Migration and Morals. Declining Birther Rate (7 April 1922) The Times
Labour Party's Programme. Confiscation and Class Hatred (letter) (28 October 1922) The Times
Efficient Denmark. Keeping the People on the Land (7 December 1922) The Times
The Egyptian Find. Tombs of Eighteenth Dynasty Queens (letter) (19 December 1922) The Times
King Tutankhamen. Reburial in Great Pyramid (letter) (13 February 1923) The Times
The Norfolk Dispute. A Truce while There is Time (letter) (3 April 1923) The Times
Rural Post and Telephone. Minister's Reply to Deputation (19 April 1923) The Times
Liberalism and Land Reform (letter) (1 May 1923) The Times
Small Holdings. Influence of Heredity (letter) (4 July 1923) The Times
Agricultural Parcel Post (26 July 1923) The Times
Country Houses for Sale. Empty East Anglian Mansions (letter) (14 June 1924) The Times
Plight of Agriculture (24 July 1924) The Times

Loans From the British Museum (letter) (30 July 1924) The Times
Zinovieff Letter. Mr MacDonald and a Political Plot (letter) (29 October 1924) The Times
Two Centuries of Publishing. Tributes to Messrs. Longmans (6 November 1924) The Times
Imagination and War (26 November 1924) The Times

Non-Fiction

Cetywayo and His White Neighbours (1882)
A Farmer's Year (1899)
The Last Boer War (1899)
A Winter Pilgrimage (1901)
Rural England (1902)
A Gardener's Year (1905)
The Poor and the Land (1905)
Regeneration (1910)
Rural Denmark (1911)
The Days of My Life (1926)

Film Adaptations

King Solomon's Mines

This novel has been adapted at least six times. The first version, King Solomon's Mines, directed by Robert Stevenson, premiered in 1937. The best known version premiered in 1950: King Solomon's Mines, directed by Compton Bennett and Andrew Marton, was followed in 1959 by a sequel, Watusi. In 1979 a low-budget version directed by Alvin Rakoff, King Solomon's Treasure, combined both King Solomon's Mines and Allan Quatermain in one story. The 1985 film King Solomon's Mines was a tongue-in-cheek parody of the story, with a 1987 sequel in the same vein, Allan Quatermain and the Lost City of Gold. Around the same time an Australian animated TV film came out, King Solomon's Mines. In 2008 a direct-to-video adaptation, Allan Quatermain and the Temple of Skulls, was released.

She

She has been adapted for the cinema at least ten times, and was one of the earliest films to be made, in 1899 as La Colonne de feu (The Pillar of Fire), by Georges Méliès. A 1911 version starred Marguerite Snow, a British-produced version appeared in 1916, and in 1917 Valeska Suratt appeared in a production for Fox which is lost. In 1925 a silent film of She, starring Betty Blythe, was produced with the active participation of Rider Haggard, who wrote the intertitles. This film combines elements from all the books in the series.

A decade later another cinematic version of the novels was released, featuring Helen Gahagan, Randolph Scott and Nigel Bruce. Unlike the book and the other films, this 1935 version was set in the Arctic, rather than Africa, and depicts the ancient civilisation of the story in an Art Deco style, with music by Max Steiner.

The 1965 film She was produced by Hammer Film Productions; it starred Ursula Andress as Ayesha and John Richardson as her reincarnated love, with Peter Cushing and Bernard Cribbins as other members of the expedition.

In 2001 another adaption was released direct-to-video with Ian Duncan as Leo Vincey, Ophélie Winter as Ayesha and Marie Bäumer as Roxane.

Dawn
The film Dawn was released in 1917, starring Hubert Carter and Annie Esmond.

Jess
This book was filmed in 1912, featuring Marguerite Snow, Florence La Badie and James Cruze, in 1914 with Constance Crawley and Arthur Maude, and in 1917 as Heart and Soul, starring Theda Bara in the title role.

Beatrice
The book was adapted into a 1921 Italian silent drama film called The Stronger Passion, directed by Herbert Brenon and starring Marie Doro and Sandro Salvini.

Swallow
The novel was adapted into a 1922 South African film.

Stella Fregelius
The book was adapted into a 1921 British film, Stella.

Moon of Israel
This novel was the basis of a script by Ladislaus Vajda, for film-director Michael Curtiz in his 1924 Austrian epic known as Die Sklavenkönigin (Queen of the Slaves).